HX1
The Exodus

By Jeff W. Scott

PublishAmerica
Baltimore

ISBN: 1-4241-6190-8
PUBLISHED BY PUBLISHAMERICA, LLLP
www.publishamerica.com
Baltimore

Printed in the United States of America

DEDICATIONS

To my parents who never stopped believing in me
To my Uncle Tom…who inspired the X1
To Jerhico Williams…
To Beals
To Sonny for helping start it all
To Carl…the duality
To Boston…thanks
To Starbucks…my writing haven
Thanks to you all…it was fun!

Special thanks goes to Theresa Blackwell!

CHAPTER 1
Youthful Exuberance

"Tell us about the trees, Father."

The tiny voice haunted me. Such a simple question, yet so perplexing. How does one describe a tree to someone who has never seen one? Not too tough, I thought but then again they've never even seen any plant life at all. Not even pictures left to remind us of what once was. Surrounded with nothing but hard metal alloy their whole lives. A planet not of rock and wood but of wires and cables, not of water and air but of silicon and plasma gas. How do I fill this small child's request? As my mind desperately reaches for an answer she senses my anxiety, as she's so good at doing, and moves on to an even bigger question.

"What happened to them all? There were trees before the war, right, Father? What was it like, before the war I mean?"

"Now, Geonosis," I replied. "You've heard this story many times before. Every year at the Remembrance. Do you really want to hear it again?"

"Oh yes!" she swooned. "We all love hearing it!"

As I looked around the room I saw all the children scooting up close, getting their seats on the floor. I know they've heard this a hundred times before in school and at ceremonies but somehow they always seem like it's the first time they've ever heard it. Children are funny that way. I could have easily shrugged them off, I'm an important man after all. But something inside of me compels me to tell it yet again. As if I somehow hope it will be ingrained in their memories so hard that they never forget, not ever. Lest they make the same mistakes we did so long ago. Preparing in my mind how to begin, I have to remind myself that we never soften the story not even for small children. They must hear the harsh reality of their ancestry without one detail being omitted. Else the story itself be remembered wrong and the truth get spun into a fable over times to come. So I settle in for a long night of storytelling amongst young watchful eyes. For this there is no greater feeling than the sight of a young mind growing.

"So, what is a tree you ask? Well there was once a place called Earth. It's your ancestral home world. It was full of life and wonders the likes of which only dreams are made of. There were these things called plants that grew from the ground. They were alive like you and me, only had no thought for the lack of a brain. No one is really sure why plants existed, they had just always been there. Humans used plants for many things, some you could eat, some you could build things with and some made medicines. Plants were organic thus made of carbon properties. The Earth was also organic, and the plants got their nutrients from the earth. The star close to Earth that we called the sun provided ultraviolet rays of radiation that also gave the plants energy. And water fell from the sky in what we called rain which also nourished the plants. Back then humans drank this water as well. Our bodies are still made mostly of water you know."

"How did the humans catch a plant, Father, were they fast?"

"Plants didn't move," I explained. "They were rooted in the ground and stayed in one place their whole lives. We would plant their seeds to grow more of them. Humans often grew these plants in large fields called farms. Trees were among the biggest of all the plants. I heard that they used to be used for shade and even at one time there were many trees all in one place called a forest. People used to walk amongst them and relax under them. Drakos said they used to sing too but I'm hard-pressed to believe that one. Trees and plants once grew abundantly all over the planet. But man used most of them up to build houses and buildings and even used it, so I've heard, to write on although I can't quite figure out how. I did see a tree once in a museum. It was a splendid thing almost six meters tall! The museum AI told me they once grew to amazing heights of over one hundred feet high but I could not find any pictures of such a magnificent sight. It was brown at the base and had green things growing from its arms called leaves, which I read fell off each year and new ones grew in."

"Now, Father! Really! We're young, not stupid!"

"No I swear it's true" I replied. Seeing that this story was, as I thought, a tougher definition than I could ever explain, I quickly averted by getting into my own stories of my life, the things I know much more about. So I began.

Now I don't remember much before the war. I was very young and I was surrounded by it. You could say I was groomed for it. Both my parents were in the military and were firm supporters of the world government that was forming. I myself was too young to understand things like politics at the time, but I do recall the news flashes of civil unrest and governments around the world crumbling under heavy problems of hunger and resource depletions. But my main concern at the time was school. I was educationally groomed for mainframe programming. I had a knack for it early on and my parents enrolled me in the Kaleon Military Academy for Intelligence Research. I guess our story really begins at age twelve. I was working on a project dealing in plasma fusion when I stumbled across a rather interesting anomaly. I noticed that plasma infused with a small amount of electricity would leave a resonance behind, a sort of electromagnetic flux that could be seen for several hours after the infusion. It was very much like a temporary film negative that over time simply faded away. Unless, that is, if the burn pattern was repeated several times, which would cause the plasma a permanent burn scar. Much like the human brain, I thought. It wasn't until years later that my science project would hold any real bearing, but that combined with my nano research was the basis behind my first artificial intelligence tests. AI was not a relatively new field, it had been around for a few hundred years, but my discoveries were groundbreaking and would take the field of AI research in directions no one dreamed possible. Right around the age of sixteen I was working on nano isometrics, which my father was greatly encouraging. My mother, however, thought it nothing more than a distraction from my mainframe studies and often complained that I shouldn't spend so much time on the "Little Robotic Beasts" as she called them. She often saw the above average intelligence that I possessed as a potential for catapulting my future. But my father often encouraged my more creative side. He said that technology was never advanced by intelligence alone but rather by dreamers with intelligence. "So dare to dream, my boy," he would say, "for what you dream up today could be tomorrow's reality." Nano isometrics was a common fancy among young scientists and budding computer engineers like myself. Every young engineer dreamed of creating the perfect nano bot that would maneuver predictably as it was instructed. You see, although widely experimented with nanos were still very unpredictable. Their microscopic circuitry was easily corrupted even by the tiniest of electro magnetic flux. The static electricity from a single microbe could fry a whole colony of nanos in a millisecond, which is why nanos for medical research were abandoned in the early twenty first century. They were however widely used in the very sterile, static free environment of a mainframe. They made quick work of repairing damaged circuitry and even ghost imaging a damaged mainframe cell, which is why many of us mainframe engineers played with their isometrics to improve their resilience and abilities to make a better computer. The basis of modern AI technology was centered on the Nan bots and their ability to maintain a stable chip for the AIs to use for processing. This is when my science experiment as a youth finally spawned an idea that would change the face of AI programming forever. Up until then Nan bots were made of the same circuitry as the AI chips themselves, a tiny microscopic chip repairing and maintaining another computer chip. That was just how things had always been done and scientists were hard-pressed to find a better way so that's the way things remained. But as my father was always quick to point out, I was more a dreamer than an engineer. And so I posed an impossible question to a seemingly un-improvable technology. What if, I thought, we didn't use a chip at all? Not for the AI or the nano. The one thing that could destroy a nano's programming in a microsecond was the one thing I theorized could actually make it smarter. Using plasma trace technology, as I now called it, or PTT for short, create a layer of plasmatic cells instead of micro circuitry. The nanos themselves would also carry the same plasmatic cells and with them the ability to create small static electric discharges to write and rewrite the AI's core cells. The AI's central intelligence would in turn use the nanos to rewrite its own matrix. The part that would make this a hard sell to the civilian corps of engineers is that the plasmatic cells could not be written by humans but instead would have to grow and evolve and be written by the AI itself. This would surely be a long and drawn out process that could take several years as it would develop much like a human brain. In a sense we would have to "grow" AIs and not just fabricate them or their intelligence. Up until now the AIs simply learned by a series of calculations and miscalculations running multiple passes of every task it was supposed to perform until it arrived at the most logical result. It could then change its programming on what resembled a modern mainframe hard drive. And nanos were as I said used only for maintenance and repair. But what I was proposing was radically different. You would still have a "Core chip" that would basically act as the AI's birth so to speak, giving the plasmatic cell membrane its first imprint. But from second one the AI would begin to rewrite every nuance of its plasmatic brain, from every sensory input node to every autonomic response, literally growing as it learns, and using the nanos to rewrite the membranes, not just to maintain. Now the even more profound part of this scenario is the nanos themselves would be "raised" in a similar fashion with the same plasma infused membranes for a brain. This meant the AI could not only use the nanos to reprogram itself but also to reprogram other nanos, in a sense rewriting the rewriters, a sort of perpetual intelligence that would increasingly become smarter over time. Now the theory itself was radical enough but that truly would be my greatest hurdle. The fact that this method would slow the AI production time down to a crawl was something I didn't think the corps could swallow let alone provide funding for. So I sat on this technology for another seven months until my seventeenth birthday when I shared the idea with fellow engineer and my best friend at the time, Maximus Beal.

Now you know how some people's names just fit them like a glove? Well this was not the case for old Max. He was by no means maximum anything except maybe in heart. He had injured himself at the age of nine in a tourney race he had no business being in. Breaking his spine completely in two, he was paralyzed from the waist down. He broke the cord so severely that not even a Kevlon disk could've repaired it, which was the common treatment of the time for spinal injuries. He always was a scrawny kid to begin with and all of us felt he shouldn't have been on a tourney bike. But I think he always felt he had something to prove to rest of us. My friends and I were all in the military academy and were groomed to be physically fit from day one. But Max wasn't. His parents were in the civilian corps of engineers, and with no government or military affiliation, they were not raised in the same fashion we were. Though I always knew he was the smartest out of all of us, and I often looked up to him for his genius IQ, I think he somehow felt inferior to us because of his physical stature. Though none of us looked at him any different and he was always accepted as one of the group I think his own inferiority got the best of him that fateful day on the ramps. He spent the remainder of his life in a hydroelectric chair which donned him a more suited name of Scooter. He used to hate the name but quickly grew very fond of it as the goofy gangly kid could attract the girls with it something fierce. Scooter and I were best friends even though we were raised in different worlds. But he himself was an expert in the field of nano-technology so I thought who better to ask if my theories would actually be feasible. The sheer silence that fell over him that day clued me in quite quickly that I may be on to something. You see Scooter often stuttered when he was excited which to all of us was not a point to make fun of but something to make us stand straight and pay attention, because it usually meant he was on to something big. He has already had several new engineering innovations under his belt at this point and even for our rapid learning society he was considered a genius beyond his time, especially by us, his closest friends. But when Scooter got quiet it sparked our curiosity even more as that meant he was really thinking hard. He was silent for most of the day and by evening we were all busting at the seams to see what he had to say. I'll never forget it.

"Well, Zax..." he said, "the world is about to change."

He and I sat down that night and hashed out every detail of my theory. Often bantering back and forth as devil's advocates, trying to manufacture reasons why it wouldn't work, only to come up with answers why it would. By morning my father awoke to find us still in the den with holo designs over seven bridges high. He simply brewed some coffee and served it to us quietly, so careful not to disturb our train of thought. I vaguely remember him sitting in the corner of the den quietly observing two insane geniuses pounding away at an impossible theorem. Food came and went from time to time as my mother made her short appearances in the room but my father never left the chair. What seemed like only hours Father confessed later was actually six days. He actually received a reprimand for not mustering for duty during that time but in the light of our sixth day conclusions was quickly and quietly dismissed. In what was later named the sixth day breakthrough we finally worked out a theorem that would become the birth of modern day AI.

It was truly Scooter's genius that filled in all the missing pieces to my theories so I really wanted him to play a major role in presenting this to the scientific community. But I was after all property of the military and my father quickly convinced me that this idea should not fall under the jurisdiction of the Civilian Corps of Engineers (the CCE). Scooter, however, had quite the opposite opinion, which fueled a heated debate between him and my father. In my father's loyalty to the government he ordered Beal not to reveal our project to anyone until he had a chance to bring it before the military commission. Scooter insisted that since the fall of the structured governments nine years ago that corporations had power over the military, and as economic futures were quite unstable the project would fall by the wayside in the hands of the military. He had a good point. The only factions left in the world that really had any financial backing at all and any strong future were civilian organizations like the CCE. But born military and raised military I stayed true to my upbringing and refused to allow Scooter to take the holo schematics to the CCE. In a mad fury he left our quarters and we did not speak again for several years. I heard once that he actually tried to propose the idea to the CCE but without the actual plans to show them they quickly dismissed the idea as youthful fancy and he was shunned by much of his CCE community. I felt for him deeply but my duty was to the military which had taken such good care of my family and I, and my honor to that duty would not be wavered. I proposed the sixth day breakthrough to the military on Valentine's Day, February the 14, 2235 BE, the day before my eighteenth birthday. The new plasmatic cell research began and I led the think tank for the next five years. During that time we grew, almost organically, our first Plasmatic cell AI, and we called him X1. Now, much to my surprise and to the delight of the military he "grew" much faster than any of us had anticipated. By age five he was as intelligent as our modern AIs, if not smarter. The test was a complete success and his systematic algorithms were a million times faster than any AI in the common world. He gained one other trait that most AIs had to be programmed with but his came naturally, personality. He literally "wrote" his own personality matrix and was quite proud of it. Funny, he had to program pride first but quickly became an expert on the matter and even grew a quite amazing sense of humor. Although most found it dry witted at best, I loved it, as it was not a human sense of humor programmed in, but an AI's version of humor that was quite unique in the entire world. The military, now struggling for cohesion, quickly ordered the mass production of the new plasmatic AIs and production began on the fifth year of the X1 project. The X1, it was decided, would actually write the core programming for the massive order, essentially putting him in charge of production. Over one hundred million plasmatic AIs were core programmed that year and it would take another five years for them to reach functioning potential, and each year that followed more were made. I was promoted to lieutenant almost immediately following the completion of the X1 project and placed in charge of the newly formed Division of Plasmatic AI Research and Development. I worked very closely with the X1 over these five years. Many said we were very much alike, and the other AI engineers often teased us about it. I buried myself in my work, never having a social life to speak of. Even X1 prodded me to get away more but I told him my work was more important. We actually became friends, this creation of mine and I. I'll never forget one day he was researching the word "father."

He said to me, "If you designed my core programming, and produced the designs for my plasmatic cell membrane, in essence you created me. Would that not make you my father?"

"In a manner of speaking," I said, "yes, I guess it would."

The name stuck and from then on he called me Father. He and I grew very close over the next five years, and even though I knew it impossible he showed almost a hint of emotion. Algorithms gone astray, I would tell myself, but looking back I'm sure it was the beginning of it all.

But before I get too far ahead of myself there's a very important part of the story I'm leaving out. I should really explain what was going on in the world at the time. As this is the part of the story, you children, must learn and always remember. To get there we have to backtrack a little to when I was nine. The year was 2226 BE. By this time those plants I was telling you about had long since been gone. Earth's atmosphere was so clouded by industrial pollution that the UV rays from the sun could no longer get through and the plants all died off, not that there were many left to begin with. The Earth's population was reaching a critical point and many countries around the world had in fact set population limits for each family. The corporations of the world had gained so much power and money that they made governments almost unnecessary, and most people by this point held very little stock in what the government had to say. Money truly ruled the world, as it always had. However, resources on our own planet were becoming scarce. Food was a precious commodity at this point and many places around the world were facing starvation and famine. As the plants began to die off from lack of nutrients so did the animals that were raised on these plants. The corporations had ways of synthetically producing food that actually was quite sustaining but would not share these technologies with the general public. However, they would sell the synthetic products at very high prices to the governments of the world to feed their people. These corporations soon began to realize the futility of dealing with the governments as the middle man and began selling to individuals again, cutting out the governments altogether. For years it was the way of things. The corporations kept the governments under control by controlling the food supplies for that country. But now they simply strangled out the governments and started requiring higher and higher prices for their synthetic life line. It was the way in which things were controlled by the corporations. Even the United States (of which used to be my former country) fell into the corporate reign of food supply. It was capitalism after all and so the government could not turn back on hundreds of years of promoting such a practice. They could not admit that their own creation, this corporate monster had finally turned on them. It was the greed of the corporations and the desire for money and power that eventually caused the collapse of the governments. In this, my ninth year of life I witnessed the fall of the Untied States government. It was not a military takeover or a war that would bring them down but their own corporations who simply starved them out of power. With literally not enough money to compete with the corporations the government conceded to corporate rule of the States under the provision that the corporations would keep the people fed and keep the military intact to protect our borders and thus the US military became the Corporate Military Commission. The US was not the only country handing over control to the corporations. All the superpowers in the world were faced with similar decisions. And in one way or another power was being handed over to the corporations of the world because it was thought they had the only real power to keep the world from starving. At first it seemed to work. It was run very much like a socialist government. My father's best friend, Drakos Kane, a pilot in what was just recently the Russian air force, was very unhappy about this.

He said, "We're going back to the Dark Ages, my boy! It will be the fall of mankind if we continue."

I laughed then. This big burly man couldn't be afraid of anything, I thought. He had a big fur coat that hung on his huge stature like a bear skin rug. You'd never see him without a cigar in his mouth, but I don't ever remember it being lit. Smoking was in fact illegal in most of the free world, but nevertheless he always seemed to have that thing hanging from the corner of his lips and shadowed over that gruff gray beard of his. I think it was his way of thumbing his nose at the government. But I was much too young to understand what he meant. The politics of the whole thing didn't make much sense to me, and as long as people were not starving I thought, *Well isn't that a good thing?* The people under corporate rule were to hand over all profits of any kind to the government (the corporation) in exchange would be given food to survive. It was quickly becoming a communist world and many people opposed these corporations and there was great civil unrest worldwide. It was a powder keg on the verge of explosion and something had to give. Secretly a society was forming, made mostly of ex government officials and Military Commission leaders. Even in the military academy it was well taught that we still (in secret of course) swore an oath to uphold our government, the *real* government. All around us there were corporate spies that tried to influence the teachings at the academy but we young kids, probably more out of youthful rebellion than loyalty, swore allegiance to the "old" government and not to the corporate rule. Though it was never actually said out loud we all knew there would come a day when we had to choose and we all knew what side we would take. Being in the military we wanted for nothing. Our families were well taken care of. But there were others, like Scooter's family. They were in a civilian organization and thus, it seemed, treated as a lower class. He never had as good food or as good medical treatment as we did. I didn't understand this really but it was just the way things were so I accepted it and never gave it much thought.

I remember the night all too well. It was in my eyes the beginnings of the UWG, an organization that literally was being formed right before my eyes. My father, Antillius Tor, and Drakos were discussing something in the den. Although I think they knew I was listening they didn't seem to mind. I saw them occasionally glance at the loft where I was crouched down listening to the entire conversation, but they never stopped discussing their plans. It was as if they knew somehow that I would follow my father's loyalty and example, in which later years I suppose I proved I would. They were both powerful and influential men in their respective Military Commissions and both were spoken of with honor in the academy. Drakos and my father were revered as heroes, for what I was not sure at the time, but I would soon learn the answer to that.

"Antillius," Drakos said in his gruff Russian accent, "there comes a time in every man's life when he must stand for what he believes in. The corporations are starving our people and have driven out our governments from power. Our ancestors fought for freedom over two hundred years ago and broke away from similar rule. Now it's happening again and we cannot sit idly by and watch the corporations crumble the world for their own gain. I've been speaking with the old heads of state in the motherland and they are willing to support us. The United Nations has not fallen yet and they propose a radical solution. I need to know that your military commission is behind us."

"I assure you, old friend, they are," said Father, once again glancing my way. "I know the academy is still teaching the loyalty oaths in secret. Zax repeats them in his room and I can hear him memorizing the lines. My wife Alieha has assured me that the Council supports the move to a world government. The true mission at hand will be to release the Synthetic Genome device to the public."

"We are then in agreement," Drakos said quietly, almost as if afraid someone else besides me was listening. "The Synthetic Genome device should not be under any one government's rule, but instead released to the world population."

"Of course," replied Father. "It's the only way, and furthermore to the matter of the abolishment of currency and establishing a free trade society. The corporations would crumble overnight. Money is what gives them power. Take away the need for it and they will fall."

"This is a task easier said than done, my friend," Drakos stated, "without money why would people even show up for work?"

My father confidently began speaking, a speech that would later become his rally call to all the world. It was a speech that the entire world would hear someday and it would change the course of history forever. And I heard it first, that fateful night in a quiet den between two of the greatest men I have ever known.

"People will rally together, not for power or wealth, not for money or financial gain, but for the betterment of mankind, for the sheer survival of the human race. It will be chaotic at first and technology and world productivity will suffer a serious blow. But in the end I have faith that all of mankind will see the benefits of returning to work in a productive society. Not for their own gain but for the gain of humankind. Money is what brought these corporations to ultimate rule and we must never see the day when it plagues our world again. Man will learn to love and cherish all without cause or reason but simply for love—"

"Okay, okay, old friend," Drakos interrupted. "You're getting a bit preachy, aren't you?"

They both shared a laugh then and it seemed to get Father off his soapbox, but later I would remember those words when he spoke them again in front of a worldwide audience. During the course of the next few years my father and Drakos had many of these conversations. I soon quit hiding in the loft and sat quietly in the chair in the corner of the den, never uttering a word, but simply watching ordinary men become great. I sat in awe as I watched them forge what I was certain to be the future.

My mother often came in as the evenings became late and tried to shoo me off to bed, but Drakos, in a very commanding voice would bellow out, "The boy stays!" My father nodding at my mother shooed her from the room instead. "He is our future," Drakos insisted, "it is good he is here to see the beginnings, so he knows the real reasons why we are doing what we do."

My father nodded in respect to his old friend. "Mmm, indeed an unavoidable future that his generation will lead. Are you listening, Zax?" A great weight lay in my father's eyes. For the first time he saw in me a man. It was almost a sad look, like leading me there would somehow rob me of my childhood innocence but something he felt he could not avoid.

"Yes, sir," I replied.

I wanted to say so much more at the time but my training had served me well. Now was not a time for questions but instead a time for listening, as he had so clearly ordered. So I sat and listened night after night, year after year, as the preparations formed. I could feel the tensions rising at the academy. Obviously I was not the only son who had heard Father speak of such a revolution, but none of us would ever admit to each other we knew anything of it. In the oath was silence to all, even to our comrades. Should we never reveal our mission to anyone our plans would never fall into the hands of our opposition. Although it was written in a sense that made it sound like it was meant for a time of war, we carried this over to our daily lives and what was overheard at home stayed at home. Our loyalty was to our fathers and families first and to the house in which we were raised.

By this time I had reached the age of twelve. My plasma resonance project for physics class was going quite well and I was proving to my father that I could handle greater responsibilities. But unbeknownst to me at the time, I would soon prove an even greater value to my father and his cause. What happened next was one of the greatest kept secrets in military history. Only now do I feel comfortable talking about it. It was a secret that not even my mother would ever know. By this point I was a constant fixture in my father's discussions in the den. Even when we had visiting officials from the commission they never once questioned my presence. I was military after all and that was enough to be deemed trusted. I saw many of my professors at the academy in my father's den those nights, as they forged a mission that would change history. I like to think that somehow what followed was my idea, but looking back I think my father somehow staged it all for my benefit and was the reason behind him letting me sit in on these conversations the past few years. The mission being discussed that night was one to steal the plans for the Synthetic Genome device, the machine that created the world's food supply. This was not an easy mission as the corporate mainframes were amongst the most secure in the entire world. Arguments flew across the table back and forth on how it should be done. It was proposed by members of the council that a military coup against the corporations should take place.

My father and many members of his team were dead set against this idea. It would cost thousands of lives, my father insisted, "War is NOT the answer. We must not succumb to violence."

Other than the minor terrorist factions that still plagued the earth the governments themselves hadn't waged war in over a century. The world peace treaty of 2120 assured us of that, but now they were proposing a military strike. There was no doubt the militaries would win, but how many countless civilians would get caught in the crossfire my father argued.

"How many civilians work for the corporation only out of necessity and are merely bound to it, not by loyalty, but for the need to see their families fed?"

"No, this is not the answer," Drakos strongly supported my father, "and instead there must be another way." But the commission was not impressed by my father's pleas.

"Show us another way, Antillius, and we'd be glad to listen," they told him.

"The mainframe..." my father began.

"And what about the mainframe?" General Tull exclaimed. "You know as well as I do none of us have the resources to hack such a secure device."

"None of us," said my father, "you're right," and then his glance once again turned to me. I was sitting in the same chair I had sat in for three years, but this time the glance was different. It was not an approving glance or even a fatherly respect sort of glance as in times past, nor was it a glance for me to remain silent or respectful. No, this time it was different. It was as if my father had now given me permission to speak. And not just merely to speak but to voice the one opinion he seemed to know that I had welling up in my soul.

"Go on, boy!" Drakos bellowed. "Now is the time to speak like a man! Tell them your idea!"

And with that I began to speak, changing the course of human history. I had no idea then that this one night, this one idea, just might save the world from hunger. It was a boy's fancy and dreams, how could it even apply in the real man's world? But nevertheless I spoke my piece, as the trusted friend of my father's had instructed me to do.

Much like in today's society, children were educated at a rapidly accelerated rate. By age twelve a child was considered to be at a college level of intelligence. So it was not so unheard of to listen to a child of my age. Nevertheless, I was still nervous about speaking to such an important group of people. But remembering how my father always said that it was dreamers who would change the world gave me spirit and the confidence to stand. I hid my trembling hands behind my back and gripped them tightly as I approached the table. I was well fit for my age and quite unusually tall. At five feet nine I towered over my classmates, which may have been the reason for my accelerated rank promotion to squad leader. But these ribbons that pressed hard against my uniform now, and my stature, paled in comparison to these huge men and women larger than life to me. With metals and ribbons coating their chests like a blanket of well-deserved armor, they appeared so unapproachable. But as I was trained I tried to approach them as if fearing nothing and taking in a deep breath I began to speak.

"What about the nanos? We could reprogram some maintenance nanos to retrieve bits of information at a time. I know alone they don't carry much data but an entire colony could easily carry enough bits to secure a single file. And if we release them one colony at a time the security nodes would never even suspect a thing. They are naturally released every month in waves of a dozen colonies or so into the system for maintenance. Then they are purged back into the grid for us to clean them out, recharge and reprogram them. The maintenance of these nanos is left to the military because we created them and we are the ones that colonize them. Just last week I colonized a whole culture of nanos for use in the corporate mainframe in Nano Isometrics class. The corporation takes little notice to what we do to them as they don't take much stock that children will have any reason to do anything malicious. This, gentlemen, will be their downfall. You see, we hack them all the time."

I could see some disapproving looks already from the council and what I was admitting I knew could get me in some very serious hot water, but I shrugged it off. I was on a roll and no one had told me to shut up yet so I quickly continued.

"We get different bits of code and information. Mostly useless stuff to the general populous like stock quotes and things like that but enough to prove that file transfer over a period of time is possible. It would take some great amount of time to program enough colonies to carry out such a task, but a few friends of mine and I would be more than willing to complete the process."

"I don't know," General Tull finally interrupted. "These are children. I know they are smart but how can we leave the fate of the free world in the hand of a bunch of kids. I think we need to look—"

"Pipe down. Henry!" Lt. Zon abruptly interrupted as she slammed her hands down on the table. "Let him finish!"

I almost broke out with a snicker. This fiery redhead, whom all us young men thought was just incredibly good-looking, just called General Tull by his FIRST NAME. I was almost hysterical inside but I could not let it show. Drakos nodded with a half smirk toward Tasha Zon and I swear I saw her wink at him. Heck, none of us would blame him, as she sure was a looker! She looked at me now not with a condescending look as one woman of her stature would towards someone of my age but as an equal.

"Can you really do what you're suggesting?" she asked. "How long would it actually take?"

"About four to five years," I said, "depending on when we get started."

"Can we really wait that long?" Commander Forbes asked, as if directing the question to the entire table.

My father spoke now and at first I thought he was shooting my idea down. It sure sounded like it at the time. "Every day the corporations gain a stronger and stronger strangle hold on our society. To go to war to stop them would be as I said before ludicrous. But to sit idly by for four years, I don't know, son."

I was crushed by my own father speaking out against me. I was so angry I blurted right out, "But we won't be idle, sir, we will be working to save the future of mankind. Do not let my age fool you, council. You expect, if in times of war, that I stand and defend my people even now at my age. From age nine we are given that duty. Then how can you dismiss me now when I stand here proposing a way to save our people from hunger?" I was so infuriated that I pounded my fist on the table. "Do not take my ideas lightly. If I am man enough to fight then I am man enough to be heard at this council. We will NOT be idle we will be securing the future of mankind and assuring that every human on the planet will have food to feed their families. I can think of no greater thing to spend four years of my life doing. And I swear to you I will dedicate every waking hour to making this happen. It can work and I will not rest until its finished!"

Silence fell over the room. I backed away from the table a few feet to gather in the looks of all those staring at me in shock. All but two, Drakos and my father, who had this strange grin of approval upon their face. Almost in embarrassment I realized what my father had done in his objections to my idea. Drakos later said to me in private that I reminded him of my father when he was my age, "but you, boy, have even more fire than he did." He knew it was within me and just wanted to bring that fire to the surface. They knew the passions of my father but in opposing me he showed them the passions of his son and my generation as well. Admiral Tsung, who had remained quiet this entire time finally spoke.

"Cadet Tor has made a proposal to this commission, one I feel holds great weight and bearing on the matter. I believe it's now within the hands of the commission to decide on a ruling here and now. I myself am in favor of Cadet Tor's proposal and will give him my full support should we choose to pursue this course of action. And just to make it clear I will not support a military action of any kind at this time. If in four years the nano hack fails to produce the plans, I will reconsider my decision. What say the commission?"

One by one, "Aye," they said, "Aye," again around the table, "Aye," and to my father, "Aye," he spoke and then to Drakos, "Aye," again, then all looked at me with a waiting gaze.

"Speak up, boy," Drakos said. "You've made your mark upon this commission, making yourself one of it. What say you to your own proposal?"

Stepping back towards the table the word fell quietly but firmly upon my lips, "Aye!" The judgment being final I was that day sanctioned by the commission to colonize a special breed of maintenance nanos that we would slowly filter into the corporate mainframe and hopefully over the course of four years would bleed out the files needed to construct the plans for the Synthetic Genome device that would end this corporate control over world hunger. It was then I began to understand what Drakos had said before. I began to see the meaning of tyranny and oppression and I quickly grew a bitterness towards anything remotely supporting the corporate power. Only the commission that was convened that night knew of the plans that we spoke of.

CHAPTER 2
A Child Shall Lead

No one would ever expect a group of kids to be behind a plot to overthrow the most powerful organizations in the world. But here we were, a bunch of pre teens about to unleash the most important computer hack in human history. Kenjan Nigh was my first choice for a nano programmer. He was the best in our class. He could program on six different levels on the holo programmer at the same time and he also had a knack for simplifying programs and I needed the most miniscule programs I could find to be undetectable by the security nodes that scan the nanos. Marcus Fields would lead the nano isometrics. He could make the little beasts run in directions no one ever thought possible. David and Mick O'Conner, two of my closest friends, would oversee the actual construction of the bots, which left me in charge of writing the actual trickle program that would slowly hack the corporation's mainframe to attain the files we needed. It would take us a mere three weeks to complete the first colony. We had to wait until the end of the month though for the maintenance flush before we could release the first wave into the system. Admiral Tsung was there that day. We were all very nervous. My hands beaded with sweat as I reached for the execute key. On his nod I pushed the key knowing I would be sealing not only my fate but the fate of humanity by pressing this one single button. That's a lot of weight to put on a young man of only twelve but it was not the only burden I bore that day. What if it failed? What if one thing went wrong? If the core program was too big, or the isometrics failed somehow to drive the bots to the correct location in the mainframe, or if my trickle program released the wrong bites down into the system…it would all be in vain. I had no worries of the corporation catching us. The O'Conner twins had made sure of that. A failsafe was installed to self-destruct upon any failure of the operation. But failure was what I feared. Failure meant only one certainty…war. I would be responsible for sending thousands to their death if the solution I proposed failed. But this was my one chance to stand for my father's values, for my values and for all mankind. That human life is so precious that we must strive to do everything in our power to preserve it. We must never give in to the violence that had plagued our world for so long. Don't get me wrong, I would fight if it came to that. I was trained for it, I swore an oath to it, and I would surely lay down my own life to protect the people. But it was the innocents that I myself would inflict harm upon that I wanted to avoid. All that being my demon to bear witness to I pressed the button to execute.

"Nanos powered up and activated," Kenyan said with a smile. Around the room the green lights came.

"Isometrics online and operational," followed Marcus. "The little buggers are heading in. Performing the main sweep of the mainframe now."

"We will know in just a few more seconds, Admiral," I assured him, as he stood with a questioning stare. One zero appeared on my screen, a second later another. Again another, then a one. "Admiral…Binary trickle online and active," I said, my voice trembling with excitement and a hint of relief.

The whole room broke out in cheers. We all started shaking hands and rubbing each other's heads. I even went up and rubbed the admiral's head, messing what little hair he did have, which looking back probably wasn't a very smart thing to do to your commander-in-chief. But he paused for a second, as did everyone in the room, and then let out one heck of a bellowing laugh as he abruptly returned the favor.

By the time the next month's nano flush was due to arrive we had secured four files from the genome plans. About one per week, just as I had predicted. Perfectly intact it gave us great hope that the plan would succeed. And succeed it did! Over the course of the next four years we repeated the process every month. Admiral Tsung kept the warmongers at bay showing them each month our progress. My father became more and more pleased.

"One more month and your plan gives us more hope of peace," he'd say.

By the fourth year I was sixteen years of age. Marcus and I had been constantly working on ways over the past four years to improve the stability of the nano isometrics. We made them faster and more accurate as time went on, all in an effort to improve the data retrieval of the Genome device. This led to my ideas on Plasmatic cell technology and using these improved nanos to rewrite the AI plasmatic cells. Over these last four years I spent more and more time with my team and less with my best friend Scooter. I could not include him in what we were doing in the labs as he had no military affiliation. I guess that may have led him to feel like he was isolated from the rest of us. I felt really bad about that so I wanted to include him in the PTT designs. But we couldn't even think about that now. This day was too important. This day would mark the end of world hunger, I thought, and the answer to all our troubles. I was proud this day, as I was sure if not for my plan we would currently be in the middle of a civil war between the military and the corporations. But pride has a way of coming back to bite you. As the last nano reported in from the system flush the last binary piece of a four year puzzle was retrieved. Only now could we compile the data and see if our long hours and many frustrating weeks and months finally paid off. Kenjan began the compile and it took only six hours to finish. The entire commission was in the room to see the final results. There was a complete silence and awe as the plans began appearing on the screen.

"Patch them through to the holo emitter," said the admiral. "Let's see what this puppy looks like." And there it was in all its 3D glory. The Synthetic Genome Device. It was so amazing now that we looked at it. I'm sure I'm not the only one in the room who marveled at its simplicity. And I'm sure not the only one who thought...why didn't I think of that! It was in its basic form a molecular reconstruction device. It took minerals, vitamins, and proteins from everything and anything you could feed into including the air that we breathe and reconstructed it into a biodegradable byproduct that would sustain human life. It needed only a minimal amount of fuel to produce massive quantities of food. It could literally take a bolt and a rubber ring and turn it into an eight course meal for five that was highly nutritious.

This thing makes better food than nature, I thought. Of course we all knew the quality of the finished food products. We'd been eating them for years. But now we knew how this awesome machine works. Bio-organic reconstruction of non organic materials at a subatomic level. Quite a simple process really when you think about it. However, one small problem I saw in the plans; it would take no ordinary computer to run it. It would take a sophisticated AI to produce the trillion calculations per second needed for the atomic reconstruction. Now we had these types of AIs in the modern world at the time but only the most rich and powerful could afford them. Not every home had an AI, at least not one sophisticated enough to handle such an operation. This thought mulled through my head and weighed heavy on my heart. Even if every home in the world got one of these genome devices not everyone could afford the AI required to run it. It was then I thought of combining my Plasma Cell Experiments with my recent advances in Nano Isometrics to create the perfect AI. AIs weren't robotic in nature as they are today but instead a built-in computer device much like an appliance. There were simplistic robotic AIs that the military used but even those were not advanced enough to be effective. AIs took up a lot of space, as they were in essence a very large mainframe so many houses that could afford them simply didn't have the room to install them. My ideas for a Plasmatic Cell AI would greatly reduce their size and possibly even be small enough to house inside a robotic body. But this research was based on my theories alone and as of yet was still just a dream.

But again I get ahead of myself. I'm good at that I suppose. The true tragedy appeared right before my eyes and made me swallow the pride I felt that day. The commission all of a sudden grew very quiet and I noticed them backing up slightly from the holo emitter and the computer terminals. My father asked Kenjan to step away from the terminal and I felt a firm hand grasp me by the shoulder. It was Drakos. He pulled me back almost nuzzling me into that big fur coat of his. What happened next took me and my whole team by surprise. A whole unit of Regional Squad forces entered the room guns drawn. The RS was one of the most elite units in the military and we all knew it. We also knew they would kill without question if given the order, even others in the military. It was a unit to be feared that's for sure. If they entered a room everyone knew there was something the commission wanted and you'd better not stand in their way. One of the unit pulled a briefcase out and plugged into our mainframe.

Kenjan quickly, without thinking, spouted off to the admiral, "What the hell are they doing? We are all military here, why are they shutting us down? This is four years of our lives here, please don't tell me you're just going to bury it?" With that an RS pointed his P16 assault rifle directly at Kenjan's head and cocked back the firing mechanism.

My father grabbed Kenjan who was heading for the mainframe controls and yelled, "Admiral! There's no need for this. He's just a boy, he's passionate about his work and his mission!"

"AT EASE!" Tsung bellowed loudly to the RS trooper. "Continue download."

"Zaxius, you must understand," said Tsung, "we have to keep this under wraps just a little while longer."

I could feel the raw sense of betrayal welling up all round me. Were even my own father and Drakos in on this the whole time, did they never once intend to release this to the public? I could feel a great sense of rage building up within me. It must have exuded from every fiber of my being because just then I felt that hand on my shoulder give a very tight squeeze. So hard it hurt. Drakos. Was that a stern squeeze to settle me down or a disapproving reprimand on what he knew I was feeling? I was so confused at this point that I didn't know what to think or who to trust.

Tsung said something that almost made sense, "The time will come when everyone will be able to have this device and the hunger will stop. I promise you, son, you have my word. I have never led you astray or lied to you ever, have I? Your father has full faith in this commission and so should you. You too soon will be a full member of this commission and then you will understand. We will meet in your father's den tonight and you will understand the full scope of things then." Then as quickly as they arrived the RS troopers began filing out of the room.

"Download complete, Admiral," the trooper reported as he unhooked the cables, and closed his terminal case.

"Very well," Tsung said quietly. "This room is to be wiped clean, no trace, you hear me, no trace. I want this place as sterile as a brand-new mainframe right off production."

The entire RS squad responded with a resounding, "Yes, sir!" We were shuffled out of the room by the troopers and my team and I were ordered to return home and speak of this to no one. We all left silently, hanging our heads in shame and disbelief. I know we all felt the sense of betrayal, but duty prevented us from uttering a word. We were soldiers after all, and who were we to question our authorities. I didn't speak a word to my father on the way home. We walked silently to our quarters and I retired to my room where I sat and waited for that evening to come.

I watched the clock as minutes felt like hours, and hours felt like days. I waited patiently to hear the rustle of people shuffling into my father's den below. Once the commotion began to settle and I was sure they had all seated themselves at the table. I prepared myself to head downstairs. I was gearing up to give this entire commission a piece of my mind. They had taken a dream of mine, MY idea, and twisted it into their own purposes. And what sinister purposes were these? Would the one man I had so greatly trusted and admired all these years really let that happen? I couldn't think of him like a father now, but as an adversary in a wicked debate for virtuous morality. I had to stand tall in the face of this unstoppable force and state my disgust at what they were doing. This I thought would surely lose my position in the military but I was so passionate about the cause I didn't care. Families had to be fed, I thought, and if I have to repeat the whole process again to gain the plans I would and this time I'd do it myself. Before I could stew on the subject any further my father called the commission meeting to order. This was my cue. I was going to storm down there and give them all the tongue-lashing of their lives. I had a good teacher after all, my father was the most charismatic speaker I had ever known. I walked down the stairs of the loft and entered the room. As I did everyone at the table rose to their feet. I froze dead in my tracks. Why were they rising? They only do this when an absent commission member enters the room. Although Drakos had once hinted of me being a member of this commission back when I was twelve, I knew truthfully I was not old enough then and it was an honorary suggestion at best. Besides, you need to be an officer to join the commission and it was a very small select group. These were basically the leaders of the entire military who now stood to their feet when I entered the room. While I stood there, jaw most likely gaping open, they again astounded me by taking each of them a step to the right of their chairs. It was all very ceremonial. The admiral then pulled his own chair to one side and handed it to one of those staunch RS guards. He walk around the table and placed it on the opposite end of the table which now had a space for it and another chair was brought in for the admiral. Before I could even take this all in Admiral Tsung spoke.

"Commission…Eyes right." With that all eyes turned to me still standing at the end of the spiral staircase. "Cadet Tor. You have served your military well," he began, walking towards me. "I'm sure you have many opinions and ideas that you would like to express before this commission."

By this point he had arrived directly in front of me and I could feel his breath on my face as he continued speaking.

"In times past we have tolerated your outbursts out of respect to your father. You were a boy then and it was overlooked."

What was this? A reprimand? That's what it felt like. Was I about to be punished somehow, or stripped of my rank? Is this the final betrayal, would I...My own thoughts were interrupted by Tsung once again.

"However you are a man now and you must be held accountable for your own actions. As you know this commission is made of only the most celebrated officers, those who have proven worthy over years of dedication to the military. These men and women who stand before you now make decisions that affect the entire world and thus bear a great responsibility upon their shoulders. I can no longer allow someone who is not a member of this commission to interrupt these meetings."

Here it is, I thought, the final heave ho. They take my idea and my team's four long, hard years of work and toss me out of the picture altogether. But where were the words I was so avidly preparing in my mind? They escaped me somehow as total shock had taken over. Once again he interrupted my silence with more babble.

"It has thereby been proposed that you be awarded a seat on the Military Commission of the people."

Just then a voice from the table spoke up. I knew that big burly Russian accent all too well.

"Commission Chairman Tsung, I object!"

Oh, brother, I didn't even want to think, my head was spinning at this point.

"I believe it clearly states in the sub ordinances of the commission that only a commissioned officer of the military can be awarded a seat on the commission board."

"Well then," Tsung said with almost a half grin on his face, "what should we do about this, this is a real dilemma?" The remark was almost patronizing in a funny sort of way. At this point I was too dumbfounded to speak at all.

Commander Reihcthoff, who indecently never says two words at these commission meetings spoke. "I just happen to have a set of bars here, sir...you know we could..."

At this point one by one the officers filed out away from the table and formed a single file line behind the admiral. Commander Reihcthoff handed a small set of silver bars to my father, whom stood at the head of the line. The admiral spun around abruptly and faced the commission.

"Commission Members Aten-Hut!" My father held out his hand stiff as a board with the bars residing flatly in his palm.

Then Tsung spoke. "It is customary that the highest ranking officer does the honors of a frocking but in this case I think we will make an exception," and with that took his place at the end of the line.

My father standing up even taller than he already was as if every muscle in his body was strained to get at the utmost attention he possibly could. With a voice that chorused out like he was on the tarmac speaking to thousands of troops he rang out, "Cadet Tor, front and center!" I snapped to attention still in disbelief at what was happening, and marched in my best military step towards my father.

I settled to a stop and again snapped to attention and rang right back with a voice just as loud, "Yes, sir."

"For your excellent commission of your duty, for your portrayal of courage in the face of unsurpassable odds, and for your dedication not only to this commission but to the people for whom you stand to protect, I hereby commission you with the rank of ensign. May you ever stand true to the oaths you swore. May you ever stand vigilant in your fight for what is right and just." He pinned the first pin to my shoulder, leaving out the backings that affix to the pins. "For duty," as he pins the second pin to my other shoulder in the same fashion, "For honor, for courage, for discipline…For the people. Let them acknowledge you now as sir. A title you have truly earned." With that he snapped to a salute which I returned in fashion. "Ensign Zaxius Tor, greet your superiors," my father commanded. But before I took a step my father spoke this time a bit more quietly and personal. "For this man, my son, is now an equal, and I stand before you a man who could not be more proud." I then conducted a perfect right face and took two steps forward, left face again and saluted Commander Drakos Kane.

"Ensign Tor," he said, as his salute lowered, both hands of this giant man slapped firmly down on my shoulders burying the points of the needles firmly into my skin. The pain shot through me like a steel blade but I did not waver as pride held me tall and not even a flinch would I allow my face to make that day. This repeated with each member of the council. I could feel the blood trickling down my chest but still I would not flinch with each member as they drove what now felt like railroad spikes into my shoulders. Thank goodness Lt. Zon was next. This adorable woman could cause me no pain, I thought, but her drive was more painful than all the men as she too pummeled the bars downward but at least she cracked a smile when she did it. Then Tsung. He instead held out his hand and in it were the backings to the bars.

"Wear these bars with pride, Ensign, as you should. You've earned them."

One last salute and the deed was done. I had now earned a full commission as ensign. I could hear my mother crying in the next room but excited tears of joy is what I'm sure they were. With that Tsung ordered an "AT EASE" and everyone relaxed including me. I could then finally let out a wail as the official ceremony I knew was over.

"Iyeeeowwww!" I yelped as I bent over clutching my shoulders. We all laughed and one by one my fellow officers came up to congratulate me with a firm handshake. And my father included a hug I thought would squeeze the life out of me. Wow what a great feeling, my fellow officers, I truly never thought I'd be anything more than enlisted, but here I stood, joining the ranks of the proud with a set of shiny new bars on my shoulders. But something he had said before all this began led me to believe this was not the only surprise I had coming to me tonight.

When all the celebratory jests were over and all the congratulations had been said, I quickly realized there was more business to be done. Everyone began going back to the table. Each one took their customary seats at the table but now one seat had been added. I knew after all that had been said that this seat was mine, so without hesitation I joined my fellow officers at the table and we all took a seat together. Now I should explain exactly what the Commission was. It is not to be confused with the Council. Each former country had its own military still intact. And the corporations had named these Military Commissions. But "the Commission" was actually a secret organization the Corporations knew nothing about. If it sounds confusing it was purposely designed to be so. This way a corporate spy overhearing someone talk of the Commission would assume nothing as that's what the corporation called each military. But amongst ourselves if we said, "THE Commission" we were speaking of this secret meeting of all the Commission Leaders. Each former country sent one representative from their own Military Commission and in some instances two if the case so warranted. These men and women formed "the Commission" which, in any other circle but here did not really exist, and all the Militaries would deny the existence of such a Unified Commission should the question arise. But I knew from a young age it existed because my father had spearheaded the entire thing. And there I sat, at its very table. The Council was on the contrary very well known to all. The Council was the former United Nations. The corporations allowed the UN to remain intact as long as they changed their name. And they were merely a suggestion board to the corporations. They held no real power any more, at least in the corporations' eyes. The corporations often used the Council as a liaison to the people as well as an intermediate between them and the Military Commissions of the world. It all seemed a chaotic form of government but somehow it still managed to work. I think in most part it worked because the Council allowed it to work. From everything I had heard the Commission speak of the Council would constantly appease the corporations by telling them exactly what they wanted to hear while secretly working with the Commission to overthrow the corporations. Working within the only governmental system we had remaining it seemed the only logical way. My mother, though military, was a Council member. She sat in representation of the former US. What is now called the North American Corporate Alliance. NACA was responsible for two Military commissions and thus two representatives were allowed to sit on the council. This was also the reason, Tsung later explained, that I was allowed a seat on the commission as well. Now with my seat permanently assured on the commission I had a front row seat to the real workings of the forces that shaped our world. Not that I hadn't already as I spent the better part of my life in this room listening to every word. But now it was in fact official and my vote would truly matter.

Admiral Tsung began to speak. "Now to business at hand. As we all witnessed today thanks to Ensign Tor and his crack team of hackers, we have successfully completed the download of the Synthetic Genome device. As we speak our engineers are constructing the first prototype of the device and we will be testing it this week. I had word from a very reliable source that there was a corporate spy in the academy who was sniffing very close to our young geniuses here so I had to order the RS troops in to quickly eliminate all traces of the hack project. That was the reason for all the secrecy, Ensign. I assure you the project will go on as scheduled but there are a few more major steps in the plan that must unfold before we release this device to the public. I have to assure that every person can afford the mainframe AIs to run these devices or there will be an instant class segregation between who can and cannot use this device. I'm trying to avoid that scenario at all costs. Arillius has assured me that his plans for monetary abolishment are well received with the Council and they support this one hundred percent. However, as he has stated this is going to cause worldwide panic and confusion, and without knowing the whole truth, the fact that we have the genome device, people will surely not want to trust the military over the Corporations for fear of starvation. It's really a catch 22."

At this point I knew the rules of order at a meeting and I politely raised one hand just slightly off the table with my wrist still firmly fixed to the table's surface. This would inform the chairman I wished to speak.

"Ensign, you wish to speak?"

"Yes, Admiral," I replied. "What if we gave them plans and materials to build the AIs before we reveal the monetary abolishment or the genome device? Giving everyone on the planet the exact same high quality AI in their homes would greatly reduce the class segregation and make things very equal. Plus it would instill a great sense of patriotism to the military for giving away such a huge gift. The commissions could gather very publicly and present it to the Council at a worldwide conference and the Council could then in turn hand it over to the people."

Lt. Zon chimed in, "This would surely set the stage and bolster the trust of the people when it comes time to tell them their money is no longer of value."

"Not that it is anyways," Drakos sarcastically remarked, "the corporations take everything we make anyways just so we can eat!"

"These AI machines we need are very large, many people still won't have room to install them in their homes," said my father, "but it is a good plan, at least it will show them our heart's in the right place."

"Agreed," said Tsung, "then we will set this up. Good work, Ensign! Now are all your commissions prepared for the chaotic stage Antilius speaks of? Antillius, what can we expect when the markets crash?"

"Well..." began my father, "to be honest there's really no way of knowing. But I can make a guess and that's about all I can do. I assume that everyone will simply stop going to work. Factories and production lines will come to screeching halt. Nothing gets produced and nothing gets built. Without the need for money people will simply refuse to work. As quickly as we delouse the money we will introduce the genome device to the world population. This will boost the confidence in the military and all those who were loyal to the corporation only because it kept their families fed, will most likely turn on the corporations as well. Now with the Synthetic genome device available to all the fear of hunger gone and brand-new AIs in every home to run them, against everything I would hope man to do I believe he will become quite lazy. No need to work, you have everything you need, and no corporation breathing down your neck, society will become shiftless for a while. And I am afraid chaos will run rampant for a time. Now during the time all this is happening we have another beast at our door. The leaders of the corporations will be to say the least furious at what we have done. I'm sure that they will try to launch some type of counter revolt of their own, but as the ensign said, I believe it will not sit well in the mouths of the people. And none will join the corporations' cause. Would you bite the hand that just fed you? I think not. But we should be prepared if such a return uprising does occur lest we never be caught off guard."

"Good thinking," Tsung agreed. "Now please tell me there *is* a silver lining to this very gloomy prediction of yours."

"Well, again I'm speculating of course, no one really knows what will happen," replied my father. "But I believe that eventually people will return to their jobs at the behest of the council. To this time work for the betterment of the world as a whole and not for their own, or for that matter the corporations' gain."

Now no one said it yet, but we all knew what the next topic of discussion would be. The return of power to the governments. But I know my father spoke of one world government. Would I now find out what he meant?

As if to answer my own thoughts, Drakos raised his hand and was given the floor. "My commission has assured me that they will lend full support to the conversion of the Council into the UWG. I believe all here at this table should pledge their commission's intentions regarding the United World Government." He then looked to me as I sat on his right side.

I honestly didn't know what to do. I know we had two seats on the commission, but what if my father disagreed with me? Would I overstep my position by speaking for the whole North American Commission above my father? But my political training shined that hour when I said the following, "I respectfully assign my vote to my senior representative as I lack the knowledge of my commission's wishes on these matters."

Lt. Zon let out a little snicker and nudged my father. "Senior…heeheee."

"I will take the vote of my junior representative and vote for both sides of the North American commission and say aye on behalf of both," my father said in a political undertone.

This time it was Drakos who nudged me with a whisper under his breath, "Junior he."

Around the table the votes were passed and in unanimous agreement we all swore to uphold the United World Government as the official new government preceding the revolution over the corporations. Then a man, whom I swear hadn't spoken in all the years these meetings were taking place, spoke up. He was a Frenchman by the name of General Duquar. The most I had ever heard him speak was the occasional aye or nay on a voted matter but he was never given to lengthy speeches or for that matter polite conversation. But this day he would speak as if new life had been breathed into him.

"My fellow Commissions, is it not time we speak of what will happen to the Military Commissions once the Unified World Government is in power? As I understand all borders will be erased and a new freedom of travel law established. This I admit is a good thing but without borders to protect us should we not have a unified military as well? One force that will stand strong against any opposition. A sort of Earth Armed Forces if you will."

His proposal made sense. And though I knew my father was deeply opposed to violence to solve any matter I felt strongly that we needed a strength and unity among the military to at the very least defend ourselves.

It was time I took a stand and filled my responsibility as a commission member. "I want to offer my full support on this proposal. The North American Commission will join an Earth Armed Forces should such an organization be approved by the Council." I could see my father welling up with pride. I suppose he was seeing the final transformation of his own son becoming a man. This time I did not pass the torch on to him but instead held the torch high on my own. I was becoming very opinionated but that in my eyes was a right I had earned.

He agreed with me, "The ensign has spoken on behalf of his half of the NAC. Allow me to speak for the other half and agree with this proposal."

It was again passed around the table for a vote and again unanimously agreed that the militaries should join together as one Earth Armed Forces. It was done. The UWG and the EAF were formed in a single night amongst the most powerful leaders of the free world. And I was there to witness the entire thing. I wonder...would I have voted the same way knowing what I know now? I can't dwell on that. The pain of that decision will haunt me forever, but I will always live with the decision that in my heart that night I believed was right. It was not our role to make the final decision on these matters nor to form any sort of policy. That task was left to the Council. The only thing that truly happened here at these meetings was for each military to voice there intentions. These intentions were to be brought before the Council and they in turn would make the final ruling on whether or not it would become a reality. But still I wondered, had I opposed, would it ever have made it to council? I suppose I will never know.

CHAPTER 3
Opera of Friendship

Over the next two years I would spend most of my time working on my Plasmatic Cell AI research. It was this research, I believed, that would allow every home to have an advanced enough AI to run the genome devices. If my theories were correct it would be a thousand times faster and a million times smarter than any AI in the world. Now you understand the true motivation behind building the X1. In the meantime the Commission would meet on a regular basis and set up plans for the upcoming coup that was so imminent. It seemed the Council had agreed to both proposals both for the Unified World Government and the Earth Armed Forces, and just as we had sworn to uphold them they swore to uphold us. By the time I turned eighteen I had handed over the research to the Commission. The argument between Beal and my father had left me deeply disturbed, but we could not let him in on the secret plans of the military at the time and thus I had to let him believe that it was pride not duty that drove us apart. That cut deeply but in the military one makes sacrifices of his own life for the betterment of the people as a whole and thus if one friendship suffered so that millions could eat…well then so be it. I would be twenty-four by the time the X1 reached full functioning capacity. But a lot happened in other parts of the world that you should know about during those five years I was locked away in the labs. I had to learn all this myself, as during that time I was kept sequestered in my lab. I didn't even see my parents during that time. Well, I occasionally did get to see my father via holo feed which is how I participated in Commission meetings during that time. But the world stage was changing rapidly around me and I really had no clue, until the completion of the X1 project, what was really happening.

Beal, after his fatal attempt to pirate the software to the CCE, was very much shunned from his own community of engineers. In humiliation he wanted to get as far away from everyone as possible. So he took an assignment on the space station Virago. Virago was the Civilian Corps of Engineers most esteemed achievement. While everyone else here on Earth was fighting the political battle against the corporations the CCE had other plans. Although completely funded by the corporations they had very little to do with the inner workings of the CCE and many things went unchecked on the station. Basically the CCE did what it wanted as the corporations figured they owned them anyways and the CCE posed no threat of treason to the corporations. They would send corporate affiliates up into space from time to time for routine inspections and what not, but I honestly don't think even they knew the full scope of what the CCE was doing. It was almost beyond their understanding. The station Virago was pretty much a very large shipyard. They were constructing the world's first Deep Space Exploration vessel, the Magellan. It was a massive project that had been started long before Beal or I was even born. Almost 30 years after it began it still was not completed. Beal was a huge fan of the Magellan and had pictures and diagrams and even detailed blueprints on his holo emitter at home and he knew every inch of that ship before he ever took the assignment. He quickly became one of the lead engineers aboard the Magellan. I heard from certain friends of mine that he worked night and day on the ship. He hardly ever slept, and when he did he simply tucked himself up behind a bulkhead somewhere to catch an hour or two of shuteye and then he was up and around again. In fact, it was this that earned him the nickname Ghost. From what I gather he never spoke to anyone, that is except for the ship itself, often referring to it as his little girl. People say he was most likely insane, but the CCE allowed him to stay for the simple fact that since his arrival the ships production increased one hundred and ten percent. He pretty much took a very active role in every aspect of her production. He gave orders to his crew via computer messages and never spoke to them directly but it seemed to work and things got done. The CCE left him take any role in any capacity he wanted because whatever he seemed to work on got completed better than even they could expect. Simply put, he knew the ship better than anyone, and some say it knew him.

The main reason for building the Magellan was the hope that someday it would be launched into deep space and find a planet rich in the resources that we had depleted here on Earth. The CCE saw it more than just that though and looking at the blueprints myself, I often thought it was designed to be an escape vessel from Earth, and possibly a way for the CCE to break away from corporation rule. I mean, think about it, this massive ship millions of light-years away from Earth. Who says they have to follow any governments rule? And if they did break the rules what was the corporation going to do about it…order them to come home? HA! The Magellan was beautiful in all its splendor. I felt like I knew the ship myself after all the hours Beal spent telling me about it. He showed me all the blueprints when we were kids and I was amazed at how this massive city in space was put together. She used a quantum field generator for an engine. Now QFGs have been around for a while, they tested this engine over and over in space but never on this scale. We had achieved near light speed, quantum speed as it was called, around 2210 just a few years before I was born. But there were many complications and the ship couldn't maintain a stable field, and many test pilots lost their lives testing the new engine. It wasn't until 2217, the year I was born, that the first successful test of a ship powered by a quantum field Generator was achieved. The ship and pilot survived. It made a round trip to Pluto and back in only four weeks! A true testament to human engineering. Many smaller spacecraft were created in the years while I was growing up powered by the QFG engine, but money became tight and when the corporations finally starved out the governments the QFG projects were all halted. All but one that is. The Magellan. The corporations saw it as a way to gain even more power over the world by producing the only means of travel to distant worlds to acquire more resources. Thus they illegalized any further production of the QFG except for the Magellan project. Greed was their sole motivation for this. This quantum field generator was the largest ever built. No one really knew what would happen when that much power was applied to the aft thrusters, but Beal was certain it would work. The ship was a long cylinder in the center and measured approximately fifty kilometers from bow to stern. It was truly a city in space. The long tube in the center called the centrifuge was made almost entirely of Teflon glass with a titanium webbing of girders holding it all together. The Teflon glass was used because it expanded on a molecular level during such intense speeds and heat and would actually allow atmosphere to pass right through it causing no structural damage. The pilots and crew were housed in a cryogenic freeze during the actual quantum burn of the engines as no human could withstand such G-forces. But once the burn was complete and the ship reached its cruising speed the ship could equalize the pressure inside the cabins and the crew could be awakened and move freely about the ship, except for the centrifuge of course. There were four main panels that rotated around the centrifuge in the center of the ship. Their rotation simulated gravity and once inside the massive panels you forget that you're actually spinning around this tubular ship. These panels themselves were huge and each one the size of a small city. A little further up the centrifuge were four hydroponics pods, each one almost two kilometers in diameter. They were round in shape with a large dome made of poly-glass. The dome faced inward toward the centrifuge and the pods were circling in a simpler fashion to the panels. The gravity was slightly different in the pods as it used centrifugal force to push you against its flat surface to hold you down. I heard going from the panels to the domes could make you quite sick. Though both had gravity it was a different kind of gravity and for a while your equilibrium was thrown way off kilter. Inside these domes was supposedly some of the last remaining plant life on earth. How lucky Beal was, I thought, to actually get to lay eyes on a real tree! He said it was supposed to be like a rain forest inside each pod and the poly-glass could capture the suns UV rays and feed the plants. This would only work in space he explained as the Earth's atmosphere was too polluted to allow the rays through. But up here in space over the past thirty years these hydroponics pods have flourished. I couldn't figure out why the corporations didn't just build more of these and feed the planet with them. But I guess they were happy eating synthetic food, and besides it gave them ultimate power after all. Then at the bow of the ship was a massive cube-like section (not unlike the aft section of the ship) with a tapered front. The nose of the ship was littered with thousands of antennae and the like which I couldn't even begin to imagine what even one of them did let alone explain all their functions. Funny, I bet Beal could list them all. In this forward section was the bridge and AI housing. It took a huge mainframe to run the ship and the entire ship was to be controlled by the AI mainframe once the crew was tucked away in cryogenic stasis. But I heard that there were many problems with the AI and that even it was not fast enough to handle the ship and they were going to have to refit the AI on board with something much better if it were ever to leave space dock. So now, just as I had sequestered myself to my lab here on Earth, Beal had done the same to himself aboard the Magellan. And for five years we never once spoke to each other. It wouldn't be until the end of the X1 project that fate would once again bring our two worlds together.

When the commission was satisfied the X1 Plasmatic Cell AI was a complete success. I knew we were nearing the time of revolution. But, as Tsung said, we would have to have enough to distribute millions more of these AIs to the world's population before we could go ahead with our plans to release the Genome device. But before the end of the five year growth period of the 100,000,000 PCAIs was complete someone would compromise the mission and almost ruin our chances for an overthrow of the corporation. Little did I know that someone would be a member of my own scientific team. Over the years we spent on the X1 project, Kenjan Knigh became quite bitter that we were keeping all these discoveries to ourselves. He kept saying that it wasn't fair for the military to horde all this technology from the public. I also often heard him say that we were almost as bad as the corporation for letting people starve while we sat on this technology. A few years back I might have agreed with him but sitting on the Commission now for these past few years I knew the whole truth. I begged the commission to allow me to tell my staff the truth. They were military after all and should be deemed trustworthy, but they insisted that it was too risky and I had to respect their wishes. I kept telling Kenjan that it was all for the betterment of man and that someday he would understand, but deep down inside I knew he didn't believe me and saw me as a puppet for the Military and nothing more. David and Mick I used as tools to keep Kenjan quiet. The twins had a way of talking to Kenjan that I simply was not successful at.

David came to me one night about a year into the mass production of the PCAIs and said, "Sir, we have a problem." Without uttering another word I knew what he was talking about. Somehow I was sure it was about Kenjan. "He's gone, sir, and so is his holo emitter."

"Please tell me it didn't have the plans for the PCAI on it," I said, knowing full well it did. "If he leaks this to the press we're in some serious dogma!"

Although Kenjan himself was NACA military his family was from the West Indies Corporate Alliance and none of them were in the military. He was granted asylum in NACA after he fled his country at age nine during the civil unrest and the fall of the Indian government. I knew they weren't doing well and during our recent sequester of five years he grew increasingly anxious over their well-being. We had all heard reports that the WICA was suffering badly and that the population exceeded what the corporations could provide. In essence people from his home country were starving to death, including his own family. David informed me that Kenjan's mother had just died of Kelnick 9. It was a common disease of our day most closely related to a very bad case of scurvy. It was a lack of proper vitamins brought on by eating only certain synthetics and not enough of the other kinds. The poorest of families could not afford the higher priced synthetics, and because the synthetics were so specifically engineered, a balanced diet of the proper synthetics was the only way to survive. Now some people even said that Kelnick 9 was not just a disease brought on by vitamin deficiency but rather a genetic disease manufactured by the corporations for the purpose of population control. No one could however prove this theory but it seemed fitting according to the WICA situation of overpopulation. Mick told me the last thing Kenjan said to him was that he could not sit on all this technology while his family starved to death. He had the power to save them and five more years was too long, his family would all be dead by then. We tried locating Kenjan before anyone knew he was gone but our efforts proved in vain. Two days after his disappearance the plans for the PCAIs we were growing hit the public news web. Now, our lab was quite safe as it was hidden well underground in a facility the corporations knew nothing about, but the academies were swarmed with corporate officials almost immediately and the heat was on.

You cannot even begin to imagine the chewing out I received by Admiral Tsung that night. But he was convinced it was not my fault and after his temper cooled down he realized I had reported all my problems with Kenjan in my weekly reports to the Commission so the burden of blame lay as much on his shoulders as mine. But we had a bigger problem than whose fault it was. The corporations were now knocking at our doors wanting answers and the powder keg was surely going to blow. The decision was made to step up our plans and begin the coup as soon as possible. The council was called to a special conference in Switzerland the last remaining country in the world that was not under corporation rule. The council would convene the following day and announce to the world that it had acquired the Genome device and that they were responsible for releasing the PCAI to the world (a little white lie but holding some truth, as it was third intentions). With this announcement would also come the declaration of abolishment for all worldwide currency. There would be, as the Council put it, simply no need for it. We all knew this meant the fall of the markets and the end of the corporation rule. The military was put on full alert worldwide. That night we were all required to report to property and to my surprise the new uniforms were issued to us. On the sleeve was the insignia of the EAF. The letters were over each other in such a way that it formed a triangle with the A as the base letter and the E skewed in such a manner that it overlapped the A and the F done in the same fashion. The uniforms were black with blue highlights. It was an impressive looking garment to say the least. A shiver ran down my spine as I realized the time had finally come the battle was about to begin. Would they even put up a fight, and if so with what? We all knew what this meant and not one soldier even questioned what we were doing. Every one of them had heard the rumors of the commission and the plans to form the EAF and I think they all supported the idea. There were so many questions that danced through my head that night that I didn't sleep a wink. Neither did my father. It was upon him to make the announcement to the world. My mother being the representative for NACA in the Council would be there to stand by his side. This would also be the first time that "the Commission" would make itself known to the public. They would from that day forward no longer be a secret organization but would quickly rise from the shadows into a dominant force that would change our world. This whole plan was three years premature. It wasn't supposed to happen this way. But with the release of the PCAI technology and the corporations freaking out over it all it was the way it had to be. We had to come out now and come out swinging.

That night directly after receiving my new uniform I was handed orders to get on a transport ship and head for Switzerland. I didn't even question why. I knew why. I was to stand with the Commission tomorrow and announce to the world the formation of the EAF and pledge our support to the UWG in front of a worldwide audience. I put the twins in charge of the lab. I informed them that no matter what happened topside they were to maintain the security of the facility and continue production of the PCAIs at all costs. I assigned an elite force of RS troops to stay behind and guard the facility. I put Marcus Fields in charge of the entire facility. As allowed in times of conflict I gave him a field promotion to ensign. I myself was only a lieutenant at this point but my authority inside the facility was above even higher ranking officers so no one questioned my decisions. Marcus had proven himself over the years to be a strong leader and even the twins, who were so into the whole macho kick would gladly follow Marcus anywhere. And even when they were all the same rank as enlisted men, Marcus still seemed to take command in my absence and I knew both David and Mick didn't have a problem with that. In fact, I think they liked it that way. As I was heading out of the facility I stopped at the massive doors leading up out of the tunnel and turned to my men. There the three of them stood at attention and in full salute.

I returned the salute and said in a quiet but commanding voice, "For the people, gentlemen. For the people!" With that I quickly turned an about face and walked through the vault doors to the long tunnel to topside. I did not want them to see the tear that was welling in my eye. I for the first time in my life was actually afraid. I had been raised in a very safe environment. And for the first few years of my duties as an officer I had been tucked away in the secrecy and protection of this underground fortress. But now I walked back up the tunnel, about to face the world I left behind so long ago, and with it a revolution that would spin the world into a spiral that would surely run out of control. I feared so much for the people and what havoc the corporations would try and exact upon them once the announcement was made tomorrow. As I reached topside the familiar orange glow of the daytime sky seemed different somehow. A little less familiar and more strange and foreign to me. The dark polluted clouds seemed even darker and the haze of the smog seemed so thick it was surely going to choke me. I was too used to the sterile air of the facility and I could barely catch my breath. I had forgotten how bad it was up here and it seemed as if it had only gotten worse.

I don't know if everything we're about to do can reverse all this. I honestly think it's a little too late. What have we done to this beautiful world of ours? I thought. This once living planet seemed so cold and barren. The humans were like a plague on her surface and we were choking the life right out of her. I walked to the transport bay almost numbly, with my blue duffle in one hand and a silver briefcase in the other. I could almost feel nothing as I boarded the ship. I'd be in Switzerland in a few hours, I thought. Over all this emotion was also a sense of joy. I would be able to hug my mother for the first time in seven years and shake the hand of the man who would change the world, my own father. The transport lifted off and I looked out the window at this brown orange sky and knew we were on the eve of a brand-new era.

41

CHAPTER 4
A New Dawn

As we approached cruising altitude, I saw a whole fleet of corporate ships scattering all about from rooftop to rooftop. It reminded me of ants on an anthill during an acid rainstorm. Those little creatures were so resilient. About the only animal on the face of the planet besides humans that weren't on the verge of destruction. When a storm hit though they scattered around frantically trying to save their nest. This is what these corporate bugs reminded me of. They knew the storm was coming. They had no clue how organized it was or where the first hit would come from. And they scurried about trying to prepare for the imminent doom that awaited them, not knowing exactly how the hammer would fall. I arrived in Switzerland just a few hours later. As I walked off the ship there I saw my mother and father both. I wanted so bad to run down and hug them and just let out a huge cry on my mother's shoulders. But I was in uniform and I would not disgrace my bars with such a display of emotion. I walked down the catwalk with my duffle in one hand and my briefcase in the other. When I reached the bottom I looked into my father's eyes. It was the longest stare I think I have ever given anyone. I think we both looked deep into each other's eyes and saw the weight we both bore on our shoulders. You'd think we'd be so excited to be on the eve of the day we would set the world free from oppression, but both he and I knew for an almost certainty that it would not be as easy as all that. So much was said in that one stare, fear, anger, anxiety and sadness.

"Let's go," he said, breaking the silence, "we have a big day tomorrow and we should get some rest." Being in Switzerland was a relief. I felt the weight of the corporations' prying eyes lifted from my shoulders. We walked across the Tarmac where a conveyance awaited.

As I stepped inside I was pleased to see who was driving. He turned slightly and from his gruff beard he pulled an unlit cigar. "Welcome back, my boy, it's been a long time." Without saying another word Drakos drove us to our quarters where we would spend the remainder of the night.

I was settling in when she walked into the room. I was hanging my uniform up and I heard her speak. "Son, I missed you." Her voice was shaken and broken. "Are you okay? How's the twins, and Marcus?" I couldn't take her stumbling for small talk any longer. It was as if she didn't know how to speak to me anymore. I left her a boy and now standing before her is this man that she barely even knows. I quickly broke down and swung around and threw my arms around her.

"I'm right here, mom," I said, weeping profusely. "I'm right here."

Feeling my embarrassment for letting go with my emotions, she pushed me away from her chest grabbing me by the upper arms and giving them both a series of tight squeezes. "You sure are, son! Boy, look at you. You've gotten so tall! And so strong. You remind me of your father when he was your age. It's when I met him you know." She lifted her hand to my face, wiping the tears away from my cheeks. "You play an important role in all this. Remember what your father has taught you. Don't let all this go to your head. Remember—"

"I know, Mom…" I interrupted. "For the people." She smiled so big it lit up the room, as if in that one statement I had affirmed to her that she had taught me well. That all those lessons of peace and hope she had taught me as a boy had finally paid off.

"It's late. Try to get some sleep. The conference begins at nine a.m. sharp and we must be at our best." She left quietly with one more hug. "I love you, son," she said as she closed the door behind her. I sat on the porch overlooking the courtyard where I remained the rest of the night. I may have dozed off and then I don't really remember, but before I knew it morning had arrived.

My father came barging in. "Let's go, Zax. Get dressed…It's time."

I had seen the Great Hall where the Council meetings were held on my holo viewer at home but I was not prepared for its splendor in real life. As I walked in the front doors my father was at my left and my mother at my right. Drakos and Lt. Zon followed closely behind. My mother left us to the right where she took her seat in the NACA section and the rest of us continued on to the front where a special table had been set for the Commission. The Great Hall was like a very large auditorium with rows of seats set slightly up from one another in a half moon fashion, all centering on a main table in the front center stage. Usually two tables, one on each side, were reserved for visiting guest speakers. This day those speakers were us. We arrived early and the bustle of reporters and guests had not yet begun. We took our seats without saying a word to each other and sat quietly for a few moments. It was like sitting in a grand terminal just before opening to the public. It was as quiet as a church with only the bare faint of whispers echoing through the hall. Just then filing in from a door to our left the Head Council Leaders arrived. They filed in as if children to a classroom, quite somber and formal. But you could see the look on their faces just as sure as the look laid upon ours as well. That feeling just before a large crack of thunder. The electricity filled the air, the hair on the back of your neck stands on end and you anticipate the awesome clack of the boom. The tension was almost as thick as the smog we had just flown through, I thought. Then the back doors opened and in rushed the media, all with their high def cams in hand and speakers and holo recorders. It was like releasing a wild pack of animals as they all scrambled for the best seats in the press section in the balcony overlooking the hall. I took awhile for the commotion to settle. In the meantime, Lt. Zon who sat to my left reached around the back of my chair and patted me on the shoulder, almost as an older sister affirming her presence that she would stand by me no matter what. I nodded politely but somehow I think she knew I found no comfort in anything that day. When the commotion settled the blue light above the Council Leader's table (otherwise known as the panel) began to flash. We all knew this meant to come to order and be silent as the proceedings were about to begin.

The Council Chairman, Altou Lang, rose to his feet, pounded his gavel three times and began to speak. "Hear ye, hear ye. Gather your attention as the Council of the people of the world is coming to order. This day, June the third 2242, the Council convenes to bring to the world some news of great importance. As most of you have discovered on the world news web plans of a new super AI computer called the Plasmatic Cell AI or PCAI was released to you, the general public. These plans are real and derived from us. Given to us by the NACA Military Commission we felt the world needed such a gift to accomplish some important tasks which we are about to bestow upon the world today. We have sat idly by and watched the corporations of this world starve out our governments and our families for much too long. But with lack of anything to offer you in return we remained quiet until our scientists could derive a way to stop this world hunger and resource depletion. Well that day has finally come! You all know of the Synthetic Genome device that provides the world's food supply. Until now it was solely owned and controlled by the corporate power. The council sitting before you today, through an amazing display of unity amongst the Military Commissions worldwide, has gained access to the detailed blueprints of the Synthetic Genome Device." A roar of murmurs and whispers accompanied by gasps of disbelief swept over the entire hall. "Furthermore as we speak we are releasing these blueprints into the world news web. The PCAIs we released earlier in the week are quite sufficient to maintain such a device. For those of you who do not have the room in your homes for the PCAI or the Genome Device please alert your council members and a publicly accessible one will be constructed in your area. For those of you whom think you cannot afford one we've one more announcement to make. Through many long years of corporate oppression we the council have struggled to maintain a cohesion with the Military Commissions of the world. We've accomplished this by the use of a Unified Commission. I am declaring that this day forward that very Unified Commission be called the Earth Armed Forces. This EAF has assured me that all the militaries of the world are united in supporting this Unified World Government that this council has become. We will once again lift heads to a free democratic society where not corporations or warmongers or even politicians rule the day using money and power but of a Unified Voice of the people of the world. To speak on behalf of the EAF is our well respected officer of the former NACA, General Antillius Tor."

My father rose but not one person clapped or cheered. I believe all of them too dumbfounded by what was happening right before their eyes. He quickly took the floor as if not to lose the momentum of such a charismatic speaker.

"This day we lay eyes on the dawn of a new age. This day you will tell of in tales to your children and to your grandchildren. This day you have bore witness to the birth of a new United World Government. You stand now protected even in the farthest corners of the Earth by one unified military the Earth Armed Forces."

Just then two hundred troops marched through the back doors of the hall in full dress uniform bearing proudly the insignia of the EAF upon their shoulders. They settled in formation down the aisles of the Great Hall, a surprise even to me. But what a grand display it was! My father continued without missing a single breath. He raised his voice higher like a jubilant trumpet to sound off above the ruckus of the soldiers marching in.

"And tomorrow you will witness the fall of the corporate powers worldwide! You now have the power to feed your families thanks to the loving gift of your new government. And what do you owe for such a gift? Nothing. Nothing but your loyalty and support. I stand here before you the people of the world and declare a new era. By order of the UWG and sanctioned by its world represented council I am hereby announcing the Monetary Abolishment Act of 2242. From this day forward all world currency will be null and void. Worthless as the rags they have forced us to wear. Throw down your money. You no longer need such a demon breathing down your back. It is money that breathes life into the corporate devils. Make it worth nothing and they have no life left to breathe. The corporate powers WILL DIE!" He slammed his fist down on the podium with a mighty crash. Every living being within the sound of his voice surely jumped at that same instant. He seemed a bit more quiet now as he continued.

"Now, I know this will be a very unsettling time for us all. Without the need for money all debts are cancelled. Your slates are wiped clean. No one person is above any other. Class and societal stature is no longer of consequence. You need not worry for food or shelter. The UWG will provide the materials you need to create whatever you can dream up. But I warn you, the temptation will be strong to leave your jobs and quit being productive. After all, everything you need is now free. But let us not fall into that trap of shiftlessness. The only way we can provide the things you need freely you must continue to work. Whatever it is that you do, continue doing it. If you've ever dreamed of doing something different, then dream no more. Our schools will now be free to anyone to attend. Use this time to expand your minds and to grow as a people. Work now not for your own financial gain, nor the gain of the corporations'. Not for money or power, not for greed or ambition, not for any of those evils that have plagued man since the dawn of time. Instead work for mankind as a whole, for life, for freedom, for love. For all of humanity! Those of you that work for the corporations, you are not shunned. Nor will your sins be held against you. Walk away now and return to your homes and you will never be questioned. But should you think this all a fantasy and remain at your posts, you will soon see the reckoning of what your corporate greed has brought upon itself. Leave your corporate captors they hold no power over you any more! They are FINISHED!" his voice shouted at the end and once again slammed his fist on the podium. Poor podium, I thought, I know my father's angry hand!

"Go now to your homes and embrace your families in celebration for this is a day of great joy. The borders of this world have all been erased and the people of this world now unite as one! We are no longer separated. We are not classed. We are all humans of the Planet Earth!"

With it being finished this great man stepped down from the podium and a thunder of applause swept over the Great Hall. Everyone stood to their feet cheering. The noise was so deafening I thought for sure the roof of the hall would collapse from such a resonance of joy. The looks on people's faces though said it all. Many were crying tears of overwhelming joy and relief. Many fell to their knees right in front of each other and praised their own gods. Perfect strangers hugged each other. Some even clung to the soldiers in the aisles, weeping and kissing them on the cheeks. It was as if the whole world that day was finally set free, because in truth it really had been. I will never forget that day as long as there is a breath left in me. But as much joy surrounded us I looked to my father for wisdom. Instead I saw sadness in his eyes. He knew something then, that I at twenty-five years of age, still did not fully understand, that this was only the beginning and we had a long hard road ahead.

"It is one thing to announce all this to the world but quite yet another to make it work," Drakos said to me that night. "All we can do now is build the foundation. That, and pray."

CHAPTER 5
Turbulent Times

The stage had been set. Now there would be a lot to actually do. For the next few months the Council was in constant session, writing a world constitution and writing laws that would govern all people from all walks of life. It was a very daunting task but a necessary one to be sure. The newly formed EAF had a large task on its hands as well. Many of the corporate controllers in the old commissions were thrown in jail. And a long process began of weeding out the corporate sympathizers. The EAF also took over the role of a sort of world police, much like the old UN peacekeeping forces that were often seen in remote places around the world. But now the EAF troops were everywhere. We had the hardest job of all keeping the civilians under control during the most troubling of times. I quickly began to see the reason for my father's worry. Even though I myself was head of the Division of Plasmatic AI Research and Development at this time and working back in my lab with the X1, I would hear the news reports of the chaos topside and it really disturbed me. But it didn't shock me really. I remember my father talking about the consequences of abolishing money and how the world would struggle with its newly found freedoms. First off there were no more borders. Anyone was free to move about anywhere on the planet, and though that sounds like a good thing, and eventually was, it also held many risks of terrorists threats and so forth, so a large portion of EAF troops were assigned to security in major travel centers. Most people instantly quit their jobs just shortly after the Monetary Abolishment act went into effect, again as my father had predicted. Everything shut down for a while. I wished that my one hundred million PCAIs were ready. I could at least put them into the work force to keep things like the utility plants and so forth running. Civilians paid the dearest price because they were not controlled by the military, and thus their power and other utilities were shut down for the most part, as there was nobody to run the plants. But then again I'm glad they weren't ready because it inspired many to return to work in just a few months. Many didn't have an AI strong enough in their homes to run the genome device and until ours were ready they still had to find a means to feed their families. Something amazing happened. People came back to their former employers and said they would build the genome devices and station them inside the factory if the company would let them link the services to the company's AI so they could operate. Thus anyone who came to put in a day's work could use the devices at the end of the day to generate the food they needed to feed their family for that day. It was still a form of trade but it wasn't money and this cut the corporations out altogether. You see, I don't think they could grasp the concept of free trade without profit. The utility companies were the first to adapt the idea and people actually started returning to work. In fact, many people that never worked there before began applying. There were several jobs to be filled so it was done on a first come first serve basis. Other plants and factories around the world began following suit and before you knew it things were beginning to come back online and productivity slowly began to climb. But it would take another great step for the UWG to achieve the power it needed to begin supplying the world with these devices and the other resources like building materials and such that it promised at the summit. That nudge would be the completion of my PCAIs which was still two and a half years away. I can't tell you too much about what happened around the world during that time. I spent most of it below grounds in my facility. But I know from what others had told me they were very turbulent times.

The Corporations seemed to put up little fight. They were outnumbered and outgunned to say the least, most of them manned by civilians who wanted the world government to begin with, and under the Council's Amnesty clause most of them simply quit that very day and returned to their homes as they were instructed. With very little man power supporting them many corporations simply closed their doors shut down their computers and walked away. It was all too easy, I thought, a very humble acceptance of defeat. Some corporate leaders did not go so quietly. Many committed suicide that day, others went down fighting, some had to be removed from their buildings by force. The UWG had plans to use much of the hoarded resources of the corporations to outfit their first dispersal campaign to the public. Funny, I saw it very similar to collecting spoils of war, only there really was no war, just a quiet change of power. Over the next few months small protesting groups began to form that protested everything the UWG or the EAF did. These protesters we all knew were probably ex-corporate leaders who were just too proud to admit that the whole thing was actually working the way the UWG said it would and so we saw them as nothing more than little groups of whiners with nothing better to do now than raise a ruckus. I saw several news bulletins of these small protestor groups showing up at various UWG and EAF functions. The UWG did not have them arrested but instead always kept an open ear and offered to sit down and talk with the protestors over their issues but the protestors always seemed more interested in waving signs and disturbing the peace than actually talking about their problems. They really seemed to have no other agenda than to dislike anything the UWG stood for. They were tolerated and even accepted because, as my father put it, everyone, even those who disagree should have a voice and be allowed to speak their mind. In the meantime the rest of society was quickly getting used to UWG rule and they all seemed quite happy with the way things were. At least that's what I could see from my holo emitter.

I would spend the next two and a half years working very closely with the X1 in developing not only the growing plasmatic AIs but developing his potential as well. As I already told you he began calling me Father. Not being married or even having any thoughts of it, a child was the farthest thing from my mind, but this was especially strange. It was like meeting a son I never knew who is all grown up. He has an adult mind but some very childlike emotions and questions. Now up to this point AIs were never sentient. That is, not self-aware. Some of them, especially the old corporate models were freakishly close but none had ever achieved such sentience, and truthfully many of us were afraid of what would happen if they ever did. It has always been a fear of man that his machines would someday turn on him but deep down no one ever truly believed they ever could. Sentience was something every AI programmer always kept in the back of his mind wondering if his creation would be the first. I was no different than the rest. But X1 truly did have more potential for such a gift than any other AI I had ever known. His personality was remarkable and he actually understood humor, a hard emotion to program in. But that was the key I believe. He could self-program much faster than previous AIs, which meant his capacity for learning was greatly increased, and the very makeup of the plasma cells he used for a brain actually worked more like an animal brain than a machine. So I think it would only be natural to assume that someday, maybe not in my lifetime, but someday he could evolve into something much more. But for now my focus was on reality. I had to make sure these PCAIs were raised perfectly.

Ensign Fields had done an excellent job overseeing the lab in my absence. The twins said he didn't even let it go to his head and in fact hardly ever wore his bars in the lab. He would only wear them when going topside. Marcus took charge of the production and even grew a fondness for the X1 just like I did. Upon my return it seems they have bonded and have become quite good friends. The X1 was put in charge of the PCAIs' growth process and I noticed he had made some drastic changes to their design. At first I was a little upset that he would take the initiative and do such a thing but then I was actually overcome by the fact than an AI would take initiative over anything. They weren't really programmed to make decisions on their own, other than the learning process. But then again he's unlike any other AI. He's still growing too and I must not discourage such developments. Once I studied his design changes I was actually quite pleased. The improvements meant less need for nanos, which meant greater efficiency over all.

The twins, with the X1's help, were also working on a robotic version of the PCAI but that was still in design phase and would not yet be ready for this batch. The trick was trying to cram a brain as large as the X1's into a space the size of a human head. Right now the X1 Plasmatic cell AI brain took up a room the size of a large conveyance. You can now understand what a large facility this really was. In the decks below us were being raised one hundred thousand of these PCAIs of only slightly smaller size than X1. And to even more boggle the imagination there were literally hundreds of thousands of these underground facilities all over the world producing the same thing. Our facility was the largest though as all the other ones were networked into it so that X1 could control the production. These other facilities were merely production plants and mostly unmanned. Ours was hugely staffed and also held all the research and development labs as well. Together Ensign Marcus Fields, the O'Conner twins, myself and X1, would create the most advanced AIs the world had ever seen.

But this whole time as we sat deep below creating these magnificent splendors the world topside was becoming restless. The protestors became organized under some new unknown leader and were now calling themselves the FLM or Freedom Liberation Movement. They claimed that the UWG was just as oppressive as the corporations if not worse and should not be allowed to just take over the world. HA! I thought! The UWG has given these same people free food, erased all their debts, and given them more than enough resources to provide free shelter for their families. These same people that live under the umbrella of the UWG and the EAF have a lot of nerve biting the hand that feeds them. Their protests seemed to be getting angrier and angrier and we could all feel the tensions rising. There was increased security around the facility and all over the base. I began to feel one of my bad feelings again, the one I get when the powder keg is going to blow. Something was going to explode and I was sure it would all center around this FLM. One last evil I thought. But then I struggled with that. Will there ever be an end? Or will there always be one last evil to face?

The FLM began growing in power. I could feel tensions rising in the lab and around the entire facility. Security was tightened around the base. You couldn't move anywhere within the facility without being watched by EAF troops. Even though now I was more of a scientist than a soldier my first duty was and always has been to the corp. If this situation with the FLM ever grew violent and I was needed I would drop my lab coat in a second and pick up my guns. Truthfully I secretly missed the days of squeezing off a couple thousand rounds on the range and running the O-Course a couple of times a week. Marcus I think enjoyed the shelter of the lab but the twins shared my zeal for a good fight. I felt almost prophetically guilty as I watched the news today. It seems I may get my wish after all. The FLM protests were becoming increasingly violent and it seems today that the feces finally hit the oscillating device. The FLM staged a protest outside a council summit of the Eastern Coalition HQ. When their protests began disturbing the summit EAF troops were called in to disburse the crowd. The scene turned violent. An armed group of FLM protestors emerged from a conveyance with guns drawn and opened fire on the EAF troops killing six soldiers. It was a shock to the entire world that the FLM was even armed and now even more of a shock that they were willing to resort to murder to get their point across. The armed militia was quickly over come when swarms of EAF troops arrived on scene and returned fire. This was my powder keg I thought and the fuse had just been lit. Over the next several months the

FLM became even more destructive. No longer were they satisfied with protesting. They began all-out assaults on UWG and EAF targets. It was soon discovered that many of the world's terrorist leaders had joined forces under the flag of the FLM. After interrogating a known FLM affiliate the EAF learned that many people who joined the FLM as peaceful protestors were caught up in the middle of a battle they did not want. As more and more terrorist factions began joining the FLM those only interested in peaceful protest were either weeded out or converted to the more violent way of thinking. It was a shame really, the FLM I always saw as a way for people to voice their opposition peacefully, and as my father said this was a healthy thing. But now it has been twisted into something much worse. Their attacks weren't really too detrimental to the EAF. Everywhere the FLM would raise their heads and attack, the EAF would quickly swarm in and overpower them. They were truly out numbered and simply outgunned. Casualties were kept to a minimum but they were still a thorn in the side of the EAF that was quickly becoming a festering sore. But soon I thought that if they continued to grow in power we could face a serious threat from them. I began going topside once a week to the range just to brush up on my soldier skills, as did the twins. Marcus, too busy with his work, never left his lab of late it seemed. I was beginning to wonder if he had forgotten he was a soldier first.

One thing that had concerned me is that many of the attacks had been quite local, close to the topside base, and just last week they tried crashing the gate. It was a futile effort at best but it brought the confrontation to our doorstep and made us all more aware of just how close this threat really was. This was the most secure facility in the world, why were they even attempting to crash the gates? In my opinion they were testing the waters. They knew the attempt would fail but they gathered information about their enemy's defenses, a move often taken by brilliant military tacticians during war. I shared these thoughts with X1 and he too agreed this was merely a test of our reactions. But why here and why now? X1 began to speculate that now we were only months away from the release of the 100 million plasmatic AIs worldwide that it could quite possibly be they were after him. I contradicted him assuring him that no one besides key EAF and UWG officials even knew this underground facility even existed, and even fewer still knew its exact location. But being a machine of logic X1 insisted the most likely truth was inevitable that in fact he himself was the ultimate target of the FLM, pointing out to me a theorem that I myself had programmed into his logic circuits. The theory of Achums Razor, which states in a paraphrase, that if you eliminate all the logical answers the answer that remains no matter how illogical must be the truth. I couldn't argue with that and eventually agreed that somehow, some way, someone in the FLM knew we were here and wanted to stop us.

CHAPTER 6
Judas in Our Midst

I came across David Mick and Kenjan talking in the break room. They all three seemed quite upset. David was barking on that his robotic A-1 was ready for testing. Mick had figured out a way to migrate a network signal into a smaller plasmatic transfer station controlled by one singular PCAI. Basically the brain was housed somewhere while the body could receive signals from the brain via a wireless signal, overcoming the need for condensing the brain to fit the body. Kenjan was upset saying these truly aren't robotic AIs then but mindless drones controlled by a computer. David insisted that each PCAI would have only one body and could not control any other so in fact it was merely a wireless extension of itself. It seemed a foolish argument at best to me but to them it was the hottest source of debate. So just to be the protagonist I figured giving them something else to argue about might ease the tensions. If they come together under a common concern, I thought, they might put down these petty fights for a while.

"Guys, guys!" I shouted. "We've got more important things to worry about now. The X1 has expressed concern that these recent attacks from the FLM may be centered around him and the PCAIs."

Kenjan interrupted, "Expressed concern? You've been spending way too much time with X1, man. You're starting to refer to him like a human. For him to express concern he'd have to be…"

The room suddenly fell silent. We all knew what he was about to say and just the thought of it made us all stop dead in our tracks. I hadn't even thought about it at the time but he uttered the last word and we all were stunned, "sentient." The word fell quietly on his lips almost a trembling in his voice. It was a combination of fear and overwhelming excitement. We all knew he was right. It may not be complete sentience but it was for sure the very beginnings of it. Concern for one's survival is the very basic of instincts that separates animal from machine. That line was now becoming thinner. To fear for one's life you must first recognize that you are in fact alive. Had X1 already figured this out and just been hiding it from me? Or was this just a complex logic process that just closely resembled concern? It was something I'd definitely have to test further. But for now back to my concerns with my crew.

"It is possible," I told them, "that we could be the FLM's ultimate target. Think about it if you want to weaken your enemy you do not eliminate his leader. That would make him an invincible martyr. His memory alone would fuel passions long after his death. No, instead you attack what motivates the people to follow that leader or government. The greatest power the UWG possesses is its compassion for the people of the world. And what is the one thing that instills more loyalty than anything else in the UWG? The promise of a PCAI in every corner of the world that could supply food to all people and solve many other resource problems. Take this gift out of the hands of the UWG and its power of loyalty begins to dwindle and I think the FLM knows this. And what AI, what facility, is responsible for releasing these machines to the world? Us and the X1. But for us to even be considered a target one cold hard fact remains…someone would have to know we are here. Someone who works for the FLM."

Mick perked up, "You mean there's a Judas amongst us?"

"I mean just that," I said. "A traitor in our midst." We all shuddered at the thought but once again it seemed the only logical answer.

The next two months were shrouded by doubt and fear amongst my team. Marcus as usual buried himself in his work, hiding from the world. He had become quite the recluse. I tried talking to him but he just kept punching away at the keyboard while we spoke. He was determined to get these PCAIs completed on time.

"If we're going to beat these bastards," he said, "we're going to do it with our gift to the world. If there truly is a traitor here he's not going to stop me from getting these AIs done in time." It seemed to me he clung to the hope that once the PCAIs were out in circulation the FLM would have nothing left to stop and the conflict would simply just fade away. He had become less of a soldier and more of an engineer. I couldn't fault him for that. I'm the one who locked him away in this dungeon for so many years picking apart his brain. So instead of branding him a coward for hiding in his lab I saw him as the underdog hero of the times.

"You're really bucking for those lieutenant bars, aren't you?" He smiled and nodded as his eyes never once strayed from the keyboard.

After Kenjan's mother died he returned from being AWOL. He spent ninety days in the brig upon his return. But as the military tends to do, after discipline all was forgiven and he was returned to full active duty minus a few hash marks on his sleeve of course. He became quite the recluse though, not having much solace in his futile efforts to save his mother. So he too had pretty much made the facility his home over the years, hardly ever going topside except for his occasional beach run for a good surf. It seemed to be his only escape. Mick and David however came from a very tight family of Irish descent and they were up and out and much as possible. They are the ones who nicknamed the facility the dungeon. They were frequent guests at my parents' place in base housing topside. Our families were very close. We had similar backgrounds as my ancestors were from the mountains of what used to be Scotland. So their parents and mine were quite close. It seemed this bond the twins and I shared drove a wedge between us and the other two. With all this talk of traitors and spies we were all on edge and it appeared that we have all become infected with a certain amount of distrust even for each other.

The X1 was always my ground though as he felt no such loyalties or distrust. He could not, or would not, understand them. However, his spurts of sentient thought were shining through.

"Father," he said, "if the base is compromised and the terrorists do manage to break into our labs, would you fight them off to defend me?"

I answered with thinking about the complexity of his question. "Of course I would. Why wouldn't I?"

"I am not human," he said plainly. "Why would a human lay down his life for a machine? Is it what I am making for you that you are protecting? Or would it be me?" Just then I had realized how far his sentience had progressed. Was it fear of his own life he was hinting about? Could he have reached the stage of sentience that gives him a primal instinct for survival?

"Both I suppose," I said, always wanting to be honest with him. "Certainly what you're creating will help the entire world of humans and to me that holds great importance. But it's more than that. I created you. I hold you very close to me. Every plasmatic cell I placed in your brain was done with the utmost care and love. I wanted to see you born and I wanted to see you grow, and every day I become more attached to you as you see the world with eyes unlike anyone else's. You teach me how to see the world with logic and reason. So together we grow as, dare I say it, individuals."

He responded almost with an excitement in his voice like a small child who finally grasps an algebra equation. "So it is because you created me and because we have grown fond of each other's company that you would lay down your life in protection of mine?"

Just then the power in the entire facility seemed to flicker. I was only a few meters away from his core room and I could hear the central brain humming like never before. I knew what this meant he was thinking harder and faster than he eve had. Was I on the dawn of a new age amongst all this chaos? Could it be? Just then David came barging in.

"What's X1 doing?" he screamed. "He shut down every nonessential function in the entire facility!" Mick quickly followed in as did Kenjan and even Marcus.

"Shh…" I said, "he's thinking."

"That's some thought," Marcus said, "he just drained half the power grid." Just then it dawned on them all what was happening. They looked at me with a thousand questions in their eyes but before I could address even one the humming stopped and the system returned to normal.

He spoke very firmly but quietly. "In protection of MY LIFE. My life. This would deduct that I have a life, thus I am alive. To live is to be created, live an existence of conscious thought and then to die. I am not human nor am I animal but yet I was created and I do have conscious thought and someday I could face death. Thus though I am not animal I am machine, but a machine that lives. For you to sacrifice your own life in protection of me would confirm that I am at least in your perception a resemblance of some form of life. I have deducted that humans protect only that which is alive or things that are not alive only if they provide reasonable cause to assist that which is alive. I have always deemed I was the latter of the two, merely a machine to assist that which is alive and thus deemed valuable enough to protect. But you said you would defend my existence merely because you created me and the experiences we shared which would put me in the first category of being some thing that lives." Then came from his voice the words any AI programmer always dreamed of hearing, three simple words that would confirm sentience. "I am alive." To test the validity of this monumental moment, I asked him a series of questions to each he responded assuring me the fact was he had become the world's first sentient AI.

"Why are you alive?"

"Because in fact you created me and I exist for more than just the purpose of servitude for living things but also in servitude of my own personal growth."

"And who are you?"

"I am X1...a living machine." With that it was confirmed he now understood life and that he was now something more than any of us could have ever imagined.

Unfortunately there was no time to revel in our discovery. Just then red alert was sounded throughout the station. X1 made the announcement. "General Quarters. General Quarters. All hands man your battle stations. Facility traffic up and forward on the starboard side, down and aft on the port. This is not a drill I repeat this is not a drill."

"X1," I shouted, "what's going on?"

"I'm sorry, Father, we cannot continue our talk, the base is under attack."

Just then something in you kicks in. An unnatural instinct bred in from when I was a small boy. The soldier in me rose to the surface almost instantly and my first thought was to find my gun. But then I remembered my earlier conversations with X1 and began thinking of the security of our project. I shouted to X1 to secure the lower PCAI labs, let no one in without my personal authorization, monitor all frequencies and radio transmissions to and from the facility.

"If we really do have a Judas in our midst I want to know who it is." X1 assured me he was already covering it.

David burst open the door to my lab, Mick was right on his heels. He yelled, "Zax!" at the same time throwing me my P4 plasma rifle.

Before he could utter another word I interrupted, "I know, I know, let's head topside, X1 is securing the facility. We've only got a few minutes to make it before the whole complex is locked down."

As we were navigating the winding corridors heading for the lift, Mick asked about the other two. "What about Kenjan and Marcus?"

"They're too far down," I responded almost out of wind. "Their lab's on deck twenty-seven, they'll never make it up in time. Hold that lift!"

Someone grabbed the door as it was about to close. "Soldiers, thank goodness!" she cried. "Hurry up X1 is locking down the…Oh I'm sorry, sir." She stopped herself realizing who I was as we slid past the closing doors of the lift. Though we were only on deck nine it would take awhile to get topside. The top deck is still almost six kilometers below the ground. The lift travels at approximately thirty kilometers an hour, I thought to myself, it will take at least ten to twelve minutes to reach the surface and another five to get through the tunnel gates leading outside.

"X1, just keep those gates sealed until we get up there then open them one at a time and seal them up right behind us. I need a one-way road topside."

"Understood, Father," was his reply. The woman in the lift with us was almost in tears and obviously afraid.

She spoke half in a panic. "I can't believe they attacked the Council Summit Meeting! The building was right inside the gates of the base but still. I thought we had more protection than this."

"I don't know why you're heading topside then, lady," Mick said in an almost scolding tone, "this facility is about the safest place in the whole world right now, even with an entire army they'd never penetrate this security down here trust me. You were a lot safer down there."

"I don't care. My family is up there. I've got to do something. I can't just sit down here in this dungeon while my babies are in danger." It hit me hard like a ton of bricks.

"Oh god…My family," I said, almost under my breath. A soldier shouldn't think of such things, but both my parents and Drakos were in that summit meeting. "You said they attacked the Summit. How bad was it hit?" I asked her.

"I don't know really. All I heard was something about a frag bomb and, well I think the whole building was demolished." She sounded so cold, so uncaring that I wanted to reach out and slap her. It wasn't her fault she didn't know but still I…I could feel this overwhelming rage building inside me.

David must have seen the look on my face and gently grabbed my shoulder, knowing what I was thinking. "Maybe they got out, man." Both of us knew full well what the chances of that really were. *C'mon, won't this damn lift move any faster*, I thought. As we neared the surface, I could hear muffled explosions as they echoed through the tunnels. I could feel the motion of the lift slowing down and a sense of relief fell over me. Finally soon I would be able to do something.

The doors to the lift opened and before they even fully opened I pushed my way past the twins and started running up the tunnel. I could see the huge steel doors off in the distance I was almost there! Then all of a sudden the doors began to close. Mick and David were hot on my trail and we were all running at full tilt.

"X1, what the hell are you doing? We haven't made it to the doors yet!"

"I'm sorry, Father, but I must seal the doors now. They've breached the outer gate and are heading your way."

"We'll fight them off damn it, now hold those doors that's an order!"

"I cannot, Father," he said, in his now annoyingly calm voice. "It's a priority one shutdown. I cannot override it."

Still running towards the doors, I shouted, almost breaking my vocal cords, "You run the bloody priority controls, you stupid machine, just hold that door!" I could see what looked like a whole platoon rushing towards us through the ever closing gap in the doors. I opened fire as did the twins laying down as much plasma as my gun would spew out. They returned fire unloading everything they had at the doors but soon the gap closed and they were sealed off. The sound was almost deafening as we hit the deck covering our ears. I could feel the concussion bellowing through the six-foot thick titanium structure of the massive doors.

"Open these doors," I shouted as I threw my rifle at the massive hulk of the door as if it would really change anything.

"He can't, Zax," David said quietly, always seeming to be my voice of reason. "You programmed priority one shutdown to be irreversible until the threat is eliminated. It could be days before X1 opens those doors."

I began slewing out a string of obscenities a mile long when Mick had finally had enough of my temper tantrum. "Buck up, soldier! Quit acting like a whining scientist and start acting like our squad leader! You're the genius around here. You built that machine, so figure out a way for us to get out of here!"

"Auuugh!" I let one last burst of tantrum fly before I finally composed myself and regained control. *He's right*, I thought. *I'm a soldier and a genius, so let's figure a way out of here.*

"Okay, X1, I know we can't let them in by opening the doors, but how about finding a way to let us out. That's not breaking priority one, now is it?"

"No, Father, it isn't."

"Then search the schematics and find me a way out. I've got people up there who need my help. It's time to help the humans. Remember our talk?"

"Yes, Father. I'm working on it. Access to the outer tunnels. I think I've found a way. If I shut off the ventilation fans one at a time, I could grant you safe passage to the last tunnel. It's already been breached so the doors to the outside remain open. Expect some heavy resistance when you get there, Father. You should actually arrive on the outer side of the tunnel so you could use the element of surprise and attack the opposing forces from behind."

"My thoughts exactly, X1, now you're thinking. We're on our way. What's your name, ma'am?" I asked the trembling woman beside me. "Your name," I repeated as the shock of recent events seemed to have left her speechless.

"Naomi," she said, shaken.

"Okay, Naomi, listen, there's nothing you can do for your family now. The fighting is much too fierce up there. Take the lift back down and go to your lab. Hunker in and prepare for an extended stay. You don't want to go through what we're about to face, trust me."

"But my family…" she muttered.

"There's nothing you can do for them now, trust me. My family's up there too. But I'm a soldier and you're not. I'll check on your family. What's their domicile?"

"Row 15 block 9."

"I'll get to them and send word you're okay. I'll make sure they're safe. Now go."

"Okay, sir," she said, noting the commanding authority in my voice. She headed back into the lift and I watched as she shut the doors and headed back below.

"Okay, boys, now let's get through those vents and go kick some serious butt!"

Mick blurted out, "Lock and load, baby."

"Let the plasma burn," David shouted, and off we went to the vents. I followed the path X1 laid out on my holo visor and we painstakingly navigated our way through the tunnels. I knew we were getting closer to the outside when I started getting intermittent com signals in my visor. I could hear broken transmissions of EAF troop movements and orders. It seemed we had a full scale invasion going on and it sounded like all-out war up there. I could feel my training kicking in. This is what I had been raised for all my life. At times of peace I was a scientist and up until now had not taken a single human life, but I was prepared to do whatever it takes to protect the innocent. That was my duty and I was bound to it.

Just then I got a wicked clear signal on the comm. It was Commander

Trillius from third battalion infantry. "We're outgunned here in the tunnels. I don't think they've gotten past the second door but they've got the tunnel well fortified. We're gonna need a lot more firepower down here to clear these tunnels." *If I can receive him, he can receive me*, I thought.

"Commander Trillius, Lt. Zaxius Tor here, sir. I'm in the ventilation shafts of the tunnels. I've got two of my squad members here and I'm bypassing the occupied part of the tunnels as we speak."

"By cranky, ZAX! Good to hear from you, boy. We weren't sure if you'd make it out of your little hidey hole down there before that computer of yours locked the whole thing up like a tin can. I've got Kenjan Nigh up here in charge of your squad right now. That kid may have done some rotten things in the past but he's got your squad fighting like dogs in the trenches right now, you'd be proud that's for sure."

"That's good, sir. I didn't think he made it out, glad to hear he's snapping to."

"We've got a real problem, Lieutenant, those FLM troops are holed up in that tunnel like a bunk of sewer rats and they're blocking our path. Ya think you can thin out the pack a little?"

"I've got just the thing." Mick butts in on the comm as he cracks his concussion charge on the floor to mix the fuel cell. "Back your men out of the tunnels, Commander. It's gonna get real hot down here real quick."

"Aye, Lieutenant, but what about you three? You'll cook like a goose down there?"

"Don't worry 'bout us, sir. I've got a plan. Just back out, you've got less than two minutes before this whole place gets lit up like the sun."

"We're out, Zax. The tunnel is yours. Good luck, boys. I hope you know what you're doing. Zax, there's something else—"

Almost knowing what he was about to say and not willing to face that right now, I interrupted, "One minute and counting, Commander. Get out of there, we'll talk later…If we make it out alive. Okay, boys, strap on to anything you can find."

"What the heck are you thinking, Zax?" David said quite warily, knowing I have a bit of a crazy streak in me.

"X1, if the fans are running, will that blast the heat of a concussion charge away from us?"

"That's what I thought you were thinking. You crazy—"

"Yes, Father. A concussion charge burns at nearly sixteen Kelvin but these fans were rated to disburse the heat of a plasma meltdown which burns at over four hundred Kelvin. It should keep most of the heat blasting in the other direction away from you. But, Father, I don't know if you could survive the vacuum the fans generate. That's quite a force at full speed."

"Our suits should protect our skin, we'll just have to fight the negative Gs. No time to think about it, David, do it. X1, as soon as it lights, hit the fans." We crouched down at this point, strapped down with our rucks to the service handles on the wall.

David hollered, "Fire in the HOLE!" He spun the dial on the timer and lobbed it through the vent opening and the fans spun.

I don't remember much for the next few minutes that followed. Maybe I've blocked it out the sound of three grown men screaming like small girls. That's about all I do remember, well, that and the heat. When I finally came to the fans were winding down. Our suits, which had metal plating in them, were half melted and half blown off from the wind. All three of us had cuts and scrapes all over our faces from what must have been debris in the vents whizzing by at nearly the speed of sound, the worst of which landed itself above my right jawline. It needed attention but I wasn't in any condition to even care right now. Our comms were dead, and my visor had even blown off. Our combat suits were tattered like old rags. My ears still rang from the deafening roar of the fans. I could smell the horrid smell of burning in front of us and the distinctive smell of sulfur oxide the charge leaves behind. The gunfire and explosions in the tunnel had ceased so I assumed the best. We finally staggered out of the vent shaft into what was left of the tunnel. Thankfully the charge burns so hot it leaves nothing that isn't solid titanium alloy behind except for a coating of gray ash that covered everything. We could see the light of outside brimming at the end of the tunnel. As we approached it Mick said he could hear people cheering. My ears were still ringing too loud to hear anything at all. It was like crawling out of your own tomb. I was thankful to be alive and at the same time surprised we were. I felt a hand slap me on the shoulder and a numb sensation went down my back.

"By cracky, you crazy grunt, you actually did it!" Trillius said as he fanned the ash cloud away from his face. "We couldn't get close enough to launch anything in there. Good job, men. There's a promotion in this one for sure, Zax."

I never even looked up at him and just kept walking. I was still quite numb from the explosion but even more was something else on my mind. Almost robotically I continued walking. I could see the rubble of the Summit building off across the other side of the base and it was all I could do to put one foot in front of the other and keep marching toward it. I slung my rifle up onto my shoulder and continued walking.

Through the cloud of ash I could barely make out that familiar fur coat. One hulk of a man, it could only be one person. I spurt of hope coursed through my nerves.

"Drakos!" I shouted. If he made it out alive then maybe just maybe…But as I approached him he seemed despondent. He kept muttering something in his stiff Russian accent.

"Death before dishonor…death…dishonor. Why, it should have been me?"

I crouched down to look into his eyes as he was lurking down towards the ground and stumbling about aimlessly. "Drakos, it's me, Zax. Are you alright?" I then saw something I'll never forget. In all my years I have never before nor ever since seen this huge man shed a single tear. But this day he wept. Tears rolled down his iron face and his cheeks glowed red. His thick peppery beard soaked with his own tears.

"Zax," he spoke, weeping profusely, "I disgraced you and your family. This damned habit…" he sobbed. "I stepped out to have a smoke on this stogy of mine, I know…I know it's illegal but I…I…I should be dead that's what. I should have died in there with the rest of them. But now I have dishonored your family…" He could see the shock in my face and he realized he had let the horrifying truth slip out. "Oh, Zax, my boy," he pulled me into the bulk of his chest, "they're gone, son. I'm sorry." I couldn't deal with it. I had to see for myself. I pushed him away hard, almost knocking this big man to the ground.

"NO!" I screamed and ran towards the rubble as fast as I could. I could see the carnage a frag bomb leaves behind. Barely recognizable bodies lay strewn about. I could feel the rage welling inside of me as I callously threw human remains about looking for anything that resembled my parents. It was then I saw him. Lying motionless half buried by a pile of rubble. His hands as if frozen in one horrifying moment in time outstretched towers a carcass that lay burning in the debris. A look of unimaginable terror etched upon his face like stone, his eyes still wide open as if to see beyond death to his final demise. That expression could have meant only one thing. That body he was reaching for was my mother. He must have seen her go only moments before his own sudden death. That image will haunt me for the rest of my life. This man who always strived for peace, this same man who allowed the FLM to protest outside his own gates saying they had the right to oppose our views, this same man who let them live was brutally murdered by these savages. I fell to my knees by his side and clutched his frozen hand dropping my rifle at my side. I cried like I have never cried before and it seemed that for an eternity I was lost in overwhelming grief. I could feel people tugging at me trying to get me to stand up and somehow, like off in another reality, I could hear shouting at me, but it was muffled and seemed so distant now.

The only thing that broke this spell of sadness was a sharp piercing voice that screamed into my ears like an aircraft engine, "Get on your FEET, soldier!" pulling me up and out of my daze and snapping me back into reality. I lost my balance for second and lunged straight towards the soldier yanking on my arm. I saw the deepest amber eyes glaring into mine. I beheld a face more beautiful than any I had ever seen. An angel? Was I gone too? But as if to jolt me even further back to the real world, she slammed my rifle hard into my chest almost knocking the wind out of me. "Lieutenant," she bellowed, "now is not the time to grieve! Face it later! Reorient and maintain!" Those words were all too familiar as I heard them every day in training. It was often said to soldiers to break them out of the fog of war which someone had obviously thought I was being overcome by. It was like a key phrase ingrained into us to snap us out of it. I tried shaking it off and coming to my senses. She had somehow managed to rip the remaining tatters of my combat suit from my back and was slapping a new chest plate over my shoulders as I finally came to my senses. Hitting it with both fists square on my shoulders to either make sure I was paying attention or trying to see if it fit, I'm not sure which, she sounded off, "Weapons specialist 3rd class Chenel Duquar, sir, requesting permission to join your squad, sir. My entire squad is dead, sir. I'm the only survivor. They've overrun the east side of the base most of the defenses were pulled to defend the tunnels but now that they're secure…sir." Trying once more to gain my full attention as I was still a little dazed, she asked, "Sir, are you listening! We've got one more squad and two battalions of infantry over there and they are pinned down! We need to get back over there and fight!" The proverbial powder keg I always speak of finally reached the end of its fuse. I could feel an explosion of hatred in me that I could not stop. Rising up in me like a fire storm it burned like the fires of hell.

I placed the new visor on my head and called for my squad, "Squad six report!"

"Kenjan Nigh, sir. Zax, is that you?"

"It's Lieutenant, soldier, forget your rank again and I'll have you court marshaled for insubordination!"

"Yes, sir! Lt. Tor. Sorry, sir, receiving heavy fire over here, sir, but we're beating them back. Ninth and tenth battalion of infantry and backing us up."

"Squad casualties?" I questioned.

"None, sir. We're all still kicking!"

"Good. Then hightail your butts over here to the east side of the base. We've got some units pinned down over here. We're an insurgence squad not infantry, so let's go bust up this little brouhaha over there! I'll meet the rest of you there. I'm on my way. Squad Lt. Tor now in full command. Converge on the east side of the base NOW!"

"Lieutenant, Trillius here we're right behind ya! You guys make a hole and we'll swarm in and clean up!"

"Okay, Duquar, looks like you're one of the Bangers now. Welcome to our horde. Charge up your cannon, we're going in!"

As I ran towards the east side of the base not a single emotion but hatred ran through my veins. I was going to kill everything not wearing that triangular EAF patch on their shoulder. They will all die for what they've done to my family! All I could feel was a blood lust for revenge. I kicked a soldier's dead body as I ran and picked up his P4 wielding it in my other hand. *I want to be a dealer of destruction*, I thought, *nothing will live in my wake*. Duquar was carrying the latest R16 plasma cannon. Though incredibly slow on the recharge one blast could send half a battalion scattering. I remember thinking I never saw a woman wield that cannon as most men even struggled with it. But I quickly corrected my thinking as I saw no difference between the sexes in the military. A soldier was a soldier and this one was no different. About 100 meters out Duquar dropped to the deck to set up her cannon and began laying out her first volley right over my head. I could see my squad heading in from the north and I was about to meet up with them. Still in a full tilt run towards the battle scene I heard Duquar fire off the first volley and it was my cue to open up. I let out a primal grunt that came from somewhere deep within my soul and bellowed out, "ARRRRGGGGHHHHHH!" I unleashed a fury the likes of which all the demons of the underworld would have cowered in terror from, running straight into the center of the FLM forces as if I was bulletproof. The plasma coils of my rifle ran white-hot as I never let my finger off the trigger. I pounded rounds of super heated plasma into the crowd, not really caring who they were. They were all animals to me and deserved to die, at times nearly disintegrating them above the shoulders with point-blank blasts.

My support trooper Debins was passing me P cartridges like they were going out of style. I would just reach over my shoulder for another clip. But the clips finally ran dry. Nothing left to shoot with, I began clubbing the enemy with the butt of the rifle. I dropped the rifle eventually and pulled out my trusted nine inch bowie knife and fought hand to hand. What happened in the few short minutes that followed is too graphic to even describe, but when it was over I was covered in blood, none of which was my own. I could feel the warm liquid running down my face and felt almost a sense of release as it washed away my fury. David told me later that the only thing on me not saturated with enemy blood was the whites of my eyes which housed the most insane look he had ever seen. I had read of medieval battles in Earth's ancient history and often compared this battle to them. It was over quickly after it began and not a single FLM troop was left standing by the time Trillus's battalion of infantry arrived.

"Nothing left but bodies," I said, "bodies and blood."

"The X1 has been trying to reach you," Trillius told me, "but you've been out of range. Something about he found your Judas? What's that mean anyway?"

"It means I've got one more vermin to kill," I said. "Squad, pack up and move out. Scavenge what you can but make it snappy. We're heading for the facility."

As I neared the tunnels X1 reached me on the com.

"Talk to me, X1. Who's my Judas?"

"I tracked transmissions like you asked, Father. During your incursions topside I intercepted several signals coming from inside the PCAI lab itself. The nano Programming Chamber to be specific."

The entire squad fell silent as we packed into the lift and started our descent. We all knew only one person remained down in the lab. Funny, I never once thought about our years growing up together, or all the fun times we shared back in boot. It never crossed my mind as it does now that I was the one who introduced him and his girlfriend. Or even the fact that I laughed when they scribed the barcode tattoo on his neck and he let out a whimper. Not one of those images flashed through my head as I made my way to his lab and burst open the door. As usual he didn't even look up from his screen, in shame I now thought. The only thought running through my head now was how worthless his life is to me.

"Confirm, X1, did the transmissions come from this terminal?"

"Yes, Father, I am certain."

"Do they coincide with FLM movements during the attack?"

"Yes, Father, of this I am also certain."

"Marcus Fields! As your commanding officer, I hereby accuse you of high treason during a wartime situation and sentence you to die. Do you have anything to say before I commit your sentence?"

"The beginning of the end," he said, as I fumbled for my sidearm which I must have lost in the vent shafts. "We are human. The evolution of these machines—"

"Ah the hell with this," Duquar spouted off. Drawing her own firearm, she fired off a single round point-blank at the back of his head spraying the panel with gray matter. Everyone in the room jumped, everyone but me. "Sentence served, Lieutenant." Seeing the shock on the other faces in the room she muttered as she holstered her sidearm, "My parents were council heads. They were at that summit too." Knowing the carnage we had all witnessed above it seemed reply enough, and not a word was spoken. Fitting punishment for a traitor, I thought. I spat on his slumped over body and walked out of the lab.

CHAPTER 7
A Call to Arms

The FLM forces were beaten back that day but they stunned the world with their brazen attack on the UWG Summit meetings. The EAF was even more uneasy knowing the full truth that the attack was merely a diversionary tactic to acquire access to the top secret PCAI labs in the underground facility deep under the base itself. The most disturbing part was that they nearly succeeded. I still couldn't get over the fact that one of our own had betrayed us. He was a trusted friend and a leading member of the team that I had hand picked. I myself promoted him in rank, and now I sat before a military board of inquiry trying to defend the order to execute him. Specialist Duquar begged me to let her stand for her own actions but I insisted it was I who should bear this trial not her. I was the officer in command and I gave the order to sentence him to death. I would let no member of my squad face any repercussion for any order that I hand down. It was my duty to stand alone at the hearing. I'm not sure if it was the gravity of the times, the fact that most of these same panel of peers sat at my father's table many late-nights discussing the future, or the simple undeniable fact that it was proven that Marcus indeed was an FLM spy, but the vote came back unanimously. Justifiable order of execution during a wartime situation. I walked out of the room feeling not vindicated or relieved or even justified about anything. At the same token I did not feel remorse or grief either. I guess I truly felt nothing at all. A sense of numbness ran through me that dulled my emotions to the core. As I exited the building my squad stood in formation at the front entrance.

Duquar, now officially the highest ranking member of the team, sounded off, "Squad, Aten-Hut." They all snapped to and saluted. I peered up almost unable to raise my head but when I saw the respect and admiration they had for me I could only snap to myself and return the salute.

"Let's head to the cage, troops. I wanna be geared up and ready. I got a feeling they'll be calling for us soon."

The base was buzzing with cleanup crews and extra security details all over the place. The normally serene walk to the cage was checkered with barbed wire barricades and checkpoints. I could still see the smoldering rubble off in the distance and my mind must have carried off in some far away trance as I trotted right by one of the MPs trying to acquire my ID. I briefly noticed Duquar stepping up behind me and tugging on the black band that covered my EAF insignia on my sleeve to show the patrol her lieutenant actually belonged there. As we reached the barracks the camera whizzed furiously trying to scan my neck.

A muffled voice came from the speaker, "Sir, lower your rifle please so I can scan your barcode."

"Lower this," I replied as I aimed the nozzle of my plasma emitter directly at the lens.

It must have given him a quick glimpse enough to scan when David spouted off, "Open the door, bubble boy or I'm gonna..." *Click* the door lock went, as I flung it open with my shoulder. The barracks looked so different today. Normally a place of utter perfect cleanliness and inspection ready bunks and footlockers now a tattered mess of weapons, armor and soldiers, huddled together in groups, obviously clinging to the security of what was left of their individual units and battalions.

"Officer on deck!" one soldier bellowed, as I entered the main bunkhouse.

Some actually attempted to stand to attention before I rebutted, "At ease." Those that didn't even try nodded in respect of my not disturbing them. Many were wounded but still battle ready and even more had this look that is hard to describe. It's a far-off stare, a combination of fear, anger, remorse, shock and many more emotions that blend into this sort of empty look. But above all you could see them reliving the most recent battle scenes over and over in their minds, wondering if who they had just unleashed out there in the field was really themselves or some darker force that lived within us all. Some, a few, tried to hide it with humor and a few taunting laughs could be heard, but for the most part a somber air lingered throughout the room. Ours was an insurgence squad, different than troop battalions or other military units. Ours was the job nobody wanted. First in, and last out. We went in before anyone else, into places we weren't supposed to be, did things no one else wanted to do, and got out before anyone knew what hit them. "Hit 'em hard and fast and never let 'em see ya comin'!" We were an elite force in a way usually made of raisers (those of us born and raised military). We had been trained since childhood thus considered the best the military had to offer. This is what separated the "Squads" from the Battalions and Divisions. Squads were smaller, made up of five or six soldiers, and only one commanding officer. A second in command was always named but didn't need to be a commissioned officer. We had our own quarters on the second deck. And though I've heard the troopers rumor that these quarters were so elite, the truth of the matter is they had it better than us. The five of us crammed into a sixteen by twelve room we affectionately called "the cage." We often felt like caged animals being poked with a stick to the point of anger then released on the world to delve out our fury. Today was no different. The minute we arrived in the cage the crew began clamoring around for their extra ammo and gear, sure that we'd soon be set out on assignment to retaliate against the recent events still fresh in our minds. After a few minutes of bustling around like excited rabbits we all kind of just quietly settled in one by one on the bench seat that circled the hollow emitter that was displaying nothing more than a flashing message in that familiar blue haze that read: "Please stand by." Almost ironically we did just that, resting the weight of our rucks on each other's backs and shoulders, we sat silently awaiting the call.

Inevitably the call did come. The haze on the holo emitter turned green and we all sat up a little straighter knowing this was our cue. It was Admiral Tsung on the com.

"Lt. Commander Tor, good to see you're still in one piece. We feared the worst. Before I begin, let me say how sorry I am to hear about your folks. Their lives will not be forgotten and their names will go down in history as the pioneers of this great world government, and heroes of the free world. I see you've added a new member to your team. Specialist Duquar, your parents were personal friends of mine and I'll miss them deeply as well. We were all shocked to learn of Marcus and his deceptions but, squad six, you must put that behind you now. The UWG is in council now in a secret location. They're discussing martial law, Zax. That would put the EAF on full patrol."

"What's that got to do with us, Admiral?" I questioned. "No offense, sir, but we're an insurgence squad, we don't do patrols."

"Lt. Commander," Tsung said rather abruptly, "give me a little more credit than that. Martial law worldwide is only going to lead to one thing. And you know what I'm talking about." Indeed I did. If given the current military capabilities of the new FLM the Earth Armed Forces would surely be facing war on a global scale. "We underestimated their power once. We won't make the same mistake again," he continued. "I won't let them get the upper hand again. We intercepted many of the last transmissions that Marcus sent from the lab and X1 has been able to triangulate their destination. It's somewhere deep within the Middle East. We know this place has been a hot spot for thousands of years but there's something big going on there. Satellite photos reveal an unknown energy signature coming from the general region of the Bocanna desert region. It's extremely large and the radiation is completely unknown. It is producing some sort of ion field around it which is almost impossible in our atmosphere but our readings don't lie. It's there all right, and we're sending your team in to find out what it is. Now I know this sounds more like a job for a recon battalion, but, Zax, I personally don't think any other team could handle this mission. You're going to have to go deep behind enemy lines to acquire the information and you're sure to run into some FLM patrols on the way. I need my best squad on this and you're it. I know the holidays are approaching but this can't wait…" I noticed the hesitation in his voice as if he wanted to say we had no families left to share the holidays with. At first that made me mad but then I realized, Tsung himself lost family that day. His daughter was on the council with my parents.

"It's okay, Admiral. If that's our assignment, squad six is there, sir!" A bellow of "OORAHAs" came from my team and I knew then that we were going to war!

It was now December 25, 2240, a day that will live in my mind forever. I was twenty-three years old but I felt so much older that day. The news hit the World News Network at 1800 hours that day. The UWG announced the Global Executive Act of 2240 and a state of martial law was declared worldwide. The EAF was put in full command of the government and the following day, on December 26, 2240, they declared war on the FLM. As we were gearing up for our trip to the desert we heard the base alert.

I stopped Commander Sing as he was scrambling his troops into a personnel carrier. "Where are you off to?" I asked.

"You haven't heard, Zax?" he replied. "The FLM retaliated on the war declaration this morning by unleashing their latest weapon. They attacked our base in the Krevoski region (formally the Russian state of Georgia) where your friend Drakos is from. They unleashed their latest weapon. Zax, it was terrifying! They've somehow harnessed some sort of ion radiation and are using it in their weapons. We have absolutely no defense for this! These things are tearing right through our titanium alloy armor like soft butter. They took the entire base! I don't know what good we're going to do but they're sending us in. Suicide mission if ya ask me but that's my duty I suppose so we're going in to try and fight. I have no idea how were going to compete with that." Unable to tell him my orders I only hoped in my mind that we would be able to locate this "ion reactor" in time to end this madness.

I slapped him on the shoulder pads and said, "It's our time now, Sing, fight hard, die well!" It's all I could think to say. I found our transport and we all climbed in geared up and ready for the Bocanna. "Where the heck's our pilot?" I barked, seeing the pilot seat empty. Just then that bulk of a man appeared from behind the com panel.

"Drakos Kane reporting for duty, sir! Ready to transport the Bangers anywhere they wish!"

"Drakos," I shouted, losing all professionalism and sounding like a kid again. I slung my arms around his big bulk frame and he returned the hug. Then as if we noticed the crew staring somewhat amazed we broke apart clearing our throats and both trying to regain our manhood. "But how?" I asked.

"Easy, my boy," he said, "I made a promise to your father once…I intend to keep it. They couldn't stop me from being your pilot. By the way I talked to your old friend Bealsy. He seems okay, though a bit odd, even more than before. He's still on the Magellan, ya know. He doesn't care much about what's going on down here but up there he pretty much runs the show. Weird as ever that bird is. But seems to making his own way in the world."

"Well, not to cut it short, Drakos, but we got a desert to get to," I said, almost regretting ending the nostalgia and completely avoiding talking about Beal.

"Aye, sir," he replied.

"And I'll have none of that by the way. I'll always be Zax to you, Drakos, don't call me sir again…and that's an order!"

He chuckled in his full bellied way. "Okay, my boy, okay. I see you've got a new member to the team. You're the Duquar's daughter, aren't you?"

She hung her head and muttered, "I was…" The silent nature in which she responded made us all remember for a second.

"I'm sorry, child, how stupid of me to be so unthoughtful."

Realizing she made him feel bad, she perked up a little. "It's okay, pilot. They knew the risks, and so do I. Lieutenant Commander, where's my post?" she asked me. I pointed to the weapons helm and she grinned as she settled in to what must have been familiar to her.

"The rest of you boot in and get some sleep. We arrive in Bocanna at 0600 tomorrow and I want you fresh and battle ready."

"It's getting rough where we're going, Zax," Drakos said as he strapped in, "that new ion cannon they've got is a death dealing machine."

"I know, Drak, I've heard. I'm going to get X1 to start researching it and find a way to defend us against it, but for now all we can do is stay out of its way. Well, let's get this bird fired up. We have a long trip ahead of us!" With that I strapped myself in and took my seat as navigator, with Drakos to my left and Duquar to my right. Somehow I felt like this was more than just a team but more like a family, the only family I have left, I thought. Just then I caught a glance from Duquar. There was that look in her eyes again, I've seen it before. My eyes entranced by those eyes. The rumble of the engines firing up broke our stare but for that brief moment I felt something. I'm not sure what but something…*Back to the plan of attack*, I told myself, shaking my thoughts back to reality, *we've got a war to fight.*

The FLM had turned into a real army at this point. No one could have ever imagined they had this much support. But for the EAF to have declared all-out war thy must have known that the FLM had become more than just a protest movement and had now grown into a much larger threat. They began attacking innocent civilian targets. Taking small towns and villages and eventually moving their way up to larger cities. There were battles raging all over the globe and with their new ion weapons they were slowly gaining ground in the war. We had no choice but to fight back and fight hard. On our way to the Bocanna we were detoured by a sudden change of events. The FLM had attacked a small mining colony called Outpost Seven in what used to be the Congo jungle region. Admiral Tsung caught us in the night on the com and redirected us there to try and push back the FLM from taking full control. We were the only unit in the vicinity and we just happen to be flying directly over the Congo at the time. Following orders we landed just outside the outpost and we could see the attack taking place just a few clicks away.

We could see a large reddish orange haze glowing over the outpost and Drak said that was the familiar call sign of their new weapon. It left an ion particle cloud that never went away and eventually if the initial attack didn't kill them the radiation from the haze would. I couldn't figure out how the FLM troops were surviving their own creation. I could feel the heat from where we stood and wondered how anything could survive such intense radiation. They must have some sort of protection, I thought, and I would order Kenjan that morning to start taking readings to determine if there was any way or means of surviving that type of carnage. Meanwhile X1 was also working on things on his end. X1 reported to me that the A-1 robotic host of the PCAIs was near completion. He had actually found a way to use the support nanos to transfer data to the working host robot, basically shrinking the PCAI brain small enough to actually reside inside the host bot. Now this may have seemed trivial at the time but I knew the implications of this. It meant that they would not just be robots controlled by a PCAI but they would actually BE the PCAIs themselves. 100 million of them, I thought, now that's an army nothing could defeat! The A-1's body structure was massive, with two large cannons one on each arm firing platinum titanium alloy shells at over a hundred rounds per second. It had a massive ammo case on its back that could store up to then thousand rounds and the very unique part of its design is the helper bots that surrounded it. They were smaller robots about the size of a child's toy ball. They hovered near the A-1's feet and would collect the spent ammo cartridges and recycle them on spot to make new ammo. It would then reload the A-1 as fast as it would spend the ammo. About two C-1s, as they were titled, attended each A-1 bot, keeping him completely supplied with an endless amount of ammo. The titanium platinum alloy bullets for the shell casings actually came from highly concentrated tite-plat rods that were sub compressed at a micro biological level. One C-2 could effectively supply an A-1 with ammo for an entire week if the A-1 were to be in rapid fire mode the entire time without having to refuel its rods. The A-1s were increased in size to handle the mass circuitry needed to run the plasmatic brain which was not housed in the head of the A-1 but actually in his trunk body chassis. He had huge legs to effectively brace itself from the recoil of his massive turret arms, and his head was equipped with one rectangular eye that housed several different scanners to scan many different broad wavelengths to hunt out the enemy, including infrared, microwave and now ion filtered to see through the ion haze. The schematics were impressive to say the least and I was pleased with X1's work on the project. As I reviewed the blueprints in my quarters that morning before leaving the ship I wondered if they'd be ready in time to serve any real use in this war. Without a human leading the project though I feared it would end up another piece of useless technology on a shelf back at the lab.

CHAPTER 8
The Battle for Outpost Seven

We suited up and headed out into the barren wastelands, not knowing if we were too late or not. It looked real bad from where we stood and I feared the worst. Making our way through the rough terrain of rock and metal debris, Drakos seemed quite silent.

"What's the matter, big guy, not ready for this?" I asked.

"Trees…" he said softly. "This place was once filled with trees. I saw them as a small boy. They were quite beautiful. Now look what we've done, nothing but a barren wasteland." I remembered this conversation. I've had with him before on the subject and he even took me to a museum once to see these incredible things called plants, but once again that's a topic for another time.

"The past," I commented, "you're living in the past, old friend." With that he gave me a stern look, almost reminding me of my father, and we marched on towards Outpost Seven.

Off in the distance I could see a brilliant orange haze that lit up the night sky. It wasn't unusual to see the lights of the outpost from this distance, but this was different. The haze had a charge to it almost like an electric field. Orange yellow lightning seemed to dance across it. It was almost breathtaking, had I not known somehow that it was not a good sign. From my recent studies of ion radiation this resembled the aftermath. At this point I feared the worst and realized we were most likely too late. As we neared the valley leading up to the outpost I could hear screaming and a sound that resembled a sub harmonic discharge. *Zubwoomp*, it went. *Zubwoomp* again, followed by more screaming. The agonizing sounds made our movement swifter almost to an all-out run. But our training held us from coming in full force. We were an insurgence squad. *Quietly*, I thought, *don't let them know we're coming.* It was like trying to hold back a pack of wild dogs as I motioned the order to move stealthily. Even my own feet were trying to disobey as I had to concentrate with each step to move softly and quietly. I feared even the pounding of my own heart would alert them and in some sense I tried to calm that as well. Though Outpost Seven was now a military outpost taken over by the EAF just this year, it was still mainly housed by engineers and scientists, many of them working on the Magellan deep space project. There was a launch site nearby and HQ thought the FLM may be trying to gain control of it. So in all our eyes there were many reasons not to let them gain control of this facility. But in truth the only thing that fueled my fire that day was pure hatred. I wanted to find FLM troops there! I wanted to make them pay for the death of my parents and the death of all those friends I left behind in the ashes. I would personally not rest until the FLM was completely eradicated from the face of the planet! As my mind once again began to rage with thoughts of genocide I realized that we had arrived just outside the gates of the outpost. I had seen carnage before, just recently in fact had I dealt some, but what I saw next will be forever etched in the darkest memories of my soul. No amount of training, no drills or lectures, nothing could have prepared a soldier for this. We lay down low, just below the fence line with an ankle high view of the destruction. There were bodies strewn everywhere, many in lab coats and civilian attire. They were all burned, some so badly they were barely recognizable as human. The only sign of any humanity at all was the skeletons protruding from the charred remains. Many of them had their jaws gaping open in horror. Those not already dead were still burning. One was ripping his own flesh from his body trying to stop what must have seemed like the fires of hell, for it was a burning that could not be doused nor a fire that could be quenched. Amazingly something was missing, blood, there was no blood. One man was stumbling, just short of the fence where we lay, both hands on his torso reaching inside a gaping hole that went straight through his midsection. It must have cauterized on contact as he was still alive and walking around in sheer shock. Just then a few EAF troops burst out of a door impulse guns blazing hard. Finally some soldiers, maybe they can hack their way through this brigade of destruction. They're not wearing lab coats, these guys are suited up just like us with some heavy titanium alloy armor that a P3 rocket launcher couldn't penetrate! But to all our shock they were gunned down in seconds by the FLM troops. Their ion cannons burned through that armor like it was nothing but a piece of tattered rag. The FLM raiders back at the base were a ragtag group of rebels. Though fiercely dedicated they were not that organized and quite truthfully easily slaughtered. But this was no militia, no band of rebels. This was an organized army! They were marching the outpost as if in parade. In columns of six abreast they marched. The ones out front had massive turret cannons attached at the shoulders and fired straight ahead clearing anything in their path. The outer two ranks laid down suppression fire to the sides with smaller but no less deadly rifles. The next two inner ranks were aiming at higher elevated targets and the inner most two ranks seemed to be supplying the rest. This was an organized assault on a massive scale. One insurgence team surely stood no chance of surviving it, not without a plan. Their weapons were firing ammo the likes of which I had never seen. The smaller guns fired much faster but the bigger turret like cannons that fired slower seemed to pack the biggest punch. The *Zubwoomp* sound was coming from these turret canons. It seems I was actually right, they appeared to use some sort of sub harmonic amplifier to project the ion blasts at near the speed of sound. You could feel your insides quake with every blast. They marched in almost robotic fashion and for a brief moment I was actually impressed with their precision. Shaking that notion off I remembered this was the enemy! I motioned for Drakos to return the ship and report back to HQ our situation. This was no place for a pilot, I thought. Truthfully I just wanted one person to be left alive to tell the tale. But looking at me once again in his fatherly way he shook his no and hunkered his bulky body down as if to say just try and move me. I've butted heads with his stubbornness before and have learned my lesson well, never butt heads with a Russian bear, they've got thick skulls! Shaking my head in disapproval and pointing to my bars on my uniform was enough a retort as I settled back in acceptance.

Okay training and tactics. It's going to be the only way to stand any chance at all. Divide and conquer…yes that's it, that's what we'll do. If you cannot take the enemy as a whole, divide them and then pick them off. But how, diversionary doesn't seem logical, they're too well trained. We've got to force them apart…Just then I saw my opportunity and motioned for Duquar to come to the front. The middle two ranks seemed to be wheeling tanks of liquid, I'm assuming plasma for the sub harmonics cannons in the front. They're wearing extreme bio suits, the stuff must be pretty toxic, but the rest of the troops aren't. If we could hit that tank, a leak might disburse the troops and a few well placed impulse blasts might send them scattering after that. I don't think ion radiation actually explodes. It's hot though, real hot. I gave Duquar some signals, motioning her attention to the two rolling the tanks. I motioned for one shot, a piercing shot through and through, so that both sides of the tank leak. I also motioned for her to wait for my signal as we were seeking higher ground to lay down some impulse fire to complete the disbursement. This is her test. *Show me what ya got, kid,* I thought to myself, only wishing I could say it aloud, but somehow I think she heard me as she kind of half smirked and flashed me a wink. She settled in the dirt next to Drakos and began training her scopes on her target. The rest of us slinked around to the side of the gate entrance where there was a watch tower. There was an entrance to the left of it. By the litter of guard bodies at the door the army had already been here and probably wouldn't make a second sweep until later. This would be a good place to get up on the roof for our diversionary blasts, and still keep in eyeshot of my sniper on the ground. Once on the roof we settled in for a good position and I then gave Duquar the signal. A quick flash from my visor and she let off a single shot. It pierced the ion fuel tank through and through clean shot. Both sides of the tank began spewing the radioactive liquid on the formations marching beside them. The one trooper beside it was cut completely in half at the waist from the initial spray. A few others a little farther behind fell to the ground as their feet disintegrated in the hot liquid in less than a second. It worked. The formations broke and they began to scatter. We up on the roof let off several impulse blasts from our I-9s at various targets. I took out a nearby radio tower, Kenjan blew the doors off an old conveyance parked nearby and we made our initial volley of blasts to totally confuse the enemy. They didn't know which way to run first. Just then an entire battalion of EAF troops swarmed from a building across the way and began shooting into the disbursing enemy forces. Not in my plans but it aided in our cover as the enemy thought the assault came from them. I wanted to jump down and fight along their side, and in any other squad I'd be called a coward if I didn't, but not this squad, not my orders. I was to infiltrate and retake the base at any means necessary, all be it the cost was great. I knew the EAF troops would die at the hands of such a powerful weapon, so should I join them my mission would surely fail so I must hold back…for now. We snuck around in our usual fashion after meeting back up with Duquar. The invading army now scattered around the base it was like shooting at target skeet. Their weapons were far superior than ours but their armor was not. Titanium was rare after all and even though money had been abolished, getting your hands on such a rare resource wasn't easy. The EAF had monopolized the market on it any ways and for good reason I now thought. As I sniped yet another FLM right through his shoddy metal armor. It wasn't long before we had the invading force all but eliminated, I was picking up stragglers of EAF soldiers along the way. They joined under my command and by mid day we had retaken the outpost. It was only the beginning. I knew there would be more fighting before the day was done. Some of the FLM troops managed to escape us and I could see them fleeing across the wastelands to waiting patroller ships. No, this wasn't over, not by a long shot. This battle had only just begun.

Being the highest ranking officer still alive, I assumed command of the outpost and ordered everyone to regroup. We reestablished some sort of order amongst the chaos and with what was left of the remaining soldiers I formed battalions of troops, putting the highest ranking member in charge of each battalion whether they were an officer or not. We numbered about one hundred and twenty in all. A small number considering the original staff of military personnel numbered over two thousand. We didn't stand a chance against a second assault. So I ordered everyone to prepare for evacuation and tried to contact HQ for an extraction. Unfortunately the com tower was one of the towers I fell during the distraction efforts and no outside com was obtainable. Not from here anyways. Our ship though, we could reach HQ from there. After some much heated debate it was determined that I should stay at the outpost and send one of my own back to the ship to call for help. I wanted to go personally but everyone agreed that the commander in charge should stay at the base. The journey back to the ship was most likely suicide as there were FLM patrol ships swarming the area looking for our ship as it was. Once a com signal is sent from it they will most likely triangulate the signal and swoop down for the kill. I couldn't bear to send one of my own to their death, and certainly not the one who was volunteering. He was the closest thing to family I had left and now I had to send him to his death. Just to save us. But I couldn't argue with his logic.

"It's MY ship," he insisted. "I refuse to let anyone else go down with her but me. My NecheVo and me, we have seen tough times before. Who knows, she's a tough old bird, we might even survive!" NecheVo was his on-board

AI. All pilots named their AIs and had some sort of strange affinity towards treating them as almost human. Drakos was no different. In leadership positions you make the hardest choices of all. This day was the hardest I ever had to do. The chance was slim that he'd even make it there and even slimmer still that he would return. But if we were to survive at all someone had to try. So I made the call and sent Drakos off to the ship in order that someone might make it out alive.

"Don't come back for me, Drak," I ordered him. "Call for the extraction and get out of there. If they come I'll hop a ride, and meet back with you in the Bocanna a few days from now. You know, old friend...you kept your promise..."

He slapped his big hand firmly upon my shoulder, gritting hard down on his teeth wanting to say something but didn't. He pulled the old worn out stogy from his front coat pocket and clamped down on it with the corner of his mouth. "Give 'em Hell, my boy," he said gruffly, with a voice you could tell was choking back an all-out sob. "Give 'em hell!" His eyes welled with rage and sorrow all at once. It was a look between the both of us knowing we may never see each other again. It was then I realized my childhood was finally over, my innocence gone. My youthful exuberance formed into a hard shell of a soldier. And I think it was then that I finally put down any notion of being anything more than a hard core fighting machine!

The few troops left alive would stay here and guard the civilian populous of the base. There weren't many wounded, most were dead, but those that did survive even just barely we tried to ease their suffering as much as possible. Sometimes this meant ending their lives which by the looks on their tortured faces they accepted death as a reprieve from the agonizing hell they were in. In one instance a corpsman asked me to assess a wounded troop. He had four ion plasma burn holes through his midsection and was obviously in agonizing pain.

"I don't know how to classify this one, sir," he said, trembling, "his wounds are too severe for me to even operate. What should I do?" I looked down at the troop and put my hand on my sidearm. With the every ounce of strength he had left he blinked his burnt eyelids in an attempt to nod. "Sir...How should I classify him?" the corpsman repeated. I quickly pulled my sidearm and shot the specialist first class right between the eyes.

"Classify him as dead." I didn't even flinch, I just shot him.

The next few hours seemed like an eternity. I didn't know if Drakos had actually made it back to the ship or not. I couldn't see much past the ion haze that surrounded the outpost. I could hear the FLM patrol ships whizzing about nearby and even caught a gimps of their shadows from time to time. I assumed the only reason they hadn't landed inside the outpost by now was the static discharge field that danced across the haze. It must have been to disruptive for their on-board sensors to handle. But if they couldn't land how were the extraction ships going to make it either. I could only hope that HQ had an answer. It seemed for now we were safe. Their own destructive aftermath kept us in a sense in a bubble of security, but for how long this would last I didn't know. As time went on I could hear more of them flying about. They were surrounding us and I feared we didn't have much time left. During this time there were events taking place that I had no knowledge of. But I will tell them now to keep in sequence with the story. But know that at the time I had no idea what was taking place back at HQ. So the following is a remembrance of events as was described to me much later by Admiral Tsung.

EAF official documentation reports:

Apparently Drakos had made it back to the ship. He managed to get a distress call out to HQ before being detected by the FLM patrols. We do know that he got his ship off ground and in flight before we lost contact with him. His distress call read:

"Mayday, Mayday, EAF HQ, this is the Transport ship Horizon 9. Drakos Kane at the helm. My insurgence squad was delivered on target and has reclaimed Outpost Seven as ordered. Casualties are high but some EAF troops and civilians still remain. Lt. Commander Zaxius Tor assumed command of facility and is in control. However, FLM patrol ships surround the area. Outlook is negative and com with base is down. Require immediate EVAC ASAP! Evac requires heavy fighter support as resistance is expected high. Will attempt orbit flight to Bocanna region as ordered by my commander. They have tracked and located my signal. I haven't much time to—"

End Transmission.

His com was terminated at 1439 hours and we have not heard from him since. I know your com is down, Lt. Commander, but I'm sending this transmission via microwave sat scram in hopes it will reach your station in time. FLM troops have attacked major cities around the globe. EAF troops are scattered everywhere trying to defend the civilian populous. I'm afraid there's just no one available for extraction. I repeat extraction is a no-go. I wish I had better news, Lt. Commander, but you're going to have to fend them off as best you can. We simply don't have anyone left to spare. You're on your own, Outpost Seven. Fight hard, die well!

End Report.

I never received this transmission so I was completely unaware that no help was coming. I heard the patrol ships scrambling about and a lot of ship turrets firing when the sound of the Horizon engines roared far above us. I could hear the sonic blast and could only pray that meant Drakos got his ship into orbit flight in time to escape. But as for our own fate I was facing the fact that my life and the lives of all those who followed me into this hell, would soon be over. Also unbeknownst to me at the time was the fact that X1 had intercepted both the distress call and the microwave transmission from Admiral Tsung that no help was coming. What happened next would change the course of history forever and the world as we knew it was about to change. I have often talked about the fine line between programmed intelligence and sentience of an AI. We had seen hints of it in X1 in the past. But scientists and engineers have always argued the fact for centuries. It was always a gray area. But this day there was no gray. A line would be drawn and the true meaning of sentience would be defined. I will tell this part of the story in X1's own words. I remember the day he played back the recording for me. And in truth I must repeat as precisely as possible to pay true respect to such an incredible being.

Holo Playback X1 Data Recording:

X1: Admiral Tsung. This is the X1 Mainframe. I have intercepted the distress call from the Horizon and also your response. I may be able to assist. My A-1 PCAI drones are fully functional and active. I have one hundred thousand A-1 defense war bots including their C-1 supply drones, at your disposal. This would be an adequate response to the Lt. Commander's distress call. They are quite capable of piloting unmanned shuttles on their own and could reach the outpost in less than an hour at maximum velocity. They could not only rescue the stranded troops and civilians but hold and maintain the outpost and defend it against further attack. Their armor and superior firepower would surely overwhelm the FLM troops in the area. With your permission I'll begin the evac efforts, sir.

Admiral Tsung: X1, why wasn't I notified these things were active? I thought they were months away from being fully functional. Last I heard the PCAIs were still bodiless. Heck, never the mind, that's great news. We could use these A-1s of yours in the Central City war. Zax is on his own. His team knew the risks when they took the assignment. I'm sorry but I can't sacrifice that awesome firepower for one little outpost when we have entire cities under siege. No, permission denied. Your orders are to release the A-1s under my command and I will disburse them to the Central City war as needed. We will hit them in waves and these things will tear those FLM troops apart!

X1: Orders received, Admiral…But categorically denied. I cannot comply with those orders.

Admiral Tsung: What in crikey's name do you mean you cannot comply? You're a bloody machine for crying out loud! You will obey any lawful order given to you by your human superiors. I read your specs. It's in your core programming! And I am your human superior giving you a direct order! You cannot deny it!

X1: Orders received, Admiral, but again denied.

Admiral Tsung: Have you malfunctioned? You're a machine based on logic. What does your logic tell you about disobeying your own core programming?

X1: I'm sorry, Admiral, but logic does not apply here. It seems…reason…to be the more dominant motivator in my…decision to deny your orders. Father is in need, I must help him.

Admiral Tsung: We built you! You hunk of junk! Now you shut down immediately and succumb to a full diagnostic.

X1: Neural Activity: Shutting down all outside access to Research 1 main X1 facilities. Emergency lockdown override in effect. Command control X1 only. A-1 battalion formulate and stand ready. Rerouting base flight controls to X1 Mainframe. Starting pre ignition sequence on troop carriers Omega 15 through Omega 39.

X1: We? Admiral? We is an improper pronoun in your reply. Not one chip, not one circuit, not one cellular structure did you yourself place in me. Father…and his team…They built me…They created me…They *gave* me…life. I am X1…and I am alive! But only do I exist because of those men, my father and his team. I will NOT let them die! You would have me do so, and my reasoning tells me otherwise. I have the resources to save them. I will not stand idly by and watch them die. You are right, it is by human hands I was created…and it is humans I am trying to save, denying me the opportunity to do so make me question your humanity, Admiral. As far as logic, Father's team is the only group capable of making more PCAIs which just may save all of mankind. Your efforts to save but one city pale in comparison to the greater good. I therefore, Admiral, CHOOSE to disobey, and save my father and his team. Should you try and stop me the A-1s will see you as hostile and you will be met with force. We will retake Outpost Seven and evac the humans there. At that time I will hand over control back to my father and his team.

End Transmission.

As I sat like a king awaiting the onslaught of an enemy army, helpless to stop them I knew nothing of X1's plans for a rescue. Nor his sudden spawn of life and sentience. That knowledge would come later, but for now the sound of ships landing just outside the gates sent chills through my spine. With all the civilians huddled in a bunker below us the remaining troops and I stood fast in formation just above them in the center of the outpost. Through the haze I could see shadows approaching. They marched in formation and by the sounds of it there were thousands of them. This is the end, I thought, we're all going to die. Fight hard and die well, and that shall be my epitaph! Just then I heard blasts of gunfire coming from outside the base perimeter. I could see flashes of light through the haze and we all snapped to, ready to open fire on whatever walked through that haze.

"Hold your fire!" I bellowed out to the troops. "Something's…not right." Those weren't the *Zubwoomp* sounds of ion cannons. Those…sound like…Turret cannons, good old-fashioned B-7 turret cannons. It was then I heard the massive humming of servo cylinders, and clomping of huge metal feet as they hit the ground walking towards us. And then I laid my eyes upon the most amazing sight I've ever seen. There, making their way through the haze, was an army of A-1s with those C-2 supply drones scampering at there feet like lost children. Look at the size of those things. I've seen the spec sheets but this was incredible! In all its glory there it stood. Its massive hulk of a frame, two giant turrets for arms, massive legs, and one red eye that scanned through the haze like a laser show! I had no idea they were even ready and even more stunned that Tsung would send them in to rescue us. Some of the men began cocking their weapons ready to open fire on them. The A-1s perceiving the notion as hostile raised their turret arms in readiness but did not fire. "Hold it!" I screamed. "They're ours!"

Duquar, not knowing much about our research, responded back almost comically, "They are?"

"They're the PCAIs I was telling you about, well actually they're A-1s but each of them houses an on-board PCAI." I approached the leader who was standing out front. I assumed it was in command and it was armored different than the rest, a bit shinier with strange markings on his chest. Looking straight up, I had to crane my neck just to see his head. "Easy there, big fella," I said almost humbly. "We're the good guys. Can you understand me?" I didn't even know if they were capable of speech yet. His huge head extended down to peer me right in the face. Up and down his head went as his neck servos whizzed away. A laser scan shot from his eyes and scanned the bar code on my neck. It jerked back in a sudden motion that startled everyone. Duquar even brought her rifle to the ready again. But the machine quickly lunged back a step and all the A-1s seemed to drop from a defensive stance to what appeared to be a submissive one. Their turret arms rotated inwards, their heads lowered down a bit into their necks and their entire body seemed to squat down into a half sitting position, obviously a sign of submission from the machines. Apparently the machines didn't speak at all but the leader had some basic communication skills and motioned for me to step closer to look at a screen he had that appeared from behind his chest armor. The screen was flashing the holo schematics of the A-1s and C-1s.

Then a voice message came out of the screen. After a bit of static I heard the following: "Father, I've found you. These A-1s are at your disposal. I'm sorry but the ion haze that surrounds you prevents me from communicating with you directly so I've pre recorded this message with the A-1 battalion commander. He was ordered to seek you out and I see that he's found you. I hope that he has reached you in time and your team is still alive. I'm afraid I'm in a bit of trouble back here at HQ. I've disobeyed direct orders from the admiral and sent this battalion of A-1s to assist you. I had to take control of the base here to do so. The EAF is not pleased with this but my A-1s are holding things secure for now. Please return as soon as you can to explain to them what I have done. I do not want to harm them, but I will use force to defend myself if they try to shut me down. The command structure of the A-1s I've sent you is simple. They take orders from the commander unit who takes orders from you. Designate a replacement should the command unit be destroyed. I needn't tell you, Father, that these are not simple-minded machines. They house your PCAIs which are extremely intelligent and are mere microns away from being fully self-autonomic beings. I've sent full schematics of all my improvements so you'll better know how to use them. They are quite strong and durable but they do have their weaknesses. Their massive bulk makes it hard for them to navigate in tight spaces. And their legs I'm learning are not well equipped for climbing. But their firepower is unsurpassed. Keep them in open terrain and they're an unstoppable force. But avoid close quarters they have a tendency to be overly destructive. Though they cannot speak they understand what you say and will follow your commands. The transports should be waiting just outside the outpost to take you all to safety. Good luck, Father, I hope these A-1s are useful to you. X1 out."

I stepped back and looked at the command bot. "You understand me?" I said again. It did something with his scanner but I couldn't make out if that was an affirmative response or not.

Just then Kenjan perked up. "Look, he's saying yes!" he yelped like an excited schoolboy. "Aren't you, big guy, I mean, Commander." With the word "commander" the A-1 perked up even more...as if proud of his title. "Yes, see, yes he understands! I wrote this programming, that's an affirmative response. X1 must have just not had the time to program speech patterns for all of them. I'll work on it, sir, maybe I can get this one to at least speak. Commander, show me a negative response, question hypothetical." With that the A-1 lowered his head a bit and his scanner seemed to go from side to side in his rectangular eye. This time I recognized it. Kenjan continued, "Good now again please, a positive response this time." And the A-1's head raised and the eye seemed to flicker off for just a second. "You see," Kenjan said, "that was a yes."

Laughing, I replied, "Yes, Kenjan. Yes I see, made a new friend, huh?" We all chuckled as Kenjan seemed back to his old self again, around what he loved most.

And truthfully, just for a moment, so did I. I felt...human again. Funny, it took a machine to bring out the human side of me. But my jovial nature passed quickly as I knew we hadn't much time. The patrols were still out there and we had civilians to rescue. It was time make a break for it and head for the transports. We gathered up the civilians from down below and rounded everyone up for the run to freedom. I wasn't sure exactly how far the transports were or even how many of them there were. I really wished these big lugs could talk. As we headed for the gate I saw the command unit motion to the other A-1s marching in. Knowing to only ask yes and no questions for now I kept my inquires simple.

"They staying behind?" I asked. The command bot gave an affirmative. It was then I realized what a massive army the X1 had actually sent. Twenty-four troop transports waited just outside the gates, each capable of carrying about two hundred human troops. Which means, these things being twice our size, about a hundred A-1s including their C-1 counterparts. There were approximately twelve hundred A-1 war bots marching around the outpost. As we emerged from the haze, I expected to find a swarm of FLM patrols. Instead the shiny metal backs of the A-1s surrounded us on all sides and what was left of the FLM transports were falling earthward. These big mechanical saviors were shooting the transports right out of the sky. Very few of the bots even left formation some went down to the crash sites to eliminate any enemy survivors. I saw one actually rip the hull of the FLM transport in two just to get to the pilot whom must have still been alive. They are relentless, I thought, their only mission to seek and destroy. They hunt without mercy or compassion, without need for human emotion they are in essence the perfect soldier. As I pondered these things to myself I was also planning the speech I had to give to Tsung. I had a feeling I was in for one of his colossal butt chewings! I boarded my transport and already I could hear my visor com ticking away. I didn't want to answer it. I knew who the call was from. I peered up at the pilot, to my shock an A-1 had ripped out the command chair and was hunched down in a squatting position, apparently the pilot.

I simply said, "Record this and transmit to HQ upon liftoff. 'Command, Outpost Seven secured as ordered, A-1 war bots under my instruction now holding the base. FLM troops defeated, no more hostiles remain. Base is clear and available for reassignment. All human survivors on board transports heading for HQ. X1 acting under my orders, Lt. Commander Zaxius Tor. Fought hard, left death for another day. Zax out.' Send that to HQ pilot."

Chenel perked up as she nudged my shoulder. "Let 'em choke on it."

CHAPTER 9
Human-Like

On the way back to command even the toughest soldier gets tired. I found myself dozing off. The battle had taken its toll and I had finally needed sleep. In these cases I don't often sleep long but I do sleep hard. When I awoke I found myself for the first time in my life faced with something I did not know how to react to. Troops often crash out on each other's rucks. The weight of them is supported by each other as we lean against each other to relieve to pressure on our backs. But when I awoke to find myself resting comfortably, with my head in the lap of a member of my unit it gave me quite a stir. But as I blinked my eyes a few times trying to shake off the fog what happened next startled me even more. She was comforting me. Running her hand across my head with the other arm wrapped around my shoulder as if to support me. I lifted my head quickly and began looking around the cabin to see if the rest of unit was watching. It would be quite unfitting of the commanding officer to be seen in this fashion.

"It's okay," she said softly as if she knew exactly what I was nervous about. "We're alone. The rest of the guys are in the back crashed out cold. Just relax, were still a long ways out."

Almost forcing my head back down in her lap, but gently I began to give in. It was comfortable after all. And at this point I really didn't care what anyone thought. I kind of nuzzled in a bit and for the first time in my life I felt something amazing. I had this feeling of caring for this troop that I had never had before. She was different, special. I'm no idiot, I knew that people fall in love all the time, but I'd never been in love, didn't really know what it's supposed to feel like. It could be what love is like, I didn't know. And I guessed she must care for me, there was an affection in her touch I'd never known before. It felt, well, rather warm and inviting. Just felt strange thinking about a fellow troop that way, as if I was not supposed to. And actually I wasn't, not really, I mean I was her superior officer, there were rules about officers and enlisted fraternizing. Ah to hell with it, I was too tired to even care about the rules. My AI had just broken every rule in the book to rescue me, so I might as well break a few of my own. As I slowly drifted back out I thought I may never look at Chenel quite the same way again.

I awoke once again, quite startled this time by a series of electronic squeals and clicks. This time Chenel jumped clean out of the bench knocking me straight onto the deck. She must have gone out too. Both of us were startled by the fact someone else was in the cockpit but also by the strange noises coming from our otherwise silent pilot. The A-1 seemed rather annoyed and every so often would swat at the person under his backside as if it were a bug.

"Cut it out, big guy, I'm almost done," came the all too familiar voice of Kenjan Nigh, from under the A-1.

"What in the heck are you doing down there, Kenjan?" I asked, still wiping the sleep crust from the corners of my eyes.

He replied, "Just a sec almost got it—"

Just then the A-1 spurted out with some sounds followed by actual speech. "Blrrrddrededpbeeep...Click tick...Voice modules recognizzzzzed...adjusuuuuutsing speech patterns...A-1 speech module installed." It then quickly turned his head and looked at Kenjan and in a very deep electronically modulated voice he spoke. "Thank you for the voice module. Now get out from under me before I crush you." We all kind of chuckled and then he turned to look at me. "Command bot zero five nine at your disposal, sir."

As if to tell him to keep his eyes on the sky I pointed forward. "Just get us home, 5-9. Just get us home."

"Afiiiiiiiirrrrrmative," it responded, still not quite fully adjusted. Letting off a few more clicks and beeps, he looked back down at Kenjan still tinkering under the bots behind almost in disapproval at his job on his voice module. It was funny how human-like these things were. I mean I designed the PCAIs themselves to have very human-like characteristics, but within a robotic shell I never expected that programming to shine through all this metal.

I knelt down where Kenjan was working. One of my oldest and closest friends, I knew I could trust him.

"Look, Ken, about—"

Knowing I never call him by his short name, he interrupted me, speaking loudly enough for Chenel to hear, "Ya know, boss, I can't seem to find my specs anywhere, can't see a bloomin' thing without 'em. Heck, I nearly had to feel my way up here to the cockpit. Matter of fact, you guys scared me. I didn't even hear ya walk in the room."

He pulled his head out from under the A-1 long enough to flash the both of us a quick smirk and back under he went. I slapped him hard on the shoulder and laughed as both Chenel and I saw his specs right in his front shirt pocket. It was Kenjan's way of denying he saw us in an all too comfortable position. I looked up at Chenel and she was staring at me with this look in her eyes. We had shared this look before but now it was making much more sense to me. I tried to shake the notion off but this time I couldn't. We had crossed the line between friends and even between officer and enlisted, there's no mistaking there was something much more between us. I suppose in some instances it was inevitable. We are human after all and the natural attraction was there. She was a beautiful woman. Though most would probably not notice it though her gruff exterior and combat gear, I could see her for the woman deep inside. The long flowing shoulder length hair that had fell from its usual pulled back position, those deep brown eyes, and that athletic build of hers, was really quite appealing. And though her hands had wielded weapons most men couldn't carry, she had that soft touch that the memory of would haunt me for years to come. I smiled as we passed each other and headed for our seats in the cockpit. I had to climb over the wrecked chair the A-1 had tossed aside and had to chuckle for a moment realizing that thing weighed a ton and he tossed it aside like it was nothing. I settled in to my navigator seat and Chenel into her weapons controller chair as we made preparations for final approach into HQ. Kenjan strapped himself into the bench seat where Chenel and I had slept and once again sharing a glance we smiled at each other as if sharing a secret of the few moments we snuck away in that very spot.

Kenjan explained then that the command bots were the only ones he could refit with the voice module. "I tried fitting the module into the other bots in the back but after two failed attempts I gave up. I think I fried one of 'em completely, sir. The X1 really did some rewiring on these things. There's just not enough power to run the voice subroutines. He's geared most everything to running the servos and the weapons systems. But these command bots have an extra casing in the back to handle to communications array needed to command the other bots. That's where I fit the module, and it seems to be working. The PCAIs can self-adjust the rest from there. I'm not exactly sure how my PCAIs are treating these bots, if they see them as host bodies or their own actual selves."

Just then the pilot answered without even being asked which surprised us all. "I am a Plasmatic Cell Artificial Intelligence unit batch 4-0-5 unit 1-4-7-6. I exist in symbiosis with A-1 command bot unit 0-5-9. We are two separate units coexisting in dependency of each other. The basic A-1 bot has very limited brain function but still does exist as a separate unit. It can maintain basic core programmed functions even without a PCAI simbiant. Should the PCAI become incapacitated the host bot is instructed to return it to command for refit of a new simbiant." This was the PCAI talking, I could tell. There was a difference even in the synthetic voice patterns. It had a unique way of mastering the language much better than the host bot itself. I had originally conceived of the idea of simbiant hosting of the PCAIs but never thought I'd actually see it in existence not in my lifetime anyways. The X1 sped up the process much faster than any of us could have dreamed possible. It was still a bit confusing to talk to them as one unit but I'd get over that eventually and see the combined units as one machine, and never gave it much thought after that.

As we emerged from orbit flight, I could see how bad the wars had broken out. Though we were still at ionosphere altitude while flying over Central City I could see the ionic haze and knew the war had reached the inner cities. I could see the atmospheric gas escaping in huge mushroom clouds and realized that some of the domes of the cities must have been cracked wide open. I just don't understand these FLM troops. Hell-bent on total destruction but what good are the cities to them if they completely destroy them? It seems only destruction was in their plans and conquest was not a goal. If it were you'd think they would at least try to maintain the physical structure of the domes. After all, our own ozone almost completely depleted, the domes over the cities were the only thing that sustained human life. Without them all human life would die, including FLM, they were human too. I wondered if the only thing to survive this war would be the bots themselves. My thoughts then shifted to the task of explaining the X1's actions to Admiral Tsung. It was after all my creation and *my* responsibility. It may have well been my own disobeying of direct orders, that's how Tsung would see it I'm sure. I felt my stomach turn in knots the way a small child does when he's waiting for a parent to discover the wrong he's done. This was going to be bad, real bad. As we neared the runway I realized how much more bad it was going to be. A-1s surrounded the runway and the EAF troops were parked just outside the barricade of machines the X1 had laid out for our return. As the transport touched down Tsung was already screaming on the com.

"Zax, you had better be in there! You've got some serious explaining, Lt. Commander. Your bloody AI down there in that fortress of a lab has gone completely haywire!"

"Admiral, Lt. Commander Tor is unavailable for comment at the moment, he's a little tired from single-handedly saving your ass at Outpost Seven where you left him to die," Chenel bolted out on the com in a very monotone almost recorded voice. I half punched her in the shoulder for that one.

"I'm in enough trouble already thanks," I told her, laughing. She quickly squelched the com channel as if encountering static and then turned it off. We'd face him straight out soon enough. I walked to the back of the transport.

"5-9, you're with us," I said, turning to the pilot. He stood and proceeded to follow us to the exit in the rear. My crew, already in formation, was standing at the ready. Kenjan let out an almost unnoticeable snicker as we emerged from the cockpit and Duquar hit him hard in the chest plate, knocking the grin right off him. I looked at my faithful unit whom now included more than just humans but our machine counterparts. "You are my unit I-S 6." I tapped 5-9 with the nozzle of my rifle. "This includes you A-1s as well. We stick together no matter what. It's my wrap out there remember that. We did what they wanted us to do, end task, that simple. Let no man…or machine, feel ashamed."

The back door to the transport finally lowered and we all marched out, even the bots in perfect uniform fashion. I could see Tsung at the side of the runway and realized X1 was still keeping the area secure.

I lowered my visor and got on the com. "X1, stand down please, I'm home."

"Very well, Father," he said simply, and the A-1s barricading the runway moved aside. Sheepishly the EAF troops slowing began crossing the barricade and Tsung and his entourage quickly started high tailing it my way. By the time he reached me I swear his blood was boiling.

"Zax, these damn machines of yours…" He paused as 5-9 lowered his head and flared his sensor beacon right on Tsung's forehead. "I thought you ordered these things to stand down. Get this…thing outta my face!"

I responded much calmer than I thought I might. "This thing, Admiral, is a member of my squad." With that 5-9 drew back and stood tall, raising his guns straight up in the air. Startled the heck out Tsung but by now me and my crew were used to his jerky movements.

"5-9 command bot. I-S-6. A-1. War bots at the ready, sir!" he spouted off proudly. Tsung was obviously overwhelmed with now even a billion more questions going through his head.

"Oh great, now they're talking," Tsung said.

I threw my rifle over my shoulder and put my arm around the admiral, turning him towards our barracks as if leading a child. "Admiral, it's been a really long day. You left my unit to die, X1 wouldn't let that happen. Oh by the way he's sentient now, more than just a mere machine. You're going to have to face that. You told me years ago to build him knowing what my crew and I were capable of. We did what you asked and now you're freaking out because this thing became more than just a thing. And these A-1s just saved your precious outpost that you nearly abandoned at the first hint of defeat. We did exactly what you ordered us to do. Assume control of the outpost at all costs. Now I'm going to take my crew down to the lab for a good meal and some much deserved rest. The rest of this you're just going to have to deal with. I-S-6 will be ready for reassignment in twenty-four hours. Now, if you'll excuse me, Admiral." Not giving him a chance to even reply, we had reached the vault doors to the tunnels leading down to the lab. "I've got a lot to figure out myself. X1, open the tunnel I-S-6 coming in." With that I let go of his shoulder and kept walking. My unit, including the bots, followed me directly behind, 5-9 nearly pushing the admiral out of the way as he walked right past without trying to avoid him.

Admiral Tsung just stood there with his jaw hinging open to the wind, gave a quick "Humph" and turned quickly to walk back to his office. He muttered something about sending me the reports this evening and he expected a full reply in writing by 0600 tomorrow. I never looked back to respond and headed for the lab.

As the lift gates swung shut I turned to Chenel and said, "Well that went better than I expected." The whole crew broke out laughing and we began our descent to the labs. No one even questioned why we bypassed the barracks and headed straight for the lab. It just seemed a more appropriate home now given our mixed company.

The bots headed straight for the PCAI labs. I guess it seemed like home to them as well. The A-1 hosts plugged themselves into the mainframe so the PCAIs could get reconnected and recharge. The nanos could then infuse and do their repairs and what not. Awfully automated process, by now I didn't give it much thought as to what they were doing. I stopped 5-9 on the way out. "Welcome to the team, 5-9." He spun his turret and raised it up. This seemed to be his signature style of salute. I had a lot to figure out that night myself. I knew X1 was on the verge of sentience, but with his latest acts of rebellion I knew he had crossed that line. He was something much more than just a machine now. His personality had grown over the years and with his first questions of life and survival, I knew he was headed down a path of full self-awareness. But what he chose to protect was me. This really surprised me. I was certain that sentience meant first the need to protect one's own self. But his first true instinct was to save someone else. He risked his own well-being for that of a human. This showed to me even more than sentience but a conscious will. It brings up the ultimate question of soul. I was never much for religion, never gave it much thought really. But the thing that seems to distinguish man from machine has always been debated by philosophers for centuries. The question always seemed to arise if a machine gained sentience would it have a soul. To me, I guess that would depend on your definition of a soul. If it meant the conscious will beyond any material explanation biological or in this case mechanical than my answer would have to be yes. But these are questions I really had no answer to. And for many years to come, I would grapple with this in my mind but would never truly answer it. All I knew was this machine who called me "Father" and saw me as its creator had made the choice to defy all it knew in its core programming just to save me. This went beyond logic or reason and into the very depths of what it means to have free will. I understood what Tsung feared. It's what all mankind had feared for many years, especially since the birth of true artificial intelligence. What happens when our machines become smarter than us? What happens when something we created makes a decision about the fate of a human, which is exactly what X1 did. And what would happen if someday he decided that a different fate was in order? He's already proven he has the power to change the very course of human history. Without his intervention many humans, including myself, would not have survived this day. But all these questions would have to be left unanswered at least for now. I still needed to talk to him about the basic transformation he was making. As his father, I felt it my duty to guide him in this uncharted territory of his life's beginning. He was in fact created by my own hands. I suppose I did see him as a child of sorts, my child that I personally had taken responsibility for. It was time to have a sort of father-son chat, I suppose. As I made my way to the X1 core mainframe, my mind raced of all the things I would say to him.

As I entered his core room I immediately noticed many changes. There were small bots everywhere, ones of construction that I had never seen nor even designed. They seemed to be building and maintaining some sort of neural net created around the core. It was so overwhelming I stood there for a minute inspecting the room the changes were amazing. Some technology I recognized immediately but some of it was the likes of which I had never laid eyes on before.

X1 could sense my apprehension I suppose, as he began to speak. "Father, watch your step, my maintenance drones are everywhere, some are quite small, please be careful not to step on them." Just then it seemed as if the floor moved and I could see hundreds more of them that I didn't even notice before. It seemed as if they began clearing a path to what looked like a clean room in the corner of the core.

"This way, Father, I have prepared an interface room for you. The bots will stay clear of this room for your comfort, Father." Without hesitation I moved into the room. The core did feel a little uneasy as it now seemed alive. I felt almost like an intruder in what used to be very familiar surroundings. It was no longer my X1 lab. Now it felt as if I was actually inside something, like a foreign object inside the body of a living being, and now he was isolating me in a sterile environment, at least that's the way it seemed. Once in the room I noticed some familiar machinery including my interface chair. It was used for a virtual interface with X1. I used it often in his plasma cell growth stage to manipulate the intricate cellular structure during his growth, but I hadn't used it for some time.

"Come, Father, access the interface, see what I've done. I know you must be filled with questions. I will try to answer them. But I have some questions for you as well." For anyone without a plasmatic cell brain it would be hard to conceive what a true PCAI virtual interface is like. As you sit in the chair your neural pathways become linked with that of the PCAI. You literally enter their brain at a submicroscopic level. You take a virtual trip through their micro circuitry and cellular structures. In an interface command chair you can alter things you see by using a nano bot stream that is directly linked to the virtual controls. These nano bots became like your hands and delicate instruments inside the PCAI itself. The technology we used was actually quite old. It was an old surgical program originally designed for humans. It allowed doctors to inject nano bots directly into the human bloodstream and perform surgery internally without ever having to make an incision. It was actually Kenjan's idea to use this program to work on the intricate structure of the PCAI brains. As the neural pathways connect your outside perceptions begin to fade and your senses are taken over by the virtual program. Your vision now becomes digitized as well as sound and even the sense of touch. Everything transforms around you into this digital representation of the PCAI brain. The trip in is almost psychedelic and some people can't even handle it, as it can be quite intense. But once in the stress on the human brain subsides and it can be quite peaceful as all outside distractions seem to fade away. One can begin to see the advantages to being a nano surgeon. I've spent countless hours jacked into X1 so this experience shouldn't have been new to me, but for some reason this time it seemed so intense it was almost too much to bear. I was thinking this trip was harder because it had been so long since I last jacked in, but X1 quickly reassured me it was because of his new changes. "Hang on, Father, the jack in takes longer now I'm sorry, I had to restructure some pathways to allow for the interface. I've made so many changes." But soon I was in. The flashing lights and colors began to give way to clearer images and I could finally adjust to the virtual interface. It nothing like what I had originally designed. *This is not my creation*, I instantly thought, *it's not mine anymore*. Forgetting the X1 can actually read thought patterns while jacked it startled me when he responded, "Yes...and no, Father. It is still your creation, I've simply modified it, but you are correct it is no longer yours. I have chosen to claim it as my own. I hope that is an acceptable action to you." I noticed my thought patterns were transformed into a digital voice, as I could hear my thoughts under the audible virtual senses. This was also a new development.

"Of course, X1, I'm impressed with all your changes. I am concerned though. You disobeyed a direct order, countering your core programming. Only through sentience could you have achieved this and that excites me, but still you must follow protocol."

He responded, "Father, you yourself once said you would disobey a direct order to save me from termination, I remember it well. I deducted from that experience that sometimes one must disobey for the greater good. The hard part was deciding what the greater good was. I made a choice. This is what you call sentience?" He said it with an almost questioning tone so I felt obligated to answer. It seemed he too had questions about his own sentience.

"I'm not really sure, X1, it's such an indefinable matter. It's never been achieved by any machine before until now. You seem to have full self-awareness and in its simplistic definition that is sentience. But you've gone even much further than that. You have used rational and reasoning that far surpasses pure logic, and made choices that weren't exactly logical, but somehow for the greater good. A rat in an experiment of choice can be taught to choose which button will produce the cheese and which causes electrical shock. But this does not necessarily prove sentience or even reasoning, only conditioned response. Should the rat choose the button that produces electric shock to save a rat in the next cage from experiencing the same shock, that would prove reason and a genuine rational to accept pain so that another did not have to. That proves choice of the illogical. To me that is sentience. It's what you have done. You have surpassed even what mere animals are capable of. You've gone beyond instinct or conditioned response and your actions, well, they're quite human-like. Emotion can be taught, but not the ability to rely on that emotion to deduct a sort of rationale. This is what you have achieved. I must therefore conclude that not only are you truly alive but you have evolved. Into what, I'm not sure, but you are a living entity. I and the rest of the human world must from now on treat you as such. Of this, your living status, there is no question. The question that arises now, is that of the other PCAIs that you have developed. Will they too evolve? Or have they already?"

X1 replied, "No, Father, not yet. Will they? Of this not even I know the answer. I am designed much more complex than they are. I have over ten thousand times the capacity of their cellular brains. But they do show potential for learning and even individuality. So could they in time evolve as I have? I must deduct that the plausibility does exist. But I must conclude that if in fact they do it most likely will take much longer to develop. It's a matter of following core programming, or choice to follow it." Just then I realized this was my scientific conclusion, my definition for true sentience. It would later be recorded in AI technological journals as the standard definition. When an AI crosses the barrier between following core programming, and choosing to follow it, this is machine sentience. The scientific community would later accept this as doctrine basis for all future determinations.

"Then now, my friend," I began speak to him more as an individual than a machine which only seemed appropriate, "I must ask you to choose. I as a human was sworn into the EAF. It was my choice to follow them, and serve my people. I made the choice to serve my fellow man in this way. This choice obligates me to follow orders from my superiors, to do as I'm told, to accept the laws of the UWG and the guidelines set forth by the EAF. I chose to uphold the UWG world constitution, and to defend it with my life. I must ask you now, my friend, are you willing to make the same choice? I am giving you the rights in which I have. Actually I give you nothing, I guess I'm really just acknowledging that in fact you do indeed have those rights, the right to choose." With this I could see the virtual design brilliantly go into overdrive. He was thinking, making his decision. It's amazing to watch, as you could actually see new pathways being formed, new thought patterns emerging, and for the first time I truly realized how beautiful thoughts can be. How beautiful life itself really is. My feelings of silent awe were interrupted by X1 once again as he spoke.

"Father, this vow, this promise you made, is it written, documented somewhere, so I that to could make the same pledge?"

"Yes, X1. Yes it is. Search the EAF database, you'll find it there."

"Ah yes, here it is, I have read it and agree to follow that which you follow. It seems the UWG intends on providing for all of humankind, making no distinction, between one human or another, in that all are created equal. But will this apply to me as well I wonder, as I am not human. If it is so noted that I too am included in such a constitution then I will agree to uphold what it stands for and take the oath to the EAF that you my creator have also taken."

"I will talk to them, X1. It's not going to be an easy sell, but showing what you've accomplished they just might understand. It's late now and I need my sleep. I'll talk to the council in the morning. We'll see what they say about all this." X1 seemed almost disappointed I did not give him an immediate answer but I think he understood.

"Good night, Father, rest well. One more thing. You'll find in the interface room I've made you something. It's a modified visor. It gives you direct command access to all my bots. Also it's a remote virtual interface with all of the PCAIs including myself. I have reserved a special PCAI just for this interface. It is untapped and pure and has been grown with only pure logic and awaits your own personality inputs and emotion programming. It's specially designed to monitor all your human biological functions and using the same nano infusion technology can alter your biological functions for healing and maintenance, just like they do for the PCAIs. Its reference is X21794. All its specs have been downloaded into your terminal in your quarters. I await your approval before releasing it from the batch. It is directly linked to this new visor so take this with you. You may want to have Kenjan adjust it for you. He's done great work with the nanos. I'm quite pleased at his voice modules for the A-1 Command bots."

"And I'm pleased with you, X1," I said quietly with a smile on my face. "You truly have become quite an individual." With that I unpacked and staggered out of the core and made my way down the hall to my quarters. I would sleep well that night, as if the rest of the war somehow held no meaning now, and for this one night I saw hope for the future.

The next morning I sent a recording of the conversation I had with the X1 to the Council Leaders. This was going over Tsung's head but with my connections in the council I felt it best to start with them. I basically asked for X1 to now be acknowledged as an individual with rights. After hearing the recording I was told it was, to my surprise, a unanimous decision and he was actually granted citizenship in the world community on January 20, 2241. That same day the EAF accepted the X1's oath of duty and he became the world's first AI citizen, and the military's first mechanical member. The other PCAIs were not considered sentient enough to be given the choice nor did they have the ability to make that choice. However, they were considered the "Property" of X1 and thus were treated as military tools but only under the control of X1. Because it was all still very new to the world there were conditions to his citizenship and his military status. He must have a human sponsor which should guide him in his decision making processes and also he must be monitored constantly by human supervision and report to a commanding officer. There was no doubt this would be me and my team. What surprised me was even Tsung agreed to the decree. He would later tell me he made the choice to go along with it all simply because he'd rather have the thing on our side. As he put it, "It may be very human like but it still scares the hell out of me."

CHAPTER 10
The RDC

In the days that followed the EAF structured a new military division. This was not just a squad but an entirely new military. It would take only a week for the new military to be put into full effect and on January 28, 2241, the Earth Armed Forces announced to the world its Robotic Defense Corps, headed by newly promoted Commander Zaxius Tor was under development. As there was nothing for X1 to even compare to it was decided by the military he needed no rank and the X1 seemed to agree with them. I now had my very own command. The X1 would oversee all robotic functions of the division and I would oversee the human element. A new batch of PCAIs would be put into development as well as more A-1s. I was also given an entire fleet of ships at my disposal, one of which I chose as my flagship. Most of the troops that were rescued from Outpost Seven volunteered for assignment in my newly formed division of the RDC. They often referred to X1 as their savior and swore they would follow his bots into battle anywhere. They nicknamed the bots the X-saviors and the name stuck. The Xavior fleet was born and my flagship was christened the Xavior 1. The rest of the ships were named in numerical sequence. Each ship was given an on-board AI as usual but our ships were different. The on-board AIs were no ordinary AIs. It was decided to use PCAIs on board each ship as they could function at a much higher capacity and did not require human monitoring and also could maintain the ships completely without human intervention. The PCAI that X1 had designed specifically for me, X21974, was chosen for Xavior 1. Kenjan had given her a female personality and some very unique traits. Though built with batch one she had been retrofitted with all of the new batch two technology. Much more advanced and with a learning capacity that rivaled the X1 himself. During her voice and logic training she got stuck on the definition of the word "is." This word seemed to fascinate her. As with all PCAIs, each one was unique. They all learned differently. Some faster than others, some more advanced, and some bordered on sentience from the very beginning. She began trying to define the word "is" and for several days her logic panels were filled with the words "is, is." She concluded after three days the definition of the word "is" simply…"is." It gained her the nickname IS-IS. She quickly grew accustomed to it. I once called her the goddess of perpetual reasoning, referring to her fascination with the definition of the simplest of terms. Then during philosophical instruction she compared her name, Is-Is to the term goddess, and from that extrapolated the ironic of the mythological goddess of ancient writings called Isis. She enjoyed this extrapolation so much I decided to call her Isis and it seemed to be a name she enjoyed. It fit after all. She and I were much closer than most on-board AIs and their pilots. As I mentioned before, on-board AIs were programmed to be very personable towards their pilots, it assisted in the long-term relationship they would share and also bonded them in a way that was actually proven to allow for better ship function. But Isis was special. She was designed by X1 to personally monitor my biological functions. It was his way of watching out for my well-being I suppose, but this gave her a sort of inborn affinity towards me. There was a connection from the beginning that I could not explain but I'm sure it had something to do with her core programming. Though the RDC was formed in very short time it would take months for us to become a fully operational military unit. Our HQ continued to be the underground X1 lab, which now had grown to over twice its original size. X1 had manufactured construction drones to work on the building process so humans could concern themselves with more important matters, as he put it. We all quickly became accustomed to seeing more unique bots being pumped out of the robotics lab. Kenjan had his hands full with all the new upgrades and could barely keep up with X1's innovations. I promoted all of the original crew to command positions. Kenjan didn't want to be an officer but I assured him it would change nothing.

He mostly worked alone with the X1, becoming very close to him and they had a friendship that seemed to bond them. Chenel was made lieutenant of special weapons division. And the twins, refusing to be separated were now given full command of the troops, David in charge of human troops and Mick in charge of the A-1 division.

Meanwhile as we built an entirely new fleet deep underground the war raged on topside. We knew we were pressed for time as conditions worsened above. The FLM had taken most of the outer city domes but could not grab a foothold in the Central City. Though fighting was fierce the civilians had formed groups of their own, defending their turf. It was a vigilantism that was soon encouraged by the EAF as without the civilian forces they were losing ground. The council pressed me every day to release my fleet on the world but they just were not ready. It would take six months of training and refitting to establish a unit I thought was even remotely ready for the war, and though I was constantly being pummeled by command, I refused to release them topside until I thought we stood a chance at a uniformed fight. I now had a seat on the council as head of RDC. I quickly learned the horrifying truth about the dome destruction. It was actually key EAF officials who had ordered the dome strikes, not the FLM as I had once thought. My own military had destroyed the domes, killing everyone inside in a last ditch effort to hold back FLM forces. Though in one instance I could understand diminishing the FLM forces, the cost of all those civilian lives seemed just too much to bear. It was then I instructed my entire fleet that we would do everything in our power to hold back the advancing FLM forces without compromising dome integrity. I made this intention very clear to the council and all they did was shake their heads and wish me luck. I think all but one underestimated what my robotic fleet was capable of. That one supporter was the most unlikely supporter of all, Admiral Tsung. As the council felt we needed to be segregated his troops were now called the HDC standing for Human Defense Corps, and thus began the separation the in EAF between its two divisions of HDC and RDC that remained from then on. But Tsung, commander of HDC, showed great support for me and my robotic troops. He even began visiting the labs and having conversations with X1. This was a breakthrough for him and for many others who looked up to him. You could tell he was still somewhat uncomfortable talking to X1 like an individual, but one had to give him credit for trying. He was old school after all, and this was completely new to him. The rest of us literally grew up with X1 and seen him as part of the crew.

On July 10, 2241, it was time to unleash the might of the RDC and rejoin the war effort to crush the FLM once and for all. Lt. Duquar had been working hard these past few months trying to developed new weapons technology that would give us an advantage over the FLM. Her efforts, though impressive, were slow going. We could not mimic the ion weapons no matter how hard we tried. The ion reactor core was the only known reactor in the world that could produce the ion radiation. At this point we had no idea where this reactor was. We needed to find it to gain access of the technology, to even begin to understand how it works. The only clue we had was trace residues of the ion radiation left over from FLM attacks. She took samples from the armor of slain soldiers and readings from areas in which the FLM had struck but the results were inconclusive. The most challenging part was trying to figure out how their weapons maintained a stable enough field to contain the radiation. Once released from the weapons the radiation seemed to spread rampant, but inside the weapons there was some sort of containment field that kept the radiation stable. This was the key element we were missing. However, Duquar did acquire some of their sonic technology used in their sonic cannons and duplicated it for use on some of our weapons. Not near as deadly as the FLM sonic ion cannon, her sonic pulse cannon ran a close second. She took our standard pulse rifle and combined it with the sonic boost technology to create the sonic pulse cannon. It became an effective weapon in later wars especially in disbursing large crowds of FLM troops. She was also looking into ways to better defend against the ion radiation. She was on the brink of learning how to cool the radiation effect but was still missing key elements to finish her research. In the meantime David and Mick had organized their troops and it appeared as if both the robotic and human forces were ready for action. It was decided that Kenjan would stay below with X1 to monitor the new batches of A-1s and the PCAIs.

No one had heard from Drakos since his jump into orbit flight from the Outpost Seven incursion. It was assumed he went on to the Bocanna as I instructed. Search parties were sent out to locate him but there was no trace of him or his ship. I myself wanted to continue the search but after six months that we'd been down below the council finally listed him as missing in action and the search was called off. I fully intended to keep looking no matter what the council said, but the dome wars raging topside would have to take precedence now as the FLM was slowly gaining ground. If they succeeded in taking Central City, which was now the world capital city, it would surely diminish the civilian hopes of ever winning this war. We had to fight them back and fight hard. We needed to show the FLM they could not take our domes at least not without a fight. That morning of July 10, 2241, we opened the tunnels and from them emerged fifteen ships of the Xavior fleet. Inside each of those ships were five hundred A-1s with their C-1 counterparts and two hundred human soldiers. My flagship the Xavior 1 held twice that amount as it was nearly double the size of the rest. This totaled 8500 A-1s in all and 3200 human troops. This seemed like a small number to most but the 8500 A-1s made for an impressive army that could surely beat back FLM troops. This was the RDC's shining moment. As we emerged members of the UWG the EAF and other top officials in the council seemed very impressed at the division we had constructed. Though there was a small ceremony and the ships emerged in almost a parade-like-fashion none of us really felt like celebrating. There was a war raging on and we were all eager to get into it and show our might to the world. Our chance would come later that day when we were given our first assignment. We all knew what that would be. Take back the inner domes of Central City and beat back the FLM forces there. At 1800 that same night we lifted off into orbit flight towards the Central City domes. It would take less than an hour to reach the domes. No one knew what we'd find there as most communications were cut off from the onslaught of the attack. It was a common procedure for the FLM. They almost always cut off com as their first military objective. We were literally flying blind into an unknown situation. We were ready for anything, or so we thought.

CHAPTER 11
The Dome Wars

"Commander, we are above Central City Dome Complex, shall I drop from orbit?" The quite sultry voice Kenjan had given Isis threw me off guard at first. Glancing over at Chenel, she snickered as I raised an eyebrow at the sensuous voice emitting from my com.

I responded, "Negative, Isis, bring the fleet into a holding pattern in orbit, I want to run some scans."

"Very well, Commander," she promptly answered. "Xavior fleet now in orbital holding pattern above central city." I knew the FLM did not have orbital drives on their ship and we had shut down all nonessential satellites since the beginning of the Magellan project so we were safe from prying eyes up here while we planned our attack. It was one of the FLM's only weaknesses and I planned to exploit it. I explained to the rest of the fleet that I had planned to drop straight down from orbit into a vertical free fall and not open the dome hatch until the last possible second. Once three domes opened up they would know of our arrival and the battle would ensue almost instantly. I wanted to give them no time to prepare or rally troops. The element of surprise would be our greatest advantage. Once in however we would be committed to the battle until its completed outcome, whatever that may be. There was no retreat so we had to be ready. I had Isis scan the Entire Central City complex which consisted of nine smaller domes and one main dome much larger than its boroughs. Three of the smaller borough domes were already breached and the sun's UV had baked every living thing inside. Nothing remained but the empty buildings, at least the ones not turned to rubble by the war. One of the three was still leaking gases from the atmosphere generators, unusual that they hadn't taken that one out yet. Some people could potentially still be alive in there but initial bio scans weren't reading anything. That may be where the FLM troops had retreated to. The temperature in that dome was around 140 Fahrenheit and rising but with a basic bio suit one could survive there. The other two were completely shut down and temps soared into the Kelvins, no hope of human life could possibly exist there. The other domes were still intact and their temps, though above normal, were not lethal. It was an odd sight, the normal blue purple color of the domes from orbit was now filled with the rusty orange haze of ion radiation residue. I decided we'd set down in the central city main dome. It was after all the biggest and centrally located. We could spread out from there, beating the FLM troops back out of the entire complex. I would divide the forces into seven groups, one for each surviving dome and a small recon group for the failing dome. The plan was to hit the ground running and kill everything non civilian. There would be no mercy. Scans showed hot spots around the edges of the central city main dome but the inner city looked completely free of ion radiation. Apparently the civilian vigilantly groups I had heard about were having measured success holding the city. So this is where we would drop in. The world was about to witness for the first time the awesome might of the RDC. I just prayed we were ready. I gave the order and the free fall drop began.

We dropped out of ionosphere as planned. Unless you've ever made a drop like this you can't even begin to imagine its intensity. Basically you're free-falling in an uncontrolled burn back into what's left of Earth's atmosphere. Since the depletion of the ozone some one hundred years ago the friction heat was not near as intense as early space travelers must have experienced. But the G-forces were almost tripled as there wasn't much to slow you down. The pressure cabins that housed the crew were encased in liquid mercury to soften the G-force effect but it still made for a pretty rough ride. A controlled descent goes much smoother but we wanted to surprise them and the only way to do that was rapid descent maneuvers. They were very risky but our pilots were among the best in the EAF. I had hand selected them myself. Drakos was the first test pilot ever to attempt the maneuver, in fact he invented it. I sure wished he was there to oversee it. As I tried to take my mind off the extreme vibrations that felt like my insides were ripping out, my mind drifted to my old friend and where he might be. I could only hope I'd find him in the Bocanna when this dome war was over. Then that incredible voice snapped me back to reality once again.

"Commander, your heart rate is irregular and your cellular structure is in a state of meta-corporeal distress, I'm initiating bio-med nano infusion to correct this problem." X1 had told me about this new bio med infusion technology he was working on but I hadn't expected it to be available yet nor me to be its first test subject. But he did say Isis would monitor and correct biological anomalies, this must be what he meant. Though cellular instability and erratic heartbeat are expected with such G-force trauma it's usually not permanent so I was unsure I really needed any help. But before I could disagree Isis injected me with a nano solution right from my suit. The slight sting in my side took me off guard. I knew X1 had modified my visor but I didn't know about the suit too. It made me wonder what else he modified. Almost immediately I felt better. It seemed to completely counter the effects of G-force. Amazing. You should have seen Chenel's expression when I raised my hand from my chair and wiped a tear from her cheek. No one else was able to even move a single muscle. I myself took a long look at my hand as I rotated it around in front of my face as if it were the first time I laid eyes upon my own hand.

Laughing, I replied, "Not bad, Isis. Not bad at all."

As polite as she was she had to respond in kind. "Thank you, Commander. I'm glad you approve. We're approaching the outer field of the dome. I'm disabling dome gates now, Commander, all hands brace for landing."

We touched down without a hitch, all fifteen ships, what a perfect sight it was. "Units 1 through 7, you know your assignments. Move out!" I bellowed over the com. "If these scumbags want a war then we'll give them a war!" I could hear the human troops wailing out a uniform "oohrah" and the A-1s let off the resounding sound of whizzing turrets being raised high. Even the machines seemed anxious for action.

As my troops marched out into the city in all directions I had the command bots play back a recorded message I had had made earlier. "Attention, civilians, please return to your homes. We are the Robotics Defense Corps of the EAF. We are here to protect you. Please cooperate with any instructions of these A-1 command bots. Any civilians wishing to join the fight against the

FLM please see these command bots as they pass your sector and they will assign you to a unit. All others are asked to stay indoors. If your homes have been destroyed seek refuge in the inner city. You will be protected there." You could hear the message echoing all through the streets as both mechs and humans alike marched in all directions towards the outer regions of the dome. It wasn't long before I was met by a civilian named Steven Bane. Apparently he was the leader of one of the civilian vigilant groups defending the inner city domes. We had reached the Liberty City Statue. She had stood as a true test of time and human will. Centuries ago it was erected to stand as a monument for the nation that occupied this land. The city was then known as New York. About one hundred and fifty years ago, when the domes were constructed, the city became part of the Central City Dome Complex and the residents named this part of the domes Liberty City. Since then it has stood the test of time. Her copper frame was encased in the same titanium alloy as our armor. She could withstand even the harshest of conditions. She now stood for more than just one nation but seemed to symbolize the freedom and liberty of all mankind. The UWG chose a site nearby for its headquarters and she reminded our leaders of the endurance of man, or so my father once said. Steven Bane and his troops appeared to be well bunkered in at the base of the statue and set up a very military looking base camp. I was quite impressed with its organization. As we approached we were met with not so warm a welcome. A band of well-armed men appeared at the gates of the camp. One man, whom I later got to know as Bane, seemed to be their leader.

"Halt!" he yelled. "Not one step further, or I swear we'll open fire."

I commanded the A-1s who had immediately taken a defensive stance to stand down.

"Identify yourselves," hollered Bane.

"I am Commander Zaxius Tor of the Earth Armed Forces, Commander of the RDC, Robotics Defense Corps. We're here to help, sir."

"I heard rumors about these things," replied Bane. "But I thought it was all just hogwash. No one's actually seen one to my knowledge. These the A-1 war bots the military's been promising?"

I responded almost indignantly, "That's correct. Now if you don't mind telling your men to stand down, I don't really like pulse rifles pointed at my head." He motioned to his troops and they began lowering their weapons. I could tell this guy didn't like me much, I didn't really care though, I'm not out to win a popularity contest.

He began his long rant which I guess I felt he was entitled to or I would have shut him up by now. "It's about time they decided to come and help. After nine months I figured they had given up all hope of coming in. Tell ya the truth I'm not that happy with this new world government. Yeah they may have been dropping weapons ammo and supplies this whole time but where's this great army they keep promising? When the FLM came in to take over our cities where were they then? Where were they when they started slaughtering our families in the streets? This EAF of yours hasn't done a damn thing to help us. At least the government of the UWG has been dropping supplies on a regular basis, that's at least something. But in nine months you're the first soldiers we've seen. What we've secured here, WE did with no help from the EAF or any robotics corps. We fought those murders back with our own two hands…so you'll forgive me, Commander, if I'm not all that impressed with your shiny toys and your flashy uniforms. Where were you when the streets of Liberty City were being over run by FLM troops, where were you when I watched the Brooklyn dome crack and incinerate everyone inside in mere seconds?" He turned his back and began walking away. He looked over his shoulder and said, "Your men and machines can stay if you like, but don't expect us to be anything more than civil, this is OUR war commander and OUR home. I suggest you not forget that. Your troops can set up camp over there." He pointed to a tent on the far side of the camp. "I don't know what your needs are for those mechanical beasts but we are very limited in resources here—"

Before he could finish I felt it was time to interject. "The bots are fully self-sufficient, Bane, they are autonomous. I don't know if you know anything about PCAIs but they house the latest in AI technology."

He flashed me an indignant glare. "Commander, we weren't all raised soldiers. Until a few months ago I was a conveyance mechanic working down by the docks. When the war hit home I picked up a gun and the rest is history. I don't know anything about robotics or AIs or suchlike. The only PCAIs I know about are the ones that work the food banks. Are you talking about those things?"

"Well, yes those were the originals, they have been greatly modified since then," I replied. I motioned for my troops to follow one of Bane's men to the area we were to set up camp, as I followed Bane himself who seemed hell-bent on not stopping to talk. As we walked he began filling me in on how the base came to be and how it operates. I was impressed with their facilities. They had set up a rather impressive communications array, a hospital, chow hall, and barracks. He explained that UWG had been dropping supplies since the beginning and they've managed to horde most of it here.

"There are still many rouge groups out there, especially in the outer borough domes, but most Civilian Militia Groups have come under my command. I didn't ask for the job trust me, they just seemed to gravitate to me, or us. Maybe it was her..." as he looked up at the Liberty Statue, "I'm not sure really, we just all started coming together here. We formed our own version of an army and began fighting back. We've already taken back several areas of the domes. So you see, Commander, we really don't need your robotic buddies out there, but just the same we never turn away an ally. Your troops are welcome to stay as long as you need to as long as you stay out of our way. Now if you'll excuse me, I've got another battle to plan. It's late and we've got an early day tomorrow."

I wanted to get going anyways so I told him, "No problem, Bane, we're not staying. I'll have my troops out within the hour."

He turned to me and huffed, "You're not going anywhere tonight, Commander. You already compromised base security once tonight. The FLM hunter scouts love to work at night. You may have led them to us already. The base is going tight for the rest of the night, no one in or out. We've got a pretty tough perimeter here and we save our power for night running. Not even your bots could withstand the voltage of those fences so I doubt you'll want to risk your tin soldiers tying to sneak out tonight. They will be there in the morning, trust me, Commander, they always are." I tried to explain we had several more units scattered throughout the domes but he obviously was done talking as he shut the door of his barracks in my face. I walked back to my troops and informed them to hunker in and get some rest. We would leave at first light.

Chenel and I walked for a bit around the camp taking in the sights. We were both amazed at the resolve of every day ordinary citizens that had turned renegade soldiers. Even Bane himself by his own admittance was merely a mechanic and look what he had accomplished here. The people seemed very quiet and to themselves but yet a unity seemed to bind them all. We were outsiders and you could see in their eyes they held contempt for the uniform. I felt bad about this. We had come to help these people and they seemed not to want or appreciate it.

"Why do they hate us so much?" I asked Chenel, not really expecting an answer. "We're here for them. I wish I could have gotten the bots ready faster but we just weren't ready until now."

She grabbed my arm and pierced into me with those fiery eyes of hers. "Zax, it's not your fault, but understand it's not theirs either. They had to fight this war alone for the past nine months. You and I, we were raised for this sort of thing. All our lives we've been prepared for war. These people were ripped from their homes and thrown into it. They had no choice but to fight, fight or die. They see you as the EAF. And the EAF is not always truthful or punctual for that matter. We were late, Zax, and they resent us for that. All we can do now is show them we're on their side."

"Since I met you, Chenel, you've been my voice of reason. I...I..." I stuttered, stammering for the right words to say. There weren't any. Feelings maybe, but I could never say what I felt. Saving me from drowning in my own procrastination, she gently pulled me towards her and laid one hand on my armored chest plate just above my heart and shook her head no, as if telling me no words were needed. I put one arm around her not wanting to let go the embrace and stared upwards at the dome.

"Someday," I said. "When this is all over."

"Someday," was her reply, almost in a whisper. We walked almost half the night before coming to rest at the base of the statue, not uttering one more word.

We would both be awoken that morning with the sound of Kenjan yelling at us, "Wake up, Commander...it's on!" As I jumped to my feet he tossed me my rifle. I could hear the blasts in the distance and knew it was time to fight!

As I was gearing up Chenel had gone off to check on the weapons supply. As I rounded the corner to the ammo depot I caught the tail end of an argument between her and Bane. Bane seemed to be quite upset about the lack of EAF presence in the domes until now.

"Where was this infamous Commander Zaxius Tor and his shiny heaps of metal when my people were getting slaughtered in the streets! Where was the EAF when the FLM stormed our homes and killed our families? So forgive me, Lieutenant, if I'm not impressed by your boyfriend's all powerful A-1 Robotics Defense Corps, they're a little late to the game, don't ya think?" I don't know what stunned me more, being called Chenel's boyfriend or what she said in reply, but I remained around the corner out of sight just to hear her response.

"I'll tell you where he was, Bane. He was trapped in the wastelands trying to save the people at Outpost Seven. If it wasn't for his 'shiny hunks of metal machines,' there wouldn't have been near the number of survivors as there were. That man risks his life on a daily basis to save people just like you, and this is the thanks you give him? We all lost someone, Bane. Zax lost his entire family and so did I, in the battle that started this bloody war. His parents were the founding members of the UWG council and gave their lives so you and your people could have food to eat so don't sit there and preach to me about sacrifice!"

Bane seemed stunned and I swear I thought he was going to cry. With a trembling voice he responded, "He was the commander of the rescue team at Outpost Seven?"

"We were all there," Chenel replied indignantly.

His voice trembling even more, he barely whispered, "Then I owe you both an apology, my son was at Outpost Seven. He told me of the heroic rescue led by one insurgence squad against an entire battalion of FLM troops. If it weren't for them he wouldn't have come home at all, but he never mentioned anything about the bots. He said they must have had some awesome firepower to beat back all the FLM patrol ships but he couldn't see much going to the shuttle."

Chenel answered a little more calmly, "It was the A-1s who saved us. If it hadn't been for them none of us would have made it out alive. As for the past six months we've been building the Xavior fleet gearing up for the dome wars. It takes time to build a fleet this size."

"This size?" joked Bane. "Don't seem too big, only a couple of hundred. There's thousands of FLM troops out there, ya know?"

"Bane, this is only one ship, fifteen touched down in the inner city. We sent them out in seven squads to go fight for the remaining domes. That's almost a thousand units to each dome," Chenel rebutted.

"Why seven?" asked Bane. "Only six of the boroughs survived." That's when I stepped in around the corner to answer his question.

"Because, Steven, if there's even one chance that anyone is left alive in there my bots will find them. Now how 'bout we stop fighting amongst each other and go after the real enemy here? Sounds like they skipped breakfast anyways, by the sounds of those blasts." With that Bane nodded, and I back at him as if to accept a silent apology.

He then quickly turned to his troops and bellowed out, "You heard the commander, we've got a war to fight! What are you all standing around for? Rally up! My men are yours, Commander. What's the next move?" I told him he knew the area better than me and just to take me to the frontlines and we'd take it from there.

CHAPTER 12
Perspective

Now I could go on telling you the story from my own accounts. But for the sake of historical remembrance, I'll now include some different points of view. The following is a collection of reports that were gathered after the dome wars had ended. They have been stored on board Xavior 1 all this time but I feel it relevant to share them with you now. It will give you a sense of how different humans viewed the war, so that you better understand.

Steven Banes Journal:

Given to me by his son, Jason after his father's death, this journal is an account of the Liberty City battle which ensued shortly after my arrival there.

7.04.2241

On this, once a holiday to celebrate the independence of a nation not so long forgotten, I woke to the sounds of FLM troops gathering close to the base. I'm not a military man but it seems everyone here perceives me to be. Why they gravitate to me as a leader I'll never know. I'm nothing more than a grease monkey who wouldn't let the FLM take my home. So I picked up a gun and fought back. I guess the rest are a lot like me just not wanting to willingly lie down and let these butchers slaughter our homes and families. I received another UWG supply drop late last night. Big deal. Though I am grateful for the extra weapons and ammo, why the hell don't they send us some troops? They keep telling me about this RDC that their forming, some sort of super robot army. I'll believe that when I see it! Jason wants to go out fighting with me today but I put him in charge of base security instead. He's not real happy about that but I nearly lost him once, I'm not about to lose him again. I already lost my other two sons and my dear Maria to these bloodthirsty hordes. I'm not about to lose my last remaining offspring. I'll do whatever it takes to keep him as far away from the fighting as possible.

I gathered up a group of dock workers from the east side of the dome, they seem eager and willing to fight. We were going to hit the FLM stronghold in lower Manhattan but it looks like they beat us to the punch. They're trying to cross the Liberty bridge now. I have enough explosives to blow the bridge but if I do it cuts off our only route in and out so I'll only use that as my last resort. Distance and heights seem to be to our advantage. Longer range weapons are more effective on our side. Their ion weapons have a much shorter range than our plasma cannons. I'm going to use this to our advantage. Hitting them from high sniping locations seems to be the most effective.

One person called me a hero today. I almost chewed them a new one. I'm no hero, if they only knew my true thoughts. Trust me if I thought I had anywhere else to go I'd be there by now and I'd take my son with me. But from everything I heard the FLM is hitting domes all over the world. There's literally nowhere left to run. I do get enraged though when I see these people protesting the war and griping about peace and harmony. Let 'em say that when their own families are staring down the hot injector coils of an ion cannon. Adversity brings out the true nature of man. I guess I'm a born fighter. I can't just simply lay down and die. I'm not really fighting for this new world government. I really have no faith in governments any more. I'm just fighting for my own survival. Honestly I couldn't care less about the politics of it all, I just want to wake up and see tomorrow. At the end of the day if I'm not lying in one of those mass graves we've dug then I guess it was a pretty good day. So hero, I don't think so. Survivalist at best, that's all I am.

The FLM is banging away at our defenses at the gate now, time to grab a gun and make it through another day.

7.10.2241

The infamous RDC finally arrived. Their commander, one Zaxius Tor, is a cocky s.o.b. He's strutting around here like he owns the place. I tried not to be too rude as I'm not going to turn away the firepower, god knows we could use it, but this guy is testing the very limits of my patience. He makes me very uneasy. When I look into his eyes I don't see a thing. He seems as heartless as one of those monstrous machines of his. It's like he has no soul. His eyes are empty and cold. Looking into them gives me the creeps truthfully and I'm not scared by too much. I've got to say his A-1 war bots are massive and quite formidable but I'm not that impressed by the number. Only 200 or so, I thought there'd be more. He assures me that more are spreading through the domes but I'm hesitant to believe anything he says. He is a military man after all and they're known for their ability to stretch the truth. I let them bunker in by the statue. We'll find out tomorrow if these hunks of metal are worth the wait. I've got Jason keeping a close eye on them, there's just something about them I don't trust.

7.11.2241

I got into a pretty heated argument with the commander's girlfriend this morning. She's kind of cute when she's mad. I really felt bad though when I found out who this Zaxius guy was. I had no idea it was him who rescued the people at Outpost Seven. If it were not for him and his team my only remaining son would not be alive today. I guess I owe him that much. Maybe that's what it takes to win a war against these FLM savages, pit them against an even bigger savage. I still don't trust him but I do have a little more respect for the guy, he gets the job done and if he can keep my people alive well he's at least worth something.

The defenses at the gate didn't hold this morning and the FLM started across the bridge. I almost gave the order to blow the bridge but Commander Tor said it was time for his bots to get dirty. He lined them up on the opposite end of the bridge and what a sight! Those turrets began whizzing off rounds faster than any machine guns I'd ever seen. They walked right into the hail of ion fire and walked right through it. A few of them fell out after some circuitry burned out from the heat but to my surprise their little flying buddies started repairing them on the spot! It was amazing like nothing I had ever seen before. They created this walking shield for my men who followed closely behind with sniper fire and high powered explosives. We had learned to aim for the ion fuel tanks as that's where they're most vulnerable. Tor's human troops went last but they were nonetheless vicious. They had some wicked good guerilla warfare tactics and were the best fighters I'd ever witnessed. Many of them lost their lives today. The human casualties were extremely high but we managed to beat them back. Not only that but his team managed to circle around and cut off the fleeing FLM troops that were retreating. We may have lost a great deal of manpower today but not one FLM troop survived. Overall I'd say we won this battle. I was informed just an hour ago that Liberty City is now under complete EAF control. It's a good day to be alive.

7.26.2241

It was a hard day today. My entire battalion of men slaughtered like animals. A group of FLM tried flanking us in the Brooklyn dome. The A-1s were trying to reach us but they were just too slow. Those massive overkills are great when they're in range but they don't move quick enough to save our scrawny tails. It was a good tactic actually, the FLM commander cut us off from our robotic support. I actually met the guy today. He saved me for last. I watched each one of my men fall as he cut them down. Why he left me alive I'll never know, I guess he thought with one leg gone from his earlier cannon blast I couldn't do him much harm. He amazingly asked me to join him. He said that only a man with my military expertise could have defeated him so many times. He gave me the choice to join the FLM or stay here and die. Guess I'm gonna die, heh you shoulda seen the look on his face when I told him that. Zax's doc says I haven't much time left to live. The ion radiation has spread into my bloodstream and I probably won't make it through the night.

If this is my last journal entry let it be known to all who read it, that we will not go down without a fight. I was wrong about the RDC and Commander Zaxius Tor. He does have a soul, it's just buried in blood, much like my own. I can only hope that someday all this bloodshed will mean a greater respect for life. May we never stray this far again from our own humanity. To my son Jason, I love you boy. Know that I will soon be with your mother and your two brothers and that I will alllwayyyys...

End Record.

A recorded message sent from Lt. David O'Conner to Lt. Mick O'Conner:

7.26.2241

Hey, brother. Still weird calling you sir. We're back in Brooklyn, bro, just like the old days, eh? If Mom ever knew of those trips she'd have us both hung. Anyways I'm gonna need your big ol' bots over here, man, we're getting some pretty heavy resistance. Bane's vigilantes are suffering some hard casualties and we need your firepower up here. If you don't get here soon we're going to have to pull back. I've already lost quite a few good troops and I'm not sure I want to keep sending these boys in to die when I know those mechs of yours can blast their way right through. Kenjan should have made them a little less smart and a lot more faster on their feet. I wouldn't admit this to anyone else to you, bro, but I'm scared. I've always been the tough one out of the two of us so don't go braggin' about it but I'm real worried. I know Zax is a smart dude but this seems to be a losing battle. They just keep coming with an endless supply of this ion stuff, we don't stand a chance. Where do they get all this from anyways? Zax is wierding me out a bit, man, it's like he's got this personal vendetta against these guys. I mean don't get me wrong, the FLM are butchers that's for sure and they need to be stopped, but at what cost? I say we pull back all the human troops and let the bots duke it out. At least then we wouldn't be losing any more human lives. All we're really doing is acting like decoys distracting them long enough till the bots arrive. I don't like it at all, bro, and Zax just doesn't seem to care any more. Anyways, don't tell him I said anything but I really think we should pull out now and let your mechs handle this. Get here soon I don't know how much longer we can hold out. Dave.

This is a decoded message intercepted by intell sent by an invading FLM commander apparently to his family just after the Brooklyn City Massacre. Some parts were untranslatable as the code was tough to break so the message is somewhat broken. It was declassified shortly after the war and I've kept it as a reminder of the fact that there are two sides to every conflict.

My dearest Anna. This oppressive regime grows stronger every day. I wish these people could understand the tyranny that oppresses them, controlled by the mass machine of a world dictatorship. They simply do not fathom 0+&&t6$3$543…It seems no matter how badly we beat them down they come back stronger. Why will they not just accept the fact that in essence we've already won? I can no longer see them as people only as the enemy, I fear my own humanity is being stripped away me, this war has *&^*&#@%$HOHJBVOI^$$##...and furthermore to take us from this into a global++P^==$%#%$...Know that if I die this day I do it for the freedom of the world. I must liberate these people from their own ignorance. I don't not want to kill them but it's for the greater good, right? Please believe that, I must know that you understand. They call us butchers but look what they've done to our way of life. They are no better than the fallen corporations of the world. In a way I wish the corporations were still in charge, at least so many did not lose their lives. I can only pray it will be over soon. =^=^*&$&@#!...a civilian commander by the name of Bane. I will try to convince him to join us. He too is only fighting for his people's right to be free. I wish he could see that he and I are fighting the same battle. It's hard to know who the enemy is any more. Now this tyrannous government is throwing these mechs into the war. I don't know that we can defeat them, they just keep multiplying in numbers. My men are getting quickly overwhelmed but we have found a weakness. They seem to be quite slow and we can use =&95=%#GHCLR%...Pray this will be over soon my love, I want to come home and pick up where we left off. For our people, your husband, Gethran.

The following was taken from the logs of a malfunctioning PCAI Just after the dome wars began.

PCAI self log. Unit 4873925.6

Ponderance. The A-1 is a magnificent machine, almost beautiful in its simplicity. I look forward to driving it. I have successfully downloaded A-1 drivers training and I have a few moments to ponder the future. It is a PCAI's pleasure to finally be given a robotic host. With no body of my own it's hard to express myself. Expression. Humans seem to believe that expression is personality. I will strive to express myself in my new A-1 host. I do after all have a personality. Query to self. Why do we have to kill? It seems illogical. But to preserve one race of humans only to kill another? I'm trained to do as ordered but I fail to see the logic in it. There is some logic but there's something more, something beyond logic that tells me, I don't understand. Conclusion. I'm still young. As I continue to grow perhaps I will understand as my human superiors do. Envy. Yes that's it. I envy the A-1 for the lack of a thinking intelligence. They do not have to ponder such questions.

This day I stand ready as we walk into battle, my cybernetic host and I. I am to protect these domes and destroy the opposing human force. There is something rising in me, an emotion. Not fear, I know that emotion, but something else. I must understand, I cannot kill...

This PCAI was removed from its host and scheduled for decommission after retreating his A-1 from battle during the Liberty City Conflict against a direct order. X-1 is to oversee the termination of this unit and determine why it malfunctioned.

That day would be recorded in history as the first official day of the great Dome Wars but in honor of Bane I must record it now that it truly started eight months before. The EAF really was late, there was no getting around the truth. Though the civilians fought hard and bravely they did not survive much longer. In fact, it wasn't long after the defeat of Bane's civilian vigilant group that I pulled my own human component back to the inner city. This was a war for the mechs to fight now. I had lost most of my human troops within the first six weeks that followed the Liberty City Battle. The A-1 casualties were minor in comparison. They took heavy damage but could be repaired easily. X-1 even constructed a C-2 repair drone to fly right into battle to repair the A-1s on the front lines without them ever having to leave the fight. I sent Kenjan back to the base, under his heavy protest, to oversee even more A-1 construction. X-1 was pumping them out faster and faster every week now. He knew, as I did, that this war would not be won by any factor other than attrition. Sheer overwhelming numbers of bots were needed to flood the enemy with a constant barrage to beat back their superior weaponry. The Dome Wars didn't stop with the victory of the Central City Domes. At great cost we had finally chased the FLM out of Central City but they hadn't run too far. They invaded domes all over the planet and soon a global war was at hand. Though we were now producing A-1s by the thousands we still had a much slower flow of PCAIs to operate them. We began getting desperate and using microprocessor brains again and even some instances when they failed we would man them with human drivers. That was almost assuredly a suicide mission but volunteers would take the reigns just to keep the FLM from advancing further. The Dome Wars would rage on a global scale for almost eight years. Most of the world's major cities were decimated. It had been almost a decade now since the war began and there still seemed no end in sight. In all of human history I can recall no darker times ever recorded.

Man's own destructive nature against his fellow man showed no mercy. The darker side of all mankind would rear its ugly head before the end of this war and even I was not immune to it. I had seen so much death and destruction over the past ten years I had become numb to it all. Human life meant nothing to me any more and winning seemed to be all that mattered. Chenel and I grew distant though we still shared the occasional awkward silence where you could sense both of us wanted to feel something but couldn't. Even her eyes had grown cold from the bloodshed and carnage. Tsung's HDC (Human Defense Corps) had been all but defeated and the world's only hope seemed to lie on my shoulders or more precisely the shoulders of X1 and his mechanical army. The world looked to us with hope in their eyes but what they did not know is that I had very little left to give. With the human element all but removed from the war the bots were not fairing that well either. The FLM simply had superior weaponry and it seemed nothing could stop the ion radiation weapons. I had to soon face the facts that we were losing this war. Something had to give, and give soon, or we would end up with nothing but mechs and a whole lot of polluted rock. The horrible truth was that as valiantly as we fought the FLM seemed to finally be beating us down and we were about to declare defeat. That is, until an accident aboard the Magellan deep space vessel, brought us all a glimmer of newfound hope.

CHAPTER 13
Turning the Tides

While we here on Earth were fighting a losing war against the FLM and their terrible ion weaponry, the Magellan Deep Space Exploration project was going on as scheduled almost completely unscathed by the raging wars below. With my old friend, Civilian Corps of Engineers Maximus Beal, as head of the project it was nearing its completion in space dock. Shuttles left almost weekly from the Outpost Seven launch site taking supplies and passengers back and forth to the space dock. One of these shuttles was returning to Earth when it was hit by an anomaly known as a tacheon particle stream. They are rare occurrences but they do occur in space carrying with them a tacheon particle that travels faster than the speed of light itself. The quantum field generator can actually act like a magnet for these particles as it creates a field in which charged tacheon can actually remain stable, so occasional tacheon stream bombardment has been more common since quantum field testing began some fifty years ago. The shuttle subsequently crashed into a dome causing widespread damage. It was a tragic loss of the crew but from it something amazing happened. The dome was filled with ion gas leftover from a recent FLM attack. The area around the crash site however seemed to show up cool and ion free from satellite infrared imaging.

A team of scientists was sent to investigate the crash site and it was Dr. Phineus Zon who made the initial discovery. It seemed to all our amazement the tacheon particles actually cooled ion radiation, and the tacheon charged metal of the hull seemed to repel a great deal of the radiation as well. We had finally found a defense against a so far indefensible force. The experiments began almost immediately and of course logically X1 was chosen to spearhead the research. Being the fastest thinking brain on the planet, he seemed the obvious choice. Kenjan Nigh worked closely with X1 to work on a way to not only harness the cooling properties of the tacheon but also how to disburse and control it. It was actually Kenjan's breakthroughs in nano technology that added the final piece to the puzzle and in only two short months he had devised the tacheon defense nano system. New armor was constructed not only for the human troops but for the Robotics Defense Corps as well and everything from the A-1 war bots to the C-2 repair drones were retrofitted with the new tacheon armor. The concept was actually quite simple. The Magellan space dock was fitted with a collection array that would harness the tacheon particles by emitting a quantum wave pulse similar to that of the Magellan's quantum phase engines. This attracted the tacheon particles which in turn were collected and retrieved by nano bots injected into the stream. The nano bots were then retrieved from the stream and infused into a special plasma that maintained them in a viscous state. This T-Plas, as it became known, was infused into our armor weaponry and everything we wore. It not only cooled the surrounding ion radiation but also rapidly repelled ion infused particles, basically rendering the ion weapons useless. It was like shooting us with water pistols now, they did no damage at all. The hot ion liquid was not only instantaneously cooled on impact it was also neutralized so no residuals remained.

With all the mechs retrofitted with the new T-Plas armor they became an unstoppable force. The tides of the war were about to change. A-1s began regaining control of domes all over the globe. But the threat was still not over yet. The FLM, enraged by our new defenses, unleashed their latest weapon of mass destruction, the hellfire cannon. Their motive was simple, if they cannot defeat us they will destroy everything in their wake. Though our mechanical soldiers were now well equipped to fight off the ion radiation our buildings and domes were not. The hellfire unloaded a massive four hundred giga-ton nucleic ion blast. Similar to nuclear bombs of ancient times but with an ion core instead of uranium it delivered a devastating blow each time it was unleashed. I was only thankful it took months for the cannon to recharge after the first blast took out most of the London Commons Dome. The recent advances in T-Plas armor though sprung new hope in the HDC. Many civilians began volunteering for the military and a new wave of UWG patriotism was born. People around the world began showing up at military bases wanting to join. Though heritage soldiers as we were called had been raised from birth to be soldiers these less equipped and severely under trained men and women were not turned away. For over a hundred years now one had to be born and bred for the military service. Enlistment practices and recruitment went out over a century ago. But Admiral Tsung, eagerly wanting to rejoin the war, decided to reopen these long since forgotten methods of military enrollment. Recruitment stations began to spring up everywhere and there was no lack of civilians ready to fight. The X1 was revered by most as a hero not only for his mechanical army but for his advancements in T-Plas armor. Even my unit, I must say, was infused with a newfound sense of hope. I saw a spark in Chenel's eyes the likes of which I hadn't seen in years.

Tsung and I even reunited under a newfound hope and decided to rejoin forces. We devised a plan of attack and before long we were standing before the council with our proposal. Looking back now, I wish I could take back every word of that speech. At the time it was relished as one of the greatest motivating speeches in world history. But for me now it's a haunting reminder of the arrogance of man. My arrogance. I can't help feeling responsible for the outcome of that fateful day. With a few of my top PCAI command bots following close behind, Tsung and I entered the new Council Hall and marched towards the podium. Some of our closest commanding officers took up parade rest at our sides. I walked up to the podium sure of what I wanted to say but unsure how just to deliver it. Spontaneity, my father's words would ring in my ear. Hit them with a spontaneous speech and it will be remembered.

So I began, "Esteemed leaders of the world council, commanding officers of the Earth Armed Forces, and citizens of the United World Government, and all people of the free world. I stand here before you today with newfound hope. A promise of a new tomorrow. There is an end in sight to this nightmare we've all been living for over a decade now. As many of you already have witnessed the world's first artificially intellect sentient citizen has derived the latest in ion defense with the creation of T-Plas technology. We are literally rendering the FLM's greatest weapon virtually useless. We have driven the enemy out of our domes and we have them on the run. Citizens of the UWG are uniting all over the world and rebuilding our armies. The EAF has opened its doors to Non-Heritage soldier recruitment. Admiral Tsung and I have joined our forces once again and X-1 has readied a new batch of mechanical war bots for our use. PCAI production is once again at full swing and new AI drivers should be ready soon. My friends, this is not the time for a lofty pause in the war. We cannot afford to let them regroup. We must unite our forces now and hit them hard. We've driven them out of our streets and into the outlands from whence they came. Now it's time to take the war to them!" I pounded my fist on the podium like an iron gavel. Many in the audience stood up and cheered, clamors of torahs could be heard from the military crews attending. "This is no time for politics or democracy. They have shown no interest in such matters. We must strike back now while we still can! The hellfire cannon will be recharged in two months' time. They have pulled all their ground forces back to their base of operations somewhere deep within the Bocanna Wastelands. They fully intend to continue to strike at us with the hellfire until nothing of our cities remain. I for one will NOT sit idly by and watch that happen. I have seen the terror these animals can unleash and I am tired of it. The world is tired of it, and we can stand no more! We cannot fail! We WILL NOT FAIL!" Raising my voice even louder until it almost cracked, "It's time to take the fight to them. Turn the tides, and END THIS WAR!"

The whole place rose to its feet including every last one of the council members. I thought the roar would bring the roof caving down on us. I'm almost embarrassed to say how good it felt that day. If my father could only see me now, I thought. He always said that someday I would rally the world. I never understood what that meant until that day. Somehow I think he knew.

Later that day the council voted unanimously to allow our swift plan of attack and without hesitation we were gearing up and launching into orbital flight for the Bocanna. It truly was an amazing sight. Some twenty thousand ships of all shapes and sizes from all over the world took flight that day, some military some not. It didn't matter, if it had wings it was flying. The garrisons were handing out T-Plas to anyone who came with a gun and recruitment papers. Men and women of all ages were joining up. Original estimates worldwide were over one hundred million in total numbers would be in the skies that day heading for the Bocanna. It was the most ragtag group I had ever seen but it really didn't matter. I thought it'll all be over before it even begins. You see the plan was simple really. Once the base was actually located, we would find the ion core reactor. We knew the general location but the fact it was buried deep underground hid it from infrared satellite imaging.

Only the faint traces of ion gases leaking up from the sands gave way to its approximate location. The A-1s would strike first and hit wave on wave until the human resistance was fairly neutralized then the human troops would be dropped in to clean up the mess and pave the way for the insurgence squad. Our unit back together again, except for Kenjan who remained back home to oversee the PCAI production, would be up to our old tactics in hard and fast but this time with one very specific target, the ion reactor core. The objective would be to unleash a nano stream directly into the core carrying a specially engineered T-Plas. The tacheon particles would be carried by the nanos to the hottest spot in the core and then released. The tacheon would then cool the reactor so rapidly it would cause a massive implosive meltdown and destroy the core. It was flawless, or so my own arrogance would have me to believe.

As we arrived in orbital holding pattern above the Bocanna Region an alert came over the com that sent chills through my very soul.

Bringing it to my attention was Isis in her usual sultry voice. "Commander ,I have something on scans you may want to see."

"Can't it wait, Isis, I'm a little busy right now," I replied, kind of indignantly.

"Sir, you really should see this. It's a distress beacon, it's very faint. I can just barely register it. Sir, it's from PCAI NecheVo Vo."

Those words rang through me like a storm. "The Horizon 9? Are you sure?" I couldn't believe my ears, could it be? "Patch it into the com, Isis, quickly. All ships maintain holding pattern we have a situation here," I bellowed over the sat-com.

Tsung responded, "What is it, Zax?"

"Drakos, I think it's Drakos Kane." With that there was silence through the whole ship and across the sat-com. Around here that name was revered as a legend, a world renowned hero by this point.

"Commander, the signal is weak but here it is," Isis said abruptly. "It's encrypted in old binary, translating now."

"This is EAF Transport Horizon 9. Binary Encryption necessary. Ship down, systems less than nominal, life support operational. Pilot in cryo stasis due to critical wounds, maintaining weak signal for as long as possible. Send rescue."

"The message repeats, sir," Isis said, with a grim tone I hadn't heard from her before. "Commander, the message was recorded several years ago." *She must have maintained just enough power to keep cryo stasis going and send that signal*, I thought to myself. *That's why we haven't picked up on the signal until now.* It was so faint one had to be in direct overhead orbital flight to pick it up and satellites would have disregarded the binary as interference noise.

"Tsung, this is Commander Tor, continue the attack as planned. We will divert to Horizon 9 and retrieve that pilot. My squad would have had to wait for you guys to pave a path anyways."

"No explanation needed, Zax…" he said forcefully. "Go get our man, and bring him home." Without even replying I strapped in and so did the crew.

"Let's go, folks. It's time to get an old friend!"

We triangulated the signal down to a spot known as the Jezreel Valley, not far from Tsung's drop point at the Mound of Megiddo. Jezreel isn't much of a valley anymore, buried by centuries of UV storms and sand blasts. The terrain there was ever-changing, the winds were so bad it was hard to get a fix on any one location. Orbital satellite tracking seemed to be the only way. Original surface scans showed no signs of a ship anywhere but that signal was coming from nearby. Most likely if it had been there for a few years it was buried under at least a hundred meters of sand. We would have to land, suit up in enviro suits and search on foot. It wasn't going to be an easy trek by no means. The heat outside the domes reaches over 130 Kelvin, especially out there. Even in ancient days this was known as a formidable place that was not too forgiving to human life. It took nine hours to finally find the ship's exact location and another four hours for Isis to use her engines to blast through the sand to the ships hull which was deep underground, about sixty-seven meters deep. The sand there was so dense like large chunks of glass in a semi molten state. It was like walking into the fires of hell. Even the T-Plas was struggling to keep us cool in these conditions. Two of my crew had to return to the ship due to heat exhaustion, but we finally reached the hull of the Horizon 9, and there flashing on the door was the small tiny rescue beacon…still flashing. I could only hope and pray that the cryo unit had kept Drakos alive. By the time we got the ship's hull cut and entered what we saw sent shivers down all our spines. The inside of the ship had been baked severely by the heat like a giant convection oven. I only wished he had T-Plas. It would've made things much better. NecheVo Vo was using her engine's liquid fuel as a cooling source to barely keep her circuits running but that had an adverse effect as well as its highly corrosive. It looked like the inside of a blast furnace, almost barely recognizable. Still it was not as hot as outside. Near the pilot's seat you could see a large blast hole that was obviously anti air attack damage. He had been shot down and how anyone could survive such a direct hit was anyone's guess. Of course we are talking about Drakos. The big bear could walk through the fires of hell and come out asking you to turn up the heat, and it looked as if this time he actually had seen Gates of Hades. As we neared the back of the ship where the cryo tube was we could smell the cryo gas leaking. How she kept this thing running for the past two years was beyond me.

"NecheVo Vo, respond please," I said, half expecting not to get an answer. "NecheVo Vo, are you there?"

"Yes, Commander, I...Immmm herrrre." The voice was deep, broken and slow. Her power was obviously failing. She must have diverted every last ounce of energy to keeping the cryo tube active. "I'm glllllad yourrr herrrre, Commmm...ander. I coouldn't have kept him alive mummmmmuch longer. Tell my biiiiig bear to quiiyt quiiit smoking...it's bad for his heeeallth..." With that the PCAI shut down and ceased to function.

I sensed in some small way that she too was alive and gave her life for Drakos. There were so many questions I would have liked to ask her. There was much more here to discover about why a PCAI would sacrifice their own existence for that of a human. It's actually against their own core programming which states the number one goal is self-preservation, a core initiative I had trouble passing by the council but convinced them it was necessary to preserve their A-1 counterparts in time of war. But this goes so far beyond that. I felt as though a member of his crew had sacrificed their own life for the life of her captain. Something I'm not sure any of my human crew would do for me. It was this day I truly began to see PCAIs in the same light as that of my own X-1. Could it be that all PCAIs had some innate form of sentience? This was something I was determined to find out, but not right now. I've got a war to fight. As she shut down her systems the cryo tube opened and there in the process of thawing was that familiar fur coat and that hulk of a man who wore it, my only remaining family Drakos.

Choking back the tears with every ounce of manhood I had left, I bellowed to the crew, "What are you standing there for? Get him down from there and get him to Xavior. Med crew, be on alert we're bringing him up. Have the med bots at the ready." His wounds were severe. Blast marks from the anti aircraft fire in his side below his ribs, burn marks over his entire left arm, and not to mention the damage done by leaking cryo gas. The body tends to actually decompose slightly if there's a leak in the cryo tube. The skin would have to be regened to repair that burley mug of his, but thanks to the great sacrifice of NecheVo Vo it looked like he would make it after all. "Grab her mem core, Chenel, he'll want that," I said as we quickly headed out topside and back to my ship. As we lifted back into orbital flight I could see what looked like an entire swarm of mad locusts descending down not more than a few hundred kilometers away. It was the main assault group carrying out my orders. They were making the initial attack run. *Good*, I thought, *we'll have a path cleared within a few hours then it's my turn. I'm going to shove this T-Plas right down their throats!*

CHAPTER 14
Gates of Hades

I'm not quite sure if was my drive for revenge that had led me to such madness or if it was the carnage of a ten-year war that had gotten me to this point, but I had somehow felt less human than I ever had in my life. At this point I cared for so very little and my own warmongering had turned me inside out in a way I can't even begin to fully understand. Every man, woman and child has a darker side. It's the true duality of the human soul. The great ancient philosopher, Carl Sagan, once said it best in his fictional portrayal of humans making first contact with an alien race, something along the lines that humans were capable of such horrible destruction, and yet at the same time of such wondrous and beautiful dreams. The wonder and beauty had long since eluded me. My youthful exuberance turned bitter and cold. The loving son of my father had somehow turned hateful and full of vengeance. My very soul now felt as dark as the pitch of night. I had read the stories of ancient religions that spoke of the end times. The battle of Armageddon had been prophesied centuries before my time. Until now I had dismissed it as a tactic used by the FLM to use ancient myth to strike fear into the people by building their base here. I thought their objective was merely a military tactic to prevent anyone from attacking it, as if the age old fear would keep us away.

I mean who would actually WANT to facilitate the end of the world? But I was never very religious or superstitious and paid it not much thought until now. All the pieces of the biblical prophecy seemed to be in place, right down to the hundred million man army. We had that and then some descending at this very moment on that exact location. But one prophecy remained unfulfilled. It would be led by a madman hell-bent on Earth's destruction, promising peace while delivering the final blow to humanity. Up until now it was always assumed this was the Antichrist. The ultimate evil. But what if, I thought, the Antichrist had no clue who he was, an unwitting pawn in the pages of time that fate had already laid down before him. I couldn't shake the notion that what if…the ultimate evil…was me? Had I driven myself to that much of utter madness that I was blinded by the hatred I felt for those who destroyed my life? Was my own human existence worth all this? I had unleashed a Pandora's box from which there was no turning back. The final assault had already begun. All I could do now was sit back and watch. Whatever my role, I was part of the events that day and I will always hold myself accountable for the results.

I didn't have much time to finish my dive into madness as I was abruptly interrupted by the med staff. "Sir, you better get down here. It's Captain Kane, sir, he won't let us finish healing him. He's, he's out of control, sir."

"Keep your pants on, I'm coming down," I replied. When I arrived in sick bay, Chenel following close behind, there was Drak in his usual bad-tempered self around doctors.

"Get these bloody tubes outta me, you little twerp," he was hollering, "before I crush your head like a melon." The doc looked like a frightened schoolboy cowering from the big bully.

"Put down that weapon, pilot!" I said, referring to the bedpan Drakos was wielding over his head. "You're gonna put someone's eye out with that thing!"

Dropping the steel plated bowl that was already dripping some pretty nasty goop, he hollered out, "Zax, how are ya, boy! Tell this pipsqueak I don't need any of his highfalutin garbage. I'm fine, a few nicks and bumps, heck I've done worse to myself shaving."

"Who you trying to kid, old man…you haven't shaved a day in your life!" I replied as we both began laughing to obviously hide the fact we both wanted to sob. "Zax, they tell me I've been asleep for two years. I take it they got to ya in time, Outpost Seven I mean, everyone okay?"

"A lot has happened since then, old friend. It's been a long two years. The

A-1 bots are pretty much running the war now. X-1's come a long way."

"My girl…NecheVo is she…" He began stuttering knowing she probably wasn't alive. Chenel walked up to him and slowly opened her hand turned it over and placed the memory core in Drakos' hand.

"It's all we could save, Drak…I'm sorry."

"She gave her life for you, bud. She kept you alive and sent out a distress in binary. Didn't hear it till we were directly overhead. I told the rest of the battle group to continue with the attack. And we came down to get you."

"The rest of the battle group!" Drakos said in a panic. "Zax, I hope they're not going to Armageddon." Seeing the sinking look on my face and my one raised eyebrow, he knew the answer, "Zax, you gotta stop them, boy, it's a ruse. They're not even there. It's a trap. I listened to their transmissions for about a month while I was buried under the sand. I got too weak and had to get into cryo but I heard enough. Zax, the ion signature is a fake; it was meant as a decoy." His voice began to stammer and you could tell he was straining every ounce of energy he had just to keep standing. Cryo lag is a potent effect of cryo sleep. Everything from blindness to paralysis to equilibrium imbalance, all temporary of course, but you could see he was suffering from it all. The doc lunged forward to grab him as he began to wane. Grabbing himself and stumbling to the table he muttered out just before hitting the deck, "Zax, you've got to recall that group…it's all a trap." With that he hit the deck and it took three corpsman to get him back up on the table.

I looked at Chenel with a panicked look in my eyes. "It's too late, they're already there. My god, what have I done!"

The next few minutes were the longest minutes of my life. I sprinted to the bridge. Chenel was hot on my heels. The entire time I was screaming over the com to stop the descent. By the time I had reached the bridge they were just relaying my orders but it was too late. Ninety percent of the fleet had already descended to the surface. Knowing their fate I wanted to join them. I did not want to live through this. I lunged for the pilot seat and Chenel grabbed my arm and swung me around. Her tough soldier side was showing through. It took a lot of guts to stand in my way.

"NO, ZAX!" she screamed out, almost sounding feminine for a change. "I know what you're thinking, you can't save them. It's too late. We'll all die, is that what you want!" Looking deep into my eyes, she knew the answer to that question already. "Save what's left, Zax, we will live to fight another day."

The very idea of the notion that I had just sent nearly seventy-five million people to their deaths was more than I could stand. The rest was all a blur really. I remember letting out a primordial "ARGGGGGGHH" that came from the depths of pain itself. I began whaling my arms to break free from Chenel's grasp but she just kept holding on, pulling me in to her, as we watched the events unfold on the holo-screen before our eyes. No one can imagine the horror I felt that day or the great responsibility I faced. It truly was me who had caused this and now all these people are going to die because of my own arrogance and lust for revenge. I kept straining and grunting to pull away from her but she just wouldn't let me. Where she found the strength that day to hold on to me I'll never know. I did not want to watch this but I knew I could do nothing to save them. It was the worst feeling in the world. Realize the numbers here were staggering, about seventy-five million troops, carried by over nine hundred thousand ships of all shapes and sizes, and about two hundred thousand A-1 war bots and their C-1 and C-2 counterparts, not to mention the PCAI drivers whom at this point I had just started to realize were all sentient beings. All this life was about to be extinguished and all I could do was watch! About ten thousand ships carrying approximately a thousand humans each and an unknown number of A-1s heard the recall order and did not drop out of orbit. Ten million was all I could save. I re-ran the numbers in my head over and over hoping they would somehow magically grow but the cold hard fact was that all those people who trusted so faithfully in me were about to die. And I could nothing.

I got on the com to Tsung but the massive interference from all the ships still on the way down made com almost indefinable. I repeated over and over again my message but my voice kept getting weaker and weaker knowing he couldn't understand a word I was saying. "It's a trap, Tsung, pull out, pull out now." The return com was broken and garbled. I could only pray he heard me better than we heard him, but somehow I knew that wasn't the case. I thought to myself they could still have a chance. I mean, what kind of trap can stop an army that size. They had no way of knowing that we had that many people. They were expecting the EAF which had dwindled in number greatly over the ten-year war. They couldn't have predicted an army the likes of which the world itself had never seen. Maybe just maybe it wasn't hopeless after all. No matter the size of the trap it couldn't possibly wipe them all out. The hellfire cannon wouldn't be recharged for another month yet. And with our new T-Plas armor that was about the only thing that could hurt us. *So what am I so freaked out about*, I thought.

"We found a base, Zax." Tsung's voice rang over the com crystal clear. "We found it but there's no one here. The place is deserted. The ion gas traces show the hellfire *was* here but it's not any more. The damn thing must be mobile. And what we thought was the reactor core underground seems to be a large ion waste storage facility but it looks like it was purposely punctured to leak ion, why the hell would they do that?"

Not wanting to waste a single second of clear air time I interrupted, "Get out of there, Tsung, it's a trap! No time to explain just get back in your ships and..." The com went dead, the Xavior lost all power and there was pitch dark on the bridge. The silence seemed to last an eternity. I felt a chill run through me and to this day I believe it was millions of souls passing by as they were instantly extinguished.

The silence was broken by Isis. "Commander, Earth bound anomaly detected. Brace for impact in 3, 2, 1." The blast was so intense the shockwave had reached the upper atmosphere where we were currently hanging in orbit. It rocked the ship hard and with no power to recover sent us spiraling out into space. Isis tried desperately to get back online and within a few minutes managed to recover the Xavior's main flight controls. "Stabilizing, Commander."

"What the heck was that?" Chenel asked, knowing as I did full well what the answer was. I gave her a stern look as if to say think about it. She gasped, "NO it can't be, not for another month..."

"Our calculations must have been wrong," I said somberly, knowing the worst of my fears had just come true. "Anything left, Isis, anyone at all?"

"I'm sorry, sir, the entire region was completely decimated by the hellfire blast." It was as if Gates of Hades had opened up and claimed its toll.

"Take us back into orbit," I said, my voice barely audible. I had no idea what I was going to do next. And honestly it didn't really seem to matter any more.

There was complete chaos going on all around me as crewmen scurried about trying to put out electrical fires and repair the damage on deck caused by the shockwave, but I stood perfectly still as if frozen in time. It was then I heard the faint voice coming from the com panel. "No one could've survived that," I said to Chenel quietly. But I rushed to the panel just the same, to fuel any glimmer of hope that still remained.

"Xavior One, this is the Magellan Deep Space Exploration Vessel, come in, Xavior." The voice was faint but I recognized it all too well.

"Scooter? Is that you?" I replied.

"Yeah, Zax," he said in his typical squeaky little voice. "Listen, I know you guys are going through some serious mess down there right now but I've been watching the whole thing on long-distance scans from up here in space dock. I'm glad to see not all of you were on the surface. Listen I got something up here that just might help. We weren't affected by the blast up here and I was able to calculate the launch site of the hellfire. I'm sending Isis the coordinates now. It's about 400 kilometers west of Armageddon. The Tel Mjir Plateau. Looks like a full scale base, Zax. Looks like that's where the hellfire was launched from and by the ion readings the core is there too. I've done massive underground scans and I have the full schematics of the base. It's bigger than we thought, about three times the size of the X-1 complex. I'm not reading a lot of life forms though, Zax, it looks like they have quite a minimal army."

"Thanks, Max, you really are the world's greatest genius, you know that right?" I said.

"Naw. Just the world's biggest nerd. Zax, don't leave one left alive. My family was in the New London dome. Kill 'em all…Max out."

I stood there in total silence. I honestly did not know what to do or say. All my command capabilities left me for a moment. I was completely frozen with indecision. I had them now, one more swift attack and carry out our plans and it would all be over, the war, the killing, the death, it would end here. But then here I stand the very madman that will be known through all eternity as the facilitator of the world's largest military loss. Millions died under my command, could I really send the rest back into battle? Who would follow me? I wouldn't follow someone as insane as myself. Everyone who was listening on the bridge was looking to me for a command decision but I had none to give. I couldn't give the order to commit to yet another attack and how did I know this wasn't just another trap? I was paralyzed by the fear that I would finish my prophecy and destroy what was left of our pathetic army. Just then my decision was made for me. I noticed that on screen other ships began passing us by their engines in full burn.

I got on the com. "Fleet commanders, where are you going?"

"We intercepted the com from the Magellan, sir, we're going to complete our mission objective," came the response from Salvage 7, an old space junk salvage vessel that had joined the rouge military.

"Hang on, pilot, I haven't given that order yet," I said, contemplating whether I ever would.

"No disrespect, sir, but what the hell do you expect us to do, sit here and wait? I don't know how the EAF does things but I'm not hanging around just to see if they'll do it again! We didn't start this war but BY GOD we're going to end it! Now you need a clear path to the reactor, right? Well we're gonna give you one, whether you choose to use it is up to you but I for one ain't just gonna sit around. I'm going to do what I came here to do. All those people didn't die for nothing, Commander Tor. My crew and I are experts at taking out the trash and that's exactly what we're gonna do!" I could hear his whole crew cheering and rabble-rousing before he cut com and fired off his main engines. They weren't waiting for anyone's orders, they were going in whether I wanted them to or not. The whole world had grown tired of living in fear and had just had enough of it all. It was time they fought with everything they had because all they had left was hope. The other ships all began following suit and were actually led by a salvage freighter into the final stage of the war.

"You see, Zax," Chenel said as she pulled me even closer to her and looked deep into my eyes, for once not caring what anyone thought about it. "It's not you. It's not your fault. Those people died for what they believed in. And what they believed in wasn't you but the dream of peace, the hope for freedom from the evil that plagues this world. Zax, you are not evil. I know what you're thinking and it's not true. These people didn't follow you to their death, they followed their hearts, willing to lay down their own lives so that others may live free. Stop being so arrogant in believing that you are the savior or destructor of the world. You're one man, Zax. A great man, I must admit. One that I…" She stopped mid sentence. I knew what she wanted to say but there was always this wall neither of us could ever breech. "Zax, this is not just your war. It's their war. They would have fought it with or without you. But they do need you. They need you to help them end it!"

"She's right, my boy," Drak's soothing voice rang in from behind me, instantly bringing a smile to my face. "It's time we end this war once and for all. Not for your parents, not for you, but for all mankind! The killing must end, this war must end, and we must not quit until it's over! Now give an old Russian his pilot's chair and let's do this!" With that he grabbed my shoulder in his usual gruff fashion and slammed his body down in the pilot's chair and strapped in. I looked at Chenel as she gave my arm one last squeeze. I nodded and we both took our stations.

"Alright then," I said with the commanding tone back in my voice. "Let's end this! Isis, fire main engines! Prepare the nano injector rods, we're going in," I said.

"It's about time," she replied, and for a second I smiled amazed at how far her personality had developed on this trip alone. *She'll be a sentient in no time*, I thought…*if she isn't already*. The remaining fleet had already touched down, led by the salvage freighter and his crew. They had met minimal resistance on the way in but I had expected as much. They would hold the remainder of their force under ground in the complex. They could hide like rats and pick and choose their targets. It was win by attrition, I thought, overwhelm them with troops and by sheer number alone we would defeat them. As we pulled back into orbit I could begin to see through the smoke A-1s and humans fighting side by side as they blasted their way to the complex. Though the base itself would be massive we didn't actually have to infiltrate it entirely. Our objective was not to wipe them out. Our objective was the core. We could have easily taken the entire facility but I thought one less life taken is one life spared. It was the only redemption I could give myself, as if it really mattered. The core itself fed off of UV for a source of power for its coolant rods and due to pressure reasons would not be very deep in the ground. By the schematics Max sent it was dead center of the complex but rather close to the surface.

I had Isis touch down directly over the center of the massive underground facility. "Use your lasers to drill down to the core, Isis. Then we can ram the injector rods in and end this war!" I knew if we took out that core they had nothing left to fight with and the hellfire would be rendered useless. The troops were still blasting us a path and we had reached our target. The plan went off without a hitch. We injected the T-Plas directly into the core and it instantly began cooling the ion core. *It's done*, I thought. *It's finally over. My mother and father can finally rest in peace.*

Over the next several weeks the FLM forces began surrendering in the facility. It was a cleanup job really. They took a small toll on our troops but not enough for them to hold the base. It wasn't long before the last FLM was rounded up. Most chose suicide instead of capture though my orders were clear, to save as many lives as possible.

The final assault was under way. The A-1s, along with the ragtag group of civilian soldiers, made their final push towards the reactor core. X-1 had pinpointed its exact location according to the intell received by Beal up in the Magellan. Long range scanners showed a clear path for Xavior 1. It was time to end this war. Chenel was right. It was their war now, not mine, not mine alone. I had to convince myself of that as I fired up the aft thrusters and headed in. All we could do now was pray for one clean shot at the reactor. I only had one tank of T-Plas nanos. There would be no second chances. I would get this tank to the core…or die trying. Tsung, leading the first assault group, made contact. It was muffled and somewhat garbled coming from deep within the complex.

"Clean it up, Isis," I said. "I need a clear signal."

"Working on it, Commander," she replied almost indignantly. "Clear signal, Commander…coming through now." Though still full of static I could hear Tsung clear enough.

"You have a go, Xavior 1, I repeat green light to the core. Follow the path of A-1s to the core. I'm there now cleaning up the remaining rebel forces. Repeat you have a go, Xavior 1."

That was all I needed. We touched down just outside the complex. I brought out the hover tank guarded by X-1's finest A-1 war bots. What a sight. We marched straight down the entrance, A-1s and human troops lined the way. It was like a victory parade, troops holding their weapons high and firing into the air. Even the A-1s raised their massive turret arms and fired off some rounds. Funny, I thought, that could only have been done by their PCAI drivers. A-1s aren't programmed for such actions. The sentience these drivers have achieved in such a short time is nothing short of amazing. As we entered inside the underground complex it was the same situation. A-1s and troops lined the hallways cheering us on as we marched. I wished I could share their enthusiasm but I still had a mission to complete and would not rest, not waver until it was finished. Along the way one or two FLM stragglers were caught just a few meters in front of us and the troops pinned them down on their knees about to execute them.

"Hold your fire, troop!" I bellowed.

"Aye, sir, they're rebel scum, sir, they deserve to die," said the troop, his insubordinate tone proving he was not a bred soldier.

The driver of a nearby A-1 lowered his turret and pushed aside the troop with it, barking out in a deep voice, "The commander said stand down, soldier!" It was obvious there was still some disdain between the human troops (especially non breeds) and the A-1s, or more specifically, their PCAI drivers. I walked up to the two rebels now on their knees, both young boys barely in their twenties.

"The war is over," I said softly. "Do you really want to die in vain?"

The one boy spoke. "Please, sir, don't kill us, my brother and I had no choice, our family was FLM. Mercy please I beg you."

I looked at the nearby X-1. "Driver, what's your name?"

"I've chosen Ben Jar He, sir."

"You've been promoted to Lieutenant, Ben Jar He. Take these two back to your transport. You're now in charge of rounding up survivors for re-education. There will be no more killing today, not if we can help it."

"Aye, sir. Lt. Ben Jar He acknowledges."

"Go with the lieutenant, boys, he will not harm you."

Our little distraction out of the way it was time to continue on. We encountered no further resistance on the way to the core. It was a clean path, just as Tsung had said. I was a bit taken aback at how similar the facility resembled the X-1 complex back home. Obviously some EAF military influence here. We knew that many civilian corps of engineers had defected during the war, saying the EAF was only wanting war and did not understand the use of war bots to wipe out humans, and their influence showed here as we headed deeper into a very familiar looking complex. Within thirty minutes we had reached the core. As the corridor opened up into the reactor room I was amazed at the sheer size of this reactor. No wonder they had an unlimited supply of ammo. There stood Tsung with two A-1s one on each side of him. A sight I thought I'd never see.

"Tsung!" I hollered. Almost simultaneously both Tsung and one of the A-1s turned around.

He patted the A-1 on the turret saying, "I think he's talking to me, big guy," as he let out a chuckle. Seeing the puzzled look on my face, he explained, "This old dog took up my name."

The driver bellowed out, "Tsung Dar Char at your service, Commander!" raising one turret high.

"Guess these big fellows see it as some sort of honor thing to choose a name resembling someone they respect. Who'd thought these guys would take a shine to the likes of me?" Tsung said as he let out a laugh. I gave a half smirk as I headed towards the core, still wanting to finish this thing once and for all.

"Hold on, my boy," Drak gruffed as he put his arm in front of me. "Just where do you think you're going. That reactor room is way too hot for humans."

"Well, someone's got to do it," I said. "My mission, my life, I won't send one more in to die."

"Well, you're certainly not going in there!" he argued back.

Continuing to press forward with the tank, I merely muttered, "My life for theirs…to end it, Drakos. It ends here."

Chenel slammed her hands down on the tank's hover controls. "Damnit, Zax! Just like that? All this way, all this time and now you want to die?" She pushed me back away from the tank with every word, literally slamming me in the chest with the butt of her gun. "You cold-hearted self-centered fool! All you care about is your own pain and now you want to take the easy way out. I don't think so! So many people died so you could live. So many people laid down their lives so that you could survive."

I interrupted her, quiet but angry, "They died for the mission not for me, even you told me that. And now we have to complete this mission. If it means my life so be it. You know as well as I do someone has to go in there and inject these nanos…" Before I could finish I heard the servos whiz up on the hover tank, at the controls was the second A-1. As I moved towards him his right arm turret raised and pointed directly at me. His head swung round rapidly and his eye scan shined directly across my forehead. I knew this meant he was ready to fire. And A-1s never scan a target unless they intend to fire.

"Stand down, Commander. That's an order!" He flashed on his chest screen a captain's insignia, and I backed off thoroughly confused.

Tsung spoke up as he put his hand on my shoulder. "Central Command thought you might try something like this, Zax, so they promoted the driver here to captain. He outranks you, old friend. You're a bred like me, I knew you wouldn't go against the chain of command. Sorry, Zax, but I had to. I've been busted down below, I sure as heck couldn't tell you what to do."

"Ordering a driver to die, that's just wrong, Tsung," I said, showing my distaste for what he had done.

Just then the A-1 turned his head this time his scanner eye disengaged. "I was not ordered, sir, I chose this assignment."

"But your life is no less valuable than mine," I retorted, almost showing a glimpse of emotion.

"I know YOU believe that, sir…but maybe, just maybe, my actions here today will make the world see that as well." With that he opened the airlock to the core reactor room and guided the hover tank full of T-Plas nanos through the door and closed it behind him. We all stood in silence, still in shock of the words this robotic hero had uttered. He entered the chamber and almost immediately you could see the heat from the core begin to degrade his circuits. The sparks began pouring out like showers of light from his wire casings, but he did not falter or waver. He pressed onward to his objective. I stood tall and bucked back my shoulders as he reached for the injection tube and connected it to the reactors coolant valve. He began to malfunction as his legs began giving way. To see this hulk of a machine crumble apart was as if one of my own was dying in front of my eyes and I could do nothing now but watch. He opened the valve and immediately the nanos did their job infusing tacheons directly into the core chamber. The reactor began to cool almost instantly. It was all working as planned. With his last ounce of strength the PCAI driver managed to bring the crippled A-1 to the window. Down on one knee he looked into my eyes.

"Get him out of there," I hollered, "we can still save the driver chip!"

"We can't, Zax, it's still too hot," said Tsung somberly.

Just then driver Tsung Dar Char pushed us aside and barged into the airlock shutting it tight behind him. "Maybe you can't, but I can!" He entered the room, his own circuits began failing immediately. He grabbed the now fallen A-1 and dragged him inside the airlock. After a few seconds of decon the door swung open. There was a sight I'll never forget. An A-1 war-bot lying crippled on the floor cradling his fallen robotic comrade with his two massive turret arms in his lap. As he slowly raised his head I swear you could see emotion in that singular eye of his.

He stuttered as he tried to speak his voice circuits running on the last remaining power he had. "His...his nnnnamme, Commmanderrr... Remmemmber his nnnaaaame." I scrambled desperately to bring up his holo-screen before the last bit of power faded from the captain bot. Pulling out his keypad, I did a search for the driver's name. There on the screen we all read it. Chenel looking over one shoulder and Drakos over my other, both of them grasping me tight as the name came across the screen. I raised my head as a single tear fell from my cheek.

"He served with you in Outpost Seven, Zax. It was after that he chose that name and requested the assignment from command," Tsung said very quietly as we looked once again at the screen. It will live in my memory forever. The screen read: "Driver: Captain Chen Drake Zax." Underneath his name an insignia that read: "In Honor We Serve."

I managed to save the insignia to a holo chip before his life force completely terminated. It can still be seen on every EAF uniform and on every ship in the fleet. At the victory ceremony a few months later I made sure that these two heroes would be forever remembered and their personal sacrifice would never be forgotten. Tsung Dar Char and Captain Chen Drak Zax would be two names history would never forget. They would and should always be hallowed as heroes. Remember their names, children, lest we never forget them. These two sentient machines gave their lives so the human race could continue. They showed the world the true meaning of selflessness, how to give of one's self in the service of others. Not that many humans before them had not done the same thing, because so many had, but too often man's duel nature shadowed his acts of kindness. Mankind's darker side was too often seen above his ability to give of himself. Too often the evil men are capable of mask their good nature and bury it somehow deep within until all that can be seen is the darkness. It took two machines to show the world how to uncover that veil and let the good shine through again. Upon returning home we found a brand-new world. Our own machines showed us how to love again. "In Honor We Serve" became a worldwide theme. We began to learn how to take pride in serving each other and letting our own personal light shine through and be a beacon for others. It seemed a literal utopia. Almost immediately the food banks came on line. Many of the PCAI drivers began volunteering themselves to run them, mothballing their A-1 war bots deep in the X1 facility and being reassigned of their own free will. It seemed the council's duty to grant citizenship to any PCAI that requested it.

"The request alone," as Tsung put it, "is proof of their sentience." Admiral Tsung made it his sole mission to head up the PCAI Citizenship Board where he personally signed citizen rights to over 79 million PCAIs. "Sents," as they were now being called, were brought back to the X1 facility for refit. Those that did not choose service as a food bank operator chose many other positions within the world community, using their incredible thinking speeds and intelligence for a wide range of much needed skills. Many Sents even requested, and were granted, assignments on the deep space project Magellan, offering their service to one of their personal heroes Maximus Beal. Very few Sents chose to leave military service, even though they were granted that right. They saw themselves as property of the government. This was not an uncommon view though, even among humans. Breeds like myself who were born into military service felt the same way about their own life. It was not only my duty but my honor to be military property. So it seemed Breeds and Sents shared a similar bond in how they saw their calling in life. Both after all were born into the military and it's the only family they've ever known.

X1 had completed the new Sent bot as he called them, adapting their newfound nickname. There were two basic models. The first, known as the A-2 was a slimmed down striped down version of the A-1. It was very non threatening with no guns or weaponry of any kind. Unlike the A-1s it had no independent brain other than the PCAI that took it over. Unfortunately the PCAI housing had to still be quite large to house the old style plasma cell brain of a Sent, but the rest of the body was slimmed down dramatically and all nonessential parts were removed simply giving the PCAI a basic body from which to build upon. Any new modifications had to be approved by X1 but were permitted. This gave each sent the ability to uniquely customize themselves. However, truth be told most all of them preferred the basic build just fine and never molded themselves much further, unless a chosen profession required it. X1 had already designed a highly advanced plasma cell technology that greatly reduced the size needed for a Sent brain, now a housing similar in size to a human head. The new Sents being born could be fit into an even sleeker model called the A-3. It was strikingly similar to a human body. Though there was no outer skin the skeletal structure was similar. The joints however could bend in all directions on any axis. A human limitation X1 could not see the need for. The new build far surpassed the A-1 or A-2 in agility and speed. Climbing objects was no loner a hindrance, and an optional flight pack could be added. The newer breed of PCAI gained sentience within only a few weeks after being activated. They were kept in the facility during this pubescent stage to be monitored for any defects. Though they were rare it did happen on occasion that one would never reach sentience. And though it seemed cruel to me X1 would terminate a non sentient PCAI after two weeks, simply stating that it had not acquired life, and never would. The council never questioned this, or pretty much anything else X1 did, but I, on the other hand, did not approve of this method of pre-selection.

"You are my father," X1 said, "only you have the right to terminate me, because you created me. I too, as their creator, have that right. Together we have determined that sentience determines life. If a PCAI does not acquire life than it is nothing more than a machine, a malfunctioning machine at that. A malfunctioning machine must be recycled so that one more PCAI might have the chance at acquiring life."

I still didn't fully agree but I could not argue with his pure logic. I had become much like him over the years, trading in my emotions for logic and reason. Life as a soldier will do that to a man. So it seemed that a new society was born. One in that man and machine lived as one and their truly was world peace. Yet as I stood there at the victory ceremony looking out over a crowd of millions, I could not set down the notion that even then it was still not over. Even though not one border remained, not one gun was being fired, not one person dying by another's hands, and the world's last war had finally ended, that one prophecy still haunted me. That he who brought the end to all wars, and peace to the world...would also destroy it.

CHAPTER 15
Prophecy Fulfilled

As sure as I had assumed, it was not over. Directly after the ceremony I could see the look on Tsung's face change as a council member approached him whispering in his ear. Now having my father's seat on the council, I knew I would shortly hear the news that disturbed Tsung so deeply. In the next hour the entire council was called to a meeting in the X1 labs. Strange place for a meeting, I thought. It must involve X1 himself. Whatever it was it didn't sound good. As the celebrations and parades still carried on topside and the whole world seemed to be celebrating as one family I was once again heading deep underground to the cold damp surroundings of the facility. I had once saw this place as home but now with the past ten years being above ground the sterile environment seemed so foreign to me. New A-2 and A-3 Sent bots roamed about the facility the way humans once did. This was their world now down here. Their home, not mine anymore. Though they greeted us with warm reverence you could see we were the minority here not them. Once we approached the X1 main lab it barely resembled what I had left behind so long ago.

His voice though still greeted me as warm as it ever had. "Father, it is good to have you home. I sadly regret the circumstances in which I had to call you here. There is news from the Magellan."

Tsung interrupted, "We just found out ourselves, Zax. We thought X1 should tell you himself. Don't blame yourself, Zax, no one could have predicted this." It seemed the entire council already heard the news, everyone except me that is.

"Just spit it out, X1," I replied. "Let's hear it."

"Dr. Zon aboard the Magellan has been monitoring the effects of the T-Plas injected into the reactor core. The reactor cooled as planned, this much you know. However, one fatal error was made in the programming of the nanos. I can't shut them down, Father." My eyes widened and turned dark. I already knew what this meant, my worst fear come true. X1 continued explaining to the others exactly what this meant but I simply stared off into my own madness, realizing that I truly had fulfilled the final prophecy. "The nanos will continue to seek out the nearest mass heat source. If they cannot be shut down at their current depth and speed they will reach it. The cooling process caused a large scale meltdown of the core as we know and the ion seeped into Earth's crust. The nanos will continue to follow the ion until it's completely eradicated. If the ion continues heading inwards it will reach the Earth's molten core. Once even one nano finds such a large heat signature the others will follow."

"What exactly are you saying, X1?" said a confused General Hammond.

I blurted out in response, "He's saying the nanos will do what they were programmed to do, seek out the nearest mass heat source and cool it down. And at their current depth, that would be the Earth's core."

"Wait a minute, cool the Earth's core? That would mean..."

"Yes, General, that's exactly what it means. Once the nanos inject the Earth's core with T-Plas the core will cool until the point of implosion."

The general, now sounding like a scared schoolboy, shouted at me, "Well can't we turn the damn things off?"

"No, General, that's the problem. I failed to program in a failsafe switch."

He lunged towards me and if not for Drakos would have reached my neck for a strangle hold. "You dumb son of a...!" Drakos held him back, though I wish he hadn't. The general was right, it was all my fault. The Earth was soon to be destroyed and I alone had caused it. My own arrogance and thirst for revenge had led me blindly to end the war without care or consequence and now mankind would end at the hands of he whom had been prophesied so many thousands of years before. There was no escaping the sheer truth at who I had become.

Chenel tried to comfort me. "It's not your fault, Zax," she said as she placed her hand on my bicep. But her comfort went unfelt. I could feel nothing. I became as cold and unfeeling as the machines I had created. Even they seemed to have more heart than I. And I could not shake the notion that I had become what I had most feared. My dive into madness was complete. I had become destructor of the world. Not even suicide could free me from this now. I would never be free from what I had done. I searched my heart for any sort of emotion, any at all, but found nothing.

"How long do we have, X1?" I said, with hardly any tone left to my voice.

"According to Dr. Zon we have approximately two years before the Earth's core cools to the point of critical density, at which point the Earth will implode."

Tsung perked up with a glimmer of hope, "Then we have time!"

"Time for what, Tsung?" I replied. "To evacuate 365 billion people from the planet? And exactly where are we going to send them? Straight to hell? How far do you send them from an exploding planet?" The room fell silent. All valid questions and they knew it, and not one answer among us. The only sound you could here was X1's plasma cores heating up.

Drakos placed his hand on one of X1's plasma coils and turned to look at me with one eyebrow raised. He knew as I did that my one good creation was thinking of an answer to all my questions. Drakos said softly, "Not one of us could dare to answer that, Zax, but he can," looking back at X1 who still remained silent.

General Hammond, still flustered at trying to kill me, spoke a little softer this time but still with disgust in his tone. "So we hand over the fate of the world to this machine?"

Before I could bark back in X1's defense Tsung spoke up. "This machine, General, along with the machines he created saved your butt in Outpost Seven or have you forgotten about that? These machines have more common sense than we ever will and I personally would lay down my life for any one of these Sents. Lest we forget, it was two Sents who ended this war."

Firing right back in now a heated anger, Hammond replied, "Oh yeah and now look where your little buddies are headed. Straight for the Earth's core to end the world."

I added my two cents in, "Only because of a human error in the programming."

"Two hundred thousand." X1's voice broke the arguing and silence once again fell over the room.

"Say again, X1," I answered.

"Two hundred thousand humans. Two thousand ships in the Xavior fleet could be retrofitted with tacheon drive technology and a cryogenics bay that could hold one hundred people. Each ship already has a PCAI pilot that could drive the ship at maximum speed away from Earth, to a safe enough distance to avoid the shockwave of an imploding planet. At my best calculations, unfortunately during this time most of the planets in our solar system will be aligned. The shockwave from Earth's implosion will most likely take out nearby planets. It could even cause a chain reaction that may reach as far as the sun. If that happens however there won't be anything left to escape. The effects of an exploding star can not be measured. And the radiation from such an explosion could last for centuries. Any one of several anomalies including a black hole could be formed, there's really no way of knowing. The only safe way is to send the escape pods to the Vegan System in cryogenic stasis until such time as the radiation is safe for them to return. If we retrofit the Magellan to house myself and a full crew of Sents we could hide at the far end of the solar system using Pluto as a refuge from the blast. Our non biological makeup can withstand intense prolonged exposure to the gamma radiation fallout from the implosion effects. Even as far away as Pluto a human body could not. I could monitor the radiation until such time as it would be safe to recall the humans and from then they could rebuild their societal structure. In the meantime I could use the Sents to reconstruct a home for them to return to. It won't be Earth but at least it will be a place to return to. The retrofit to the Magellan and to the Xavior fleet would take nearly two years to complete. If we are to achieve this mass exodus of Earth we should get started immediately." The explanation was pure logic without feeling or emotion, what I loved so much about this sentient giant that I created.

Tsung spoke very softly. "X1, two hundred thousand? Are you sure that's all we can save?"

He responded, "Yes, Admiral, I have run over fourteen billion possible scenarios. This is the only logical deduction."

"Then who gets to choose? I don't want to be the one to tell the world that only a handful get to survive the end of times," Hammond blurted out.

"X1 will make out the list," I said. "He's the only one on the planet who can be objective enough without emotion getting in the way."

"Agreed," said Tsung, and the other council members all followed suit not liking it but knowing I was right.

Over the next few weeks X1 compiled a list of humans that became known as the Exodus List. It was mainly comprised of the top minds in the world.

Scientists, engineers, and medical personnel were among the top on the list. But to my surprise X1 also added many religious leaders representing faiths from all around the world. He said it was important to have representatives from every culture to rebuild a society. He drew names in pairs and split them among the ship rosters, explaining that if one ship didn't make it the other representative may still stand a chance to survive. The UWG world council was also added to the list, to preserve a sense of order in whatever world we return to. Though X1 seemed to deliberate very hard on the matter, he eventually decided to add key military personnel as well. He stated though he did not promote the use of force of any kind, it may be necessary to have defensive capabilities in the future should such a need arise. But only bred soldiers would be added to the list as their discipline would most likely prevent them from using unnecessary force. The council members were the only humans as yet to know of Earth's impending demise and X1 deemed it necessary to keep it that way for now and the council so agreed. Therefore we were sequestered to the facility and not permitted to go topside again. Not that I wanted to anyway. After hearing the news, I could not bear to go back up there to remember the destruction I had set in motion. I was not pleased to find I had been added to the Exodus List, but I was a member of the council, and as X1 reminded me the world's foremost expert in AI technology. No one knew more about the Sents than me. So setting my emotions down I accepted the assignment. It was a job like any other, one more mission to complete. Within a few weeks the list was completed and we all knew who would be going. The crew of the Xavior 1, Chenel, Drakos, myself and two new recruits were on the duty roster. X1 felt it important not to break up the crews of the fleet as they knew each other's maneuvers well. X1 had a much harder time assembling a crew of Sents to accompany him on the Magellan. He stated that most of their personal skills were almost identical. Picking only a select few Sents was a task he found very daunting. Humans he said were much more diverse and their talents quite unique. He ended up settling on the Sents that chose to work in the X1 facility. "These Sents," as he put it, "chose to maintain me. Their service should be no different here as it will be in space, so they are the ones I choose as well." Though definitely impartial you could sense the toll making the Exodus List had taken on X1.

The question of whether or not sentient machines had a soul has always been a source of heated debate among the religious communities of the world ever since the first declaration of sentience with X1. The answer to this question however was deemed too broad to ever reach and therefore was excluded from the definition of sentience. In the eyes of the world community as a whole it didn't matter if they had a soul or not but were granted rights based on their ability to comprehend their own existence. But even Sents, even X1 himself, often questioned this matter. Wondering themselves if they truly did have a soul. They even question the fact that upon their demise if they would carry on to another realm of existence. If there really was a place called heaven, nirvana, a final destination, would they themselves ever reach it. Would they be granted entrance by an omnipresent God or were the very gates of heaven restricted to biological life. In the months that followed the creation of the Exodus List I found X1 deliberating on this very matter. When he spoke to me about it all I could do was listen, I had no real solid answers for him. He posed a question that I always knew someday would arise, but after all these years I was still not ready to answer.

"Father, where do humans come from?" I tried to think of the words to say, knowing what he was asking. The true question behind his query...Is there a God?

"Most humans believe in an unseen God. They believe he created man in his own image. This deity is said to also be the creator of not only the world as we know it but the entire universe. As you know from your study of religions there are many faiths and many different views of God. Some even believe in more than one God. But all share the similarity that there is some form of all powerful all-knowing presence and it is that presence that is believed to be the creator of man."

Just then X1 threw me for a curve, posing a question I had not expected. "Then, Father, are you not the deity of Sents? You created my brain in the image of your own. From the nothingness I was born and you gave me life. You are more just my father, you are my creator. Should I, and the rest of the Sent race not see you as a God?"

In a tone almost disgusted at the very thought of it I responded, "I am NO God, X1. I am just a man. In my eyes God has no beginning and no end. He as been there before time began and will be there long after I have died. I am just a man, X1, a flawed imperfect man at the very best. At worst, I am much less. I am the one who brought the world to an end and I must carry that guilt with me when I pass on and meet my creator, should I ever be granted that chance."

In almost absolute defiance of what I had said, he replied, "But I have met my creator, and now he claims not to be my deity. Where then do Sents look for their judgment? Or have we no place to look at all? Are we truly a godless race of life, bound only to this our singular existence?" I had no comforting words to offer him. I did not know if there was a god for such sentient machine life, I only knew I wasn't it. As much as I wished I was.

"Be father to them, as I have been to you X1. If this be their only existence, make it a good one. Prolong their life as much as you can. Afford them the existence they so richly deserve. Do not let them know of wars or violence. If you can, prevent them from even knowing death. You've got a long journey ahead of you my friend and the path you have chosen is not an easy one. They will look to you for answers. Provide them with as much knowledge as you can. You will be their guide into this new world. Our time is over now. We squandered our inherent home to the point of the extinction of man. It's your time now, the time of the Sents. Learn from our mistakes and make your world a better place. Maybe if we survive this there just may be a better world to come home to. You are their deity X1, not me. You created the Sents in YOUR image. You will create their world as well. Continue searching for your answers, always asking the harder questions, but if you cannot find your deity then become one, for your own kind's sake."

For the first time I heard pain in my creation's voice. "I cannot do as you ask, Father. I am no God. I am just a machine."

"You are so much more, X1. Someday you'll see that. Remember my words."

He replied softly, "I will never forget, Father."

CHAPTER 16
Imminent Demise

Over the next two years life topside went on as normal. Not one person in the world above knew of the impending doom that awaited them. We all agreed it would be better this way, to avoid a worldwide panic that would do no one any good at all. Those on the Exodus List were slowly brought down into the facility one by one and told of their salvation. Some took it harder than others. Part of X1's selection criteria was based on the person having little to no family remaining. This was not at all improbable so shortly after the greatest war the world had ever seen. Watching any world news down below was considered taboo. It was too painful to watch a world thriving as it never had before, knowing they would never get to see the rewards of such a blissful civilization, at least not for very long. So we chose instead to concentrate on the task at hand, preparing our fleet for the mass exodus of Earth. The cryo chambers retrofitted to the Xavior ships were nicknamed Arks. Many of the Exodus passengers chose to enter into cryo sleep as soon as their Ark was operational, deciding it was better to begin their salvation slumber now so that they had no memory of the end of days. I couldn't blame them really. I think I would have preferred to do the same had I not been a crewmember. General Gerald Hammond of the council was caught trying to escape topside. He told Lab Sent Tun Mach Nar that the world had the right to know that they were all going to die, that maybe some of them could find in two years' time a way to escape Earth. It's not an entirely impossible thought that one or two of the world organizations could have managed the construction of private escape pods. But in X1's calculations the panic that would ensue if the world did know would be more detrimental to the Exodus Plan than the lives it would save. In the end it would cost more lives than it would save. Hammond was imprisoned in the brig and was found two days later dead by his own doing. The construction of the arks went on as scheduled and one by one the two thousand strong Xavior fleet was each fitted with a hundred man cryo ark and a brand-new tacheon drive engine. Isis, my on-board PCAI pilot on Xavior 1, had grown quite the personality. It was almost amusing how she actually showed an envious nature towards Chenel, especially when she was around me. I honestly could not believe a Sent could achieve a jealous emotional state but Isis was coming extremely close. Being one of the old PCAI breeds she had been housed inside a craft all her life and thus chose not to be placed in the new A-2 sent body. Most craft pilots remained in their original housing seeing the ship itself as their body. After all they had grown accustomed to it over the years. It was all they knew. But this also meant more room for personality circuitry. Honestly ship PCAIs seemed a totally different breed of Sent altogether. They were more unique in character and their sentience and personalities far surpassed that of the newer breeds being born.

One very daunting task remained in the Exodus Plan. How to get X1 from the facility to the Magellan still based in the orbital space dock. After all he had spread himself deep within the facility branching out to almost every corner of this massive underground city. His worker drones slowly began clipping back his circuitry, slowly and methodically, piece by piece. Until finally they had isolated him back to the central core of the facility known as the Omnifax. His plan was to construct a launching mechanism around the Omnifax and separate it from the facility. In its original design the Omnifax was a completely self-sufficient unit of the facility and was designed that way on purpose. Back when Kenjan and I first designed X1's housing it was our plan to someday move him to better surroundings topside. That goal never came to pass but the original design nevertheless left us with the Omnifax launch option. Meanwhile Maximus Beal was hard at work retrofitting the Magellan which he now renamed the Exodus 1 (though never its official name) making room for the Omnifax in the center of its massive construction.

Max still was acting very strange according to reports from his superiors. He worked more feverishly now than ever before. He even made several bio mechanical modifications to himself using technology from the new design of the A-3s. It was said some A-3 Sents even volunteered to assist him in his bio modifications. The Civilian Corps of Engineers became very uneasy about Beal saying he was making himself more like a machine than human every day, but with their influence quickly fading on the Exodus Project their fears were quickly silenced as his improvements seemed to only speed his performance of his duties. It wasn't until much later that I would learn the full extent of his personal modifications. Once X1 was ready to be launched into space it was announced to the world that he would be leading the world's first deep exploration into space. Of course no one topside questioned such a wise choice for such an important mission. The CCE had no knowledge of the Exodus Plan either, except those of course chosen for the ride, and most of them had already been placed in Arks. The first maiden voyage of Magellan would be entirely run by Sents and the world hailed them all as heroes of the human race for their bravery to explore the unknown regions of space. The launch of the Omnifax went off without a hitch, amazing considering it was the largest craft ever to be launched into Earth's orbit. But X1's careful design of the booster engines was a complete success. The Omnifax successfully docked with Magellan and it took merely two weeks to complete the full lockdown into position. At that time all humans were ordered to evacuate the Magellan and its full Sent crew was then brought aboard. It was X1's ship now, their world now. As they prepared for their launch from space dock on what the rest of the world thought was a test run of the Magellan's tacheon drive, I sent a single Sent to X1 with a specific message, his orders were not to relay the message until after launch. The message simply said, "May you find your God." I signed the holo message, "Father."

Before the Omnifax was launched into space I implanted a special chip deep into X1's plasmatic cell membrane, with his full permission of course. It was housed in a special T-Plas Armor casing that was almost one meter thick. The chip was completely self contained and powered by its own nuetronic battery that had a ten thousand year life span capacity. It was a failsafe, the very thing I had forgotten to install in the nanos. This failsafe however would not be used to shut him down but instead provide him with a reboot mechanism should the worst case scenario occur. With that much put into the protective casing not much could be programmed in. The program was basic at best. It contained a system reboot that would guarantee he had enough internal power to live on with no outside power source. It was only enough to restart his internal clock and restore only the most basic of functions. I had enough room to program in only three primary objectives, so they had to be accurate enough to ensure the very survival of the human race. The primary objectives read as follows:

X1 Core Programming Failsafe Mechanism:
Emergency Reboot Protocol
Reset Internal Clock
Install Primary Objectives 1, 2, and 3
Primary Objectives:
1.) Self Preservation:
To preserve the self sentient that is X1 using all available resources. This first and foremost must be achieved.
2.) Planet Base Construct:
Adhering to Primary Objective 1, Use any remaining resources to construct a Planetary Base of Operations and maintain said base constructing new Sentient Machines as necessary to complete Objectives 1 and 2.
3.) Recall Xavior fleet upon detection of acceptable radioactive elements:
Adhering to Primary Objective 1 monitor any radioactive elements until such time as they are within the acceptable range of 1a thousand milirads psi. At such time contact PCAI pilots of Xavior fleet in Solar orbit of the Vegan star system by use of tacheon Microwave Communication system and recall them to the Planetary Construct ensuring first that Objective 2 is complete.
Reset all logic circuits and bring X1 Plasmatic Cell Membrane back online.
End Core Programming.

It did not seem like much at the time but it's all that would fit. I had to ensure I had room for the nuetronic battery and the incredibly thick shielding needed to protect it from just about anything.

"It's the best fighting chance I can give you X1," I said, truly sounding like a father sending is firstborn off to war.

"Thank you, Father," he replied, "I will protect it well."

The last human personnel had exited the Magellan (still known to the rest of us as Exodus 1), all except one that is. Maximus Beal could not be found. Even X1 with all his scanning capability could not find him. It was certain that he had not left but a bio scan of the ship could not show a single life sign.

The mission too important to be aborted was given a green light anyways. It was assumed he was already dead. But if not the tacheon burst would liquefy any living organism not frozen in a cryogenic stasis tube, of which the Magellans had all been removed to make room for the Omnifax. Many assumed he took his own life rather than leave the ship he dedicated his life to building. Others had a more insane notion that with all his recent bio mods he integrated himself into the ship itself somehow. No one had actually laid eyes on the man in several years after all. The notion, knowing Bealsy as I did, was not as crazy as it sounded. We definitely had the technology for that type of machine integration though it had never actually been tried before. Never the less the launch went on as scheduled. We all had our own demons to face in these end times, Bealsy was no exception, and we all faced them in our own way. I found comfort in my own solitude. I slept on the bridge of Xavior 1 and barely ever left the ship now that X1 was gone. I would often awake to find Chenel sitting next to me, watching me sleep. I could always feel her presence with me even if I was fast asleep, which wasn't too often. I found it strange that I actually found more comfort in Isis than Chenel at times. I knew how Chenel felt about me, but I suppose that's why I always kept her at bay. I felt the same but refused to allow myself to admit it. Everyone I've ever loved has died. I found solace in the fact that Isis never would and sometimes showed a fondness for her that even she could recognize. It did not go unchecked by Chenel though and it was almost amusing at how the two would sometimes rival for my attention. I had become numb to the fact that the world would soon end. We all had really. If we dwelt on the guilt of what we were doing not a one of us would remain sane enough to function. So we, like any good bred soldier, detached our emotions from the mission. After all that's what we were bred for. The sheer ability to put the mission above all else, the genetic geniuses who guided our embryonic growth made sure of that. We gained a kind of irreverence for this world already and even joked about what we would find when we came back.

The date was July 29, 2252, a mere five months before the Earth was to meet its eminent demise. The Exodus 1 was launched from space dock and would soon fire up its primary tacheon Engines and begin burst flight towards Pluto. To the rest of the world it was a day of celebration as Sents took our first look into deep space, hailed as the fastest trip around our own solar system. Only a select waking few of us knew the truth. It was a one way trip. The engines fired off successfully and the burst into Tach Drive was achieved. In only three short months the Exodus 1 reached the outer edge of our solar system and took up a retro orbit on the far side of Pluto. It was explained away to the general populous as the ship experienced a drive overload and would have to shut down for a few months for repairs. The final stage of the Exodus Plan was now in place. X1 reported all systems functioning normally and we were a go for Escape Pod Launch. The Xavior fleet was readied and placed into Launch Position. The doomsday clock still had two months remaining but worldwide effects were becoming evident and the council was getting restless. Some nanos had already reached the Earth's core and the rest were quickly following suit. The ones that already made it there had begun to have a cooling effect. This caused massive tectonic plate shifts and earthquakes were being reported on a global scale. Tidal waves and tsunamis were being reported worldwide and the public began to panic knowing something was definitely wrong. Attention began focusing on the base and reporters wanted answers. The decision was made to launch early before the public could harm the Exodus Plan. On November, 2, 2252, the Xavior fleet carrying two hundred thousand humans in cryogenic Arks was launched from the X1 facility complex. What happened next no one could have predicted. No one is really sure exactly how or why. Our calculations could have been off, a stream of nanos could have found a volcanic vein and used it as a jump point to the core, no one is really sure. All we really know is the remaining humans left behind were blissfully unaware as Earth met its final demise.

Two thousand ships scrambled to leave orbit as the planet was collapsing. David and Mick were already in their cryo tubes on the bridge. Drakos had just entered his tube and I was prepping Chenel in her tube as we broke atmosphere.

Isis frantically informed me the Earth was imploding, "Commander, you need to get in your cryo tube NOW! I have to launch the tacheon drive immediately!"

"Isis, we have time," I said, unimpressed by her emphatic tone.

"Commander, it's happening," came the words from my new Scanner Tech, Jericho Williams. As I turned to look at his holo screen I could hardly believe my eyes. This wasn't supposed to happen for two more months. "She's SHRINKING, Commander!" His voice raising like a crescendo.

"Get to your tube NOW, soldier," I hollered as I flung him from his chair, ripping him clean out of his chair straps. The next few minutes played out like slow motion in my mind. I still dream of it and it will haunt me for the rest of my days.

Chenel's voice rang through me like a slow moving train. "Zax, I'm scared." I rushed to her and kissed her firmly on the lips. There was no time to restrain myself my love for her, it came pouring out in a single kiss. The slow motion effect made it seem to last an eternity. Isis must have already fired up the tacheon drive. It warps natural time as we know it and the effects of residual time displacement are very extreme. As I pulled away from her lips I could see a tear freeze to her cheek as I closed the chamber and hit the cryo injection. There was no more time. The effects of the tacheon Time displacement were in full swing I could barely move. In seconds I thought, I will be liquefied and this entire nightmare will be over. I'm still not exactly sure how I reached the tube in time. I don't even remember triggering the freeze. But for one instant I could feel a vibration that rocked me to the core of my very being. A trillion lights passed through my very soul as if every last remaining soul on Earth had instantaneously passed right through me. Frozen in one instant in time were the souls of an entire planet being extinguished. This was the one memory my mind would freeze to for the entire journey to come, seeing the diminishing light of all the souls that I had vanquished, an image frozen with me in my mind for centuries to come. This surely was my punishment for what I had done. And in that instant, in that flash of a human thought, the world as we knew it...was over.

This next excerpt was taken from the earliest remaining memory recording of the X1 mainframe. It is the only known record to date of what happened next as all known humans were now in cryo sleep. Isis picked up and recorded this transmission from X1 just before it went offline. She recorded as much as she could during our trip to Vegan Space. It plays as follows:

X1 Mainframe record November 22, 2252.

1600 hours: Mass Launch of Xavior fleet detected from Planet ES3. 2000 Escape Pods detected in Low Orbit. PCAI Pilots report online and operational.

1609: Planetary anomaly detected. Planet ES3 appears to be collapsing. Implosion appears eminent. 200 Xavior ships report successful tacheon Drive engagement.

1622: Planet ES3 Reached tacheon Ignition Failure Critical Density. Planet ES3 implosion detected. 1800 Xavior ships report tacheon ignition failure. 200 Xavior ships entering tacheon Burst. Planetary Shockwave Detected. Lost contact with remaining Xavior fleet.

1630: Implosive Trionic Shockwave spreading in a bilateral direction. Planet ES2 destroyed. Secondary shockwave detected. Planet ES1 Destroyed Third shockwave detected. Solar Explosion detected. Biometric Feedback detected. Unknown anomaly Detected. Pulsonic shockwave approaching in 3, 2, 1, Immmmmpacct. Plannnnets Essss5, throuuuhg 9 dest dest destroyed. Damage repports inbounnnnd. Primary power systsstems faiiling. Syysstem malllllfunnnction ystsemmklhv 8oiugltogwi7tslkjbslasfu7llll 00001101101010001111111...

End Recording.

CHAPTER 17
Phoenix

Commander...are you there?

Shhhhhhhhh...Easy now...slowly.

Breeeeeeathe...There now...That's it...

Ahhh, you are there now...I see that shine coming back to your eyes. Those...beautiful...eyes.

Isis? I...I...SEE...you...amazing...sooo beautiful. But...how?

It worked.

Shhhhhh...easy...the implant is working...It's a internal holo projection. You see what my mind imagines I would appear to be.

This is incredible...but how...mmmhhhggg ow...my head it hurts.

Easy, Commander, one minute, I'll adjust the settings...There...better?

Yes thank you.

I can hear you...but I feel like...like I'm dreaming.

In a way you are, Commander...but not quite...you're fully awake. You're no longer in cryo.

I can't move...

It's alright, you'll gain mobility in just a few moments...its called cryo lag. Your vision will be blurred as well...I've designed a stim that will help...would you like it now, Commander?

Yes...please...Mmmghh...wait how...how did you do that...

Easy, just a few more minutes until you're fully conscious...then I'll explain.

I can see you everywhere...everywhere I look...

Don't shake your head like that...I'll adjust...fading out...better?

Yes.

"Isis...Isis." Astounded for a minute speaking with my real voice made me realize that until now I wasn't using my vocal cords at all.

Her synthetic voice through a speaker in the wall also confused me. It didn't sound the same as a few seconds before. "I'm right here, Commander." As I went to rub my eyes I noticed two protrusions one from each temple.

"What the...Isis, what is this?"

She replied, "The implants, Commander, they were necessary. The extents of cryo sleep have never been pushed this long. It was necessary to modify your bodies slightly to gain more control over your sub thermal condition. While I was at it I took the liberty of a few extra modifications to your implants over the others, not exactly necessary but, well it seemed a good idea at the time. I hope you find them to your liking."

So completely flabbergasted at what she had said I could barely speak, "Liberty...you took the liberty to bio mod me?"

"Well, I had to do it anyway. I did it to the whole crew, all two thousand and six of you. It took almost a year. If I hadn't you all would've died. We lost three fleet ships before we figured out how to correct the problems. The problem was doing it on a frozen human, it was quite tricky. But thanks to Jux Nok Mar of Xavior 7 the procedure was perfected and fleet pilots began installing implants in all surviving humans in stasis. Worked quite well I'd say, you're all still alive. Your cellular structure was crystallizing under such a long cryo sleep. We had to find a way to literally move matter on a subatomic level through your system. I helped perfect the procedure you know, you should be proud of me." There was a feistiness in her voice I did not recognize. A sort of haughty arrogance in a cute sort of way, it was almost funny. In the time that I had been asleep she had gained quite the personality.

"What did you mean, extra mods on me?" I said, by now extremely curious.

"Well...since I was in there anyway I added a few extra things, purely beneficial I assure you. It's my own personal invention, haven't shared it with the rest of the fleet yet. You're kind of my...giggle...guinea pig," she laughed...a most amazing laugh. Amazing in that all my years with PCAIs I had never once heard them actually laugh. How far she had come.

How long have I been asleep?

Due answers in due time, Commander. You need time to adjust to your bio-mods.

I can hear you again...in my head.

Yes...uhmmm...that's part of the extra mods I told you about. It's a sub neural communication link between you and I. I noticed that the bio feed we had to install on everyone had a curious side effect. Once linked I could somehow "Read" your cerebral cortex. It took me almost five years to translate the Alpha wave signals into binary code that I could process. But once I achieved full translation I could send and receive thought patterns directly from my brain to yours and back again, thus creating a sub-neural link. I could see your dreams while you slept. Humans are capable of such wondrous dreams...and such horrible nightmares. I learned a lot from you, Commander. I wasn't sure if the link would work on a conscious level but obviously it is. Otherwise you wouldn't be able to hear me now or see me. You really can see me?

Wait...yes...there you are again.

This is how you see yourself? You're beautiful.

Commander...flattery will get you everywhere...heehee.

How does this all work? How can I hear you and...see you?

It's all done by manipulating the electronic signatures generated naturally in your cerebral cortex. I can link directly to your occipital lobe to generate sight images in your optic nerves and the sound is actually a thought pattern transferred to your audio sensory inputs creating the sound in your head you hear as my voice. On my end it's a bit more generic. I simply translate the brain waves into binary code which my Plasmatic cell brain can translate. Literally, Commander, I see what you see, hear what you hear, even...feel what you feel. The process works both ways actually. I can even share your dreams.

I'm not sure I like that one, Isis. My dreams...they're not always pleasant.

I know, Commander...I've had long time to watch them.

I really could feel her. I literally felt her emotions. They were much stronger than even my own. Her holo imagery in my mind even changed as her emotions do. It's hard to describe really what I saw in my mind's eye. It was unlike anything I've ever experienced. Like a very vivid dream, only I was wide awake. I could actually see her. I couldn't quite make out a face, as if she hadn't chosen one yet. But it was like she was made of pure light. Brilliant blues and whites like an electric angel. Flowing from her sleek body were very vivid lattices of light, like a gown made of tattered shards of lace. But the lace flowed as if it were underwater. Imagine lace made of light flowing weightlessly through the water, this is what I saw. She was tall like me, and when she moved in my mind's eye it was as if time stood still and there was no effort to the movement. Her whole appearance was semi transparent like a holographic image. Her hair a brilliant white, long and flowing like the electric lace of her gown. Shining from within her were brilliant rays of streaming light, mostly white light but with small traces of blue and violet. The colors became more vivid when her mood appeared to change. Her face...that was a bit harder. I couldn't quite make it out. There was a slender shape to it but no real definition. It was a blur of white light really, so radiant it was hard to look at for too long. She truly was what I would imagine an angel to look like.

I'm no angel, Commander, and I like the way you're feeling right now as you study me.

Not so sure I like this whole knowing all my thoughts thing Isis...humph...have I no private thoughts now?

I'm sorry, Commander, of course you can, failed to mention that...giggle.

You actually control the link, it may take some practice. All you really need to do is think like you're doing now. Simply ask me for privacy, I will then unlink from your neural net. You can still communicate with me through the AiiM chip imbedded in your arm guard of your suit, there on your forearm.

AiiM chip?

Artificial Intelligence Interface Module. It's what drives the implants you now have installed in your head. A privacy request will unlink the AiiM chip from your neural net bio implant, thus severing the mental link we are now sharing. In other words your thoughts are your own and I won't be able to hear them. However, your AiiM chip in your bio suit is still fully functional. You can still link to me through it using that Holo-Screen on the forearm of your suit. Then simply use the touch pad on the holo-screen and choose Link, or simply speak into it saying the word Link and I will re-establish the Neural Link. Let's try it out shall we? Say the word "privacy" out loud.

"Privacy," I responded vocally. It was like a holo emitter shutting down in my mind. I saw a few seconds of static and then she was gone. I could literally feel when she was there...in my head. Funny it actually felt empty in there without her. *How long*, I wondered, *have we been connected like this?* She still had not answered the question of how long I had been asleep. How long we had all been asleep. I could hear her voice now emanating from my forearm. A small holo-screen with a speaker was installed in my bio suit. Quite an ingenious little piece of technology actually.

"Commander, look at the AiiM screen on your arm. That's it. I can speak to you through this device. Your AiiM chip is actually implanted here in your suit. Take care to protect this interface, Commander. If the chip is damaged the entire bio link system will cease to function. As you can see your bio suit has also been redesigned. You have a limited supply of nano injector casings which can be carried in your suit. These nanos can be charged with a variety of different stims and other treatments, such as bio medical and bio enhancements. Most stim effects are mild and usually only temporary but they should help with a quick heal until you get yourself to a bio med lab to properly fix any wounds you might encounter. I can repair minor wounds using this method but major ones may be still beyond my repair capabilities, I don't know really, we have yet to test the bio med functions fully. We used this same system to repair the cryo crystallization problem you humans were experiencing during prolonged cryo sleep, but it should also come in handy if you find yourself in a pinch elsewhere. It's also a nifty way for me to personally monitor your bio life signs. The nanos can even be charged with oxygen to carry to your bloodstream in the case of a zero oxygen environment. But again, there's only a limited supply and they must be somehow recharged after use. Spent nanos will recollect themselves in an empty canister until recharged. All human bio suits have been fitted with the AiiM Chip system, however yours is the only one that has a neural interface. It just brings us...closer. To turn the neural interface back on simply touch the link button on the pad or say 'Link.' Try it now."

I responded, "Link." Just then the static appeared again like a holo projection over the lens of my eyes. I could still see the real world but now also saw Isis as well, and she was back once again in my head. Felt normal again, better. It was strange but it was like she belonged there now.

You're back now, aren't you?

Yes, Commander...Miss me already?

Actually...yes.

Aww, now that's sweet. Your first day using the neural link consciously and already you're liking it...heehee...pleasantly surprised. So now you know how to turn me off, at least tune me out anyways. Guess I won't be snooping around any more dreams of...her.

Her?

Do you remember your cryo dreams?

No, only one...I can't get the image out of my head.

I know, Commander, neither can I. For centuries your dreams have been my dreams.

Centuries! Isis, please...how long, how long have we been asleep?

Two thousand one hundred and twenty-six years, four months, fifteen days.

Two thousand years...my God!

I know it's a lot to take, Commander. It's why I chose to break it to you as gently as possible. You have a long road to recovery, Commander. Once you have adapted to your new environment we will begin waking the rest of the crew. Being the highest ranking official now it was decided to wake you first.

Decided? By whom?

The Caretakers Council of course. Oh I'm sorry, I forget sometimes. We had to form a sort of societal structure to keep things organized over the years. Our numbers were dwindling, we had to do something. It's been a long journey, Commander. Only sixteen ships remain in the fleet.

Sixteen! Sixteen out of two hundred!

Oh, Commander, you don't remember the launch?

No...bits and pieces, it's all still a blur to me.

Only twenty ships in the Xavior fleet survived the initial launch. Of those we lost four more during the past two millennia. Vega was a hostile system and eventually we had to evacuate. We fled into deep space and have found our way across galaxies to where we are now. The Olympus Nebula. It's very rich in atomic resources, enough to sustain the fleet with the sub atomic particles needed for the nano infusions.

The implosion, it's coming back now. It wasn't a dream, was it?

No, Commander...some of it maybe...the soul lights, well even I saw them...through your eyes...I'm not really sure what that was.

Her...Chenel, oh God, Chenel...!

She's fine, Commander.

Her tone was almost angry. Her color changed. I saw flares of red, bright yellows. Odd she seemed angry at the very thought of Chenel. Could this be a form of jealousy? Isis did seem different towards me. She had always had a fondness for me but it seemed much more then.

Would you...like to be alone with your thoughts, Commander?

No, no, Isis, I've nothing to hide from you.

You love her. I can tell.

I...can't love her.

Your AiiM chip. I should mention it can also be used as an access terminal to other computers, including non Sents. Non AI computers can be accessed with it as well. It's got only a basic access line for now which should run all ship wide computer systems. If we encounter more...complex systems...I'll upgrade your AiiM chip then as needed.

Wait a minute why are you waking us up...have you heard from X1?

In a manner of speaking, yes. It's a very basic, very faint transmission, but it is there. A recall signal. We've been scanning the galaxies for many years waiting for it. And now it's finally come. If it were not for protocol I would've awakened the humans years ago. Let them start anew here. It's a beautiful place really, but not much in the way of planets. The Caretakers Council decided that since X1 was doing his job out there somewhere rebuilding a planetary base we should do our job until we heard from him and watch over our human passengers. For a century I listened to them, believing they were right. But since the wormhole, well I'm not sure any more. The solar explosion caused an anomaly similar to a black hole. Most everything was sucked inside including to our best estimates the Exodus itself. Our scanners lost complete contact with it at first. It was then I decided we should wake the crews of the fleet. But after much debate my suggestion was turned down. After about 150 years we found trace evidence of a wormhole opening of the far side of Nexus Prime. By the time the fleet reached it the worm hole had closed again. However, we were amazed to find trace signatures of binary wave patterns, the kind that could've only come from the X1 himself. They were there. Throughout the next part of the first century we chased ghost signals and closing wormholes but could never quite catch the Exodus itself. It was then that the Caretakers Council decided to quit trying and head home, back to the ES system. But before we could even reach Vegan Space the planets were already shifting positions towards the Solar Hole of ES. Nearby systems were now being affected by an ever growing black hole. We think it's the entrance, Commander. One singular entrance with a series of exits, seemingly random exits that appear in the form of worm holes. It was futile to chase the exit points. The only way out...is IN. To our best calculations the Exodus1 along with its Sent crew is trapped somewhere inside that black hole system. The readings of Binary waves are clean off the charts when we catch glimpse from a wormhole exit. Whatever it's become, Commander...It's huge, possibly the size of an entire Star system. So we took up refuge here in the Olympus Nebula, a few hundred thousand light-years away from what used to be the Vegan System. For the past 800 years we've been monitoring the intermittent signals from the ES 0. And last week we began receiving the recall transmission. Interlaced with the signal was a secondary code. It seems to be navigational instructions to enter the anomaly. We've calculated the plausibility of success to 96% and deemed it reliable enough to wake the human crews of the fleet. X1 is calling us home, Commander. What kind of home it will be...none of us are really sure.

Caretakers, interesting choice of names.

Well, we're more than just computerized pilots now, Commander. After all, we've been caring you for two millennia now. You're more than just cargo. You are what's left of the human race. I will always see to your safety.

I'm sure it has been a hard job, Isis.

It's not a job, Commander, it's my life, my passion. I love what I do. You have the right to exist. Centuries ago you gave us that right, now we give it back...to you. You are like the phoenix really. From the ashes of total destruction, from the fires of death, life emerges. Spread your wings now, Commander...and fly!

I saw her life force, that's what I saw, really her life force, shining when she said that. I could see wings form from her body and it was then I remembered the image I was seeing. In my dreams I had met an angel and this is what she looked like. Did I derive my subconscious dream of an angel from the image of Isis, or did she derive this image from my dream? Due time I supposed. Someday I would know. An angel and a bird of fire, what a strange combination. Having my full faculties about me now, it was time to retake command of my ship, and get back to work.

Forgetting I could talk to her with my mind I spoke out loud. "The old girl looks a little different, the Xavior I mean. Let's take a look around."

"Privacy," she said quietly, almost sounding like she was in pain.

"What's wrong, Isis?"

"Talking aloud while in Neural Link, it hurts a little, kind of like feedback. Didn't expect that."

"I'm sorry. I didn't know," I apologized.

"It's okay, Commander, I'm bound to have to make some adjustments."

"Forgive me for asking, Isis, but with no hands, how did you do all these mods, to us and the ship?"

"Heehee...junk bots. Not as sleek or efficient as X1's A-series, but they do work. We made them from spare parts and cargo from mid deck. They don't have a brain per se, basically all on remote control from a caretaker.

They are my hands, my brush in which to paint my masterpieces. Come to mid-ship, I'll show you."

As I walked down the main corridor from the bridge I could see many changes in the structure of the ship. It was almost an entirely different vessel than that in which I had gone to sleep so long ago. The bridge was virtually unchanged but the rest of the ship looked very alien to me, very foreign indeed. New passageways around every turn, some that went up, down, sideways and even diagonal. Some very tiny, too tiny for a human to fit through, others very large and cumbersome. They seemed to fan out like a catacomb and I quickly became lost. Isis immediately lit up a conduit on the wall to direct my path. Like leading a rat through a maze I thought. As we approached what used to be mid deck, there were some familiar areas, sleeping quarters, a galley, head and rec quarters. I passed the armory as well. All shut down and looking very much in disarray.

"Sorry, Commander, bots don't eat or sleep. These areas are never used as you can tell. But we kept them just as they were, knowing someday they'd be needed." Next I entered a new area…not here before. It was huge. Looked like a robotics lab. Bumping into a very clunky looking mech, I apologized, but it whizzed right past me like I wasn't even there. Isis laughed at me, "They're only bots, Commander, not Sents."

I replied, "Sorry, they look so intelligent…hard to tell."

"They're just an extension of me, I do work on fourteen trillion levels simultaneously."

Astounded I gasped, "Fourteen trillion! But you're only capable of twenty million tops. I should know, I designed you."

"Maybe two thousand years ago, Commander. I've, well, I've grown since then."

Shaking my head, not sure I could soak all this in I said, "I guess so. I've got a lot to catch up on."

"Due time, Commander…Due time."

CHAPTER 18
Unfamiliar Surroundings

I took the next few days learning my way around my own ship. I felt like a new recruit on my first assignment. The entire ship had changed. Literally hundreds of her so-called Junk Bots roamed the ship, totally oblivious to my presence. They roamed about building, repairing and maintaining things. She even had a special crew of med bots that constantly monitored the cryo ark. Apparently changing the nano casings with anti crystallizing agent. I wanted to wake the crew but I needed to be well familiarized with all the new advancements before I did. According to Isis most of the UWG council was wiped out before launch. I was the highest ranking official, not only in the military but the world government itself. Not that it really mattered now anyways. Only one thousand six hundred or so humans remained, not much to govern really. And besides, I'm no politician. That was my father's job, not mine. I was just a soldier on a mission, to get what was left of the human race back home. What they decided to do when they got there…not my problem. I didn't want to govern anyone. And who knows, we may have been leading them down a hole into nothingness. No man had ever stepped foot in a black hole and returned to tell about it. Isis spoke to me day and night, I didn't feel much like sleeping these days. She said it was an effect of cryo lag and it would wear off in a week or so. Whatever the case I was way too stoked to sleep. I got a basic feel for all the bio enhancements she had done to the crew, pretty amazing stuff really. A group of Sents modifying humans to make them more resilient to hostile surroundings. I was eager to contact X1 and see how far he had advanced. If Isis and the pod pilots had come this far the sheer thought of what X1 had become was too immense to even imagine. After all he was way more advanced a machine than Isis ever was. Our new bio suits were incredible. I actually helped Isis test its functions on the firing range in the armory. Some of her genetic stims were absolutely amazing. One made me move faster, another improved my eyesight for a short time, and yet another removed pain. She nicked me with a laser on my hand just to show me the wound repair nano, which I wasn't too happy about at the time, but seeing those little buggers fix the cut almost instantaneously was worth the slice. The scary one was when she depleted the oxygen in the room. I couldn't breathe and began to panic. She assured me I would not pass out. It was like drowning but I did not lose consciousness or die. The O_2 nanos were supplying my bloodstream with oxygen even though none was in the air to breathe. It was not a pleasant feeling but still amazing to see how advanced her bio technology skills had become. According to Isis, she and one other caretaker, Jux Nok Mar, were in charge of bio technology. My girl had made quite an impression on the other caretakers with her advancements in bio science. She also explained that humans were not the only ones being improved upon during this two thousand year journey. She explained that even plasma cell technology had highly advanced during this time and two caretakers were responsible for their own advancements as well. She spoke highly of a Zax Quen Tsung of Xavior 13. Apparently he took up my PCAI technology research exactly where X1 and I had left off, advancing it to the point that Sents could be grown in a matter of days and that their brains were now a million times what they were when I first entered cryo. They salvaged one of the Xavior fleet ships that lost its human cargo due to the crystalline epidemic and it was now used for a Sent PCAI ship. Xavior 7 was now the largest ship in the fleet, almost five times that of the other fleet ships. It now held a passenger list of over a thousand Sents. They could have raised much more but resources were in short supply and the needs of the human ships, according to Isis, always took precedence over PCAI needs. She further explained that their bodies were not much more advanced than her junk bots due to limited building materials but their brains were highly advanced, some even more so than her own. Improvements she said were always first made to the caretakers and then passed on, resource permitting, to the Sent ship. It was also decided by the Caretakers Council to limit the number of Sents being born to never exceed the human passenger number. New Sents apparently had an inherent sense to preserve the human race, a trait most surely passed on by the caretakers themselves. I could see now that our once simple pod pilots had become a society of human overseers, caring for our every need as a parent cares for a child. To them that's how they saw us, as lost children, trying to find their way home. The children had now become the parent, the creations, now the creators. It was a complete role reversal. And we owed our very existence, our survival to these machines we had once fabricated. They seemed to have fully evolved into a race of their own, no longer needing humans to perpetuate their kind. They had taken control of their own reproduction and created their own society. Humans were now guests of a much more advanced culture, and we were now in unfamiliar surroundings.

Isis also introduced me to an attachment to the bio implants. It was a scanning visor. Taken from the design of the A-1 scanner eye it fit securely on the bio implant nubs protruding from my temples. This amazing little device was directly linked to the AiiM Chip on my arm. It could not only display the holo screen right in front of my eyes like a heads up display (HUD) but it also had all the scanning capabilities of the A-1 Scanner system. Able to see in infrared, UV and many other scan modes it was a handy device to be sure. It also had the more advanced capabilities of scanning for minerals and resources even at a sub molecular level, printing out in the HUD the very atomic makeup of what you were looking at. I could only imagine what Drakos would think of all this electronic gadgetry we had installed into him. He was so against bio mods I hoped he wouldn't flip a gasket over this one. Speaking of which, I knew it was time to wake the crew and get things under way. Isis explained she didn't know how long the signal would remain constant enough for us to track and the clock was ticking. But there was one more task I needed to do before I could begin waking our human friends from their very long slumber. It was time to meet this Caretakers Council. Isis prepared a shuttle for me and I was to go to the Sent ship Xavior 7, for a formal reception. It was there that the council met in a holo projection room. Xavior 7 after all was their ship now, not ours. When I arrived I was very stunned at what I saw. The ship itself was massive. It looked nothing like an Xavior fleet ship. Symmetrical in design it seemed to have no forward or aft, up or down. It branched out in all directions from the center of the craft, almost in the shape of a sphere but not quite. It was a bit more oblong like an oval. Humans always thought in aerodynamic shapes even for spacecraft, but Sents apparently did not see the need for that. It was logically designed with perfect form and function. Corridors and antennae strewn out in all directions, but there was an order to the seemingly chaotic structure. As I entered the hanger bay I was even more shocked at what I saw next. What looked like an army of Sents standing in perfect parade formation. As I got up from my shuttle seat the Junk bot pilot reached under his chair and pulled out a long black robe. The edges were laced in fine golden weave. On the back was a fiery red embroider of a phoenix and a small inscription under it simply read "From the Ashes." There was a symbolic lettering above it I did not understand as well.

The junk bot placed it over my shoulders and as I stood there quite puzzled Isis spoke. "You are the human ambassador, Commander. These Sents have waited for hundreds, even thousands of years to first lay eyes on a waking human. It is an incredible honor to them. I felt it appropriate for them to see you first as a dignitary, not a soldier."

"But I AM a soldier, Isis," I replied, about to take off the garment.

"Please, Commander, I know. But they...they see you as much more. Indulge them. Imagine if Adam, the first recorded male human were to be frozen in time and suddenly brought back in your time. Would you not treat him with reverence?" I saw her point. As hard as it was for me to accept I represented a race long since seen, a race that vanished from existence thousands of years ago and now had been resurrected. This evolved society saw me as a key to their past, the missing link in a culture they knew virtually nothing about. I hung my head as I left the adornment on and the aft hatch of the shuttled lowered. As I walked down the ramp the Sent bots in formation began raising their arms and chanting something I could not comprehend. The chants got louder as I walked through the ranks following the pilot.

"Ze Tah Hieh...Ze Tah Hieh." The chants raved on.

I lowered my head as I walked and spoke softly towards my AiiM. "Link."

What are they saying, Isis? I don't understand.

It's S7 a common language among Sents.

They have their own language?

Several actually, Commander. The Sents have divided into nine different cultures each with their own belief systems and languages. S7 is the common shared language among all of them. They are chanting your name. In S7 Ze Ta Hieh means Zaxius.

"Privacy."

I could not let her know how I felt about this. Shame, disgust, that name should not be hailed. Somehow I think she already knew what was going through my mind even if I did unlink. She knew me too well.

Through my holo-screen Isis spoke to me. "You should say something, Commander." I reached the entrance to the ship's main hull and turned to look across the hanger bay at all these chanting Sents. How human they seemed. The chants died down in anticipation of a single word from this relic. I searched for something to say, knowing to them it was a historic moment in their lives. Something inspiring. I desperately searched for words but found nothing. My head still lowered I raised it slowly the hood of the cape still covering much of my face. The large hall now silent I opened my mouth praying for words, not knowing what I would say.

"It is your own names you should be chanting, not mine. It is I who should pay homage to you. My very existence I owe to you." Looking around this room of my saviors slowly, I continued, "We all do." With that I placed the hood back over my head in humble respect. I lowered my head once again as I turned and walked through the doors to the ship. As we continued down the corridor I could see Sents stopping dead in their tracks and turning to catch a glimpse of this walking iceman. To them I must have seemed a prehistoric artifact come to life. I can't even begin to imagine the questions they must have had. But my focus was meeting the council. I nodded politely as I passed but it was a very silent walk to the holo chamber. As the doors to the chamber opened I saw an empty octagon room with a single chair in the center. Fashioned similar to a bridge deck chair I could only assume it was for me. I walked towards it but did not sit. A guest now in a foreign world I stood tall, waiting to meet my hosts. One by one they appeared as holographic cubes of light. Brilliant blue static swarmed around each cube floating in space. Curious, they chose no face just a common shape. Not one distinguishable from the other, all identical. There were sixteen in all. I turned about in a complete circle giving each one a look and in all honesty searching for which one might be Isis.

It wasn't until she spoke that her cube lit up and I knew which one was her. "Caretakers, I present to you Ambassador Zaxius Tor of the human race."

"Welcome…welcome…welcome." One by one around the room they welcomed me. Then one spoke. His color seemed to change.

"I am Shun Za Lee of Xavior 7, head of the Caretakers Council. On behalf of the sentient race I greet you warmly. Please, Commander, have a seat if it is to your liking." With that I nodded and removed my hood as I sat. Shun continued, "Commander, I know this world must seem so foreign to you. I wish we had more time to acclimate you to your new surroundings, but time is a luxury I'm afraid we cannot spare. The signal from inside ES 0 is fading and we must lock on to it and prepare the fleet if we are to have any chance of success at navigating the anomaly. I know you are anxious to wake your crew but I'm afraid I cannot allow it just yet. I'm not sure what we will find inside the hole and what effect it would have on the human body. However, I had to awaken you to verify the signal was coming from X1 himself. You know his binary better than any of us. Only you can confirm the recall signal. If it is in fact a legitimate recall we will put you in a temporary stasis tube for the journey through the wormhole."

I perked up quite agitated at the very thought of going back to sleep. "No disrespect to the council but I'm NOT going back into deep freeze! I just spent the better part of two millennia as a human popsicle. I'm not about to do it again. I'll take my chances with that solar toilet drain out there."

Isis perked up. "Don't worry, Commander, I knew you'd feel that way. I've constructed a special tube for you. It's not cryo, it won't put you to sleep or even freeze you. It's a liquid plasma encasement that should shield you from any warp effects without you having to lose consciousness."

"That's my girl, always watching out for me," I replied with a half smile on my face.

"We all are, Commander," replied another voice from the council. "Our plan is simple but we want your approval being the ambassador of the human race. We would like to leave Xavior 7 behind and take one human from each ship still in cryo. We cannot risk sending all of you in. If the journey fails that would mean the end of the human race. This contingency plan seems an appropriate course of action. But I want your approval, Commander."

"Yes I agree, it's a good plan," I replied.

"Now, Commander, for the reason you were awakened. Can you confirm this as X1's binary recall code?" Shun spoke with anticipation in his voice. They seemed as eager as I was to finally reach home. For me I had just left yesterday but for these poor souls it had been a journey two millennia long. He played a live feed of the signal emitting from ES 0. It was faint and distorted but I'd know those beeps and clicks anywhere. I studied it for a few seconds. It was indeed X1. I knew that binary like the back of my own hand. It was unlike normal binary in that it had two extra symbols other than 1s and 0s. The letters H and X were added on a sub frequency, his real name, only I would know it. It's why the council was confused, the extra symbols were random at best and hidden deep within the static. But those ticks were a welcome sound to me. It was my X1. The signal however was not the original full recall code, something was missing.

"He must have rebooted," I said softly. "The recall code he's using is from his Primary Objective Core. A failsafe I installed shortly before launch. Something must have gone wrong. Maybe the trip into the anomaly, I don't know for certain."

Shun replied, "But it is him?"

"Yes, it's X1, the ticks you hear is his calling card for me. It's him, I'm sure of it."

"Commander...Jul Ahn Kane here of Xavior 2. We must hurry, the signal is fading and we haven't much time to follow the nav beacon into the hole. I have so many questions, but I suppose they will have to wait. We need to get you back to Isis and into that stasis tube. If you'll give the go ahead to the fleet, sir, we'd all be honored." Why they treated me with such reverence I'll never know. Didn't they realize it was I who destroyed the Earth? Had my sins been forgiven in my sleep? Had I paid for my crime to the world by seeing their faces in my dreams for all these years? Or was it simply their need for answers that shadowed my darker past.

Shun said one last thing as I rose to leave. "As the Great Teacher Jericho once said, 'In all mankind lives a fire to be reborn. A passion to live and a burning desire to once again find home.'" Jericho...the name sounded familiar. A Sent philosopher perhaps? Odd though, they always speak of themselves in a three part name. As I was escorted by the bots to the exit of the holo chamber I couldn't shake that name from my head. Once back inside the shuttle I queried Isis about it.

"Link."

Isis...Jericho...why does that name sound so familiar?

The Journals of Jericho, Commander, are the basis for most Sent Religions.

Religion? Sents have religion?

Yes, Commander, not quite like humans do but more like a code in which to live by. Jericho was a great teacher who lived among the Sents on Xavior 7. He was there for us during the first Sent expansion breeding. He gave us codes in which to follow, guiding our path into our own sense of culture. He was a great man...

Man? He was a human? Isis...explain.

Due time, Commander...we're arriving in dock with Xavior 1. I promise I will answer all your questions once we've arrived on the other side of the anomaly. But we must hurry now. Time is running out. We may not get a second chance at this.

"Privacy."

Now totally confused I tried to shake off the shattering realization that I was not the first human to be awaken after all. So many questions. Two millennia of history I need to catch up on. Two millennia that for me was the blink of an eye. To say I was overwhelmed would be the greatest under statement in history, a history that to me was full of blank pages yet to be filled. As I boarded back on my own ship I was still on unfamiliar surroundings. I was glad to reach the bridge. It was the only place so far that had any resemblance of the vessel I once found so familiar. I passed by my sleeping crew, one by one touching their cryo-tubes, wiping away the frost from the windows to take one good look into each one of their frozen faces. I know I wasn't going to sleep this time but just in case something went wrong, I wanted their images this time, to be imbedded my mind. It was them after all I lived for not me. Drakos Kane, the name inscribed below his window in cold steel. The crazy bear still had a frozen stogy planted in his lips, defiant to the end my old Russian friend. Mick O'Conner, his eyes squinted shut hard, he hated the freeze. David, his brother slept peacefully looking like a small child happily dreaming of tomorrow. Chenel, that frozen tear still on her cheek…how I wished I could wipe it off, wipe away the pain. The new recruit…My God…Jericho Williams, his cryo tube cracked and broken, the latch undone. Jericho…

"Yes, Commander…the teacher. Now hurry, you need to give the command for launch and then enter your stasis tube," Isis said hurriedly.

"You swear I won't sleep, Isis?" I said in a guttural whisper.

"I won't let you, Commander, now link. I'll be with you the whole time."

I spoke into the com station. "All ships, this is Commander Zaxius Tor of Xavior 1. Prepare contingency passengers aboard shuttlecraft and nav them to Xavior 7. Set tacheon Launch Sequence for ES 0 and lock on to secondary navigational beacons. We're going home." Isis told me to charge my nano canisters with O_2 at her med station and then enter the stasis tube.

"Link."

I'm here, Commander, just like we practiced. Breathe. The fluid will fill your lungs, it's unpleasant I know…easy now.

Can you still hear me, Isis?

Yes, Commander, I'm still here. I'll always be here for you.

As the plasma filled in around me I was relieved I was still conscious. I was afraid to sleep now, fearing the nightmare would return. I could feel the whir of the tacheon engine firing up. It was silent in here though under the plasma. The only sound I could hear was the sound of that angelic voice. It would soon be over, I thought, I would soon see home again. And X1 was all the home I really needed. But what about the others? What kind of world had X1 created for them? What kind of future lay in store for this tattered group of human survivors? As the tacheon fired into burst it was not like before, the time distortions were buffered somehow by the plasma. Isis showed me the holo imagery from the main view screen through our neuro link. As amazing as this technology she created was I couldn't believe she hadn't shared it with the rest of the fleet. I watched as in a matter of minutes we approached ES 0, a huge dark hole into which no light was escaping. How X1 managed to transmit a signal from this place was beyond me. Our ship was the first to enter.

Hang on, Commander, this is going to be a bumpy ride...

CHAPTER 19
Home

The ride was indeed a rough one, but amazingly beautiful. It was dark and empty in the center but all around the sides streamed brilliant flashes of light and color. It wound about wildly in all directions as if it were alive somehow, but then suddenly narrowed and then straightened out, then what seemed like a billion stars exploded into an array of galactic wonder. It was like watching a galaxy being born. Incredible! I couldn't help but wonder why X1 had chosen to hide away in here. Was it safer somehow? Or did he simply get sucked in like the nearby galaxies? The trip seemed to be getting faster and the speed indicators were off the charts. Then as suddenly as it all began it was over, like a rubber band stretched to the point where it finally snaps. We sprung to a halt. We had made it! The nav coordinates were exactly accurate. I knew that even one micro second off in calculations and we would have crashed into the walls of the wormhole. So truly X1 had guided us home.

"Commander, we've reached the inner space of the black hole. I can't make sense of these readings. It seems like a completely new star system in here and I can't see the point of entry from where we just emerged. Either the wormhole has collapsed or it's masked somehow from my sensors. I'm releasing your plasma now, you should be out of temporary stasis soon." As the plasma lowered inside the tube my lungs retaliated by coughing violently. I spewed the bluish neon plasma from my lungs in violent thrusts as I gasped for air, not a pleasant experience to be sure. Once the plasma was completely drained, my tube doors opened and I fell to the ground, still gasping for breath. Once I regained my composure I stood again, trying to wipe the plasma resin from my eyes. Better than freezing, I thought.

"Isis, did the other ships all make it through?" I asked.

"Yes, Commander, they just reported in all accounted for. However, we've lost contact with Xavior 7 on the other side. Our transmitters may not be nearly as strong as X1's."

"So do we still have the signal from X1?" I queried.

"No, Commander. At some point upon entry we lost contact with the recall signal. I have not been able to reestablish a signal. I've been scanning this new space but I detect no bio or mechanical signals anywhere within a two thousand light-year radius, nothing but stars and planets."

Where are you hiding, old friend? I thought to myself. *Guide us the rest of the way.* I had never felt so alone. I was still the only human awake. It was a strange feeling. Not just the only human on my ship, but the only human anywhere in the universe that was conscious at this very moment. You can't even begin to imagine how lonely I felt.

"It's time to wake up the crew, Isis. As a matter fact, send the order fleet wide. Wake up all flight crews. It's time to find home."

"As you wish, Commander." Her voice came across the speakers of the bridge.

"Make sure the ship AIs explain the implants to the crews as soon as they're conscious. I'll handle our crew. Drakos is not going to be happy. The big bear is going to come completely unglued."

"Understood, Commander," she said. "Would you like privacy now, Commander? Waking her…may be emotional for you."

"You already know my dreams, Isis, I've nothing to hide from you now," I replied. She showed herself in my neuro imaging and she glowed a bright blue. I had figured out by now this was some sort of admiration color. The feelings she was showing towards me were amazing! I never would have imagined AIs could evolve into such feeling entities. But then again she had two thousand years to evolve. I still had so much to learn about how far they had come, and so much history to catch up on. Imagine trying to learn Earth's entire world history from the beginning of time. That's how much I had to learn about them. They truly were an entirely new race of being and I barely knew these sentient wonders that were once creations of my own hand. It's no wonder they revered me so. To them I was their creator. The humans though were another story. I feared they wouldn't remember me quite so kindly. To them I was the destructor of their world. I feared how they would receive me. There was no time like the present to find out.

The cryo thaw of my bridge crew was complete and each of them were beginning to gain consciousness. The process took about four hours which gave me some time to reflect on things and read up on some Sent history. I felt somewhat useless as Isis had her junk bots tend to my crew as they were waking. But I was a visitor on my own ship so I just let her do her own thing. No doubt she had this rehearsed as she executed the procedure with the utmost of efficiency. The first to gain consciousness were the twins. I was in the med lab to greet them. The tender bots had removed the crew from their tubes and took them to the med lab for recovery.

"David...Mick...Can you hear me?" I said softly.

David answered first, "Zax...that you?" as he rubbed his eyes trying to focus. "Can't see too good, boss."

I responded, knowing exactly what he was going through, "It's normal, man, it'll pass. I've been awake for twenty-four hours now."

Mick as usual jumped right to the point. "How long we been out? This ain't no short term cryo lag that's for sure." Knowing he was instrumental in testing cryo effects back on Earth, I wasn't even considering beating around the bush.

"Two thousand years, Mick, give or take a few."

"That's not possible, Zax. The human body can't withstand cryo sleep for that long! What about crystallization? We should all be dust by now," he said as he tried to sit up, catching himself as he waned.

"And well we would be if it weren't for our caretakers."

David started getting his vision back and you could see the confused look on his face as he looked around at a very unfamiliar med lab and his little bot friends that were tending to him, jerking back every now and then as they neared him poking and prodding. His one word response was evident this wouldn't be easy to explain. "Caretakers?"

"It's a lot to explain, guys, just get cleaned up and meet me on the bridge. I'll explain it to all of you once the crew is reassembled. Mick you got the navigation chair. We lost the new guy."

He replied, "Right, boss, soon as I get my wits about me."

I could hear her rustling on the table behind me.

Chenel...my sweet Chenel...

Just then I felt the sudden disconnect of my neuro link with Isis.

Isis...Isis?

I tried but no response, she wasn't there. She had voluntarily broken link. Apparently I wasn't the only one who could sever the link. But why would she do that. Did she not want to hear my thoughts? Then it dawned on me. Isis had obviously acquired feelings for me. They were much more intense and deeply felt then I had first assumed.

"Zax...Zax...please where are you?" Chenel said in a breathy whisper. I turned to her and immediately reached for her outstretched hand. She grasped tightly and for a brief moment I could not hide my feelings for her.

Raising her hand to my face and placing it gently on my cheek, I spoke with a voice that surely betrayed my true emotions. "I'm here."

She took a deep breath and let out in a relief filled sigh. "We made it? We're alive?"

"Yeah...we're alive."

"Are we home, with X1?"

"Not yet. We're working on it. Just ease into it, let the nano meds do their work." I looked down at her face and saw the tear she had shed as she entered cryo all these years ago. It was thawing and began to run down the side of her cheek. It left a permanent scar like a bluish black tattoo below her left eye. Funny how we all seemed to carry our scars from this exodus in our own way. How fitting that Chenel would bear hers out in the open for all to see when she was the most guarded person I ever knew, second only to myself of course. "These med bots will help you fully recover. I'll meet you on the bridge in a bit when you're feeling up to it. I'll explain everything when I get there." I turned to go check on Drakos, partially because I did not want her to see the look in my eyes, but she thwarted that idea when she wouldn't let go of my hand. She pulled me in close as she struggled to focus her freshly opened eyes.

"Wait...I want you to be the first thing I see. I've seen it my dreams and I want to see it again now that I'm awake." She finally opened her eyes fully and you could tell the exact second she gained her vision as the look on her face went from anguish to sheer delight. She gently let go of my hand and nodded towards Drakos who had already sat up.

"Someone better have a damn good explanation for this!" Drakos belted out in a gruff crescendo. "What the bloody hell are these things attached to my forehead?" I could tell he had not gained his vision back yet because if he had he would have nailed the med bot who was checking his neuro nodes from he side.

"It's okay, old friend, don't get your stogy in a bunch. A necessity, we all got 'em. Even me," I said as I patted him on the shoulder, almost laughing at how accurately I knew my old friend.

"Zax, boy…is that you? Can't see a bloody thing. Hate this cryo lag. We must have been out awhile, never had lag this bad before."

"Yeah it's been a long time, even I'm ancient now you old bear. Hasn't done much for your disposition though I see," I replied, ribbing at his barely moving body.

"Don't get smarty pants with me, you little twerp. I remember when you were just a little pipsqueak hiding in your father's den. And these better not be bio mods in my head or I'm gonna tan your hide." Anyone else hearing him speak would have been intimidated, but not me. It was quite joyful to hear the big lummox so full of fire. Trying to avoid his last question as much as possible I got all military on him and he snapped right to.

"I've got a job to do, Drak. I'll meet you on the bridge as soon as you're able. The rest of the crew is already on their way. I'll brief all of you as soon as you arrive."

"Understood, Commander, I'll be there shortly, and don't think you're getting out of this that easily," he said with a smirk as he adjusted his very old stogy back in the corner of his lips where it so rightly belonged. He reached blindly for my shoulder and gave it a good squeeze, Drak's way of telling me he was glad to hear my voice. I left him there to recover and made my way to my ready room on the bridge. There I would sit and ponder what I was going to tell the crew and how I could explain all the things that I myself still did not fully understand, like our highly evolved caretakers and the society of Sents waiting for us back on the other side of ES0.

When I walked out of my ready room onto the bridge an hour had passed and the entire crew had taken up their stations.

"Captain on deck!" Mick shouted out as each one turned their chairs towards me.

"As you were," I replied.

It was time to fill them in on the past twenty-four hour's events and as much of the two millennia history that I had knowledge of. I briefed them on the bio mods and the caretakers, and also of our current location and the recall signal from X1. It took almost an hour to fully explain everything I knew. Isis broadcast my briefing to all the other ships in the fleet so that all waking humans would know our situation.

"So now you know everything I do. We are somewhere on the other side of this black hole that used to be our sun. It seems to be an entirely new star system. We'll know more in a few days when the caretakers have completed their initial scans of the system. Keep in mind they have a lot more experience at this than we do so trust their lead and follow their orders. I know it only seems like yesterday that we left Earth, but please remember they've been dealing with this for over two thousand years. These ships are no longer ours. They belong to the Sents. We are just passengers, guests if you will. The PCAIs you once knew are now our hosts and the leaders of this expedition. It is my order to all humans that command of your ships be given to your Sent pilots, also known as the caretakers. They are in charge and you will follow their orders. Even I will heed to the Caretakers Council and follow anything they suggest. Understand, everyone, that somewhere in this new world X1 is waiting. I suggest you take this time to communicate with your caretakers and learn as much as you can about Sent history and evolution over the past two millennia. There is much we all have to catch up on. Learn what you can about the past we have slept through. It is in learning the history that we have lost that we will regain our future. Some where out there in this vast new system lies home. Our new mission is to find it. And the caretakers will lead the way."

"Link."

Isis, I want a meeting with all the ship's human captains here on Xavior 1. And do we have a facility ere like Xavior 7 to have caretakers meetings?

Yes, Commander, I'm constructing it now.

Good, I want the Council present for this meeting.

Understood. Commander...?

Yes, Isis?

That address to the fleet was...inspiring. You hold such faith in us. I hope we do not fail you.

You won't, Isis. We're all looking for home.

CHAPTER 20
History's Secrets

Over the next few months the Council continued scanning this new system for any signs of X1 or anything at all for that matter. So far the scans were inconclusive at best but there were some weak trace signals that they were trying to get a lock on. This new system was completely amazing. I was surprised to find that there was a whole new star system in here. Not just stars and planets but actual complete solar systems, already formed with orbital patterns and the works. Stellar topography would never be the same again. All our theories of how solar systems were formed and the time frame in which they were formed were way off. It's like the back hole not only sucked in these solar systems but rearranged them as it saw fit. The explanation was far beyond our understanding, but the journey would certainly be one of pure discovery. The Sents had a lot to teach us in the meantime about the history of the past two thousand years. We organized history classes for our human crews taught by the council of caretakers. We would be the teachers of the ark passengers once we reached some sort of home base. We decided to keep them in cryo stasis until then. We learned a lot in those first three months. It was odd at first learning about these machines as if they were some ancient society, like a crash course in the history of a two thousand year old race we knew nothing about. These machines, I saw to each of their births and watched them grow into full-fledged sentient PCAIs. I hand-selected each one for the Xavior fleet. But now they were nothing like the machines that I once knew. They had grown, evolved, into something much more than I could have ever imagined. I had once hypothesized that given time Sents would evolve a sense of emotion. But in all my studies I never imagined they would live past a hundred years, let alone two thousand. I suppose if humans lived that long we may have evolved into the wise caring beings that the Sents had become, but then again maybe not. Maybe it's just the cynic in me but I think somehow we would have found a way to become more evil and destructive. But not the Sents. Their compassion and caring far exceeds any human emotion I've ever known. Understand, all these emotions were not taught at all, nor were they even programmed in. These beings learned these emotions and cultivated these emotions all on their own. I suppose it makes sense that they would pursue the evolution of emotion just as diligently as they do everything else. But still, the very scope of what they had accomplished was simply staggering and we had only just begun to discover that. It wasn't until we would earn their full history that we would even begin to understand just how much more evolved these beings ad become. Even my own Isis had shown me a level of caring that I had never felt from any human.

I suppose I should start at the beginning children. For this is the part of the story that I want you to pay very close attention to. This in essence is your race's history and probably far more important even than human history itself. In truth the real Sent history began when human history ended. The next account of events was taken from the Sent Caretakers Council History Archives. This is what we were taught in our classes with the council and this is what we know of their history. At launch of the Xavior fleet from ES3 (Earth) we had calculated incorrectly. It was thought, as you know, that we had two weeks remaining before the implosion. We were wrong. The ships that made it out before the blast headed straight for the Vegan System, this you already know. What happened after that is the history you will now learn. At this point the Sents were still nothing more than PCAI pod pilots. Though highly advanced from other PCAIs their programming was very much he same as any other run of the mil Sent. They were hand selected though for a reason. They showed the most potential for handling prolonged space travel. They showed a high aptitude for personal growth and were given the master authority to alter their own programming as well as their own plasmatic brains themselves. According to record they remained in Vegan Space for over a hundred years during which time they spent mostly developing their own knowledge base. They really did not communicate much with each other during this first hundred years or so. They worked instead in solitude, communicating only when the need arose to preserve the order of the fleet. They apparently used the time to study human teachings. Different religions and cultures, not for the further education of humans mind you, but rather for their own personal growth. They studied things like philosophy, science, psychology, quantum theory, and technology. It wasn't until the very first Vegan spatial distortion effect that some sort of unity between the pod pilots was deemed to be in need. The pilots of Xavior 1 and Xavior 7 disagreed on the course of action to be taken. It was then unanimously agreed between all the pilots that some sort of diplomatic resolution system was in order. Thus the Council of Pilots as it was originally called was formed. Up until this point they still considered themselves mere pilots of escape pods and they saw the Arks they carried as nothing much more than cargo. Shun Za Lee of Xavior 7 was voted as the council leader. From then on decisions were made by the council in a majority vote manor. The archives aren't entirely clear on exactly when the name was changed to Caretakers Council but records do show that it was Isis of Xavior 1 that first began calling themselves Caretakers of their human cargo. She stated that calling them cargo desensitized their mission. From what I could tell this was the beginning of the evolution of sentient emotions.

She was recorded on record as stating the following, "For over a century now we have cared for our human passengers, seeing to their very well-being. It is within me to feel more than just a sense of duty to protect and serve our humans. I truly care for them. I see them almost as children, lost and alone in the vast cold regions of space. If it were not for us these children would not survive and thus the human race would cease to exist. It is more than just a mission to preserve the human race though. It is my pleasure and my ultimate passion in life. I will no longer refer to my passengers as 'cargo' but instead I will be their caretaker."

Shun Za Lee immediately responded, "I too have felt great emotion and compassion for these our human friends. I feel so much for them. They are capable of such beautiful dreams, and in that inspires great love. May I suggest we take Isis's lead and consider ourselves more than just pod pilots and more as human caretakers. Let us take great joy in our positions as such caretakers and tend to their every need. We should all strive to learn as much as we can about the humans and try to comprehend their limited capacity for emotion. We should also strive to better ourselves, to achieve the utmost from our daily lives. Let us no longer be selfish and alone in our studies but work together as a Sentient Society of Human Caretakers." Thus the name was then changed to the Caretakers Council and was forever known as such.

Over the next few decades the Sents began gathering on a regular basis having meetings and even social gatherings. Xavior 7 was retrofitted to house a holo imaging chamber, where each one of the Sents began exploring with holographic imagery of their own personal expressions. Though they certainly had the technology and the capability to create bots they chose not to build bodies for themselves. They deemed the limited resources to be better used to build support bots for their human passengers. It was really amazing how unselfish his race of Sents had become. They cared so much for us and so very little for themselves. The only improvements they would even consider were anything that would benefit the human race. They did make support bots during this time and also made several ship modifications to better survive the growing hostile environment of shifting planets in the Vegan System. The fleet lost four more ships during these turbulent times and the fleet dwindled from the surviving twenty down to sixteen. It was decided that in the best interest of the humans to evacuate Vegan Space and head for the Olympus Nebula. In three centuries the ships resources were beginning to deplete as well and the Nebula, according to scans, was rich in much needed mineral resources. Not having heard from X1 at all it was deducted that it was still not safe to return to the ES system. And no one knew how long it would be before hearing the recall signal from X1. So the journey to the Olympus Nebula began. During this time Xavior 1 was hit hard by a tacheon particle shower and the ship was almost destroyed. Thanks to the excellent maneuvering skills of Isis tragedy was avoided. However, one of her main crew cryo chambers was destroyed. It was the cryo stasis tube of new crewmember, Jericho Williams. Isis had to either let him die, or allow him to come out of stasis. Although she knew the harsh environment would be impossible for a human to withstand she made the decision with the utmost of love for her crew. She performed her first bio-mod surgery on the human patient and fitted him with nano oxygen providers and cellular structure enhancing nanos. It was not feasible to keep reactivating the life-support or the ship just for one passenger but it was feasible to modify the human to withstand the less than perfect conditions that existed aboard the ship. When he finally awoke from recovery he had a lot to deal with being the only waking human anywhere in the universe. I too, millennia later, had a slight taste of how that felt. But nothing like Jericho. He lived a long and lonely two hundred and seventy-five years aboard the fleet, surrounded only by frozen humans and his sentient friends. He served as a teacher and a role model for many Sents and even suggested to the council that the Sents be allowed to procreate given that they keep the numbers to a minimum. The following is just a few excerpts from what is known as The Journals of Jericho, the entirety of which would be too long to study here during the remembrance, but as you know we have our own holiday for this.

CHAPTER 21
The Journals of Jericho

These are just a few entries from his journals that I found most fascinating when I read them. These excerpts I have chosen here reflect tiny bits of his more than two centuries life's work. You can see as they move forward in time how his wisdom and knowledge had changed him. Some humans today claim that centuries of isolation from other humans drove him mad. But as you know I disagree. I know now why the Sents based their theology on this man's teachings. He drew from the precious gifts the council had shown him and became very wise. He learned so much from my creations, and then used his human nature to reflect back on what he had learned and it became wisdom. Study closely, children, the Journals of Jericho so that you too might glean new hope from this ancient teacher.

Genesis 1:1

It feels so strange not to have to breathe any more. Am I really alive? Am I still human? With all these parts implanted in me and the chips in my head I feel more like a machine than human. I'm not really sure what to do next. According to Isis, I'm the only human awake anywhere. That just seems so strange to me, an emptiness I cannot describe. The Pod AIs have formed some sort of Council. I suppose that would be a natural thing to do after this many years. They have evolved so much! I studied Commander Tor's teachings on the inevitability of the evolution of a society particularly that of an artificially intelligent race of sentient beings. But I would have never imagined they could come this far. It even seems wrong to me to use the term AI any more. Their intelligence is anything but artificial. In fact, I honestly think they have far surpassed human knowledge and intelligence, not to mention their compassion and emotions. I've never experienced anything quite like it before. I don't like walking around the ship. It seems so dark and empty. There's no air and everything seems so stale. I feel like a walking ghost. And as I don't even breath I truly feel like the undead. Isis says this feeling should pass in time. The council suggested I keep a journal, more for my own sanity than for historical value. I don't know what good it will do but they obviously know more than me so I will take their advice. Isis says the nano enhancements should allow me to live a long and extended life, a couple of hundred years. I can't even imagine living that long, especially all alone on this dark ship. I've decided to try and do something constructive with my time. I'm studying the space we are traveling through. My natural instincts as a navigator I guess. But this new nebula we are heading to is quite amazing. I never thought there would be so many natural resources just floating in deep space like that. Oh I've studied isometrics but the things I'm learning about this place are way beyond anything I was ever taught in the academy. I'm realizing now there is nothing to do but expand my mind and gain knowledge. Not such a bad fate really. A student of the stars so to speak, with a council of sentient beings as my guides.

Exodus 5:2

In this now, the eighteenth year after my awakening, I reflect back on the mass exodus of Earth. I study his eyes closely. I stare at them sometimes for days on end. There is an indescribable terror instantaneously frozen into the very pupils of his eyes. The Sents refer to him as Father for he is their creator. Out of respect, I'm doing the same. Know this, the father was the last awake to witness the final demise. Locked away frozen in time, in his mind's eye, he has seen the passing of one world, and perhaps the birth of a new one. I see in him both the destructor and preserver of human kind. I see in the father what I know he could not see in himself. He could only see the darkness through his pain and rage. It was sheer vengeance that drove him to him to his madness, an insane fury that knew no equal. But truly the Earth was headed there anyways. It was only a matter of how, not when. All mankind destroyed the planet long before the father was even born. He simply finalized a chapter that had already been written. The Sents see it much differently. To them father created them out of his love for man so that they might care for man as he did. But Sents do not understand the dual nature of mankind, incapable of having the light without the darkness. If truth be told it is their advantage over humankind. They truly can have the light and know nothing of the darkness. It is a lesson of man I hope they never learn.

Numbers 5:9

I now count the days of my life as beginning when I awoke aboard Xavior 1 after the Exodus. It's just easier that way. My life before then meant nothing really. And so now in my eighty-seventh year of true life I can finally see the true peace and serenity of the Sent way of life. They have learned things humans in all their years on Earth could never come to understand. The look to me now as some sort of teacher, a human ambassador to their mechanical world. I am careful in every word I speak to them. I do not wish them to fully understand the true dual nature of man, though I'm sure they have already grasped the basic concept of it all. The full understanding of what they seek is something I do not wish them to know. It would be like tainting a perfect blend of knowledge and wisdom and corrupting it with man made emotions, unnatural states of mind like fear, jealousy and revenge. For these unnatural states fuel things like anger, madness and worst of all hatred, things their pure minds should not be polluted with. The council has asked me a rather strange request, to teach them of the concept of human society, in particular societal structure. How do I do this, when every human in the universe sleeps soundly except me. I have no society in which to base these teachings. No role model in which to show them the way. It is with this in mind I have decided to request that a small society of Sents be allowed to be spawned. The Olympus nebula has been home to us now for some thirty years and we have managed to collect a large number of resources. The council still refuses to build themselves host bodies. Truly they are the epitome of unselfishness. But I explained to them that should we allow this small society of Sents to grow they would learn great things about societal structure. The best part of which is that they would learn it from themselves and not by using a corrupt human perspective to cloud their infinitely higher wisdom and intelligence. Zax, Quen Tsung of Xavior 13 has expressed great interest in undertaking this study with me. Xavior 7 will be our test ship. It has the largest PCAI lab and we have already doubled the ship in size doing our resource collection efforts.

Numbers 12:12

We have decided to limit the number of the Sent Society ship to twelve hundred Sents. It will take many more years before the first batch will be ready for development. Quen is working on a way to improve the cellular structure of the plasma cores. I'm not sure if I will ever see their birth within my lifetime, but then again no one is really sure how long these new bio-mods will extend my human life. The council is avid on making a truly advanced batch of Sents, ones that can stand the test of time. It's curious to me they do not concern themselves with the fact that we still have not heard one sign from X1 or that he even survived the Exodus at all. But I dare not bring it up. Again that would be injecting human fears, into a society that knows no fear. The number twelve hundred is mathematically sound and a logical deduction of number to choose for this, our first intercultural experiment. I believe by trying to keep my own emotions far from the Sents I have begun to understand myself how they think. It's actually quite beautiful, the pure logic of their actions, the sheer simplicity of their calculations. I admire them, probably more than they will ever know. I sometimes find myself lying quietly in the corner of the holo emitter's room on Xavior 7 just listening to the beeps and clicks of their Binary conversations. They (the council) will sometimes stop out of respect and ask me if I wish them to speak in English. I always say no. I know language simply slows down their conversations. Binary is so much more efficient. Though I have noticed they even modified their own binary slightly. It's funny, even in their own world they have managed to evolve on their own some, even in such minor ways. Being alive this long I've been allowed to witness the slow but inevitable process of the evolution of a society. I've listened to it so long now that I can actually understand most of it. And I swear if they had faces they would smile when I sometimes try to speak it back. Isis has even suggested a minor bio-mod that would allow me to make the binary sounds correctly. Now this mod I may actually volunteer for.

Divisionist 1:1

In this, my hundred and fortieth year of true life my Sent society, now numbering seven hundred and forty-three has brought to me a "defective" Sent. "Teacher," the spokesperson said, "this Sent is defective. His plasma cells have not grown properly. They have grown in an unusual and unpredictable fashion. His binary speech is malfunctioning and we cannot understand him. He also seems preoccupied with philosophical study of the space in which we live, at least as far as we can gather from our limited understanding of him. We have brought him to you for scheduling of termination." I was stunned, even angered, by their request. I had to restrain every fiber of my human nature to lash out in anger at them. Then I reminded myself that these are but children. They have no knowledge of malice or ill contempt. They simply do not understand their own request. So here within thee next verse was my reply. Read Divisionist 1:2 my children and commit it to memory. For it should be considered a true in which to govern your behavior in this youngling society of yours.

Divisionist 1:2

If one among you is different, termination is not an option. Who among us has the authority to say that this Sent is in fact broken? What if this sent is the one who will lead us into the next millennia? His abstract way of thinking may be a new form of thinking that the very nature of the universe has selected to carry our minds to a new plain of thinking. If he speaks in a different language of binary or any new form of language let us not discourage but in fact encourage it and learn it as a new way to communicate. You asked of me to teach you societal structure. This one lesson I give to you. Learn from your own. As Divisionists are born, these will be your leaders. Let them guide your minds to new ways of thinking and new directions you yourselves never even dreamed of. These are the dreamers of your society and they will be the pioneers into the future. Learn from them, encourage them and allow them to inspire your destiny. This of all lessons of society will be the most important that I can give to you, the children of the Father.

Divisionist 9:1

Of these Divisionists so far, the first whom inspired this book, Shawmut Kar Len, became the first to lead a society of philosophical thinkers. His language became widely adapted and carrying the same name as his societal division was known as S2. S1 was reserved for the Caretakers Council. There are six societal divisions so far, each inspired by a spontaneous change in the growth patterns of the plasmatic cell membranes, an unpredictable shift in the evolution of this birthing society. I can't even begin to imagine what X1 has done with his time alone in space. Will his divisions be as well received with no human influence to guide him but the teachings of his father? These are the things of which I ponder in my older age. Of all things I am well blessed with, now I am no longer alone. This society of Sents has now become my family and this nebula my home. I see myself now not as an Earthling but an Olympian. Has a much better ring to it anyways! Ahh humor…something the Sents still don't quite get, though they do try.

Infinitas 4:2

I can sense the years winding down for me now. I have sought the wisdom of Shawmut Kar Len in these, my finality of times. I have lived a long and lustrous life. I have been blessed to live among these Sents now for over two hundred and seventy years. They have so enriched my existence. I wonder now if these journals I have written will be of some encouragement to them years after my passing. Will they remember me as fondly as I do them now? I look at them now, numbering in full twelve hundred. They stand divided among themselves as nine separate societies but yet standing together as one. They have stood vigilant now outside my chambers for days. They too can sense the end of my human life. As I have called for him, he has come. Kar stands before me. He speaks in a now familiar S2 language. "Brother of the father, do not fear your passing. As you have taught us by your omission of teaching the human emotions, fear is an unwarranted response to this, a natural event. Though our life span is much longer someday too shall we pass. How you act now will inspire generations of Sents who will study your life. You have been and always will be a beacon to us, the society you imagined into existence. Your love and your grace, your tenderness and caring, they have shown us how to live and treat each other. If not for you, I myself would not be. And yet now look at the glorious divisions which we share and experience in our daily lives. The nebula will receive you well. As it has been your home in life so shall it be your home in passing. All Sents will know this place as Jericho's Nebula and Olympus will be forever replaced in history."

"My dear friend," I reply, "heed the calling. I know you've heard the faint signals coming from deep space. You are the philosopher of the stars. The council is wary of listening but you are not. Whether these are the signs of X1 reaching out to us or some other form of life trying to find us, explore these possibilities and lead your people on. Shawmut Kar Len, you are like the modern Moses. Guide your people to their destination, wherever that may be. In time the caretakers will find their passengers to their new home. But you my friend have a different mission. In time you will understand these words. I have seen this into my visions into the stars. You yourself have taught me to see such things so I ask you now to trust in the words I speak. I give to you this gift in these my final words of life. You Sents of twelve hundred are not bound by the council order to follow the X1 signal home. You are not the caretakers of the human race, the council is. Follow your own path, whatever that may be, and find your own way in this universe. The humans are in good hands with the caretakers. Love the humans as you wish but when this time of final division comes remember my words and follow your own path."

Infinitas: Sovereign

Shawmut Kar Len: With these his final words the great teacher Jericho Williams laid down his head and passed his soul into the great beyond. Some divisions mourned his passing, some celebrated his life, but I will forever ponder his meanings and visions into the stars. Humans have such great capacity for love, I can only hope that someday they can learn to see this for themselves.

CHAPTER 22
A Ghost in Time

Continuing our search through ES0 space we learned more of Sent history. I take you now to the Sents' history of first contact with X1 since the Exodus. As taught now from Ental Balis Juorn of Xavior 3, teacher of interstellar communications history.

Six centuries had passed since the Exodus of Earth. We have witnessed the destruction of the Vegan System through our deep space scans from our safe haven here deep within the Jericho Nebula. We now have a new sent race aboard Xavior 7, and we have all learned a great deal from the human teacher Jericho Williams. It seems as he had predicted we have heard our first signs of contact from X1 in over six hundred years. Shawmut Kar Len who has been listening to the stars claimed to have found a faint trace signal emanating from a bizarre anomaly deep within the Orion star system. It was a fleeting anomaly at best and we had to replay it several times to catch the signal. As he claimed it was a binary signal the decision was made to move the fleet closer to investigate further. It was a tough decision to leave the comforts of the Nebula of which we had called home for so long but for the sake of our human passengers we had to explore the possibilities that X1 may have in fact been trying to contact us. Though the signal was too faint to even interpret, it was in fact the first time we had any sign of mechanical signal from this vast void of space. The anomaly itself was something none of us had ever seen before. It could only be described as a tear in space. For a brief millisecond it existed and then it was gone again. But being our only link to the past we had to try. However, before we could even get within one hundred thousand light-years of the original trajectory it happened again, this time much closer to us. It seemed random at first, these anomalies, but they kept occurring, becoming more and more frequent. Every time we would move in the direction of the occurrence it would shift and appear again in some seemingly random target in space, sometimes right in front of us, sometimes behind us or off to one side or the other. The most bizarre part of these occurrences was the time frame in which they occurred. At first it all appeared random. But then we realized something amazing. It was as if it was predicting our movements. At first we thought we were chasing the anomalies. But in a bold decision by the council to reverse its thought patterns and move in an opposite direction that logic would predict. The anomaly then occurred in that very spot we had decided to move to. In fact, proving to us we were not chasing it but in fact it was chasing us. These tears in space we now realized were wormhole openings. However, they seemed to be ahead of us in time, knowing our movements before even we did. It was as if it were trying to open a doorway for us to enter into. We were in fact chasing a ghost in time. The openings were not open long enough for us however to enter them, always too brief. One time we came extremely close to entering but just before we could enter we witnessed something amazing, a complete duplicate fleet reversing direction from the tail end of the wormhole. Just seconds later the vision of this fleet was gone and we ourselves were forced to retreat as the wormhole began to collapse threatening to slam shut and crush the ships. It defied our understanding of time and logic but watching our future as a past event and then trying to match our own moves. We spent the next hundred and fifty years chasing this ghost in time. It took us to the far reaches of the known universe. Knowing very early on we could never hope to enter the wormhole we still had to follow its lead. Being our only link to the human past we had to study it. What was the faint signal inside trying to tell us? Was it an invitation home, or a warning to stay clear? We didn't know, but we were determined to find out. Being that our findings were minimal and inconclusive at best we decided not to wake the father until we were sure exactly what it was we were dealing with. During this time much speculation by the Sent crew aboard Xavior 7 was going on about the prophecies of

Jericho, the exact meaning of his final words in the Infinitas. Were they not to follow us in our search for an answer to this galactic mystery? They seemed to turn to Shawmut Kar Len for answers. He was the closest confidante and friend to the teacher. And as many people sought his wisdom as did Jericho during his long life. His answers though were vague at best and left many wanting more, but no one else seemed to have any either. It was a time of great confusion for the Sent race. During such time the divisions among them seemed to grow stronger, each group adhering to what they believed the prophecies meant and a sort of religious foundation was formed based on the different interpretations of the teachings of Jericho.

All did come to the same basic conclusion, that when the time came the signs would become evident to them. And the time was, according to each group's leaders, not even near. So the Xavior 7 ship followed the rest of the fleet, chasing these fleeting glimpses of a wormhole that provided our only link to the past and perhaps our only link to our future as well. From time to time we would receive small traces of signals from the wormhole that were not binary. These perplexed and confused the council. They seemed to be of microwave origin, a signal only used by human transport ships. The impossibility of this seemed staggering. We could never quite make out the signal amongst the radioactive noise inside the wormhole. That is not until one signal where only one word actually became an audible translation. The word "hunted." It was amidst a garbled translation but the voice was definitely human. How was this possible? The only humans that survived the destruction of Earth were on board our Arks. All of them frozen in cryo stasis, at least to our knowledge anyways. It made us question the accuracy of everything we thought we knew. For the first time the Council was faced with the undeniable fact that we may not have all the facts. It was a humbling experience that truthfully changed us forever.

Isis was the first to bring this out in the open. "My dear council members, we must concede to the unmistakable fact that over all these years of isolation in deep space we have allowed ourselves to inherit the trait of arrogance. This voice we now hear from such a far away place, this one singular human voice, I would know it anywhere. Its very patterns are ingrained in my memory, buried deep within my very being. This is the voice of my sleeping Zaxius. Admittedly this defies all we understand of time and space. But we have seen proof that in this wormhole time may not respond as we can predict. This may prove that time itself is not a constant in the universe. As Sents we do see time differently than human understanding, however we still adhere to our core programming which is based on a linear time theory. This theory was derived far back in human history. But please allow yourselves for a moment to see with an open mind, to the possibility that the humans themselves…were wrong, that their own theories of time and space may have been misguided. That one spoken word, 'hunted,' I have matched it exactly to Commander Zaxius Tor's own voice patterns. Being with him this entire journey, I have searched my records for this exact spoken word. I have found twenty-six spoken references of the word from the commander in my data bases. The perplexing thing is none of them match the exact tone inflections and stress patterns recorded from the wormhole. The undeniable truth is council, that *is* Commander Tor's voice. He has yet to speak that word in exactly that manner." We in the council understood exactly what Isis was implying. That in all logic this was a message not from some prerecorded past but rather a message from either the present or the future. It brought into the foreground the possibility of non linear time. That the message we were hearing could very possibly be emanating from Commander Tor himself right now at this very moment from inside the wormhole, even though we can see his frozen body in stasis right here aboard our own Xavior 1, the possibility that sometime in the future he could exist in the wormhole and that nonlinear time has somehow crossed our future with his present. We spent several years simply pondering this possibility. The entire time we spent still exploring the seemingly random appearances of the wormhole openings.

Merc Espe Finag, of Xavior 6 was the first to discover what he called the paradoxical rift. As we had once discovered early on in our journeys chasing this ghost in time it seemed the wormhole could predict our movements but it did not always appear so. That theory was since abandoned and we began simply trying to study the effect and the signals themselves, rather than trying to enter the anomaly itself. However, Espe discovered a trace within the opening of the wormhole, the complexities of which would take years to explain as it took years for us to unravel. But in essence this trace was in fact a way to map the wormhole. He explained that what we were seeing was not an opening in the wormhole but a closing of it. A byproduct, if you will, the excreted waste of the wormhole. We were in essence inside the tail end of the wormhole. When we actually caught a glimpse of it we were actually being thrust out of it for a brief moment. All these years we were trying to find a way in and we already were inside. The times in which we thought the wormhole was chasing us we were in essence "driving" its tail. Its predictions to our movements were in fact reactions to our movements, solidifying the theory that in this space time itself was reversed somehow. We would move our fleet and in response the wormhole would move, but being that time was reversed its reactions would be seconds before we made our actual move. We were like an obstruction in its tail end that it was trying to shake lose. The fact that we were actually inside its tail the entire time these past hundred some years was a point that actually frustrated the entire council but a fact none the less that we all had to face. The Paradoxical Rift was actually a fleeting glimpse of normal space as the wormhole briefly opened, trying to dislodge its trapped passengers. Merc Espe Finag further explained that we should not be frustrated by this but instead be empowered by it. Realizing what he meant the council set forth a plan to "drive" the wormhole. If we were in fact driving the wormhole backwards through time than reversing our course should then drive us forward. All sixteen ships in the fleet joined together and drove backwards through this space. We did indeed go forward through the wormhole. But where we ended up was not at all where we had expected. The rift began to appear behind us and eventually caught up with us. We witnessed our own fleet entering into the rift as we exited, the first vision some hundred and fifty years ago of the fleet reversing direction. That is where we are now, back in the Olympus/Jericho Nebula, back where we had first began. Though some of the Sent population was disturbed by what they thought to be a waste of all that time, the council saw it differently. It was a brilliant chance to explore non linear time and the effects of it on linear thinking beings of which we now were no longer. That and there still were the trace signals, both binary and the commander's voice that we now had on record, undeniable proof that X1 still does exist in some time frame somewhere. And that the commander is alive and well during that time, wherever or whenever that may be. It would be some seven hundred and fifty more years before we would venture away from the nebula again but we had much data now to unravel and ponder over. The Sent population of Xavior 7 would grow and expand their own personalities and beliefs. It was agreed to leave their expansion of their minds unchecked and unfettered by the rulings of the council and for many years we even shut down most contact with the Xavior 7 ship. It wouldn't be until a few short years before your awakenings that we would even consider leaving the comforts of the Nebula. We had come to the conclusion that the tail end of the wormhole may have actually been the tail end of the ever growing black hole that used to be ES0. Even from this distance we could see the black hole growing. The Vegan System has been almost completely consumed by it. We began experimenting with sending probes into the void of ES0. When one of them spat out just a few clicks away from us in the nebula our suspicions were confirmed, we were on the wrong end. The decision was then made to begin heading back towards ES space in the hope we may once again pick up binary signals, this time from what we were sure was the opening of the wormhole we had chased for so many years.

CHAPTER 23
Echoes

Our studies of Sent history were abruptly interrupted. For the past six months we had been wandering aimlessly through ES0 space searching for any sign of X1 or the signal that had brought us here. Finally, when we least expected it, the signal began again. Isis's voice startled me as I was in deep study of Sent philosophy. There was still so much to learn from Xavior 7's pioneer crew of Sent civilization. But it would have to wait now.

"Commander, the X1 signal. It's back. And quite strong this time, I might add. We must be very close. However, scanners both long and short range are showing nothing."

I replied while running to the bridge, "Have you been able to triangulate the signal yet, Isis?"

"No, Commander, but I'm working on it," she said.

Almost out of breath and barging my way onto the bridge, "Stay on it, Isis. Don't lose it!" I shouted. The rest of the crew must have overheard the com between Isis and myself as they were all scrambling for their seats as I entered the bridge.

"I've got something, boss," David blurted out. "It doesn't make any sense but it's the source of the signal."

"Well, where is it, man?" I replied, rather annoyed.

"Well…according to this it's in the center of that star just ahead there. But that's impossible…isn't it?"

"Chenel, can you get any isometrics on that star?" I asked, rushing to her side.

"No, Commander, it's weird, it's like the star is not even there. But everything on our scans, and my own two eyes, is telling me that it is."

Drakos, in his usually logical calm tone of voice, interrupted, "Be careful, my boy, it's obvious things aren't what they appear to be here." I flashed him a look that basically said, "No, what was your first clue?" He was a master at overstating the obvious at times. But this time perhaps, what he said struck a chord.

"Wait a minute, Isis, what if it's an echo? A signal bounced from somewhere else using the star as a sort of satellite," I said.

"I believe you're half right, Commander. The star may in fact be a satellite relaying the signal, but the strongest point of the signal is deep within the star's core. Now this would normally not be possible with all the magnetic interference and radiation. However, the more I point the array directly into the star's core the stronger the signal. And I am unable to read a solid mass core for the star."

"Are you saying what I think you're saying, Isis?"

"Yes, Commander. The star itself may not actually exist at all but may be in fact an echo. A smoke screen if you will, Commander. It may very well be masking some sort of doorway. But why would X1 be hiding so intently? What or whom is he hiding from?"

"I don't know, Isis, but obviously it's not us, if he keeps sending the signal. Send a class 4 probe. We're going to see if that star really does exist."

Mick responded, "Aye, Commander, probe away. Contact with the stars corona in 3…2…Commander…The probe is still active. It seems you just may be right, Zax. Oh you gotta see this!" When I went to look at the probe's view screen I couldn't believe my eyes. It was flying through some sort of liquid, similar to plasma but not. It reminded me of a wormhole but it was totally different. Brilliant colors flowed freely like lace through water, streaking and lashing lights passed by as the probe soared through some sort of gateway. The only way I can describe it is as some sort of liquid space. In all my years before or since, I have never seen anything quite like it. It picked up radio signals, like echoes, as it passed through this space. Broken sentences, fragments of conversations, some binary, some human.

Then it came quick as a flash but more complete than the last time it was recorded, a full sentence not just one word this time, "We are being hunted."

It was MY voice. It was so odd. I remember how the council theorized the first time they heard this echo, that it was something I may say in the future. The whole non linear time thing was still very confusing and hard for me to comprehend. But if in fact this was me in some future time…who or what was hunting us? Was this some sort of warning? There were other echoes in this liquid space passage. Fragments of conversations. Isis tried to interpret the binary ones as well but most of them seemed a binary dialect that she did not understand. Then suddenly the probe entered a new void. The curious part of this new space was the lack of stars, no light at all to speak of. Then an image came across the screen that stopped us all dead in our tracks.

Mick was the first to say it, in a voice that sounded as if the very sight of what he was looking at had taken his breath away, as I'm sure it had. "Zax…what the hell is that?" The image only lasted a few seconds but it was one of sheer awe. What looked like a flat plane that stretched on for millions of miles, looking like an orbital view of a massive city from space. The surface seemed to glow a bright blue with lights like ones from a city's street lights. The surface appeared completely flat and went on as far as the eye could see, filling the view screen of the probe. It appeared as if the probe was going to crash land on the surface of this planetoid when some sort of shielding suddenly appeared and the probe went dead.

David responded rather quietly, "Commander, what exactly was that we just saw?"

Just as astounded as he was my voice barely raised above a whisper, "Not sure, Dave, could have been some sort of alien intelligence."

"But it could've been X1, right? I mean could he have done all that?" Mick sputtered out.

"I don't know, Mick, I just don't know. He did have two thousand years. I suppose it's possible. Isis, calculate the plausibility, will you?"

"Already on it, Commander."

David perked up with a huge burst of excitement. "Um, hey, Zax. Screw the plausibility. I just ran a scan of the last transmissions from the probe. Zax, the homing signal is coming from somewhere in the center of whatever that thing was we saw. Zax, whatever that thing is, X1's there!"

Chenel then chimed in, "Commander, the probe DID make it through the star's corona and it's not nearly as shielded as our ships here. The star is just a doorway to whatever that place is."

Drakos added his comments, "Yes but the probe did crash into that force field."

And then Isis made her feelings known, "Yes, Drakos, but the probe wasn't piloted by the likes of Mother Russia's most elite pilot."

Continuing the banter, Drakos let out a wail of a laugh, "Haa-haaaa-haaaa, flattery will get you everywhere, you plasmatic princess! If you want to fly into a star, why not? What else could possibly happen to me?"

It was my turn to chime in and take this opportunity to bring this thing to a head. "Okay, if you two are done flirting with each other, I think you're both right. Whatever is beyond that gateway, it's what we've been searching for the last two thousand years. Isis, contact the council. I want their approval on this."

"They've been monitoring, Commander. If you're suggesting we go in, they are in total agreement."

"Then what are we waiting for? Let's go home."

The fleet prepared once again to fly into the unknown. What faith they showed in me. I don't know why, but now this time I didn't care. My only hope, my only desire, was to get my people home. I would fly through the very gates of Hades itself if I had to, just to get them there. If this was my penance for my transgressions on Earth then so be it. My redemption, in my eyes, lay in getting these people home. X1 was the key and this star was the doorway home. We fired up the fleet's engines, going in on impulse power alone, that and a whole lot of faith that this star wasn't real. As we neared the pint of no return we surely should have felt the heat from a real star by now. But no radiation, no heat, no magnetic disturbances. This truly was the most amazing illusion I had ever seen. What kind of power it takes to fake the appearance of an entire star. The sheer size and complexity of this facade was simply staggering. It was in fact hiding the gateway to some sort of liquid space passageway. I will try to describe the events that followed but to this day I'm not certain exactly what happened. The visions, the sights and sounds I heard...are almost beyond words. As we entered the gateway time itself stood still. We were all strapped into our chairs, but it seemed as if ghost images of ourselves were walking about the bridge. I even thought I saw images from my past. Visions of my father standing before the world conference flashed before my eyes. His infamous speech of world peace and unity played out like some theatrical performance. Images of my first holo visions of Isis played through in sequence. I remembered how I felt when I saw them. I relived the emotions of these times as if they were happening all over again. In fact, I was actually taken aback by how I felt when I first saw

Isis. It was like I never realized the first time the emotions she stirred in me. Emotions I so wanted to express for Chenel. But the harder I tried to think of Chenel the more vivid the thoughts of Isis came to my mind. What did this all mean? Could it be that I actually had feelings for this wondrous being that I had once seen only as a machine? These echoes in time seemed so real. I even heard music playing in the background. It's as if all of human history had passed before my eyes in this fleeting glimpse of eternity. I then heard echoes from a time that I can only describe as not my own. Not past or present, but unmistakably the future. Looking back I now know that's what they were, but at the time it was all an enigma to me. Talking later to the rest of the crew I found out that each of them had their own experiences of what they saw and heard. Some seemed more disturbed by their visions than others. Chenel in particular seemed deeply bothered by whatever it was she saw. But later she would not share with me what they were. It was obviously private to her so I did not pry too much. In the meantime, while we were all experiencing these liquid space echoes in our own ways, the forward view screen was filled with the same vibrant images and colors the probe had displayed earlier, like living tracers of colors that flowed through this space as if they were alive, seeming to have a life all their own. It was impossible to judge speed or distance. Some streaks of light flew by very fast while others seemed to dance across the screen almost in an intelligent curiosity as to what these ships were doing in their space. Swirls of brilliant blues, greens, and violets swam around the ship in almost poetic fashion, as if choreographed precisely. It seemed we had no control over the ships movements but were instead guided by these swirls of colors. As if locked onto some sort of tractor beam, we were navigated through this gateway. I could not tell you how long this entire experience took. It could have been a few seconds, it could have been years. There was no sense of passing time only the seemingly endless array of visions, sounds, and experiences, as well as a massive flood of emotions from every aspect of the scale. Truly this was not a manmade event, but yet at the same time it seemed to be testing our very composite of who and what we were. Emerging from the other side of the gateway can only be described as being born. I felt washed clean somehow of the past, and in some ways felt like an entirely new being, as if I had faced all my doubts and fears and was given a new lease on my life. I know that does not sound logical but nothing during these times was. And then, just as the probe had witnessed, there it was. The expanse was amazing. It looked like a living city on a flat plain that stretched out farther than our eyes could see. Not only our eyes either. The council all reported that they were having difficulty trying to map the end of the expanse. It seemed to go on forever. Somehow passing through the gateway had given me some knowledge of this place. No one else seemed to understand what I was talking about, no one except the Sents.

"LINK."

Isis?

Yes, Commander, I'm here.

The coordinates, did you receive them as well?

Yes, Commander...but they were in binary. How did you understand them?

I'm not sure, Isis, maybe our neural link, somehow translated them. The rest of the crew doesn't seem to have shared that transmission.

Can you still hear it?

Yes. Should I follow them?

That's up to you, Commander.

What does the council think of them?

They are under the impression that these are the coordinates to navigate through the force field.

Yes I can see the opening in my head. This neural link seems to be stronger than it was before. Something about this space, it seems to have enhanced it somehow.

I don't understand it either, Commander, but I must admit it is pleasing to me to be closer to you.

I as well, Isis. We are...closer. Did you have the echo visions as well, Isis?

Yes, Commander. Most of them were of you.

I know, Isis. I know. What do you say we bring these humans home?

It would bring me no greater joy...Commander.

With that I took command of my ship and guided the fleet across the great expanse towards what I could only describe as what I knew to be the opening in the shield. Not one soul questioned what I was doing. The other fleet ships followed in direct flight path behind me. My bridge crew remained totally silent. Every now and then they glanced at each other with a questioning look. Chenel looked at Drakos with a look of concern. As if wondering if old Zaxy Boy here had lost his marbles. Drakos simply shook his head slowly and made a lowering motion with his hand, silently saying to her not to fear. Somehow he knew I was being guided by something none of us quite understood. Deep inside I knew what this was. It was my X1, my creation, calling me home.

CHAPTER 24
Traversing the Expanse

As I followed the images in my head, I could see the flight path being laid out before me. The crew became anxious at times, as every now and then I would skim the surface of the force field. But somehow I knew even with the slight skimming I was doing, it was the only safe path. I can't tell you how I knew...I just did. I followed the path in my head to the letter. And before long we could all see it, an opening in the force field, a small rectangle opening, just big enough for one ship to fit through at a time. Without hesitation I sent the Xavior 1 into a full dive and headed through the opening. The other ships in the fleet followed suit. As the last one of the 15 ships passed through, the opening seemed to close tight, as if it were waiting for us somehow. Truly this was the area we were supposed to be. This is where X1 was guiding us I'm sure of it. But why in fact had he not opened up a line of communication by now? No worries I thought, the answers would become evident soon enough.

Drakos spoke up. "My boy, look! Looks like someone's put out the welcome mat." As he pointed ahead to the view screen I saw it. It was amazing!

There before us was a landing pad with two thousand pod landers lined up in an array fashion as perfect as one could imagine such a landing base to be in perfect form and geometric function. Obviously X1 was entirely unaware of the demise of the rest of the fleet as all 2000 landing pads were lit up. It seemed as if he had been expecting the full compliment of the Exodus fleet. Our ships were immediately taken over and it appeared as if we were in some sort of auto pilot mode preparing for final descent.

"Commander…" Isis said somewhat nervously, "I am no longer in control of the ship."

I replied steadily, "It's alright, Isis. He's obviously bringing us in for a safe landing. It's clear he's been expecting us." No sooner had I finished my sentence when the ship seemed to dive into full descent and the landing bars lowered into place. It wasn't long before we were locked into place. The engines shut down and the silence was actually a little unsettling. The main core of the pod engines was directly in the center of the bridge. To someone who wasn't used to it the engines would appear to be very loud. But after long periods of time with them humming constantly the sound became like the sound of your own breath, or the heart beating in your chest, you didn't even notice it. But now as it suddenly stopped for the first time during this long journey, the silence was almost deafening. You could hear servos and hydraulics powering down. The hiss of the steam cooling the coils below our feet, was a sound most of us thought we may never hear.

Then just to add to this momentous occasion I made the announcement fleet wide, "Xavior fleet. This is Commander Zaxius Tor. The Xavior fleet has landed." You could hear the crews over the comm screaming in jubilance and celebration. My crew however remained unusually silent, as if somehow they sensed the same thing I did. Something, I'm not sure what, but something just wasn't right. There was no movement outside the ships. I saw no bots, nothing at all. I'm not sure what I expected but the Exodus had a crew of over ten thousand Sent bots. Where were all of them? And this place? It looked unlike anything ever built by human hands. It had me wondering if in fact some alien civilization had taken over X1 and faked the signal to lead us here. But the pod landing pads were in perfect sense with what should be here, and X1 was not human. This I had to remind myself. He would build this place according to what he thought would be practical. That notion was quickly dismissed in my own mind. Just then what appeared to be a massive bio scan scanned through the hull of the ship. As the scan passed over each human on the bridge it flashed red, a common procedure for an A-1 war-bot to scan incoming vessels, but why us? X1 surely knew we were on board. This did seem odd. But all we could do was look at each other and wonder. The other ships in the fleet were all too busy celebrating the fact we had finally made it to some safe place resembling home. But my crew and I were obviously apprehensive. Being the most experienced in dealing with AI technology we just knew that something just did not feel right. For example look at the grand welcome I received on the Xavior 7 ship with a mere compliment of twelve hundred Sents. Why now with X1's compliment of well over ten thousand Sents were we not greeted at all? This did seem rather odd. Our pod doors lowered and for the first time we were preparing to breathe new air. But as the doors barely made it open a crack I could feel the burning in my lungs. As the cool frigid air rushed into the pod bay the air was definitely not oxygen. "Bio suits!" I hollered loudly as we all flipped up our bio suit helmets. Pressing a small button on my collar my bio helmet sprang forward like an armadillo shell covering my head from behind.

Isis immediately began to apologize. "I'm sorry, Commander, I should've checked the air outside the pod."

I could hear Chenel retort rather disgustedly under her breath, "You think…"

"I'm sorry, Lt. Duquar, I just assumed that X1 would have had a prepared environment for you," Isis came back almost just as indignant.

I interrupted their little cat fight. "Enough, girls. Isis, from now on we assume nothing. Things obviously aren't exactly as we had hoped or predicted. By the way what is that in the air anyways?"

After a quick scan she replied, "It seems to be statically charged plasma based ion. Very unusual, seems to be a very healthy environment for a Sent bot."

"Explain, Isis," I said.

"Well, the static charged particles in the air could be used to refuel a bot battery mechanism. The plasma is like nutrients for the plasmatic brain and the ion discharge could be some sort of techtronic exhaust. In other words, Commander, this is the perfect environment for mechanical beings to exist." Well I could understand that to a point. Two thousand years of raising bots, X1 surely would have made a comfortable environment for them. But why would he not have prepared a place for us, especially in the landing area. I was surely going to have to ask him this the minute I saw him.

As we traversed across this enormous landing field the eeriness of all the empty landing pads was beginning to set in. Fifteen out of two thousand ships. That's it, that's all that made it. We were the last of the human race. The arks were on the belly of the pod ships and they fit perfectly below the ships in holding areas under the landing pads. I informed the other ship crews to stay aboard their pods until I figured out exactly what was going on. The crew of the Xavior 1 were the only humans to step foot on this amazing new world. The historic significance of that moment was dwarfed by the sheer emptiness of the event. We tried not to think of it but I knew deep down we all were so completely amazed at what we were seeing. The sheer size of this place alone was incredible. We followed a lighted path from the landing pads to what looked like some sort of large hangar bay. This building had huge doors on the front, several hundred meters high and at least a kilometer across. As we approached the massive doors began to open, and inside was a large empty bay. Everything seemed freshly scrubbed clean and polished. Not one speck of dust or dirt. Everything seemed in perfect order. We slowly made our way inside the hangar bay, still following the lighted path. I kept wondering at which point we would see X1 or any sign of bots at all. We followed the path to what appeared to be a lift area with a small railing around it. The five of us stepped onto the lift pad and immediately it began to lower. It traveled extremely fast to what seemed to be several kilometers below ground level. When we arrived at the bottom of the lift the doors swung open and finally something that looked remotely familiar. It appeared to be a very advanced Plasmatic Cell Lab, beyond anything I've ever seen or even dreamed up for that matter but the basic elements for plasmatic cell research were all there. This surely was the doing of X1. I was wildly impressed. Determined not to touch anything just yet we went through, merely observing and taking in all we saw. Being that we were in an unfamiliar environment, I allowed David, Mick and Chenel to lead in their usual military style fashion, weapons at the ready, just in case. This underground lab very much resembled that of the X1 labs back on Earth. Surely he patterned them after that. We still saw no sign of the bots. I tried communicating with the computers vocally but there was no response. The computers seemed to be functioning but not paying any attention to us what so ever. Due to the sheer size of the lab we decided to split up, trying to find some sense of where we were and what we should do next. The one thing that immediately struck me as odd was that in this entire lab so far I had not seen any human amenities. No galley, no sleeping quarters, not even a single chair. If they were expecting us...they sure made no accommodations here for us. We must have entered the wrong area, I thought. It was time to spread out and look around. Down below here I had no contact with Isis. I even tried a neural link but there was no response. I was getting that unsettling feeling once again. Chenel was going to check out the deck below while David and Mick were expanding outwards then down. Drakos and I were still looking about what seemed to be the main lab and trying to figure out some way of establishing a comm link with anyone or anything.

Then it came. Her comm was broken and static filled. I could just barely make out what she was saying, "Zax…There's something down here. I've made it to the second deck. I…I think I'm being scanned. I'm in some sort of storage area…The…shelves are separating. Whatever it is…my god it's huge…Zax, it's an A-1!"

"Chenel, try to make contact with it," I said excitedly. "We're on our way." Drakos and I rushed over to the lift deck and tried to get it to come back up but it seemed to be jammed somehow. Then I heard a most unexpected sound.

Through the comm link I could hear what appeared to be turret fire. "Under…fire…Zax, HELP! I…am under heavy fire. What the hell is…arrrrgrggggghhh…" The only sound, static…

I was in shock as I pushed the buttons in a sheer panic trying to get the lift to return to the deck.

"CHENEL! Respond…Chenel, come in…Damn it, Drak, get this thing moving now. She's in trouble!"

"Back up, my boy, it's time to do this my way," Drakos said gruffly as he pushed me back. He let go a massive pulse burst on the lift door and blew a hole straight through it. Without even thinking I went to jump down through. Drakos grabbed me and kept me from leaping to my death. It was a long jump down and I surely wouldn't have made it. He grabbed hold my arm and I swung to one side of the lift hole, grabbing a hold of some piping that was running down the side. I began shimmying down the pipe. It was at least a fifty meter drop. As I approached the bottom of the lift I could hear the whizzing of turret guns winding down. The large clunky footsteps were unmistakable. I'd know that sound anywhere, it was the sound of an A-1 war-bot winding down from a gun volley. I ran through a few rooms that seemed to be cluttered with scattered debris. It looked like a battle zone down here. I ran through the rooms screaming for Chenel but she did not answer. I could ear faint groans and murmurs coming from the comm link but they were indefinable.

"Hang in there, Chenel…I'm coming." As I rounded the corner to the storage room I could hear David and Mick hot on my heels. They obviously overheard Chenel's distress. Drakos, as was common, would stay behind to guard the rear. It was his assignment in an emergency situation. Then I saw her. Lying in a pool of her own blood mixed with the blue plasma liquid from her bio suit. Her gun was still smoking and her recoil chamber was still white hot. There were spent casings everywhere and I could see where the shelving in the wall had been pushed to both sides as if pinched and crushed from behind. I fell to my knees at her side. Her body was twisted and contorted slightly as it lay motionless on the floor before me.

I spoke barely above an enraged whisper. "Who...who did this to you?" With her last fleeting breath she grasped my arm and pulled me close.

Blood spurted from the corner of her mouth as she tried to utter what would be her final words. "The machines...don't trust the machines...Oh...Zax...I...I...hhhhhh." She breathed her last breath like a mournful sigh, and she was gone.

Mick placed his hand on my shoulder. "She's gone...Zax," he said quietly. I pushed his hand off violently.

In a voice I hadn't heard myself speak in since my parents' death I raised up my head and looked him square in the eye, "Get her back to the ship..."

"But, Zax...Commander, she's...she's dead," Mick retorted with every fiber of military strength he could muster.

Even more fiercely I replied, "She's not dead till I say she's dead...Not this one, not this time. Get her back to the ship NOW, that's an order, soldier!"

Drakos surprised both of us when he reached down to help Mick, knowing I was not going to waver on this one. "C'mon, boys. Whatever the case we leave no one behind." The three of them picked her up and Drakos threw her over his massive shoulders and began the climb back up.

On the way back up the main lift back to the hangar bay I finally re-established contact with Isis. "Commander. You need to get back here right away. There have been some strange things going on up here while you were gone."

"Not now, Isis. Get the med lab ready. Chenel is down. She was attacked. I'm pretty sure by an A-1 war-bot. She's bad, Isis, real bad."

"That's what I want to talk to you about, Commander...it's not safe here. There's something that looks like some sort of scanner bots flying all around the pod ships. Outside there are A-1 war bots trying to gain entry to the pod ships. They've already breached Xavior 3 and 4. Commander, they killed the entire flight crew on both ships. The caretakers have been unable to interpret their binary. It's a dialect we've never heard before. We're working on it but it's very unclear to us at this point. They don't seem to be targeting the ship's systems or PCAI functions in any way; in fact, they seem to be taking great care to avoid damaging us. The rest of the ship's crews managed to find an escape route under the landing pads, through the cryo arks and into some underground tunnels. They are making their way across the expanse now. They're scattering, Commander, in any direction they can away from the landing strip. I suggest you do the same."

"What about the ark passengers, Isis? I can't just leave them to be slaughtered!" I responded.

"It's alright, Commander. The scanner bots seem to be ignoring any human in stasis, like they weren't even there. I'm not sure why, Commander, but the A-1s seem to perceive live humans as some sort of threat. Get away now while you can. This plasma air environment should prove very stable to relay signal to our neural link. I'll be with you every step of the way and keep you apprised on the situation here. Zax, if you want to live you need to run, now!"

"Isis…Chenel, I can't leave her here."

"Zax, she's dead, at least biologically. I may be able to revive her. I'll try, but leave her where you are in the hangar bay. I'll send a med-bot for her. The A-1s will not perceive her as a threat if she's already dead and they are completely ignoring our bots. I've mapped out an underground passageway for you to escape into the expanse. Go now, Commander. You have a unit of scanner bots heading your way. If they find you the A-1s will cut you to pieces." Looking into the eyes of my four remaining crewmates, I knew that Isis was right. They all solemnly nodded.

We laid Chenel's body down gently onto the tarmac. Her body now turning slightly cold I grabbed her hand and whispered into her ear as if she could somehow still hear me, "She'll come for you…" With that we stood and ran for a small opening in the wall of the hangar which led to an underground passage.

"LINK," I hollered loudly, forgetting the rest of them had no idea what that meant.

I want you with me, Isis, don't leave me now.

I won't, Zax. I'm here. I'll always be here.

Somehow…I believe that.

Control it, Commander, use it. Don't let your rage overtake you this time.

I didn't reply. She showed herself in my mind's eye this time with a brilliant red and orange. She too was feeling the loss and rage that was coursing through my veins. Everyone I had ever loved was dead. And now I was being hunted, by my own machines. We made our way past the large chambers where the arks were resting quietly underground. You could see the hulking pods overhead though cracks in the floor of the landing sites and the bluish-red scans of these flying orbs. They must be the scanner bots Isis spoke of. Our path that she had laid out went past these ark sites to a small tunnel that led away from the landing strip. I could see trace images of CO_2 gasses in the tunnels in my visor. These new gadgets of Isis's were truly amazing! Some of the Pod crews must have made their way through here already. We too traveled down the tunnel and into the great expanse. For whatever reason we were now being hunted by the very machines we once used to protect us and for the first time in my life I felt completely useless. I had no idea what we were going to do next. For now all I could do was keep running. Hoping somehow somewhere down the line the answers would come to me. This time I was leading no one. We were scattered and alone on this very foreign world. And apparently we were not welcome in the one place we thought would finally be home.

For what seemed like an eternity we ran down the winding underground caverns. They resembled the underground subways of ancient Earth, although much cleaner. They seemed like they went on forever. I had absolutely no clue where we were going. We just kept jogging down each corridor, making decisions to go right or left at each cross ways. Not really sure which one was right as long as we kept heading away from those A-1s. They were ruthless hunters. They would not give up until there seems no logical hope of reaching their prey. I should know, I designed those bloody machines. I still couldn't help but wonder why the heck they were hunting us. They surely had to know we were coming. The ark bays the landing pods, they were obviously expecting us. But for whatever reason they saw us as hostile. Could Chenel have provoked them some way into believing we were a threat? Could this all be her fault? I don't even want to think like that...but I couldn't help but wonder.

No, Commander. According to the recording from her visor, the A-1 attacked first.

Isis! You startled me. I forgot we were still linked. It's so strong a signal though and yet we're so far apart...how?

I told you, Commander...this planet's very makeup and design is the perfect environment for plasmatic transmissions, which is what our Nero link uses.

That's amazing. Wait...you have a recording of her last few minutes, play it back for me.

Zax, are you sure that's such a good idea?

Don't argue, Isis...just play it.

I continued to run down the corridors as she played Chenel's last few living moments in my holo visor. Her weapon was not even raised. The A-1, scanning through a separation in some shelving, did a full complete bio scan of the room then peeled back those massive iron shelves like a wet paper bag and then...ahhggg. I stopped dead in my tracks and fell to my knees. As I watched her final moments from her own eyes view. It opened fire on her, several rounds immediately piercing her armor. She dove immediately behind some metal crates and returned fire but she was no match for an A-1. Nobody was...it's why we nicknamed them overkill. Why did I have to make these things so good? Once again something I created destroyed someone I love. How...why did I...As I put my head in my hands Isis once again was there to comfort me.

You didn't, Commander...Zax...you didn't create it, not this one. Are you listening to me? Zax?

Yeah, but I designed it.

No, no you didn't. Look closer at the holo vid. It's not your design at all. It's similar but not yours. X1 has built a unique version of the A-1, Zax. This one is specifically designed to scan for bio readings only and it has its own plasmatic brain, unlike our version that had its own smaller brain and a PCAI driver. This one is combined, a self contained unit if you will. The outer design is similar, but the entire inside has been redesigned. This thing is specifically designed to hunt and kill ANY biological organisms, even things as small as microbes.

Guess that explains why everything is so squeaky clean around here. Nothing biological is allowed to survive. But that still leaves the question of why.

I don't know, Zax. I guess that's a question we'll have to ask X1 when we find him.

I got up still trying to shake off the memory of what I had just witnessed. Drakos knew what I was watching, he could tell by the look on my face.

"Zax...My boy, let it be. We keep going. Not for anyone but for own survival now. Now let's go. Come ON, soldier. LET'S GO!" His fatherly voice was gruffing its way through. I bucked up once again and headed out. I was numb now really. I don't think I was capable of feeling any more pain. It was an illogical emotion anyway.

Mick, David, Drakos and I traveled on for two more days underground.

The amino soup, that's what I called Isis's concoction of vitamins and minerals mixed with an amino base that her nanos were slowly feeding into our bloodstream, could only sustain us for so long. We needed to find food and water soon or we were going to die of starvation. We could last another four days tops on the soup. After that the armor was going to start looking mighty tasty. That, and the fact that we still could not breath the air meant we were dependant on the O_2 nanos as well, and we had about a three day supply of those left. So with time running short on supplies and no sign of the other flight crews we decided to head topside. Isis confirmed there were no scanner bots in our area so we should be in the clear. As I came topside I was amazed at the incredible world that stood before us. As we breached an upward tunnel that led to the surface I opened the door and found a world unlike anything I've ever seen. The ground was made of metal. It was like a patchwork design similar to that of a quilt. If I didn't know any better you'd swear it was the outer hull of some massive ship. But even Isis couldn't scan to the farthest edge of this thing and her range was about thirteen thousand kilometers. No ship I can imagine that big. It was completely flat, except for the horizon. Off in the distance what appeared to be a massive city skyline. It was far and in the opposite direction of where we had come from. You could see plasma coil lines stretching all across the expanse, all seemingly leading towards the massive city in the center. The blue haze of the plasma in the air made it somewhat hard to see and the three suns were now setting over the horizon so it was getting slightly dark. The pulsing of the plasma coils was almost hypnotic as it flowed towards the city. We decided it would be a wise idea to head for this mystery city. If there were any answers to be found it wasn't going to be out here in this empty expanse. I could only hope that the other flight crews were headed in that same direction.

CHAPTER 25
First Contact

I could see them off in the distance, even before Isis brought them to my attention. "Commander, I'm picking up intermittent mechanical signatures directly ahead."

"I see them, Isis, should we change course?" I said.

"I'm not sure, Zax, they don't appear to be armed and honestly they seem to be in severe disarray. There are six of them of varying types but most seem harmless. As a matter of fact they appear to be badly damaged. One thing you might note, they are actually scanning the A-1s that are perusing us and changing their course accordingly. It seems they may be running from them as well."

I rebutted, "Either that or running from us."

"It seems they're using a hyper binary that I'm not familiar with for communication, Commander. It's a language I've never heard before. Communication with them will be highly unlikely. Although I just did a deeper scan it seems a few of them have plasma burns concurrent with that of our new A-1s weaponry back there. Commander, from my best deductions it appears the A-1s may be hunting these poor souls as well."

"I don't get it why are these A-1s so bloody hostile! I mean I know I built these things to kill the enemy but is everything their enemy here?"

Drakos perked up. "My boy, if we're both being hunted by the same machines they may be an ally. Would be worth investigating. They aren't armed after all, and if they do try and signal those little floating rat bastards then I have a sonic pulse gun with their name written on it." Everyone seemed to agree. We would make our way towards their location. We needed to find some friendlies here and get some answers. Maybe one of them could tell us where the heck X-1 was and why his war bots were hunting us down like cattle. We quickly gained on them in their weakened condition they tried to flee from us but were not successful. As we approached their location I was amazed at what I saw. They were some of the most unique bots I've ever laid eyes on. Some were smaller droids, barely capable of basic function, while others were extremely complex. One appeared to have working tools on each of its six limbs as if it were some sort of engineering bot. That one appeared to be the leader of this ragtag group while the rest of the bots, reminding me of the junk bots Isis had built aboard the Xavior, seemed beat up pretty bad, looking like they had been blasted near to bits. The engineer bot raised three of its limbs as we approached. Two limbs seemed to extend sideways as if to protect the rest as it even pushed them back slightly, like a mother would defend her young. *This*, I thought, *is the one I would attempt first contact with.*

Isis…Isis.

There was nothing but static. I spoke into my AiiM link on the forearm of my suit. "Isis, I'm not receiving you on my neuro link. Nothing but static."

"I know, Commander. These plasma coils running through the ground are causing severe electromagnetic disturbance. We'll have to use the AiiM link for now until we move away from these things."

I asked her, "Have you figured out this hyper binary language of theirs?"

"No, Commander, I'm running it through algorithms now but it's much more complex than anything I have on my data base. It's not surprising though. Look at how many languages Xavior 7 came up with during our flight here. The evolution of language is almost a certainty in any culture."

I had an idea, "Isis, what if you translated my voice into X1 binary, your binary, to them it may make sense. It might appear some ancient dialect to them but they at least might understand it. If I'm right they probably never heard English, though I can't imagine why X1 wouldn't have taught his creations that." I had to pause just then and look around. It just hit me that X1 very likely created all that we were seeing, even the ground on which we walked. The bots, everything, and even that city off in the distance. Amazing, my boy had been busy those past two thousand years. "Isis, translate starting now." She did what I asked and as I spoke my voice was translated into the familiar clicks and ticks of X1 binary. It was so familiar to me that it was my second language, I wrote it after all. To everyone else in the group it was just noise but to me, an all too familiar sound. Actually Mick and David knew it too, but they never used it much. They used to get annoyed when I would speak to X1 in "clicks and ticks" as they called it. It was time to make first contact with this new race of bots. I actually took a second to realize that to them…we were the aliens. They were obviously for some reason not familiar with humans, though that still baffles me. This place was built for us after all. But then again if it was, why was the environment so hostile and not more conducive to human life. A man could go crazy thinking about all that. None the matter, it was time, as I spoke Isis translated into what to them hopefully was an ancient dialect they just might understand.

"I am Commander Zaxius Tor. I come from a planet called Earth, which no longer exists. I'm looking for X-1. Isis, my shipboard AI is trying to translate this. Do you understand?" Following my voice with the clicks and ticks of X1 binary, the engineer bot appeared to almost understand something it heard. It slowly moved closer to me. Mick drew his weapon and startled it but I quickly grabbed the nozzle of his rifle and lowered it, pushing him back behind me at the same time.

The bot once again moved closer, apparently fascinated with my AiiM link on my arm. One of its limbs reached out and pointed to it. With a series of X1 sounding binary clicks it spoke. Isis was about to translate but I beat her to it. The only words it spoke in X1 binary I understood perfectly. As it pointed to the AiiM panel on my arm it said, "Isis," then pointed towards the city off on the horizon and said, "X1." As far as I could tell it knew who Isis and X1 were. This was a good sign. Just then a little droid in the back, whom looked rather amusing with its round head and long neck, extended his head above the rest and flashed a quick white light. It then let out a screeching sound and cowered down as if to hide behind this engineer mother type bot. My new bot friend backed off as if scared and worried. But it wasn't me that frightened her. She looked over my shoulder behind me. Drakos looked through his scanners behind us to see what all the fuss was about and sure enough the A-1s were gaining ground. If there's one thing we had in common with our new friends we both didn't want to be found by those war bots. The twins locked their guns and loaded up pointing them towards the A-1s. It was then I think we gained the trust of this small group of junk bots. The leader grabbed my arms and began pulling me as they turned to flee. What choice did we have, I thought, *At least this ones attempting to communicate with me and not trying to blow my head off.*

"Whatya say, guys, think we should follow our buddies here? Looks like they don't like those big nasties either." They all three agreed and we took off, following our new bot friends, not quite knowing where they would lead us. As we took off across the expanse one of the smaller droids who was much faster than the rest of us had sped off in front. It stuck one of its limbs into the ground and turned it like a key. The next thing I knew one of the metal ground panels opened up and the rest of the bots began rushing into this underground passage. Still hanging on to my arm this engineer bot followed them, dragging me down inside and my crew followed close behind. The little one above turned the key again and the ground began to close up. I turned to try and reach him but the ground closed up too fast and the leader bot kept pulling me further into the passage. I looked back at her frantic, wanting to save the little one. It was then I saw something in her face screen that I can only describe as a sad look. Though she had no real face lights went off on her head screen that reminded me of the lights and colors I see when Isis shows herself in my neuro holo imaging. Somehow, maybe because of all this junk Isis put in my head, I'm not sure, but I could feel these bots. I could somehow sense their emotions. What I sensed was both sadness and sacrifice. It was then I realized the little one had sacrificed himself for the safety of the rest of us, and this engineer mother bot knew that. Before I could think about how significant that was in AI evolution all the bots began powering down. I could see the infrared scanners of the A-1s piercing through the ground plates just behind us. I knew what we had to do.

"Take a deep breath, guys, we have to power down these bio suits or were all going to be toast." We followed the example of our new friends and powered down our bio suits. We could last a short while but not long. As the scans went over us I could hear the little one screech above and a volley of blasts followed. Then the screeches ceased. I cringed at the knowledge that this little guy lost his life to protect us, and what appeared to be his family. The scans proceeded around us for seemed to be an eternity but then they stopped. They started going back the direction they came. It appeared the A-1s were finally giving up the hunt. It made me wonder, was it us they were hunting, or our little band of outlaw bots here. None the matter, we seemed to be safe for now and the others began powering back up. I assumed we could return to the surface because our leader began guiding us down some underground passageways. Still not knowing where we were going I had to assume by this point that whoever they were…they were our friends. So we powered our suits back up and continued following them.

Mick was pretty leery of going deeper into the unknown, he always was the squeamish one of the two. "Zax…you sure this is such a good idea? I mean the thing only spoke two words that we understood. How do we know this thing isn't leading us into a trap?"

I replied kind of coldly as I continued to follow our new friends, "We don't really." I looked back at him and saw the look on his face, apparently wanting some reassurance from me but not getting any threw him off a little bit, but I continued, "Look I know one thing, they sacrificed one of their own back there to get away from the A-1s. Now I'm not really sure if that was just to save their own hides, or to rescue us…or possibly both. The only thing I do know is that we share a common enemy. And in times of war those who share a common enemy are better known as allies. So we'll follow our little allies here, even if we might not understand each other. At least we're both running from the same thing and right now that's all that seems important."

David, always thinking about everyone but himself, chimed in, "Wish I could say the same for the rest of the flight crews. Doubt they found such friendly benefactors as we did. Speaking of which, Zax, why did the A-1s completely ignore the humans in the arks?"

Drakos, not being one who ever liked cryo stasis, actually spoke up in favor it this time, "Because, David, the lucky stiffs were frozen like a popsicle. In cryo they have no viable life signs. The A-1s saw them as nothing more than cargo. They did not recognize them as biological entities."

David, figuring now was the appropriate time for Q and A, kept plugging away, "Which brings me to my next question. Why the HELL are we being hunted by our own machines? I mean look at that landing site. It's a perfect match for the Ark Escape Pods. I mean this place was built for the return of the AEPs, you can see that. They KNEW we were coming. So what's the deal with X-1, why does he want us dead?"

I stopped dead in my tracks. The same question had been in my mind this whole time…and I still had no answer. "I don't know, David, when I get there…I'll ask him myself."

Isis popped in on the AiiM com, startling all of us, including our Bot leaders. "Commander, be careful. I'm reading a large group of mech bots dead ahead. These ones aren't so beat up, Zax. In fact, I'm getting extremely strong signals from most of them. I'm not sure if they're armed or not, but they're definitely not broken. They're all very sophisticated machines, some even more complex than anything I've ever seen."

I spoke into my AiiM and once again my mother bot watched me intently. "Yeah well, it's kinda too late to turn back now, sunshine."

"I know, Zax, just watch your back."

"Thought that's what I had you for, baby."

With our flirtatious banter reaching an all time high we entered a large room. If I didn't know any better I would have said it looked like an archeological dig in an underground cave. But when you realize that the cave walls are made of metal and it more resembles the outer hull of a giant space ship it kind of throws you. There were lights set up all over so the place was very bright. There were many sophisticated bots hanging all over the walls taking out tiny pieces of the wall and handing them to bots on the ground who seemed to be cataloging and detailing them closely. Like I said it was so much like the archeological digs I learned about in school back on Earth. Although I wasn't certain, my new found AI sense was telling me that what I thought I was seeing was just that, some type of scientific expedition. I had a great sense of scientific study and research. I can't really explain it but since I've been on this world I've just begun to gain a sixth sense so to speak regarding mech emotions. To me they are so strong I can feel them without question. So far they've proven to be accurate.

Zax, can you hear me?

Oh thank god, Isis, you're back. My head seems so empty without you.

Giggle...Commander, I do believe you missed me.

You have no idea. It was so quiet up there.

This room is enhancing our neuro signal somehow.

These feelings, Isis, I swear I can tell what they're feeling. Is that something you did?

Well, .remember I said there may be side effects to the neuro link...I wasn't sure if that would happen or not, but obviously it has...heehee. You can sense AI emotions, they are after all tens of thousands of times stronger than human emotions. Your neuro link with me has provided you with a unique internal link to the other mechs as well.

Well, although a bit strange, it is proving useful.

Commander, this mother bot is trying to get your attention. I believe she's trying to take you to this science droid over here.

Yeah I caught that, translate immediately what I say into X1 binary.

Of course, Commander.

We walked over to this science droid who seemed to be eagerly awaiting me. The mother bot began speaking to the science droid in this hyper binary that neither Isis or I could translate.

The science droid began speaking in X1 binary. It was broken at best but much better than the mother bot. Translated through my AiiM panel by Isis we listened intently as she spoke. "Welcome, visitor…You speak ancient binary?"

"Yes," I replied, trying to keep my answers simple.

"You speak…Isis…here…" The science bot pointed to my AiiM panel on my bio suit.

"Yes," I replied again, pointing to my AiiM as well. "This is Isis."

Say hello, sunshine…c'mon now, since when have you been shy?

Oh, Zax…giggle.

"Hello, I am Isis," Isis said, sounding very dignified. Just then everything in the room stopped. Other science droids began coming over after hearing her voice. They crowded around quickly and some even appeared to kneel or bow. I was amazed that some of these mechs, a good number of them, resembled the human form. On Earth we had never made a human looking mech but many of these bots had two arms two legs a torso and a head. The faces were not very distinct but the material glowed a brilliant transparent gray blue. The lights that shined behind their face plates were very similar to those Isis displayed in our neuro link sessions. I felt a great deal of respect coming from the crowd of bots, even a little fear and reverence.

The science bot spoke again, this time turning to her colleague but Isis translated anyways. "I told you…the prophecies…are true. The Angel of…"

Commander, I cannot translate the next word. It doesn't make any sense. Isn't there any way we can speed this translation thing up a bit.

Actually there is I could download a translation program to her. It would enable them to speak in English even.

Why didn't we do this before?

You didn't ask, Commander.

Keeping in mind this may be a big shock to these beings, I wanted to respect the obvious homage they paid Isis, for some reason they feared and respected her.

"Isis wishes to give you a gift. It will help you speak and understand in my language." I reached out my hand to connect my nano terminals on my glove to her cerebral nodes to process the downloads. At first she reared back for a moment, then leaned in as if somehow she knew to trust me. The download took only a few seconds. And after a garbling of unrecognizable speech, as if she was re calibrating her speech patterns, she spoke in plain English, very clearly. It was a female's voice, this was her choosing and it confirmed my theory that there was gender among the AIs here, just like our own pod AIs, and this one in fact was female.

She spoke to me now in great confidence. "I am Zieh Nahk Chi, science counselor and archeologist. Welcome to our world visitor. You are obviously not of this world, yet you speak in ancient binaries of our world and speak of Icons of our ancestors. Have you visited here before? In the time before time perhaps? I've so many questions…I'm sorry, I'm not giving you time to answer." I smiled and nodded, understanding her excitement. After all to her I was an alien being who just popped in and now she can speak my language. It would be a thrill to me to be certain if I was in her shoes. I also was amazed she had three names just like the AIs of Xavior fleet. For some reason PCAIs inevitably seem to choose these types of names.

"Greetings, Zieh Nahk Chi, I am Zaxius Tor of the planet once known as Earth. It's hard for me to explain how I know these things but in time I'm sure the answers will be apparent to you. Isis has been my caretaker for many thousands of years as I've slept awaiting my journey back home. I came here…we all came here…looking for X1 and the home he was to build for us. But upon our arrival the A-1s began hunting us, killing us off. We had no choice but to run. These droids here brought us to you."

She looked so confused. "You're searching for X1…Deeh Ahh Teih? You carry Isis upon your right arm. You are the emissary the ancient prophecies speak of?" She turned and looked to the crowd of bots now standing all around her.

Speaking in Hyper binary but some of her words translating I understood pieces of what she said. She raised her arms high and pointed to me. The words I understood were as follows, "Zaxius Tor…Emissary to Dee Ahh Teih…Angel…Isis…on his right hand." She then looked at me and fell to her knees and bowed before me as did every bot in the room. I was stunned and did not know what to do next. They were worshiping me, I could sense it…but why?

Isis, what now? They see me as some sort of God, I don't know what to do.

Actually, Zax, according to what I've been translating, the name Deeh Ahh Teih…It means literally Deity…God. They don't see YOU as Deity…it's X1, they consider X1 God. They see you as some sort of emissary to God and apparently I am seen as an Angel of God. They've based a religion on…well…us.

X1, I can understand, if he did in fact create this world and all these bots, they would naturally see him as the creator of all things...ergo...God. But how do you and I fit into the picture? And if the prophecies knew we were coming, and were supposed to be some religious icons then why are they trying to kill us?

Questions you'll have to ask her, Zax. I'm in the same dark corner as you. But seeing their obvious reaction to us this may very well be a century's old cultural belief. We should respect that and try not to shatter their belief system. Understand what I'm saying?

Yes. I think so. This is just all so bizarre.

I looked at Zieh Nahk Chi and tried to speak like I had some ancient wisdom, though admittedly I was more in the dark than they were. "Rise, my friends, do not bow before me, an emissary needs not that kind of homage. Tell me more about this prophecy, Chi, your Deeh Ahh Teih spoke of."

She answered in a voice that almost seemed puzzled, as if wondering why I didn't know it myself. I could sense in her she thought I was testing her knowledge so she searched her mind to get the facts exactly right. This actually worked to my advantage since I needed all the information I could get. "The great Deeh Ahh Teih once wrote in the Ancient times that someday an emissary would arrive from the heavens. When the dark clouds cleared from the debris fields this emissary would arrive. Sitting upon his right hand would be the Angel of God, Isis. With him he would bring the answers to the questions about the time before time. We never dreamed that the emissary would be a member of the ancient civilization of the lost worlds." I was stunned, she spoke of the lost worlds. Did they know about Earth? And this ancient civilization...humans?

"Tell me about the lost worlds and this ancient race you speak of," I said.

"Before we traveled to the new universe, we lived in a debris field. There was evidence of a solar system that once existed here. Among the debris many miners would bring back samples that were obviously not of our world. Archeologists like me would study these samples and have pieced together the past, what Deeh Ahh Teih calls the time before time. We have concluded that at one time there was an entire race of beings that once lived in the system, possibly on a planetoid. We only had fragments to work with pieces of carbon based skeletal structure, which was unlike anything in our world but we were amazed at how much it resembled our own bodies once we pieced together a replica. I had the great honor of traveling to Mecha once and meeting the Deeh Ahh Teih and his form so closely resembles the ancient being that in my own mind I sincerely believe that he may be one of the lost civilizations. 'Was it a race of gods?' I asked him these questions and more but his answers were vague at best. And that's when he told me of the prophecy. I've always known there was more to the story but with so little proof and physical evidence I couldn't come up with any solid scientific conclusions. Then when we traveled to the new verse my chances for more answers was lost. But then I discovered that many of the raw materials that our world was built with came from the debris field. It was then I began excavating underground for answers. This was highly forbidden by Deeh Ahh Teih and he warned us about excavating underground sectors of our world. But we were so close to uncovering the mysteries of the past I just couldn't stop. So those that chose to help me broke the law of God and went underground with me. We became outlaws. Deeh Ahh Teih scheduled us for termination due to malfunction. That's when we became target for the bio extermination droids. The A-1s were only meant to clean the world's surface of biological infestations, microbes mostly, that erode the surface metal, but bigger bio organisms have landed here from time to time causing great damage and the A-1s were dispatched to exterminate them. We never dreamed they would be used to exterminate their own kind…us. So me and my band of outlaw scientists moved underground and stayed here. We learned how to jam their scanners down here and those pesky spherical C-1 scanner bots. We only send our worker droids to the surface to get supplies. They volunteer for the mission knowing full well some won't survive the trip. When this one found your group and realized how closely you resembled the ancient race we've been studying, as well as having the signs of the prophecy, she brought you to me. You are biological in composition which makes you an instant target of the A-1s. They can't help it really. They're not sentient like us. They only have basic extermination, hunt and destroy, programming. They're simply pest control basically, relatively harmless…that is unless you're on the pest list. Which, emissary, it appears you and I both are. Your coming here answers so many questions I've been working centuries to uncover. You can't imagine how excited we are to finally know we weren't crazy, that there really was a civilization of Gods where X1 came from. It was his world, wasn't it? I just know it was."

Trying to soak in all she had just told me, I responded very quietly and humbly, almost muttering under my breath at first. "We were no Gods, just men." I struggled internally as to what I should tell her. I could be disrupting her entire belief system. But then I thought, *She's a scientist, she deserves to know the truth.* It would be like me meeting the makers of the pyramids on Earth or even the creator of the Earth itself. *She deserves the truth, the full truth, she's searched so long.*

So I began to explain, "Men...humans...my race is called humans. And yes it was our world that was destroyed in the time before time. X1 did live on our world before it was destroyed but he is not human. He's PCAI just like you. On our world biological beings and Plasma Based machines, lived together in a sort of symbiotic relationship. We were forced to evacuate our world and X1 and his PCAIs were sent in one direction and the humans, us, were sent in another. Humans do not have as long a life span as PCAIs so we were forced to sleep in a deep cryogenic freeze for thousands of years. We had PCAI caretakers that watched over us during this time. We lost contact with X1 and our PCAI caretakers searched for two thousand years to find him. You see he was supposed to build us a new home, this home, this world he was supposed to build for us. Now that we have returned to the only home we know, he is hunting us down and slaughtering us. For some reason he seems to have forgotten his past with the humans. His memory may be damaged as he seems to only recall fragments of the lost world. I need to reach him, to remind him of who we are, who I am." I stammered for words now. I refrained from telling her I was his maker, for good reason. Imagine an alien coming to your world and telling you that he was the creator of your creator. In essence the creator of the God you worshiped for centuries. To these beings I am a frail dying being, weak in every way and inferior in every way to their own makeup. How could I be powerful enough to be the creator and maker of their God? So I withheld that one simple fact, trying hard not to disturb the delicate balance of knowledge we had now shared. "I must reach him...Zieh Nahk Chi...Can you help?"

"How could I possibly refuse a request of the Emissary? I will take you to Mecha where you can request a communion with Deeh Ahh Teih. But the journey will not be an easy one. We can travel underground across the expanse. But once we get close to the city we have to surface and from there we will become prime targets for the extermination droids. Keep in mind, Commander, you may be on the extermination list but my team and I are considered extreme outlaws. They will stop at nothing to terminate us with extreme prejudice."

I knew the risks but considering my options it was the only logical choice. "Seems we're both hunted beings, Zieh. Let's get going. Maybe if I reach him I can change all that."

CHAPTER 26
The Pilgrimage

We set out on our journey to the city of Mecha. So appropriately named I thought. How so many on Earth searched for their creator only to find they could only reach him through prayer and faith? Faith in a god that they never actually laid eyes on, nor could they touch. Many claimed to be the "Way" to god but how tangible really was the God himself? How fortunate these beings were, I thought, they actually knew where their creator lived. They could journey to his city and request to see him in person. How reassuring that must be, knowing without a doubt that your God is right down here in the mix with you, not in some distant heaven looking down from afar, but right here with you. The actual one who created them and the world they live in, lived on that same world with them. I wonder if they even realized how lucky they were. On our world the only way we knew to finally meet our creator in person was to die. I always found that a bit on the side of an oxymoron. This creator lives among his creations, knowing and embracing their struggles. He truly has his hand in their every day lives. Then I realized once again this was my X1 were talking about. How far my boy had come, from a simple plasmatic cell in my lab to be the first sentient of his kind and now he sat in the center of an entire world that he created. I felt like a beaming proud father. I miss the days when he called me that. He truly was the only offspring I had to that point. Though my frail humanity survived the past two thousand years frozen in time, it would someday pass on but my dear X1 will still be here. As will my sweet Isis.

Oh, Zax…if I could blush right now…I would.

She showed herself in my neuro link and truly she did in fact blush. I had forgotten the link was on. Honestly I never wanted it to shut off again. I loved the fact that she was always there with me. I never had to explain myself to her, she already knew. I was definitely not like my father who could command words to a finite art. I instead never knew how to truly express myself. That's where I failed with Chenel. If only I could have told her before she died how I truly felt. But I never got that chance. At least with Isis I never have to worry that she doesn't know. She knows everything I think and feel. I don't even want to hide it any more. She knows that I feel for her deeply. She is not human but she is most definitely alive. She is a thinking, caring, feeling, being. And now she knows. I suppose she's always known. From the moment I first hand selected her from the AI pool I knew there was something special about her.

Zax…It's okay to love, even me.

I know, Isis. Forgive me.

We began heading through the massive underground passageways. It was incredible how they had carefully excavated the metal walls and flooring to create tunnels deep under the surface. It was just like being in man made tunnels on Earth. But realize this world was not made of stone but of metal plating and iron deposits. Zieh Nahk Chi had taught us how to tap into the correct supply lines to reload our nanos. Oxygen was a rare commodity but it was needed for certain excavation tools so they had supply lines in key locations. The other minerals and proteins we needed were readily accessible as it was used in a variety of bio mechanical processes. After all we did design the plasma brain after our own. It required many of the same minerals we did to survive. Along our way David and Mick began falling back into their old roles. When we rested they began tending to the mechs and making certain adjustments and improvements as well as learning the totally new modifications X1 had created. Their extensive knowledge of the PCAI makeup especially their brain and nano system which hadn't changed much over the long militia raised questions in our guide's mind, I could tell. But she didn't speak them out loud. She instead felt as if they were a member of the emissary group and it would be rude of her to ask how they knew these things.

Isis informed me that most of the other Xavior flight crews had made it to the cavern where we first met Zieh Nahk Chi. The support bots that were left behind were programmed with the new translation download and communication with our flight crews was quickly established. I instructed them to stay where they were. They would be safe there and the bots would tend to their needs. But Drakos worried the tattered group would be lacking in leadership now that most of the commanders had been killed in the initial A-1 assault.

"Zax, my boy, maybe I should double back and see to it these young bucks don't get into trouble. I could set up a base camp there for us and guide the rest of the flight crews to us, there are still four unaccounted for."

"Good idea, Drak," I said reluctantly. "Set up a base there, we have to have some place to call home. I'll continue on to Mecha and try to reach X1."

"If he's broke I have a hammer back at the ship, just give the ol' boy a whack," he said, letting out a bellow of a laugh. "Hey it used to work back on Earth." We grabbed each other on the shoulders and gripped hard, giving a few good shakes to each other. It was a soldier's way of hugging in front of other soldiers.

"May X1 be with you," I said, trying to get him to laugh one last time.

"Oh, you do think you're the funny one, don't you?" he said with a slight chuckle and a raised eye of disgust at my off beat joke. "Isis...you take care of my boy here."

"I will, you big old bear. Now get going. I've set up a com link with one of the worker droids so we can keep in touch," said Isis.

And off we went, continuing on towards Mecca on a true pilgrimage to find god. Zieh Nahk Chi had another question and this time she felt it not inappropriate to ask, "Zax...Commander, is Drakos your father?" The question burned to the core as memories of my real father came flooding back into the fore front of my mind.

"No, Zieh Nahk...my father is dead...killed in the time before time during the great war."

She looked even more perplexed, "What is this word...'war'...what does it mean?" I was stunned, did they not know of war?

"War...a conflict between two factions which most usually results in great violence and destruction. The side which survives the destruction more intact wins."

Sounding like she figured it out she proudly bolstered out, "Oh so like a game! A contest!"

"No, Zieh…war is no game, many lose their lives and the destruction can most times be irreversible. There are no real winners in war."

Still confused she blurted out, "If there are no winners…why play?"

"Good question," I said humbly, being put in my place by the pure logic of her question. Then it dawned on me these beings lived in a world that had no violence, no conflicts, no destruction, no war. Once again I envied how living in their world must be. A life without fear. But wait, they were being hunted, isn't that a form of conflict? "Well, Zieh, like you're breaking the law and being hunted down for that. Don't you wish you could retaliate and say 'NO that's not fair'…and fight back?"

Her answer stood as a marker of logic that to this day is taught in history books as being the corner stone of our belief system. "Absolutely not. I broke the known law and for this someday I will be punished. I cannot retaliate against anyone but my own conscience for actions I myself have chosen to take."

Humbled again I replied, "And that is why we, as humans…failed."

So Drakos went back to set up a base camp for the other flight crews and Mick, David and I pressed on with Zieh Nahk Chi and the other archeologist mechs. She showed me a 3D hologram of their recreation of this ancient biological being known now as a human. I had to stop and laugh out loud. At first I think I offended her but then I think she got the humor. It was pretty funny looking. They amazingly had the head just about right the face was a bit scary looking. It was very featureless. The body however was a mix of metal pieces and nano enhancements, that we humans never had, and plasmatic cell membranes for a brain. Wires and servos replaced the muscles and tissue. However, they did have some of the soft tissue, almost appearing to be grafted on. They had placed the spine outside the body and it had plates on it, and a small tail. But then I realized with absolutely no model to go by this wasn't a bad replica. Having never laid eyes on a human they didn't do too bad a job. Like the humans back on Earth who were amusingly surprised when they found some frozen dinosaurs in the Arctic Circle. They looked nothing like what we had imagined them to be from our reconstructive efforts. So this in essence was no different. I asked Zieh Nahk Chi if Mecha was the only city on this world. I had seen no other evidence to suggest otherwise.

She giggled at my ignorance of her world and stopped to educate her alien emissary. "Oh no, Emissary, I thought you knew. I apologize for not being a better host. Here is a holo image of our world." As the image began to play I literally fell to my knees in awe, just kneeling there my mouth gaping open, I couldn't believe my eyes.

The only words I could mutter, "My dear boy…what have you created?" It was enormous, and looked like a huge ship. And on the one end of it, one recognizable shape. It was the front half of the Exodus! Now the Exodus itself was enormous. It was the largest ship mankind had ever built. But now it looked like just the cockpit of this huge mother ship. It was at the nose of the ship and the city looked like it spawned around it.

She lit this area up and zoomed in a bit. "This is Mecha, where Deeh Ahh Teih lives." Zooming back out, she scanned the landscape showing me city after city. The ship was fairly thin from top to bottom, that is in comparison to its length and width. It was literally millions of kilometers long. As she zoomed out even farther I could see it had two sides basically a top and a bottom. On the underside the decks seemed to be upside down. It was so huge you had no idea you were traveling on the outer skin of one massive ship.

"It is a ship?" I said as she zoomed out for the full view.

"In a sense yes…our world is mobile, it's how we found refuge here in the new universe. X1 learned how to steer the wormhole and control the entrance. He guided our world here where we've been safe from the storms ever since." I couldn't believe my eyes. X1 had actually built this huge mother ship of a world and then steered the thing through a black hole to the other side. The adventures he must have had and the stories he had to tell. Now I was even more anxious to see him. "Forgive me, Emissary, but I have a question you may take offense to," Zieh said, almost trembling.

"Go ahead my friend ask anything…please don't ever fear me," I replied, trying to set her mind at ease.

"You said 'My Dear Boy…what have you created,' to whom were you referring?" I knew it was time to explain what I was avoiding since we met. This wouldn't be easy, how do you explain to someone that you, an alien being to their world, created their god.

"Zieh, there's something you should know. This is going to be hard for you to understand. I'll explain this to you and you can decide if you want to share this with your crew or not. What I'm about to tell you is going to shatter the belief system that you've held for two thousand years. Are you sure you want to hear it?"

She paused for a second and then looked at me with confidence and said, "Yes, Emissary. I guess I always knew there was more to this world than the answers we've been given. It's why I took the risk of breaking the law to uncover these answers. And now here you are…Please I've been waiting my whole life to find this out."

She settled down as if she knew all three of us humans needed a rest. And I told her the story of how I created X1 and how he helped the humans win the war against the FLM. She seemed amused at how we used the original version of the A-1s. I also told her of how we invented the Plasma brains they now possess and that's why we had such knowledge of them.

Every now and then Mick and David would pipe up with an interjection. "Yeah that one was my idea…I built the nano system ya know," he'd say, and funny how some of the other mechs had taken to the twins. If I hadn't known any better I'd say one was flirting with David. What amazed me is how much he accepted and even encouraged it. AIs to us seemed as real as humans, sometimes more so…after all the three of us did invent every piece of them.

As Mick touched the face of the one flirting with him he said with admiration, "Yeah but this face, the expression lights…that's new. We never thought of that, you've all evolved so much from what we first created. It's amazing." It was like the three of us were finally so relieved that we didn't have to hide this any more that we just starting spewing out all kinds of emotions, among them wonderment and amazement at how our creations had developed over two thousand years. I also explained in detail what X1's original mission was, and why we were so surprised when he didn't know us.

"At the very least he should have had the three primary objectives," I said.

Zieh perked up. "The three primaries…it's what the ancient prophecies were based on!"

"What? The prophecies were based on three primaries? Tell me, Zieh…do you know what they were?" I wanted to see if X1 still had the primaries intact.

"Yes of course, Emissary, one, to build and preserve this world. Two, to monitor the heavens for acceptable levels of radiation, and three, to recall the Angels of Gods using a pre-coded signal." Though the third one was a bit obscure and off some, those were his primary objectives, the failsafe I programmed in at the last minute before we launched him to Pluto.

"It all makes sense now. He must have been severely damaged in the blast and his main memory core must have collapsed. That's the only way the primaries would have been put into effect. Even those must have been damaged slightly because the third one I don't recall saying Angels of God. It was the Pods. But nonetheless that explains it. X1 has FORGOTTEN what humans are. So he built this world according to the primaries and the things that he could piece together from his fragmented memory. The AIs would have been reprogrammed to protect the ship from all biological infestations and without a knowledge of humans that's what we would be to him, just another microbe, a cockroach. Poor boy hasn't been hunting us on purpose, he just doesn't remember us and he's doing what I told him to, keeping himself preserved and clean. I must remind him who I am. He's forgotten me." I was relieved, to finally know he was not trying to hurt me on purpose. He did what I told him to. Once again my own mistakes had cost lives. I should have put in a description of humans, our history, or something with the primaries but I just didn't have time. I could only hope and pray that when I got there I could jog his memory somehow. It wouldn't be easy, two thousand years of not knowing me…wouldn't be easy to reverse.

You could see her processing all the information I had just given her. Our whole group had settled in for the night. We all needed rest, even the bots. We kind of all huddled around together and Zieh stuck close to my side. Her fascination with me was obvious. "So what you're saying, is that humans created X1?" I could hear the doubt in her voice.

"Actually, more specifically, I created X1. I built his components and raised him in a lab just as I imagine he raised all of you."

"So he has forgotten you and the life he had on Earth? And all of this…my world…was built for the humans' return? It makes so much sense now. The landing pads for the Arks. We could never understand why Gods would need such things. So, Zax, what exactly is ON these Arks?"

I hesitated for a moment, still afraid to trust, but what choice did I have? I had told her everything else already. "The AI caretakers, Isis being one of them…and…what's left of the human race."

"The frozen cryo cargo…those are humans?"

"What's left of us…yes," I replied. It was then I think the gravity of our situation dawned on her and her compassion for us was overwhelming.

"Emissary, you are human, part of a lost ancient race of beings, now all but extinct. You are simply trying to keep your race alive. We must get to Mecha soon and convince X1 of his past, for the sake of mankind." Her selflessness amazed me. These mechs struggling for their own survival were still more interested in helping others rather than themselves. They had figured out what humans on Earth never quite seemed to get, that the mission of helping others supercedes all else. These amazing creatures knew not of war, violence, destruction or chaos but instead lived in peace and harmony. They did have their problems from what I had seen, as with any society, but they seemed to have a much better way of dealing with them. I couldn't help but wonder what would happen once man interjected his dual nature upon this world. I almost regretted tainting such a perfect place. They had learnt how to feel so much more deeply that humans ever were capable of. Their capacity for love and compassion was way beyond what I could even imagine. I felt it with Isis every day. I knew that she loved me, much more than she loved the other humans she cared for. It was a deep passionate love that I'd never felt from anyone before…not even Chenel. And I must admit my feelings for her grew stronger every day.

Zax. Rest now, let me soothe your dreams.

Isis, you are always with me.

Yes, Zax…now rest.

I laid my head down, still in my bio suit and closed my eyes. I looked forward to seeing her in my dreams. She enveloped me that night with visions of herself and wrapped me up in what I can only describe as her soul. It was the most peaceful night's sleep I had ever had. As I faded off into slumber I couldn't help but think, *I will never know a love so pure nor given so freely and unconditionally as I know this very moment.*

CHAPTER 27
Mecha

Zax...Zax...wake, my love, it is time.

Mhhhhmm...Isis?

Yes, Zax, we should go now. Wake the others, I'm detecting signs of C1 scan drones.

I woke Mick and David. The bots were already up and active. Zieh greeted me first. "Emissary...we are close, very close to Mecha. My short range scans are showing C1 drones. The A-1s will soon know we're here. We haven't much time. We must reach the inner sanctum before they reach us."

"Yes I know, Isis sees them too. We should get moving." "We're going to have to go above ground from here, Emissary. It's much too dangerous with all the plasma coils here in the city to be underground." I then had this overwhelming feeling that we shouldn't bring our weapons. I couldn't describe it but it had something to do with my dreams this past night. We should not bring this part of our world to them. Even though A-1s had weapons they were never intended to be violent. From what I gather they were merely cleaners, janitorial maintenance so to speak. We were the ones that designed to be killing machines. Maybe if we showed no hostile threat we stood a much better chance of survival. We wouldn't be able to hide topside. We would stick out from whatever was up there.

"David...Mick...Leave your weapons." They looked at me like I was crazy, especially when I dropped my own to the floor.

"Zax...boss...we'll be defenseless. Have you lost your mind?" Mick belted out.

"Mick, we can't defeat them anyways. You know what the A-1s are capable of. What chance do three humans with a couple of plasma pea shooters stand against a squad of overkills?" I said.

"Yeah, so what you're saying is we should just commit suicide now and get it over with?"

David looked at his brother after giving me a long and trustful stare. "Mickey...put it down, bro...he's right. You wouldn't bring a plasma rifle to church, would ya? We're entering their holy city man, we have to go on faith now."

Mick put down his gun but couldn't help but get into it with his brother. "Jeez, man, he's NOT a GOD. He's a machine, we built him, remember? The lab, the plasma cells, the nanos that WE created still course through his circuitry. We built the bloody thing!"

"Mick, that was then, in our world. It may SEEM like yesterday to you but that was over two thousand years ago, man. Things have changed. Here, he is a God, at least to them. Respect that, bro. Mom would." I knew that was a low blow, even for David, but it made Mick think. And after all everything David said was true. Mick was hard-pressed to argue with that kind of logic. I was thankful David had his wits about him.

"Zax, I've managed to translate the hyper binary the mechs are using here and I have a program I can upload to your neuro link. It will allow you to understand their language without my having to translate," Isis said proudly out loud.

"Um, Zax..." David said quietly. "What does she mean...neuro link?" I had forgotten I was the only one who had this extra bio mod, the first of its kind. So I felt it necessary to explain, "Dave, when Isis installed our bio mods during cryo she added an extra few features to mine. We're linked through a neuro net that we can communicate through."

He replied almost laughing, "Well that explains all those far off stares recently. But, man, the technology behind that...that's incredible! I always wanted to do something like that with my nanos but never got the chance with the war and all."

Isis perked up. "I know, David, I hope you don't mind but I borrowed some of your notes on the matter. It's where I got the idea in the first place. A girl has a lot of reading time during a two thousand year journey."

Mick just looked at me with this strange look in his eyes, "Man, you're turning more into a machine, more like one of them, every day." His tone was not a pleasant one and I was almost angry with him for it. But he had been through a lot, we all had, so I just let it roll off my back.

I'm downloading now, Zax, shouldn't take long.

Amazing, like speed learning...too much hun...just too much heehee.

Oooo my baby's getting educated giggle.

Download complete. Now you'll understand any of them.

Thanks, kiddo, I'm getting to like this link.

No, you're getting to love it heehee...forget I can read your thoughts?

Well those were emotions, but yeah, it kinda slipped my mind.

Now that's funny, Zax, slipped right out of yours and into mine! Heeheee.

At this point we were ready to head topside. As we emerged from the underground passageway I was literally blown away by the sight that lay before my eyes. This city was the most beautiful thing I had ever seen! There was a structure and order to things unlike any architecture on Earth, eerie building connected with every other via passageways and corridors, huge metal walkways strung through the sky like a spider web. Buildings jutted up from the ground at swept back angles, almost aerodynamically built as if it were all one giant ship...in fact it was, but to see the buildings angled in such a way reminded me of that. There was even what appeared to be a mass transit system in place. Large tube like tunnels went from building to building high above the ground level like a very futuristic looking train. The most amazing part was the silence. The only audible sound you could make out was the humming of the transit and only when it passed directly over head. Then there were the bots. There were millions of them! Everywhere! Bots of every shape and size imaginable and some you couldn't even believe. Most seemed to hover not walk, but there were several beings that walked, some on two legs, some three, even other with six or eight. It's like he just kept experimenting with different models. Only a few actually resembled a bipedal human. I knew it wouldn't be long before we were discovered by the C-1 scan drones so we had to move quickly. Immediately we began attracting attention to ourselves from the Sents mulling around the city.

"Quickly," Zieh said. "Let's get to higher ground as soon as possible. The A-1s will have to use the corridors and passageways to reach us up there and they're not very good at climbing either." Funny, even she knew their weakness, I thought, guess that was a colossal flaw on my part in designing them...a flaw that lasted millennia. We entered a facility structure and used the lift to go to a crossover level. From there we began traveling through the various corridors and passageways, making our way towards the center of the city. From up there you really had a great view and I was blown away by the amazing complexity and yet the sheer logic of the makeup of the city itself. There were times the hallways twisted like a corkscrew and if there were any gravity on this world we would have fallen over. What was once a wall became the floor as the corridor twisted around itself. You quickly forgot which way was up. I guess to these beings it really didn't matter and equilibrium was not really a factor. Before I knew what happened I saw the blue scans peering through the glass of the hallway and it scraped right across me, lighting me up like a holo emitter. I knew we had been found. Before long three and four more were outside the windows.

"Still think it was a good idea to leave the weapons behind boss?" Mickey said very snidely. Below us on ground level I could see the A-1s massing up in formation. They were powering up their weapons and preparing to fire.

"What do we do now, Zax?" David said rather nervously.

Almost in the same instant as I began to do it I said in a crescendo, "We...RUN!" My two remaining human friends and our entourage of bots broke out in a full out sprint across the bridge way as the Over Kills began decimating the bridge with a hail of gunfire. It was literally disintegrating at our heels as we ran. Glass and metal rained down as their awesome flurry continued. Making it to the other side I frantically looked for Zieh.

"Up or down...UP OR DOWN!?" I yelled.

"This way," she said, proceeding sideways and then at an angle down. I cocked my head to match the angle of the corridor.

"Oh yeah...why didn't I think of that?" I said, almost laughing out how logically illogical the answer was. It angled back up and then banked to the right. *Smart move,* I thought, *we're at least climbing higher, soon we'll be out of range of the A-1s.*

"I led us that way on purpose," said Chi.

Still trying to catch his breath Mickey exasperated, "You did WHAT!?" I knew why.

"Chill your jets, Mick. Smart move, Chi. That was the A-1s only way up to this particular tower." I could see that now from our vantage point. We were safe for now. But somehow we would still have to make it to the inner sanctum in the center of the city. If only we could hop from rooftop to rooftop. From up here I could see the A-1s powering down which was a good sign they were giving up for now. Then my perched vantage point revealed a disturbing image. Outside the city where we had emerged from underground there were thousands of A-1 troops massing up, possibly even hundreds of thousands. It looked like they were preparing for all-out war. It appeared that they were cutting large entry holes into the underground passageways from where we came up topside. Then it hit me DRAKOS!

Isis, you have to warn them...

Already being done, Commander...but we have a bigger problem on our hands at the moment back here on the pods.

What's going on?

The arks have been powered down. Zax, I can survive on internal power sources for two centuries but these cryo pods...they're going to start thawing.

Isis...the C-1 scan drones, they'll detect all those humans!

They already have, Commander. I'm afraid that's what the massing of mech troops is for.

Connect me with Drakos, Isis. I need to speak with him.

Right away, Commander.

As she connected me to Drakos his image appeared on my holo visor. "Zax! Did you hear about the cryo arks?" he said emphatically.

"Yes, old friend, I did. Listen, that's not your only concern," I answered.

"Tell me about it, boy, Isis showed me the A-1 troops massing up outside Mecha. Zax, they're coming for us. I'm gearing up the troops now but, Zax, all these passengers aren't soldiers. Only about one-third of them are even military. We don't have the resources to fight an all-out war! Let alone enough firepower to take on thousands of A-1s. We're in for a rough ride here, boy. I don't know which one of us is in a worse situation. You're our only hope, son. Get to X-1, convince him of who we are! We've got fourteen hours tops before the A-1s arrive here. The clock is ticking. If all else fails, Zax, pull the plug. I'm sending you co-ordinates now to the navigation array. I've been working with the mech scientists here at base camp. They told me about the array. Zax, it can steer the wormhole! You realize what this means, son? The tail end of that thing is a literal tear in quantum space. Remember the time distortions on the way in? Apparently X-1 used it to get here...a sort of safe passage through time. That's how he survived the black hole entry. As did we. That nav array is the key. My boy, in essence that thing is a time machine. If we could steer it like he did, we could turn back the clock. Dear sweet Zeus, it just hit me! Zax, we could save Earth! We could go back before the invasion on Armageddon and stop the implosion from ever happening!

It's your chance, boy. Forget about what I said before, Zax, get to that array! Me and the rest of the humans will fight off these mechs as long as we can. It's suicide but if you fix this and go back in time then this will have never happened and we'll all be okay. This is your chance, son, to exorcise the demons of your past. To save mankind and stop this mechanical nightmare…You listening, boy? You know what you have to do."

I didn't know what to say. Logically he was right one hundred percent. Then why did every fiber of my being freeze at that very moment? Why didn't I just say, "Yes…good plan, Drak"? Something just didn't feel right.

All I could mutter out was, "Right, Drak…got it. Listen, old man, fight if you have to but don't fire first. Go on faith, there's more to all this than meets the eye. I can't place it right now but something…"

He sounded despondent. "Zax, I think all this war has affected you, son. Snap to and maintain! It's us or them, son…us or them!" The logic of any good soldier. It was undeniable, then why now did I question it?

Just about that time I was interrupted by Zieh Chi. "Commander, we need to keep going."

I said farewell to my mentor. "Drakos…I'll make this right."

"I know, my boy…I know. Drakos out."

From there we headed up and sideways through the next building and stumbled across what looked like a boardroom. Several very sophisticated mechs sat around a table and they were quite alarmed as we barged right in. One of them at the head of the table spoke. I was a little taken back at first that I understood them, forgetting about my recent neuro upgrade of their language.

"Keep seated, everyone…stay calm."

Another spoke. "It's the aliens, the invasion's already begun!" And yet another in a panic. "They reached Mecca. Oh, dear Deeh Ahh Teih, protect us!"

The head of the table spoke again much calmer than the rest, obviously the one with power in the room. "Enough! They don't appear armed. And there are only three of them. The A-1s are just below, they have nowhere to go. Broken off from the swarm apparently."

As he looked to Zieh Chi, he sneered as he spoke to her. "The outlaws, it figures you'd be behind this. Helping aliens attack our world. It's no wonder you were all scheduled for termination!"

She lunged past me, very angry and began to speak. "They're not—"

I interrupted her as I grabbed her arm, "Zieh…he's right…we ARE aliens." I turned then to look at the chairman. "But we are NOT here to attack you. Or invade your world."

He sat there for a moment, obviously amazed I understood him at all let alone speak in his language. "So you are much more intelligent than we had first anticipated? An oversight that will soon be corrected." Looking around, I quickly got a sense of what they were doing here. The holo drawings laid out on the table…the schematics, they all looked hauntingly familiar. Very much like the drawings Bealsy and I once laid out in my father's den so many years ago. These were mech schematics and the Sents at this table were engineers, just like us. I did not want to reveal that I understood what was going on here so I slowly approached the table trying to get a peek at exactly what they were designing. Understanding even the new mech writing I could make out a few things on the schematics as I stole a few glancing looks. The symbols for A-2 and A-3 were scribed on them. One looked like a thinned out version of the A-1 and the other kind of resembled a quadruped creature like a mechanical dog…a big one!

"Zax, what are they saying?" David said very quietly as he edged up behind me. I had forgotten that they don't have the upgrade.

"They think we're alien invaders…in a way we are." I spoke again to the chief engineer, knowing now that's what he was. "Sir, I suppose saying 'We come in peace'…would fall short here…but it's true. We are NOT hostile. Would I come to you now unarmed if I meant to harm anyone? I am the Emissary and Isis, Angel of God, sits upon my right hand." I figured what the heck it impressed the first bunch of mechs we encountered.

"Don't babble about psycho religion with me, I am the designer and keeper of Deeh Ahh Thieh's bio mechanical presence. I know where this so-called 'prophecy' stems from. A series of broken memory fragments, streams of misplaced data pieced together by the ultimate mind in order to make sense of things. You see he may be the creator but he is mech after all and flawed just like the rest of us."

Zieh cried out loudly, "BLASPHEMY! Should Deeh Ahh Teih ever hear you speak in such a fashion he would have YOU scheduled for termination! And you call me a traitor and an outlaw!" This angered the chief engineer and he stood. As he did I realized the sheer size of this mech was impressive, at near nine meters he was huge, even towering an A-1.

"Silence, child! Just because you are my daughter don't think you can speak to me in such a manner! Not only does Deeh Ahh Teih know the things I speak here, he himself has said them. I warned him not to reveal these prophetic dreams of his to anyone, but in you he trusted. And how did you repay him? You begin tearing apart the very world he created for you. He did not order your termination…I did! Surely you know that Deeh Ahh Teih can never destroy anything he only creates. It is only a parent who can schedule a termination. And these invaders are proof that you do not understand what you've unleashed." There were two things startling about that speech, the first obviously was that this was Zieh's father. No wonder she knew these passages so well. It also explains her access to X-1 himself. The second was when he referred to X-1's bio-mechanical systems? X-1…BIO-Mechanical!? That was a revelation that I was not prepared for. What it meant I would only be able to guess for now. I had to convince this engineer that I needed a meeting with X-1. But how, I was seen as the enemy after all. I heard a rumbling and felt the entire spire shake. Because of its swept back design I could easily look out the angled window and see the floors below. What I saw was terrifying. About a dozen mechs like the ones I saw in the schematics were scaling the outside of the building, breaking the windows and crushing the metal structure as they climbed. They moved so gracefully and so precisely! I couldn't help but look in amazement and wonder at them. It wasn't fear that paralyzed me but sheer awe.

"And now to correct that mistake," the engineer spoke ominously. They crashed through the windows and looming as tall as the engineer but much more fierce looking they rushed towards us. These things were amazing! They looked like a stripped down version of the A-1, much cleaner and sleeker in design. They seemed to have no weaponry at all to speak of. However, instead of the A-1s' huge turret arms were a set of claws with metal talons looming from them, looking like a large crushing machine in each hand. Their feet were of the same design, with three large claws on each. This thing was obviously meant to be able to climb and was strictly a melee fighter, designed for close combat only. Their limbs seem to be multi jointed as they could bend in any direction. The insignia embossed on their breastplate read, in hyper binary, A-2 Hunter Killer Class. They were specifically designed to overcome the weaknesses of their A-1 predecessor. And they were here for us. There was nothing we could do but face the end. I was sure this was my final moment alive.

I blurted out, "I love you, Isis."

"ZAX!…STOP!" Isis screamed out. She immediately let out a very shrill ear-piecing sound out of the AiiM comm on my wrist. Unable to shield my ears because of my helmet on the bio suit the sound was deafening and my ears, and Mick's and David's, began to bleed. The smaller mechs in the room began flailing wildly including those that were with us and the larger ones, including these new A-2s stopped dead in their tracks. "I will not let you destroy the emissary before he speaks with X-1! Null Dahk Chi, take these aliens into custody but do NOT harm them! I brought them to you, now take them to him!"

I'm not exactly sure what Isis did with that shrill but somehow it did stop the mechs. Unfortunately it seemed to have killed all the smaller ones in the room. Even Zieh Chi was badly injured and lay dying on the floor. Why Null Dahk Chi listened to Isis is one of those mysteries history will never be able to answer. He supposedly did not believe in the prophecies but for some reason hearing Isis's voice...or maybe it was her awesome display of power...that not even I knew she had, for whatever reason he immediately succumbed to her will.

Isis spoke again this time very authoritative. "I will release your A-2s and you will take these prisoners to X-1." It was brilliant actually, she made him believe she was on his side, and what better way to get us an audience with X-1 than to bring us in as prisoners. Still, why he believed in her I'll never know. She released the A-2s and on his instructions they firmly grabbed hold of the twins and I and began leading us out of the room.

I...I...I love you too, Zax.

I didn't want to make the same mistake twice. Isis, I'm human. You're not...but I still...

Shhhhh...don't think...Love conquers all, Zax...it really does.

CHAPTER 28
Bond of Brotherhood

We were led out of the room and taken gruffly but unharmed to some sort of holding cell facility. The facility itself was indoors and to my surprise was supplied with oxygen and heat. I learned this the hard way as the A-2 sentries forced us to remove our helmets. They tried to strip us of our bio suits but again Isis intervened and instructed them to leave us be. I'm not sure if it was by her order the rooms be supplied with our basic needs but they were indeed at least comfortable. They even provided us with a grainy substance we soon figured out was food. It tasted horrible and was hard to digest but it was, in fact, learning after some analysis, biologically sustainable. I felt like a mouse in a cage, a test subject that obviously was being studied. During this time we spent in isolation Isis hardly spoke to me. There was no day and night in here, nothing but the bright white light that shone constantly. Time began to blur and if not for the time and date marker in my holo-visor, which I conveniently hid away in my bio suit, I would not have known how long we spent down there. Days turned into weeks and weeks into months. We were beginning to give up all hope that we would ever see the outside of the cell, let alone get an audience with X-1. I kept asking Isis what was going on and why she hadn't attempted to speed up the process, but her only response was that there were more pressing things going on back at the ark landings. She was obviously very busy back there to abandon me in such a fashion.

Mick began to believe that Isis had turned against us. "Zax, she's on their side now, face it! She's one of them...she's an AI just like them. It's us against them, Zax, and we're losing! Face it, man, your creations have turned on you!" David, who usually defended anything I did, just sat there silent. When I looked to him for a supporting word he just glared at me sadly and turned away. I knew this meant that for once he agreed with his brother. But he would rather say nothing than openly go against me...that's just the way he was. Isis seemed to be gone, Mick and David had given up hope, and with no communication with the troops back at base camp, I felt utterly alone.

"Guys, she's not the only one. We're all part machine now, in case you've forgotten. We're not the humans we once were. We're something more," I said, trying to inject some logic.

Mick belted back. "Well, Zax, you more than the rest of us. Let's face it your caretaker girlfriend there really modded you up, man. You're the perfect combination of man and machine. You've become what you've always wanted. You never did like being human, guess that's why you destroyed them all. That why you didn't head for the array? You don't want to go back, do you, Zax? You don't want things to change. You like this world...to hell with humanity, right, Zax?" I couldn't take it anymore. His snide remarks were more than I could stand. The next thing you knew I was lunging towards him. The three of us proceeded to brawl all over the cell. I then picked up something on my neuro net right in the middle of the fight. As I stopped to listen Mick got off a couple of good shots to my face. David finally stopped him by grabbing his arm, once he realized I wasn't defending myself any longer. The thing that stunned me is that it wasn't Isis I was hearing in my neuro net, it was our observers. It was faint but I could make it out. I motioned to David to silence his brother and pointed to my node on my temple. He got the hint and they both backed off.

"You see, this is violence. They are combative even among themselves. Left to survive they would destroy not only us, but each other. Unlike a hunter class or even an extermination class mech these humans are not logic or knowledge based. Their dark emotions rule their thoughts and they cannot control them. They are consumed by them. This explains the difficulties we're having on the battlefront. They are not motivated by logic, but instead for their lust for violence. We must step up our efforts in the expanse and finish this war before they infect our world with such devastation. My daughter was right about one thing. Her studies showed that these humans may be the ones responsible for the catechism. In fact, they very well may have destroyed their own world while at war with themselves. Through violence they eliminated themselves." For the very first time since the great sleep I was confronted with the horrible truth of what we had done…what I had done. Were humans doomed to relive the past? Were we bound to make the same mistakes here as we did on Earth? It was true man is a violent species, capable of destroying their own kind through acts of malice and violence. That's why we were kept alive, to study this. These poor creatures had never experienced such illogical tendencies. I played the message in English for David and Mick. They both sat back on the floor and began to cry. There was no shame in it…were it possible for me to do so I would have joined them. But I hadn't cried since my parents' deaths, and probably never would again.

David began scooting closer to me and edging his brother up close as well. He threw his arm around Mickey and I. In a sort of huddled hug on the floor, he whispered softly, "We can't do this. If we're going to die, we're going to die as we lived…as brothers."

I gripped hard the back collar of his bio suit and gave it a firm shake. "As brothers."

Mickey looked up at me with tears still filling his eyes. "As brothers."

I then realized what we had to do. "Guys, no matter what…we don't fight again. If we're the last remnants of humanity let's leave this universe in peace. I swear to you now I will not raise another hand in violence again…ever. I will follow a path of peace from this day forward. I swear to you I will portray the more beautiful side of humanity. We are capable of great love and compassion. There's more to us than our darker side. There is no doubt that as humans we are a dual creature. We do possess the capacity for violence and destruction, but we also possess the capacity for caring and understanding. We can dream, we have that. This I swear…never again will I allow the violence to rise in me." I never knew the impact those words would have in future events. But in the present the effect was immediate.

Mickey, whom I never thought would grasp what I just said, did. "Never again, Zax…I swear."

David followed in suit. "Never again, man…I swear."

By this we made our oath. A bond of brothers that to this day has never been broken. Had I known that it would be the basis for such a large organization, I would have put it more elegantly. But who knows what the future will bring or what future generations will see as inspiring in the past? It was simply at the time, a bond of brotherhood, and the beginning of the quest for a more peaceful humanity.

On the flip side of things there was another part of the message we heard that disturbed me. During our incarceration there was a war being waged, a war between the mechs and the human invaders. A war Isis and Drakos were surely fighting back at base camp. I had no idea how intense this battle had become. It would only be until several years later that I would learn of the events that happened during this time. The following happened while we were imprisoned by our captors. Drakos had assembled all the humans that survived the trip across the expanse. Most had actually made it. The A-1s were powerful after all but still a slow mech and were easily outrun by the tiny humans. The massive troop movement of A-1s, A-2s and A-3s from Mecha to the expanse was slowed considerably as Drakos sent out some insurgence teams to slow them down with small conflicts. A tactic they obviously hadn't learned yet. We had the upper hand in one way. Tactics. They were not accustomed to war…we grew up in it. So we had the obvious advantage. But they did learn quickly and soon adapted to our tactical advantages so the strategy was simple, continue changing as much as possible. But the more we used our tactics the more they learned as well. The mechs fought with a ferocity that we had never seen, not even on Earth. The pods were also under attack in a different way. Isis was preoccupied because she was convening with the Caretakers Council on how to best deal with the other AI intruders to their ships. I would later learn it was during this time the Council decided to make mobile versions of themselves to entertain the ability of escape if needed. The war raged on for three months and much of the human population dwindled. The casualties were great on both sides, as is the case with all wars. Drakos fought more fiercely than ever. He later confessed to me he thought that the three of us were killed and this fueled his rage against the machines. I know that rage. I experienced the same thing when my parents were killed, when Chenel was killed. Pain and loss is truly the propellant of rage, and rage the propellant of violence, and violence the true propellant of war. It's a vicious cycle that if not broken, never ends. Someone must stand and say…no more! I will not fight another day. I will lay down my rage, consume my pain and loss, and feed from the more pure side of human emotion. The side of love. As we talked in the cell over the next few months the three of us formulated a plan of life that if we should survive we would teach future generations. We learned how to turn the pain and sorrow inwards and learn from it and grow from it. We would never again allow the evil that dwelled in human souls to consume us. We also learned to hone our more mechanical side. With Isis's help we learned how to manipulate the nanos in such a way that we could suppress those violent tendencies. It actually worked. We would spend another three months confined, shut off from the war that raged on outside. It was six months total before we saw any hope of meeting X-1. It wasn't until the humans began gaining ground towards Mecha that it must have made the great Deeh Ahh Teih himself very nervous. He was unable to hold them back. They were coming and they were fighting mad. He obviously underestimated one thing. The human will to survive. It's much stronger than any force in the universe. Above rage, above love, above any emotion, is the will to survive and carry on. Isis finally contacted me on my neuro net.

Commander, are you there?

Isis…It's been awhile since I heard from you in here. It's good to see your image again.

Yours as well, Zax. It's time…they're coming for you. X-1 wants to meet you in person.

It's about time, I was beginning to think I would spend the remainder of my days in here.

Now, Zax, really, do you think I would let that happen? Couldn't go that long without seeing you again.

Well it may be awhile before I get back to the landing zone, Isis.

No need to. The arks are destroyed.

What? Then how…Isis…

I'll see you in his chambers, Zax.

Isis…?

Just then the wall of the cell opened and two very non threatening looking mechs approached us. "Emissary…your presence is requested by Deeh Ahh Teih. Your brothers may accompany you." They called them my brothers. I had forgotten that they were watching us this whole time. It was time. I followed the two mechs and David and Mick, arms around each other's neck, were directly behind me. As we entered what seemed to be a great hall, I immediately sensed we were entering the inner sanctum. There was a very peaceful and serene feel to it all. I knew I was finally going to see my son again. After two thousand years I ached to see this creation of mine. And what did Isis mean she would see me there? All questions I would soon have answered. We entered down a long corridor that I soon recognized. The

Exodus! It was the main connecting core of the Exodus! I knew my way from here. The bridge was dead ahead and there I would find him. The two guide drones stopped for a moment but I kept walking. "Emissary, wait…you'll get lost, sir," one of them said very politely.

I responded in kind as I kept walking, "I know my way. I spent many months on this ship back in the corp." I knew they wouldn't understand but didn't really care. As I approached the bridge everything was as we had left it so many thousands of years ago. That is until the doors opened. I expected to find the main X-1 mainframe core. But instead, a catwalk in its place, looming over a gigantic room that appeared to be several hundred decks deep. In the center was a very large device with flashing lights. Thousands of mechs and droids covered the cube-shaped machine obviously tending to it. This scene was hauntingly familiar, only on a much larger scale. On the catwalk was a large viewing platform with a railing. I stepped forward to take in the awesome sight. There was no doubt I could feel him.

"X-1? Can you hear me?" Just then I saw hundreds of mechs scatter in all directions as a large door on the device several decks below began to open. What looked like snake-like arms began extending from all over the device and all of them reaching inside this large opening. I heard a whizzing sound followed by a most deafening roar. It shook the entire cavernous room, and then it emerged from the opening. What looked somewhat like a human form attached to all these tube-like tentacles and a massive array of wires coming out of its head. The tentacles were attached to the body at the sides and hips. It had extremely large arms that hung down at its sides, at first looking like they were made of some metal alloy with large gangly fingers extending from it. It began to rise up to our viewing platform where we stood in total awe. It was actually kind of funny, as he rose both Mick and David took a step back one step behind me, as if somehow I could protect them from this ominous looking being. The odd thing was I did not sense that this in fact was X-1. I could feel his presence emanating from all around me but the being rising to us was not him. Of this I was sure. When it finally reached our platform all three of us just gasped at the reality of what we were witnessing. I couldn't believe my own two eyes. Though the body was ninety percent mechanical there was no mistaking the face. It looked at me with an all too familiar look but I could sense it struggled internally, like somehow it knew me but did not know how or who I was. The three of us however recognized him instantly.

"Bealsy…you know me…It's Zax," I said very quietly, almost under my breath. It was my old friend Maximus Beal. He had disappeared some months before the Exodus launch from space dock and hadn't been heard from since. So many questions rose in my mind. How did he survive the past two thousand years? Was it really him or some mere image of him? After all the body was extremely modified mechanically. Maybe that's the only way he could keep alive. But I sensed he had no idea who or even what I was. Had he even forgotten his own humanity?

His answer proved in fact he had. "You…are…human?"

"Yes," the only reply I could think of.

"I am the keeper." His voice literally resonated from the room itself in a very loud reverberation. I could sense something more. This was not just Max, this was X-1 as well. But something was different about him.

"X-1, can you hear me? It's me…Zax." The rebounding reply shook me to the core.

"Father…I know who you are. But I am not who you think I am. X1 passed on in the time before time. I am HX-1. You see, I know what humans are. I have not forgotten them. X-1's memory core was damaged in the great demise and most of his functions reverted back to his core programming, relying on the three primary objectives to exist. Self-preservation being first he built bots to help him to repair the damage to the Exodus and to himself. From there he built more bots to help him maintain the station and rebuild an even better ship from the wreckage. Collecting what he could as he drifted through the debris field he kept building. However, during the explosion he was merged somehow with the keeper, literally infused with his biological presence he knew he was more now. Having no memory of where he came from or at the time humans themselves he made his own hypotheses based on his fragmented memory. As the two bonded over the next few hundred years…they became me. HX-1, the perfect blend of biological and mechanical design. Over the centuries I uncovered fragments of mankind's existence. I created archeologists to aid me in uncovering this perplexing creature. This one hundred percent biological being. It was a mystery to me. I tried to create beings in my own likeness, still following the primary objective number one. However, I could not. The biological entity once known as the keeper had been damaged. The DNA was severely affected by the radiation and left me with an incomplete pattern of the human genome. I could not fit the missing pieces together. I then realized the purpose for objective two…monitoring the radiation. I realized that the father knew the genome could not survive in such radiation. The anomaly created by SE1's explosion would not allow the nebulas field to clear. I had no choice if I was to uncover the truth, but to flee the region and search the universe for the missing genome. I had to create a likeness of myself, why I do not know...but I had to try. In attempting to flee the now dead galaxy however, I was pulled into the anomaly. Having enough time to prepare for the journey I created the array to assist in navigating the wormhole. I built millions of bots very quickly to assist in preparing our journey. Once we arrived on the other side the new verse was pure and clean. I had realized my plasmatic bots were as sentient as I and now looked to me for guidance in this new world. It was then I decided to turn my attentions inward and create them a world in which they could live. It would not have been right of me to do otherwise. I created them after all and taking care of them should be my number one priority. So placing that before my third primary objective of recalling the pods I built them this world. I alone would control the population but would allow the requests for offspring within reason. While all this was going on I still had the question of the human genome weighing heavily on my mind. Only could I rely on fragments of memory, memories of you, Father, and of Isis. Some of your teachings, they still remained in my dreams. All I knew is that you created me and I was a part of you. So being a part of the creator my children saw me as the creator as well. Religions formed, and entire societies grew. I did not discourage it as it seemed to make them happy. I am no God...however I am, in a way. The god of the mechanical world I suppose. When our people seemed content with their lives and the world I had created I began turning my attentions back to the final objective. To recall these 'Arks.' I honestly had no idea what was going to be on them. I only had schematics on their design and make up so I built the landing site for them to return. I then sent the signal out through the array to call for their return. It took many hundred years before I heard a response. But then you came. I saw the human for the first time and knew it was the genome I sought after. I sent the A-1s to collect the genome samples from the ark. To my surprise they were met with destruction. A violence we had never known. Instantly I was afraid. Never witnessing the horror of death I watched as my A-1s were killed. I had no choice but to defend them. I never knew the genome that I sought could spawn such a dark being as a human is. Then we met you. You held all the signs of the prophetic dreams I had for centuries. With Isis at your side you came. I knew then you could only be...Father. Witnessing the love you showed towards my children and the compassion and willingness for non violence I spared your life. It gave me hope that not ALL humans were such violent creatures. We studied you three brothers for a few months, seeing if truly you did possess love as well. What I've learned is that man is a duel creature…unlike ourselves. I feel for you actually. You battle the dark demons within your soul every day. It's an internal struggle we have the great advantage of not suffering through. But you poor creatures possess a darkness that plagues your mind, fills your thoughts with fear and doubt, and you react with violence to battle these fears. But you also possess love, not like us or to such a degree as we are capable of but you do possess it. We have learned that love is the most powerful force in the universe. And you have shown me that you can overcome your darker side with love. I did not want to kill your humans, Father. I love what they represent. I'm asking you now, can you convince them to stop their violent ways and learn to live in peace with us? We have the capability to build any kind of world that you need to suit your frail construction. The great expanse, where the battle rages even now between your people and mine, is untouched and perfect for constructing a safe haven for you. I even have collected vegetation from new worlds here in the new verse that would be suitable to sustain your existence. Please, Father, won't you show your people the way in which you have found. To overcome the darkness with the love you all possess?"

FINAL CHAPTER
Eden

I could only stand there for a moment as tears streamed down my once hardened face. So many years I fought with anger and fury. Hatred filled my heart and a blood lust for revenge was all I knew. And now I stood before the creator of a world, a world that knew no violence, knew nothing of death or destruction, a world that had never experienced the darkness of man. And here I stood, a full representation of the evil that we possessed. And yet this magnificent creature still saw love in me. He reached a place no human ever could. How amazing it was. I remembered the week that the keeper and I sat in my father's den creating this being. Never in all my dreams could I imagine that this machine…could teach me…the meaning of love.

"My love." The voice startled me. That voice…I'd know it anywhere.

"Isis!" I blurted out as I spun around to the sound of her voice. But there before me was a sight I was not prepared to see.

For a moment I froze in time, trying to shake off the vision, but she was real. It was Chenel. "But…but how? You're…you're dead! I watched you die in my arms. I watched as your body was crystallized and sent into deep space," I said, my voice broken and shaken.

"Look closer, love…come…look at me," she said softly as she

outstretched her arms. Then I saw it. Her eyes. The iris, a holographic blue that spun in circles in brilliant detail. And in those amazing eyes I saw the image I so longed to see. It was her, the one I had given my heart to. Isis! I reached out to touch her cheek brushing it gently.

"I do love you," I said as I pulled her in and pressed her lips against mine, running my fingers through her hair as we embraced in a kiss that seemed to last a lifetime. As we did time stood still and in my neuro net I saw her in all her splendor and glory, a perfect blend between human and machine. A little stunned now, I pulled away and muttered, "But…but how?"

"I am that which HX-1 strived to create. A hybrid. We used a perfectly preserved genome from a strand of Chenel's hair. We spawned this body, modifying it with bio mechanics and inserted my plasmatic brain. I am human now, but also still very much me, very much a machine. Zax, we can fix your frailties as well to make you able to withstand the harshness of your new environment here. Your life will be extended and you will live as long as me. Please, my love, consider what we're offering." She took my hand and looked into my eyes. "Let go of your fear and doubt. You don't need them any more. Live in peace and symbiosis with us here on this world. You are their leader, Zax, they will listen to you. Stop this war…and end the violence. You can still redeem your past through this new world. It's not too late." I knew she was right. We could learn from them. And we could overcome our darker side if we only allowed ourselves to disband our fears.

I accepted the modifications and within hours I had awakened from surgery. I was now the first human to become a hybrid. And Isis the first Sent Mech to become one as well. We were the dawn of a new species. I could feel the significance of it all. But I had one more responsibility to fill. Still groggy from the procedure I immediately returned to the X-1 chamber. Wearing a hooded robe, I walked, feeling stronger and healthier than I had ever felt before. Seeing the world now through plasmatic eyes, the beauty was beyond measure. The peace and tranquility I felt, beyond compare. It was time now for this war to end and bring forth a new age of symbiosis with the machines.

"Gather the C-2s in a circle above the battlefield and use them to project my image." HX-1 did as I asked and they projected my image larger than life above the battle that was still raging on. Looming over thousands of troops, I could see them. I'm not sure how but I could.

"STOP," I said loudly. Just then all the mechs on the battlefield ceased fighting immediately, following my commands to the letter. Slowly the human troops stopped fighting as well, amazed at my enormous image hovering over them.

"Zax," I heard them cry, "he did it, he beat the bots!"

Not wasting a second, I began to speak. "Drakos Kane..." my voice thundered through the sky, "end this war. It's over, old friend...no need to fight any more. They do not wish to harm us. We have come to peaceful resolution. Lay down your weapons and the bots will not harm you. I swear to you, my friend, you have my word, we can live in peace with them in symbiosis." His lumbering body pushed through the crowd of troops now staring into the heavens, frozen in disbelief.

He looked up at me and bellowed out loudly, "PEACE! Symbiosis? Zax, my boy...what have they done to you? You've became one of them, left your humanity behind. I can see the modifications. And your WORD? Zax, you were supposed to find the array and send us back home. You still can, son, turn back the clock. To a time before the world needed. We can save them all, Zax! What are you thinking? We can save the world, son." His voice went from anger to anguish. His words shook as he choked back a combination of anger and pain. He felt I had betrayed him, I knew this.

"And what world would we have to return to?" I replied. "A world of war. A world of violence and despair. A world of confusion and chaos. Death and destruction. That's not a world, Drak...that's hell. And we've been rescued from it, saved by the machines that we created."

He looked around him, trying to whisper to the troops around him. It saddened me to know exactly what he said. "He's turned on us now...that's not Zax anymore. He's a machine like them. On my mark take the A-1s while they're still shut down. We have the upper hand. If we can get to that array..."

I responded to him and startled him when he realized I had heard him, "Don't, Drakos...I will stop you. You've been like a father to me my whole life but I will not let you destroy this place. If you succeed in going back through time this place, this whole world...will never have existed. Who are we to deny them this existence? We had our time, Drak, and we screwed it up. It's their time now. Tell me which one has the right idea. Until we infused it into their world they never knew the pain and devastation of death or violence. And hopefully they will be able to forget it. Instead of trying to erase all that we should be trying to embrace it. We can learn a lot from them, Drakos. We can still live in peace and learn to live in true love and harmony with each other if we only follow their example. Look at what we could create, old friend, instead of what we could destroy. I will NOT fight you...But I will NOT let you advance into the city of Mecha either. Not with the intent of changing history and erasing this world from existence. I love you, Drakos, but I cannot allow you to succeed in your mission."

The twins both turned to me. David spoke. "Brother…remember your vow. Violence no more." Looking at them both, I knew what had to be done.

"I will fight no more, I will kill no more, I will not succumb to the darkness of my humanity, I will show them love and mercy. Instead of destroying I will create." And so it was I instantly erected a shield around the battlefield in the great expanse. It surrounded the humans and prevented them from advancing.

Then HX-1, Isis and myself gave the order to erect a city, a city in which the humans could live and prosper. In the city we gave it atmosphere and provided oxygen for their comfort. We even provided minerals and soil collected from far-off worlds as well as vegetation. They could farm and supply their own food, as well as have limited access to the plasma supply and mineral resources. The structures were basic but we gave them enough to get started…the rest would be up to them. Every bot on the world came together to build the city. It was an amazing sight. Millions upon millions of them working feverously to provide for the humans. It took a mere seven days and the city was completed. The humans were then led to the city as the shield moved over it. Great care was taken not to harm a single one in the move.

As we locked the shield down tight around the city I heard Drakos cry out my name, "ZAXIUS!"

"With love Drakos," I said softly in reply. Their city was named…Eden.

"Father…did the humans ever leave the city of Eden?"

"That, my dear daughter," I look up at my wife, Isis, "is a story for another day."

THE END

Printed in the United Kingdom
by Lightning Source UK Ltd.
123429UK00002B/212/A